Book Cover by Leoneh Charmell at The Book Savant

Developmental Editorial Assessment by Leoneh Charmell at The Book Savant

Line Edits & Proofreading by Kimberly Dawn

First Edition 2026

For the friends and family who read Jenna's story and INSISTED I publish it. It makes me so happy that you all felt so passionately about this book.

This one is for you guys.

BOOK ONE

LORYN MOORE

Content Warnings

For the Love of Demons and Katanas is an adult urban fantasy novel with romance. The story contains mature content and the characters have difficult experiences that may be triggering for some individuals.

- Sexual content
- Violence
- Death on page
- Explicit language
- Fictionalized depictions of demonic possession & demons
- Fictionalized depictions of witchcraft

Old Willow
Glen
Falcon
Lake
Sombra
Hills
Relics &
Roots
Santa
Sombra
Midtown
East Santa
Sombra
Downtown
Shipping
Yard
The Delta

Contents

Chapter 1

Rain poured in drenching sheets from the sky, its sheer force making me blink in rapid succession. The onslaught of water plastered my dark hair to my skull and my clothes to my body, but I didn't have time to worry about that.

I had a demon to kill.

Deciding to ignore the shiver rolling through me from the January chill, I reached for the sword at my back. I grasped the hilt with my frozen fingers and unsheathed the katana from its scabbard in a smooth, practiced motion.

Its sharp, metallic surface gleamed in the streetlights of the darkened alleyway, and I sliced it through the air. The blade whipped in front of me with expert precision as I took up a fighting stance that would have impressed even a karate master.

But I didn't need to impress any weapons expert. No, I just needed to show the hell-spawn staring me down from the other end of the alley who was boss. Maybe if she witnessed my badassery right off the bat, I could scare her into immobility.

A long shot? Sure. But a girl could dream.

As I went for another swipe of my sword, furthering the display of my prowess, the katana broke in half. The hilt remained clutched in my fingers while the blade shot four feet into the air, executing a deadly succession of three-sixties. I jumped back, my quick reflexes saving my leg from the blade's descent, right before it landed in a puddle with a loud, metallic plop.

I looked down at the sharp, disembodied blade, mouth agape.

The demon looked at it too, eyebrows raised. Safe to say I hadn't impressed her.

That was so embarrassing.

"Goddamn eBay!" I growled.

Idra, the demon I'd spent the last three weeks hunting, looked up and grinned at me. Her shoulders shook with gleeful laughter. She probably thought this gave her a better chance at survival—a miscalculation on her part. I almost felt bad for her, but then again, not really.

She was a demon, after all.

Chucking the useless hilt on the ground, I glared at her. "That was supposed to be a one hundred percent genuine katana, and that seller had five stars on eBay! Who can a girl trust these days if not five-star sellers on eBay?"

Idra's demonic nature still hid beneath the illusion of humanity as she sized me up, apparently liking her odds. "Looks like you got cheated, hunter. Now you'll have to fight me hand-to-hand."

She appeared like your garden-variety woman to the untrained eye. Her dark hair and creamy skin all but glowed with youth and beauty in the dim streetlights behind her. But I could see the darkness seeping out of her, the black aura that surrounded her, and the slight crackle of fire on the Earth beneath her feet. It looked as though hell followed her wherever she went—a byproduct of a demon in its incorporeal, spirit form.

To a regular person, demons, like Idra, could appear or not appear whenever and however they wanted to. But those same illusions, no matter how strong, never fully hid the beast inside them from me.

With my eye on the prize, namely Idra's exile from my world, I rolled my shoulders and shuffled my feet, a warrior preparing for battle. "I've faced worse odds."

Idra's red lips stretched wide in a dazzling smile right before she dropped the illusion. As the mirage of it shivered around her, pulsating with unnatural power, her body and face transformed. It happened slowly at first and then faster and faster until it built into a horrifying crescendo.

Her body lengthened, stretching as she grew taller and her skin mutated into a luminous red vapor, streaked through with black mist. Elongated teeth speared through the once sensuous mouth and narrowed into razor-sharp tips as her glistening blue eyes sank deep into her skull. Their sockets filled with smoky darkness within seconds, and a thin red dot glowed in the middle.

At last came the pièce de résistance and the reason I fought her kind with blades—her nails. One black fingernail on each hand extended, drawing out into the length of a deadly sword. I knew Idra's particular variety of demon, the kind that amplified fury and rage for sport, had an unfair advantage in hand-to-hand combat. I imagined that accounted for her smugness when my katana had broken.

But that didn't matter. I'd learned a long time ago to always have a backup plan. We stared each other down across the narrow alley and I remained unmoved, my face expressionless as I tamped down the anger that permeated the air around us—a familiar byproduct of a wrath demon's transition. Idra growled, baring her razor-sharp teeth, clearly hoping her true form might scare me stiff.

It didn't.

Rather than turn tail and run, I pulled out the .45 caliber handgun hidden in the waistband of my jeans. Offering her my cheekiest grin, I scratched my chin with the butt of my gun. "You know, I was looking forward to the exercise of nail-to-sword combat. It would have been nice to get those steps in. But now, I think I'll settle for blowing your head off."

Idra snarled at me, the red in her eyes flaring bright with what I recognized as fear. Aww, she had heard about me. At least enough to know my weapons could kill her.

She spun in the narrow space between buildings, unable to disappear in my presence. As she tried to flee, her elongated body still looked graceful and lithe despite the super grody nails. But before she could make it two steps, I pulled the trigger once, then twice. She was no match for the charmed bullets in my chamber. They hit home, one through the heart and one through the head.

Her not-quite corporeal body slumped to the ground, lifeless and immobile. Within seconds, the earth shook, and I fought to keep my balance because I knew what came next, and I didn't dare get too close. Fire roared to life where she landed, burning so hot and bright that it turned the rain to steam around me. Stepping back from the scalding heat and bracing a hand against the dumpster beside me for balance, I watched as it sucked her essence back to where she belonged.

To hell.

Or at least I had always assumed the fire that took demons out of this world was hell. It looked hellish, so one assumed. When she finally disappeared, the scent of sulfur lingering in the air, I slipped my gun back into my waistband and pulled off my leather jacket. I swore under my breath as an icy wind cut through my soaking wet t-shirt.

Crouching down, I used the protective coating of my leather jacket to pick up the blade. The truth was that, though I had guns if I needed them in a pinch, I always preferred not to use them. They lacked... how do you say... eloquence. And also, they made a hell of a lot of noise.

As though on cue, a man shouted from the darkness, his puffy parka swishing as he turned the corner to stare down my alleyway. "What the hell's going on out here? I heard gunshots."

His eyes locked on mine and I froze in the act of sliding my blade into the scabbard still strapped to my back to gawk at him. And that, ladies and gentlemen, summed up the reason why I hated guns. They brought out the lookie-loos, the rubberneckers.

Thankfully, I didn't think he could see what I held through the material of my jacket. Nor did I have any reason to believe he had superior night vision to any other human, so I let out a breath of relief. Thank God I'd already stowed away the gun.

Securing the blade of my katana into its scabbard as fast as I could, I effected a doe-eyed look of innocence as best I could. It proved far more difficult than I would have liked, considering the onslaught of water falling from the sky and my presence in a darkened alleyway.

"You know, I think I heard that too. It sounded like it came from that direction." I pointed to my right as though I wasn't lying through my chattering teeth.

The man nodded, and I wished I could see any telling details about his expression. But I couldn't. Not with the position of the streetlight directly behind him. "You should get inside and be careful. If those really were gunshots and not just some assholes lighting off fireworks, they sounded close."

Fireworks in late January? In California? Fat chance of that.

With that last bit of parting wisdom, he pulled a cell phone out of his pocket and began to dial. I blew out a sigh of relief as he walked out of the alleyway. I knew he'd call the police to report what he'd heard. So I swiped my bullet casings from the ground and pocketed them. No sense in leaving those little nuggets of evidence behind for the boys in blue to find.

Muttering under my breath, I tugged my jacket back into place. Not sure why since the rain had soaked it through, along with the rest of my clothes and body. But I didn't question it because my mood had taken a turn for the worse. I was more than a little miffed by the whole anticlimactic face-off I'd just endured. Not to mention the humiliation of it all. I'd probably dream about Idra's mocking grin for at least the next few days.

Cheekybastard115 would get a piece of my mind the minute I got back to The Office, and he could bet his pretty ass that I wouldn't hold back in my scathing one-star review.

CHAPTER 2

After a few blocks of walking through the pouring rain, I yanked open the door to the 1994 Subaru Outback I'd borrowed for this occasion and slumped inside. I turned over the engine and cranked the heat to full blast as sirens sounded in the distance.

The owner of this little beauty, *she said facetiously*, was my best friend and partner in crime, Gaby Perez. Well, maybe not crime, exactly, since I considered what we did more of a public service than anything. Hunting down the demons who terrorized Santa Sombra, my hometown, and sending them back to hell counted in that direction. At least, I liked to think so.

As for me, I'm Jenna Torrence, and I'm a demon hunter.

Hi, Jenna.

Just kidding.

Before you ask, no, I don't belong to a secret society of demon hunters or an underground demon hunting club or anything like that. Honestly, I don't know that any such things exist. But even if I did, I'm just not much of a joiner. You may ask how I found myself in this line of work and I would have two reasons for you. Poor life choices and natural ability.

From the natural ability side of things, I can see demons. No matter how hard those icky critters try to hide, I can always sense them. Add to that, I'm much stronger than your average Jane, or Joe. Not to brag or anything, but I know how to take a beating, get up, and come back for more.

Which is important because demons can tell that I'm different too. And that means they can touch me, pummel the shit out of me, or cut me with their disgusting nails. A problem regular humans don't seem to have, unless they've already succumbed to a demon's influence. Or unless they're possessed.

Oh well, you can't win them all.

Punching the car into drive, I headed back toward my second job, i.e. the one that paid the bills—a downtown cop bar called The Office. Gaby and I both worked there most nights of the week because demon hunting did not pay as well as one might imagine and we liked to do frivolous things like eat and have electricity.

As I drove the ten blocks it took to get there, I muttered under my breath and gestured irritably about the katana. Maybe someday I could look back on everything that had happened in that alley and laugh. Sadly, today was not that day.

A few minutes later, I pulled into the residents only parking area behind The Office and threw Gaby's car into park. Getting out, I stomped all the way to the entrance, my temper still fuming despite the freezing rain that pelted me.

When I flung open the door, I saw Gaby wiping down small wooden tables and getting ready to open for the evening. She took in my bedraggled appearance for a moment, along with the pissed-off expression on my face, and decided not to comment.

Points for intelligence.

Instead, she continued to wipe before arranging napkins and coasters on the aforementioned tables. She could probably see the steam coming out of my ears, but I didn't have it in me to talk. So, maintaining my stony silence, I tossed the scabbard behind the bar and headed up the stairs and into my apartment.

Yep, that's right, I live right above the bar where I work. Best commute ever.

I pulled out my keys and opened the door to my humble abode—a petite one-bedroom apartment. The layout combined the kitchen and family room, making for a nice open living space. Or it would have, if the apartment didn't resemble a shoebox from a sizing standpoint. My furniture was secondhand, not all that comfortable and nothing to write home about. But that worked for me. It kept any visitors to a minimum since no one ever felt comfortable enough to stay for too long.

Stalking back to my bedroom, I pulled off my wet clothes, tossing them into my chocolate-brown bathtub, an unfortunate relic of the seventies, as was the rest of my bathroom. Honestly, whoever came up with the idea for brown toilets should be exhumed and slapped.

I grabbed fresh clothing from my closet, selecting skintight faded black jeans, a clingy burgundy t-shirt, a soft black leather jacket, and steel toe boots. Still not quite ready to face the world, I blow-dried my burgundy-tinted brown hair before sliding my gun into the back of my waistband. One could never be too prepared in my profession.

Hair dry at last and teeth no longer chattering with cold, I felt a teeny tiny bit better. Good thing too because we only had a few minutes before the bar opened. Stomping back down the steps and into the bar, I watched as Gaby turned on the electric red Open sign.

"You will not believe what happened to me tonight," I said, forcing my teeth to unclench in the process.

Gaby settled her large brown eyes on me as we both moved into our positions behind the bar. "Does it have something to do with your impression of a drowned rat?"

I arched a sardonic brow at her. "You think?"

She snorted a laugh, and her signature tight ponytail slid over her shoulder as she did. She ran a hand down its long silky tail, flipping it back into place behind her in an apparent attempt to distract me from the twitch in her lips that gave away her amusement at my expense. "I take it your final showdown with Idra didn't go as planned?"

Her eyes flicked to the blade I'd deposited behind the bar, and my teeth clenched yet again of their own accord. I bent down, snatched the scabbard off the ground, and dumped the contents onto the bar for her viewing pleasure. The blade clattered and the hilt thunked, the pieces of my katana no longer attached as God intended. She pressed a fist to her mouth to hide her laughter.

Too bad it didn't work. I could still see it.

I explained what had happened, and it didn't help my disposition that during my entire story, Gaby kept her fist pressed against her mouth to cover her smirk.

"And the worst part, you may ask? Idra *laughed* at me. That's right. *Laughed*. Demons should never laugh at demon hunters, you know. It goes against nature and all things holy. So then I had to take my gun out and shoot her instead and you know how I hate guns." I blew out an annoyed breath, feeling a little bit better for getting it off my chest.

"Hey, how did those bullets work for you anyway?" she asked, moving past my humiliation for the moment in favor of checking on her latest upgrade to our arsenal of magical weapons. Because Gaby wasn't your average Jane either. She was a witch or, as her family called it, a bruja, and a pretty powerful one, too. Her magic made my charmed bullets, enchanted blades, and the anti-demon wards that protected both of our homes, along with this bar possible. Without her, my swords and guns would have had no impact on the incorporeal demons, and I would've had to fight them hand-to-hand.

"Like a charm," I replied, with an internal snicker at my awesome pun. "And thank God too. Can you imagine if I'd had to enter an entire clip into Idra like we did into that incubus after we exorcized him from that hot snowboarder guy in Truckee? I mean, middle of nowhere, no problem. But in the middle of downtown? Yikes."

"I shudder to think."

"So, how'd you make them so much more effective anyway?" I asked, snagging the broken katana off the bartop and depositing both pieces in the supply room a few steps away, at the far end of the scuffed bartop.

"I used more of your blood this time, along with our holy water reserves. I think I need more of it than I do with the katanas because the wounds the bullets make are smaller, maybe? Anyway, the extra blood works as an amplifier for the holy water, which makes them pierce the demon's spirit more thoroughly. Too bad I couldn't do anything about the workmanship on that katana, though."

"You know, maybe next time you should. I'm holding you accountable to keep me from looking like an asshole. If you can enchant the blades with your witchy business, why not make them unbreakable while you're at it?"

She shook her head, chuckling. "You know that's not how this works. My magic operates in the spiritual realm, not the physical one. I'm a witch, not a blacksmith, JT."

"Oh. Right. I knew that."

"Sure you did."

I dropped it after that, unsure what else to say. Even after fourteen years of friendship, I still had only a minor grasp on how all her magic stuff worked. Or how my power worked, for that matter. I had no idea how I managed to remain anchored in both the corporeal human world and the ethereal demon world. It boggled the mind, but since I'd never known any different, I sort of just took it for granted.

With my curiosity and desire to complain satiated, I watched as Gaby's lips quivered once again and her eyes grew distant. I could tell she'd moved back to my mortifying encounter with Idra. When her wide, dark eyes watered, and her normally tan skin turned a rosy pink, I sighed.

I waved my hand at her. "Go ahead, laugh it up. I can tell you want to."

She did, the sound bubbling out of her in a loud burst. She doubled over, making twisty motions with her hands. "I can just see you. Then I can see the sword," she wheezed, gesturing at the floor. "Plop. It's just too much." A few tears slid down her rosy-bronze cheeks as I stared at her, stone-faced.

"Yep, don't worry. This isn't the first time I've lost my dignity. I'm sure it won't be the last. But I tell you what, that Cheekybastard115 better give me a refund or it's his ass I'll be hunting down." Okay, so not really, but a girl can threaten. And fantasize. Then a thought occurred to me. "Hey, back to the gun. Maybe you can try making it less noisy too? You know, since we can't afford a silencer slash we don't want to go to prison if we ever get caught with one."

"Like I told you, I work in the spiritual realm. Not a blacksmith. Or a gunsmith or whatever."

I leveled a finger on her and clicked my tongue. "Oh. Right. I knew that."

The bell on the door chimed and a couple of off-duty cops I knew all too well entered. Gaby shot me a meaningful look before walking down to the other end of the bar. I tried to busy myself with cleaning an already clean glass, doing my best not to make eye contact with the tall, blond, and built one.

Luke Parsons.

A plainclothes detective with a penchant for ending up in the wrong place at the wrong time. We'd once called each other friends, until he caught me in a few compromising positions while doing my demon hunting thing. Since then, he'd made it his personal mission to figure me out. And from that moment forward, I'd made it my mission to avoid him like the plague. Admittedly, that had proven hard to do since he was a regular at the bar where I worked.

My gaze lifted as he slid onto the stool right in front of me. Our eyes locked for a brief moment as Bud, his husky middle-aged partner and my longtime friend, settled in the spot next to him. My stomach clenched with dread and I tried not to let it show.

"Hey, JT," Luke drawled. "It's been a while. I feel like you've been avoiding me. So have you?"

I decided to feign ignorance. "Have I what?"

"Been avoiding me?"

I glared at him. He damn well knew the answer to that one. "Only when I can help it."

Deciding to ignore his amused chuckle in response, I turned my attention to his much less irritating partner. I placed an empty beer glass on the counter in front of Bud and raised a brow. "The usual?"

"You bet," Bud replied, as Gaby took care of Luke's order for him. For Bud, I slipped the glass under the Miller Lite tap and poured. Most of the cops who came into The Office lived on cop salaries. In California, that meant they drank domestic. Or at least those who wanted to feed themselves and put a decent roof over their heads while still enjoying a few post-shift beers at a bar, drank domestic.

I slid the glass a short distance to Bud, a trick I mastered eons ago, while Gaby brought Luke's glass over and set it in front of him all proper-like. Before I could say anything to excuse myself, Bud's voice stopped me cold. "You know, one of these days, you're going to have to tell me what happened between the two of you. I thought we were all friends. But now it's just uncomfortable and tense during our after-shift beers." He shook his head as though baffled, his gray beard and jowls jiggling a little. "Did you guys have sex or something?"

I'd poured myself a glass of ice water in that aforementioned super clean glass and was in the middle of taking a sip when Bud dropped that doozy on us. I choked, coughing as I pounded a fist to my chest.

"You did, didn't you?" Bud asked, staring in disbelief between Luke and me. "Goddammit, Luke, I told you that JT is off-limits. Didn't we all tell you that JT is off-limits? This is our bar, and you don't shit where you eat!"

When I finally cleared my lungs, I fixed my attention on Luke. He had a big shit-eating grin on his face, as though he didn't have a care in the world, and my fists clenched at my sides. "We didn't have sex."

Luke didn't bother to deny it or agree with me, and to add insult to injury, I could hear Gaby snickering behind me as the door jingled and more cops entered the bar. I turned to glare at her instead. "You, go help the rest of the customers."

Thankfully, she did as I asked, shaking her head in amusement while she started taking orders.

"Then what the hell happened?" Bud asked.

Luke gave me a lazy look, his sparkling blue eyes trailing over me, the laughter at my expense clear in them. "You wanna answer that?"

I chose to ignore him and give my attention to Bud instead. I still liked Bud. "Luke and I are fine. Nothing happened."

Luke snorted. "That's what you're going with?"

Bud ran a hand over his military buzz cut. "A bunch of bullshit, if you ask me. I know tension when I see it. I'm a fucking detective for Christ's sake."

Luke kept his gaze pinned on me. "So, I didn't catch you with a back seat full of knives and swords? Or an illegally concealed firearm on your front seat? And what about all those boxes of bullets on your floorboard?"

I opened my mouth, then promptly closed it, irritation spiking. He did not just say that in front of Bud.

Why hadn't I taken the extra five seconds I would have needed to put those weapons in the goddamn trunk? I'd berated myself at least a million times for that mistake. I'd planned to just cover them with a blanket and drive the five-minute trip to Gaby's place so that she could put refresher charms on our demon hunting arsenal. But then Luke had come by the bar to talk shop with me and saw my entire collection just sitting there, pretty as you pleased. That had led to oh so many questions. Man, did that guy have a lot of questions.

Trying to keep my cool, I forced a smile that may have looked more like a snarl. "I explained all that already. You need to work on letting things go, buddy."

"I can't," he said, tapping two fingers to his temple. "Detective, remember? Besides, your explanation leaves a lot to be desired."

"Well, desire all you want, that's the only explanation I've got."

He leaned closer, and I felt the warmth of his body sweep over me. "Liar."

I gripped the underside of the bar to keep from hitting him. The temptation was real, because I could feel that he'd piqued Bud's interest too. The senior detective stared at me in open curiosity, as though he wanted to hear my explanation as well.

Sighing, I gave in and forced my back to straighten in preparation for the lie. "I was just transporting the weapons for a friend. A collector, okay? They weren't real or anything." I rolled my eyes as though the idea that I owned a collection of swords with an actual purpose in the twenty-first century was absurd, which it would be to most people. "And the concealed gun was my registered weapon, and it was sitting on my front seat, which I'd accidentally covered with my jacket. See? Perfectly reasonable, am I right?" I asked, appealing to Bud, certain he'd take my side on this one.

He squinted one eye, letting the silence linger for a moment. "You're right, she is a liar. And a bad one, too. What did the swords look like?"

"Not collector's items. She had them piled in the back seat, and their scabbards looked beat to hell... well used. And then there was the matter of all those bullets too—"

"I told you, I planned to head to the shooting range after I dropped off the swords. I'm a PI for fuck's sake! I'm allowed to have a gun!"

Bud looked at me with a level of suspicion I didn't quite care for. "Hmmm."

The last thing I needed was the attention of the cops—plural—rather than Luke—singular. Of course, that wasn't the only strange thing Luke had witnessed in recent weeks, and it surprised me a little that he hadn't discussed the other incidents. Probably because it would make him look just as bad as it made me look.

"Alrighty then, fuck you very much," I said, turning to walk away from both of them to help the plethora of other customers who'd entered during our tense and irritating conversation.

"Hey, hey, hey," Luke said, rising to stand and putting his hands up in surrender. "I'm sorry. How about we call a truce, for Bud's sake? Stay and talk for just a few more minutes. Like old times."

I hesitated, chewing on my cheek. He just had to go and throw *for Bud's sake* into the mix, didn't he? I'd known Bud for over five years, since I started working at the bar just after I'd turned twenty-one. He'd been the one who encouraged me to get my PI license in the first place, and I had a soft spot for him. Not to mention, I had honestly liked how things used to be between the three of us.

Old times for us meant they'd pay me a dollar to invoke my PI privacy policy, and they'd run their cases by me in hushed tones. They both asked for my advice more than either of them probably cared to admit. But now? Bud had a point. Things had gotten tense, and I didn't like my newfound status as one of Luke's unsolved cases. Not one little bit.

I leveled a finger under Luke's nose, leaning over the bar to get closer to him. "Only if you promise to stop snooping around my life, showing up at odd hours, and trying to catch me in the middle of doing... whatever it is you think I do. I'm a PI. I can't do my job with a shadow."

"Now where would the fun be in that?" he asked, that smarmy dick-headed smile still firmly in place.

I all but growled at him before I turned on my heel and strode down to the end of the bar to find Gaby. I heard both Bud and Luke laughing as I left. When I reached Gaby, I let out a frustrated breath. "Tonight is not my night. First Idra and now Luke. He just won't let this unsanctioned investigation into my life go."

Gaby grinned. "Well, to be fair, he did see you fighting with air that time, and shit-talking yourself in the alley. Then there was the other time with all your swords and guns and bullets in the car. And remember when he walked in on us at the end of that exorcism? He didn't seem to like how we had Tracy tied to the chair."

I sighed, pinching the bridge of my nose. "Thank you for the blow-by-blow, Gaby. I appreciate that. But why can't he just let those things go? I had perfectly reasonable explanations for all of them."

She rolled her eyes. "Right? I mean it's like he's a detective or something."

"You are hilarious."

The bell chimed on the door before I could really get going and a rush of cold, wet air blew through the cozy barroom. Gaby and I both turned to see a woman hurry inside, dodging past a few of the regulars who filed in ahead of her. Her flushed cheeks, wild eyes, and soaking red hair made me do a double take and stopped anything else I might have said to Gaby on the matter of Luke. The woman looked frantic as she hurried to the bar, and I could all but sense the desperation rolling off her in waves.

"Excuse me?" she said, her voice breathy as she fingered the golden crucifix at her throat. "I'm looking for Jenna—" She broke off and pulled out a card from her purse. She looked down at it and back up to Gaby and me. "Jenna Torrence."

The card looked familiar, mostly because it belonged to me, but I didn't remember giving it to this woman. I crossed my arms over my chest warily. "I'm Jenna Torrence."

Despite her obvious anxiety, a skeptical look slipped over her features. "Of JT Investigations?"

"Yep, that's me."

Her brows shot straight into her hairline in shock. I had a way about me that screamed degenerate petty criminal, or at least that's what my friends had always told me. So I didn't hold her astonishment against her.

To her credit, she stepped closer and pressed her palms onto the bar, my card still clutched in her fingers. "Could we go somewhere private to talk?"

Seriously? I looked around at the crowded bar, filled with impatient cops waiting for their beers. "We're kind of at peak hours here. But if you leave me your number, I will call you first thing in the morning to set something up."

The instant I finished speaking, her face fell into a mask of total despair. Her eyes watered, and oh my God, she was going to fucking cry! I hated it when prospective clients cried.

She sniffed. "Please, you don't understand. It can't wait until morning. He—" Her lips wobbled and even more tears filled her eyes as she fought for composure. "He'll kill me."

Startled by her admission, I observed her more carefully. I didn't give out my card to just anyone, and in turn, the people I helped in the past only recommended me for certain situations. As a result, my clientele had very specific needs, normally of the supernatural variety.

That had a tendency to bring both the deranged and the desperate to my door—of which we had plenty in Santa Sombra, considering the excess of paranormal activity we seemed to have here.

I just needed to figure out which of the two categories the mystery redhead fit into. But before I could decide, the tears threatening in her eyes spilled down her pale cheeks.

I groaned inwardly, knowing I'd lost all hope at objectivity until the tears stopped. I held up my hands in mock surrender. "Of course, we can meet now." I lifted the entry to the bar and stepped out from behind it. "Follow me." And then I turned to Gaby. "Call Tony and see if he can swing by and pick up my shift tonight."

Gaby nodded, her eyes soft with empathy for the woman. I was right there with her. All the lady had to do was shed a few tears and I turned to putty in her hands. How pathetic was I?

Badass demon hunter, my left butt cheek.

Mentally chastising myself for my softy nature, I led her back to my apartment. A few of the cops at the bar cat-called me good-naturedly as we passed. "Looking good tonight, JT!"

In response, I offered them a stiff middle finger, never once turning my head in their direction. Laughter erupted behind me as the tearful redhead followed me up the steps. My lips twitched at their raucous behavior. Who was I kidding? I loved that cat-calling shit. It did wonders for my ego.

When we reached my apartment, I unlocked the door and held it open for her to go inside first. She did and I flicked on the lights, gesturing toward the small bistro table off the kitchen. It was all I had space for in my tiny place.

She sat down and looked around, clearly disoriented. “Is this your office?” she asked, her hands trembling as she clasped them together.

“Nope. This is where I live. Normally, I take my appointments in the bar during off hours,” I explained. Then I pointed at the kitchen. “You, uh, want something to drink? Tea? Coffee?” I hovered halfway into the kitchen, which was basically partway into the living and dining rooms as well.

She shook her head. “No, I’m okay.”

I pulled out the chair across from her and sat down, resting my forearms on the table and shifting from surly bar-wench into comforting PI with some effort. “What’s your name, hon?”

She sniffed, dabbing a finger under her eye to catch a stray tear, and opened the purse on her lap to pull out a tissue. “I’m Tara. Tara Bronsen.”

“Nice to meet you, Tara. Now, do you want to tell me why you’re so upset? And what you think I can do to help?”

Leaning forward, her pretty face looked just a bit haggard. “Someone is following me. Everywhere I go, he’s there. I can’t leave the house. I can’t go to work, and I can’t do anything without him watching. He’s always watching.”

I let this settle for a minute, once again trying to determine whether she qualified as deranged or desperate. I decided I needed more information before I could make a solid assessment. “Have you gone to the cops? This sounds like stalking, which is illegal. You could get a restraining order.”

She shook her head, her wet hair whipping from side to side. “No, I tried. They don’t believe me. They think I’m crazy. Everyone thinks

I'm crazy." She hiccupped, the sound breathy in her throat, and I was leaning in favor of the deranged column just before she slipped her hand into her purse and pulled out a photograph. "I showed them this, but they said there's nothing in here to incriminate anyone. It's like no one else can see him, but I swear he's right there!" Tara's finger jabbed into the photograph, the gesture desperate, and I followed her line of sight.

I could tell immediately that she'd taken the photo in a residential neighborhood, likely her front yard, and as my gaze settled on the spot her finger indicated, I did a double take. Without thinking, I reached out and pulled the photograph closer. She released it, not bothering to put up a fight as I squinted at what I saw there.

Chills prickled up my arms.

It was impossible, and yet what I saw standing beside the lone oak tree in her front yard made my stomach drop all the way to my toes.

Because what I saw was a demon.

CHAPTER 3

Tara did not miss the look of utter stupefaction on my face. "You see him, don't you? Can you really see him? Does this mean I'm not crazy?" On what seemed like a desperate impulse, she leaned forward and clasped my free hand in her bony grip. "Does this mean you'll help me?"

I extracted my hand from hers as kindly as I could and held the photo up to the light as I peered at it. Even from a distance, I could see the dark aura that surrounded him. Impossible. Demons who hadn't taken up residence inside a human body only showed themselves when it suited them. Otherwise, only people like me, humans with the ability to see into the supernatural realm, could see them. That included any and all photographs, too.

But this demon looked different. I set the picture down and leveled my attention on Tara once more. As I surveyed her, I could see that her face had filled with hope, and I worked to school my own expression. "How long has this been going on?"

"Almost three months," she answered, her anxiety morphing into something akin to jittery excitement. And who could blame her? She finally found someone who could see what no one else could besides her.

I nodded, trying to pretend that the photograph in my hand didn't shock me to my core. Because I knew that whatever she had following her wasn't an average run-of-the-mill demon. In the picture, he looked human, aside from the aura that swirled around him. Hues of deep bloodred intermingled with black smoke emanated from him, licking along his skin.

I shook my head, trying to make sense of what I saw. Normally, when someone took a photograph of a demon, they looked like their true selves to me—their spirit form. And if the asshole inhabited a human body, then anyone who bothered to look at the photograph should have seen him too. Confusion twisted in my gut, and a sense of inexplicable foreboding pulsed through me.

Aside from the strange, but captivating aura and the crackling hellfire beneath its feet, the demon looked absurdly human and strikingly handsome. Even from afar, I could make out the chiseled features and strong body. A sudden urge to crumple the photo in my hand welled up inside me, and I frowned down at the image.

Tearing my gaze away once more, I fixed my attention on Tara. "Has he done anything else, other than follow you?" Aside from my burning curiosity over what the hell kind of demon it was, I needed to understand its motive, its goal. Why Tara? What did it want with her? Maybe that would give me some kind of clue to follow. Something to get me started.

She shook her head. "No, but it's like this is all building to something. I can't explain it, but I feel like something is about to happen, and the possibility of what comes next... it terrifies me."

I chewed on my cheek as I thought about what that could mean. Demons typically had simple goals and they pursued them with ferocity. They either wanted to possess a human's body, corrupt a human's soul, or they wanted to sow discord and chaos in the world, tempting people into whichever of the seven deadly sins they embodied. Killing a human, though? They only did that after they'd accomplished one of their other three goals, if at all. The human's collapse into degradation usually ranked as their primary goal, and they didn't care what happened to their victims after that.

"There's nothing you can think of that would make this guy want to come after you? No deals with the devil or anything?" I asked, only half joking. Believe it or not, I'd seen it before. People did crazy things when desperation took hold.

"You can do that? Make a deal with the devil?"

"Maybe not *the devil*, but a demon, sure."

A line formed between her brows. "But why would that be relevant?"

And we'd gotten to the tricky part. I leveled a serious stare on her, knowing that what I had to say next could send her screaming from the room. I needed to deliver the news in a way that didn't sound ten shades of crazy. But how did you tell someone they had a demonic stalker without sounding at least a little batshit?

"When I tell you this, you have to promise you'll keep an open mind. Can you do that?"

"Why? What is it?"

"Promise me you'll keep an open mind?" I asked again, tapping the picture once more for emphasis.

She nodded, though I could tell she had no idea what she'd just agreed to. Oh well, I couldn't help that. I'd just have to deal with the fallout of her reaction, whatever that might be.

"I ask about deals with the devil because the creature that's following you isn't human."

She blanched, her light skin going even paler in response. "Wh–what?" She shook her head in denial. "But that can't be true. It's just a guy."

I shook my head, the gesture firm and final, full of authority. "I'm sorry to have to tell you this, but that's not a guy. That's a demon."

"That's impossible. Demons don't exist—" She opened her mouth to say more but hesitated right before her wide doe eyes narrowed. She looked down at her hands, clearly thinking through what I'd just said. As I watched her, I could see a combination of fear mixed with confusion and disbelief cross over her features. At last, she looked up at me and asked the million-dollar question. "And even if they do exist, what would a demon want with me?"

Exactly. What did a demon want with her? But I decided not to open that can of worms just yet. "So, you believe me when I tell you that your stalker is a demon?"

I had to admit, her reaction surprised me a little. She'd come around quicker than most, but then again, she did have an invisible stalker no one else could see except her. So maybe she was willing to believe just about anything, if it provided an answer or a possible solution to her problem.

She lifted a shoulder in a noncommittal gesture. "I don't know what to believe. But if you can see him, and I can see him, and no one else can, then there's either something wrong with the guy or something wrong with me."

Tears welled in her eyes again and she sniffed, trying to stifle the emotional reaction. "And this is the first explanation that doesn't point to me being the problem. The only one that doesn't mean that I'm losing my mind."

Despite her best efforts, the tears continued past her fingertips and slid down her cheeks. I leaned forward and grasped her hands in mine, sympathy for her pushing to the forefront of my mind.

I could relate to everything she'd just said. It had taken me a long time to figure out that other people couldn't see what I could. And growing up in the foster care system like I had, had forced me into a steep learning curve when it came to my abilities. I'd learned young to hide my true self from everyone, to ignore all the insane shit I saw every day that everyone else had no idea existed.

"There's nothing wrong with you. You aren't crazy. He is there. I can see him just like you can." I left out how he didn't look like any demon I'd ever seen before. And how he exuded a kind of danger and power that felt so potent I could taste it, even from a photograph. I didn't know how I picked up on all that from just looking at a picture, but I felt it deep in my gut. And I always listened to my gut.

Tara let out a strangled, desperate laugh, then she nodded and sucked in a long breath in an apparent effort to control her emotions. "Thanks. You have no idea how relieved I am to hear someone else say that they see him too. I'm glad I found your card."

"Me too. I promise, I'm going to help you. This is what I do," I said, as a question popped into my mind. "But speaking of my card, how did you get it? I usually work on referrals, given the specialized nature of my... expertise."

Her brows furrowed in clear confusion. "Oh. Someone put it through my mail slot along with the rest of my mail. I thought it was an advertisement or something. You didn't send out mailers?"

Well, that didn't seem suspicious at all. Hairs rose on the back of my neck in a natural response to that level of coincidence and my stomach burned with wariness, but I didn't let my discomfort show. "Oh, no, you're right. I forgot I had Gaby send out some cards around town." I waved it away, not wanting to alarm her any further than I probably already had.

"Who's Gaby?"

"My research assistant. We work together." *Research assistant* usually went over better than *witch* with my more normie clientele.

"Oh, okay," Tara said. "But if this is a demon, do you know why it's following me? I'm just a regular person, and I still don't understand what it could possibly want from me." She gripped the cross at her neck once more, apparently a nervous habit.

"I honestly don't know for sure, but it's safe to say that he doesn't want to braid your hair and give you a mani-pedi."

She cracked a smile despite herself and shook her head. “Yeah, I think that’s safe to say.”

“Look, I know we just met and you don't know anything about me, but from what you're telling me, I don't think it's safe for you to go home tonight. Do you agree?"

She nodded.

"I suggest that you stay here, where I can keep you safe, and we can talk more in the morning. It's getting late, and I bet you're exhausted. It sounds like you've been through a lot."

She hesitated, looking down at her sopping-wet jeans and black sweater. “But I don’t have any clothes.”

“I’ve got something you can wear. Look, I want to help you and I know that he can’t get to you here. That much I can guarantee.”

Her eyes darted toward the door, probably thinking *stranger danger!* But she looked back at me and hedged. “Are you sure I wouldn’t be imposing at all?”

“Well, it’s a small place, so it won’t exactly be comfortable. But I’m pretty sure we can both agree that a little discomfort is worth it, if it means keeping you safe, right?” I raised my brows as though looking for her confirmation. I hoped that her certainty that the demon meant her harm would convince her to stay where I could keep an eye on her. Where Gaby’s magic would keep the damn powerful demon out and a safe distance away from her.

Her mouth opened and closed again, as though debating her response. “I guess I always knew it was bad. But after all this time, after everyone telling me I was making it all up, even I thought maybe it was just me. That maybe I was just delusional. I never imagined—" She broke off, staring down at the glossy paper that trembled in her grasp.

My expression softened. "But you did. Whether you knew it or not, you did. That's why you insisted that I see you *tonight*. Listen to what your gut tells you. It's your natural survival instinct imparting what you need to do to keep yourself safe. So, what is it telling you to do right now?"

She chewed on her lip as though unable to think clearly through the fear. Her eyes slid downward for a few moments before she looked back at me. "I think you're right. I should stay."

"Perfect, I'll make up the couch, unless you'd prefer the bed?" I asked, praying she'd say no to my offer.

"No, the couch is fine," she assured me, and I said a small internal *thank God* because I already had enough trouble sleeping at night without getting relegated to the couch.

"Okay. I'll get you some pj's and a fresh change of sheets. Is there anything else you need?"

"A toothbrush, if you have one."

Coincidentally, I did. I bought a pack at Costco a year ago during a supply run for the bar and still hadn't used them all.

"You got it." I left her in my kitchen and moved to my bedroom. As I gathered a pair of boxer shorts and a t-shirt from my dresser, I couldn't help the surprise I felt at how easily she'd given in to my suggestion to stay the night. Fear would do that to a person, I knew, and I felt a little relieved that she'd made the right decision. I would have hated to have been forced to knock her out and chain her to my brown toilet. Not that I would have done that or anything. But if I had, I would have felt totally justified in my actions. I couldn't very well send her back to that demon, now could I?

Moving toward my bed, I pulled out the drawer underneath it that housed my only pair of extra sheets and warm blanket. I snagged those and grabbed a fresh toothbrush with a travel-sized toothpaste from my bathroom vanity.

I brought my haul out to the living area, where Tara had moved to the kitchen. She had a cabinet open and turned at the sound of my approach, looking guilty. "I'm sorry, I didn't mean to impose. I was just looking for a glass."

I shrugged. "No apology needed. *Mi casa es su casa*."

She smiled weakly, blushing a little in what I guessed was embarrassment. "Thank you."

"But the glasses are in there." I pointed to the cupboard next to the fridge and she nodded gratefully. She removed a chipped pint glass, the only kind I owned, from the cabinet and opened the freezer while I watched, curiosity filling me.

"So, have you always seen things other people can't? Or is this the first time?" Though I knew she was new to this whole *demons exist* thing, I wanted to understand if her ability to see the demon had to do with the creature's will or her natural ability. The distinction could change my approach to her case.

She held a handful of ice from the tray and hesitated, debating how to answer me. Then she placed the ice in the glass and shrugged. Moving to my sink, she turned on the faucet, filling her cup with water. "I'm not sure. I guess I used to see things when I was a kid, maybe? But I always thought it was just my imagination playing tricks on me. Eventually, it went away."

Great, she was one of *those. Those* meaning the people who probably suppressed their gifts as kids, only to have them rear their ugly heads later in life. Either that or she had no gifts and an overactive imagination. It seemed I'd just have to figure out which camp she fell into on my own.

She pointed at the clothes I'd left for her on the top of the couch. "Are those for me?"

"Yep. Bathroom's that way if you want to change."

She moved to pick them up but hesitated. "You're not leaving, are you?"

"Nope, I plan to stay right here." I would stick around until she fell asleep. Just to make sure she didn't change her mind and go gallivanting into the night alone. That demon in the picture didn't sit well with me. Not that any demon ever sat well with me, but something felt very off about the one who stalked Tara. Call it a hunch. And that hunch told me that I needed to solve this case fast.

CHAPTER 4

Two hours later, Tara had fallen sound asleep, and I listened as she snored softly beside me. I sat in one of the bistro chairs, which I'd moved next to the couch so we could watch Netflix. Feeling confident that I wouldn't wake her, I clicked the TV off and tiptoed over to her purse, which she'd left sitting on the table. I slipped my hand inside and grasped the photograph, feeling a little sleazy as I did. I didn't love the idea of sneaking into another woman's purse, but I had bigger problems to worry about. Namely, the strange as fuck demon in that picture, which I slid into my jacket pocket. The picture, not the demon.

I crept past the couch, careful not to wake her as I slipped out of the room intending to find Gaby and fill her in on our newest case. Also, I wanted to see what she made of the photograph. When I emerged from the back stairwell and into the bar, I saw her washing glasses in the soapy water that filled the bar's sink.

It looked like Tony had cleared out earlier, leaving her alone to handle closing up for the night and I made a mental note to chew him out later. Deciding to join her in the task, I went to the storage room and grabbed a broom. Together we swept, mopped, wiped down the bar, and cleaned the dirty glasses.

As we worked, I relayed my conversation with Tara to her. I told her all about that bad feeling in the pit of my stomach and about my hunch that this could get ugly. After my explanation, I took the picture out of my pocket and placed it on the clean, dry bartop. “What do you make of it?”

She moved closer to me and leaned down, staring at it with pursed lips. “I don’t see anything, but you know I can’t just see them all the time, like you do. I have to use magic. But—” She broke off, teeth sinking into her bottom lip in thought. “Doesn’t it seem like we’ve had more of them to put down recently? I mean, I know Santa Sombra always seems to draw any and everything paranormal to its doorstep, but it feels like we’re up to our ears in demons these days.”

I considered her question, fingers rubbing my jaw in thought. “I think you’re right. I feel like I’m tripping over them everywhere I go.”

Gaby reached out and picked up the photograph, brushing her slender fingertips over the glossy paper. “I don’t know, JT. I’ve got a bad feeling about this.”

“What do you mean? Like a witchy one?” Gaby got hunches too, but hers tended to lean more toward premonition territory and thus proved way more accurate than any I’d ever had. And honestly? I’d hoped that direct contact with the picture might trigger something for her.

"No, it's of the non-witch variety. It's more that I always get a bad feeling when you say the word *hunch*. Your hunches never end well." She handed the picture back to me and I pocketed it again.

"That's not fair. That was just that one time with Mr. Smith."

"Mr. Smith ended up working for the demon he hired you to 'kill.'"

"Yeah, but I knew I was supposed to do something about him. Shouldn't that count?"

"No, because he tried to incinerate you with hellfire after you killed his demon boss."

I snorted in amusement at the memory. "Who knew a mortal dude would have access to that much power? Besides, it's not like he succeeded."

"Your eyebrows didn't grow back for a month."

"Yeah, but he ended up burning himself to death in his own hellfire. So no harm, no foul."

She let the silence linger for a moment. "You have a very disturbing ability to downplay even the most horrifying events."

"Comes with the job description."

She sighed in response and steered the conversation back to the point at hand. "Look, I agree that you need to help her. She seemed desperate. But just... *be careful*."

"You know I always am."

"No, you're not," Gaby disagreed, clearly exasperated by me. I tended to have that effect on people. "But what freaks me out is what you said about the demon."

"What about it?"

"Don't you think it's a little weird that it looks human to you?"

"Of course I think that, ergo the whole reason we're talking right now."

"But JT, what if that's just how he looks? What if he never transforms into his demon form? From what you said, he looks like a regular guy to Tara. So, wouldn't that make slaying him a little awkward, should she happen to witness it?"

"No way, she knows it's a demon. I'm pretty sure she believed me. Like seventy-five percent sure."

"But that's not one hundred percent, right? Look, I'm just saying, you've never confronted one like this before. You don't even know if it has a corporeal body anchored in our world or not, and that complicates things. So, just be careful. You don't want to get arrested. Or worse, outed."

As her words settled, I wondered if maybe she had her priorities just a little out of order there, but I didn't bother to correct her. "Alright, I promise I'll be careful and I'll try not to slay any demons in a way that compromises my secret identity."

"How many times do I have to tell you that you're not a superhero? You don't have a secret identity and you're not fucking Clark Kent."

"How about Bruce Wayne?" I asked, loving how annoyed she got when I pretended to believe I was invincible.

"Closer, but you don't have enough money."

"Okay, okay, okay. Deadpool."

"I'm pretty sure your limbs wouldn't grow back if I cut them off."

"You know, we've never actually tested that theory—"

Gaby's eyes widened in horror. "And we're not going to start!" She looked genuinely concerned that I might grab the fire axe from the back room and give it a go. I loved that she found me so spontaneous.

I scoffed, feigning offense. "Jeez, no one said we would. Sensitive much?"

"Can you please just promise to be careful and not make a joke about it? I don't want my best friend to spend the rest of her life in prison. Or the nuthouse."

"Aw, thanks. But don't worry, I have no intention of going to prison or to an asylum for that matter. And I promise, I'll be careful."

"No one ever does." With my promise secured, she made her way to the back office to get her coat. We'd finished cleaning and had prepped for clients of a different type in the morning—our PI business, where she was the Robin to my Batman. Only, we looked better in tights.

After we said our good nights, I tiptoed back upstairs and opened the door to my apartment. Soft snores still came from the sleeping form on my couch, and I breathed a sigh of relief that I hadn't woken her. I slipped off my boots and padded across the room, depositing the photograph back where I'd found it before hurrying to my bedroom. Once inside, I closed the door with as little noise as possible. Stripping down into my skivvies, I slid under my covers. The open window across the room allowed a cool breeze to flow through the small space and I could hear rain pinging on the metal AC unit as I sighed.

Gaby had a point. I needed to proceed with caution during this case. There was something different about it, aside from the demon and his strange appearance. I just couldn't seem to put my finger on it. I had a sense of déjà vu and wondered what the hell that could mean. I tossed and turned for a few minutes and finally flipped onto my back and stared at the ceiling.

Closing my eyes, I recalled the image of the demon once more. He'd been too far away to get a detailed read on what he looked like, other than a general sense of attractiveness. But something about that dark aura, the swirling smoke, and the vague burn of fury that swirled in my gut as I'd stared at his image... it made me uneasy.

He reminded me of a particularly strong wrath demon I'd encountered a while back. Only, even through a simple picture, I could tell that Tara's demon was far more powerful than that creep ever could have hoped to become. The furious rage of that wrath demon hadn't seeped past my natural defenses. Most demon magic had little to no effect on me. Like with Idra pumping out her rage earlier, I could withstand it. Even if I could feel their draw toward the seven deadlies, it never got further than that. I always remained in control.

But the demon in the picture? Strength and potency seemed to radiate from him, and I could even feel its latent effects just by looking at his image. A kernel of fear licked its way up my spine as I lay in the dark, the steady drip of rain and the icy January breeze making me shiver.

In the morning, I would ask Tara to send me the original picture. I could all but guarantee she had it on her phone, and maybe then I could get a closer look at him. Get a better idea of exactly what we might be dealing with.

I pulled my blankets farther up and reminded myself of all the demons I'd faced down in my time. I'd taken on all manner of hellish creatures and had always come out on top. This time would be no different, I promised myself, pushing any fear or worry I might have felt down and back. The best I could do tonight was get some rest. Tomorrow, I would start on the case for my new client.

Elliott Grove Middle School, East Santa Sombra, Fourteen Years Ago

I hitched my backpack up higher, trying to ignore the giant demon staring at me from the chipped navy-blue lockers across the breezeway. I could feel its presence hovering like a plague all around us, unable to mistake the white-hot rage it exuded.

Awesome, a wrath demon. Just perfect.

If I could have chosen a demonic emissary for any of the other seven deadlies, I would have. Sloth, gluttony, lust? Still dangerous, but much less lethal and a lot less urgent to kill.

My thoughts stayed fixed on what the heck I was going to do about the thing as I watched more of my classmates walk by it. Not a single person glanced in its direction. Which made sense. They couldn't see it. No one seemed to see the things I could. Bitterness coated my mouth as I recognized the unfairness of that fact for about the millionth time in my short life.

A strong wind whipped through the open-air hallway between classrooms, causing two meathead jocks to bump into each other in front of the demon. It smiled, a horrid row of razor-sharp teeth visible, and rather than laugh it off, like they probably would have under normal circumstances, the two jocks started pushing each other. Demons sure knew how to kill the mood. If no one intervened, these small outbursts of violence would escalate into something far more sinister.

Before the rest of my fellow students could get in a circle around the jocks and start yelling 'fight, fight, fight' like they did in all the movies, a teacher came out and broke up the whole thing. Everyone pretty much went about their business after that. Except for the two in the fight, they followed the teacher to the principal's office while he chewed them out.

The demon seemed to vibrate with glee, and I let out a long sigh, knowing that I would have to kill it before really bad things started to happen.

Like they had the last time I'd left a wrath demon to its own devices on a school campus. Dread pooled in my belly, knowing that I had about a fifty percent chance of getting my ass kicked again.

It didn't seem fair that, as a twelve-year-old kid, I had to be the one to step up. Also, the fact that I had to face a monster like that with nothing more than my bare hands, holy water, and a few crucifixes really pissed me off. The deadlier weapons that worked on everything and everyone else didn't seem to work on demons. I'd learned that the hard way, and buying holy water in bulk at my age didn't exactly ingratiate me to my peers. In other words, they all thought I was a freak. And in all fairness, they had a point.

I was a freak.

I sucked my teeth, my resolve stiffening, as I prepared to walk by the evil creature. It had taken up a menacing position in front of my homeroom class, and I couldn't exactly avoid it without looking like an asshole. So I took a step forward, eyes shifting from left to right to make sure I didn't get plowed over by some eighth-grade jock. Or in a more likely scenario, said jock would bump into me and fall straight on his ass, sucking air from the collision with my freakishly strong body, thus furthering my loser status in the middle school hierarchy.

As I glanced to my right, I saw my archnemesis, Gaby Perez, in all her Lisa Frank glory. I groaned inwardly, about to turn my back on her, when I noticed her staring. Her dark eyes had gone wide, and her face had drained of all its normal color. I stopped right in the middle of the busy breezeway when I realized that she was staring directly at the demon I'd worked so hard to ignore.

Within the span of a second, it turned its head, dark smoke swirling around its elongated body. It fixed its horrifying red eyes on her and opened its mouth to show its sharpened teeth. She didn't move. Instead, she froze like she'd grown roots to that very spot and her mouth opened in what looked like a mixture of shock and terror. The demon moved toward her, sensing her awareness of it. Never a good thing. But I moved faster.

Taking my life into my own hands, I stepped into its path, far too close for comfort, and waved a hand. "Gaby! Over here!" I jogged the last few feet to her, putting a little distance between me and the demon. Despite my best efforts, I could still feel the beast's presence hovering behind me, an icy chill crawling up my spine. I reached her before the demon could and looped my arm through hers, spinning her around. "Thanks for waiting for me! We're going to be late." I dragged her forward, forcing her to unfreeze as I half carried her away from the demon and our homeroom class.

Apparently, we were ditching today.

"What are you, my sweet little dove?" the demon at my back hissed. I gritted my teeth, ignoring its question, pretending that I couldn't hear its terrifying voice. I couldn't afford to show myself to it too soon. Before Gaby's

freak-out, I'd planned to blend into the crowd, to hide in plain sight as I passed it, but its sudden fixation on her had made me abandon my plan.

I leaned my head toward hers and whispered so low even I couldn't hear my own voice over the whipping wind. "Keep walking. It can't know you saw it." I remembered the first time I'd let a demon know I sensed it. The memory of a long, nasty gash that had spanned the full length of my back burned on my skin.

I turned my head to the right, pretending like I was checking for foot traffic before I crossed the breezeway. But really, I wanted to check to see if the demon still lurked behind us. The rage it exuded had died down a bit, and I could see that it had stopped, setting its sights on another unfortunate student. I let out a sigh of relief that it hadn't found either me or Gaby too interesting and we kept moving. The bell rang as we passed the last gray stucco building and crossed into the teacher's parking lot. Gaby finally got her feet under her and I no longer had to carry her—thank the Lord for that. She was heavier than she looked.

I guided us behind an old red Suburban before tugging us to a stop. When I did, Gaby spun on her heel and stared at me with her mouth open. "You saw that thing, too?" she asked, eyes still wide as saucers, though some color had seeped back into her olive skin.

My heart hammered in my chest for an entirely different reason, and I rolled my eyes, trying to play it cool. "Obviously." Awareness tingled along my skin at the realization that, after my entire life of going this alone, I'd found someone else who could see them.

Of course, that person would be my archnemesis. The Riddler to my Batman, the Lex Luther to my Superman. That just freakin' figured. Only, now I saw something different when I looked at her with her baby pink puffy parka and super flamboyant Lisa Frank notebook. I didn't see the girl who'd thrown the gum into my hair that caused me to shave half my head, or the one whom I'd tripped face-first into that puddle of muddy water during spirit week in retaliation last year.

Instead, I saw the possibility of a confidante. Someone I could tell the crazy shit I saw every day to, and who might just believe me. I closed my eyes, taking a quick, steadying breath. I couldn't afford to get too far ahead of myself. I needed to remember who I was dealing with. Just because Gaby Perez could see them didn't mean I could trust her. I knew that all too well.

"Ey yo, Gaby!"

We spun, each turning as one of Gaby's friends, Justin, waved from a couple of cars over. Probably out getting high and ditching class. Douchebag. He was one of the more popular kids in school and firmly believed he was God's gift to girls.

For the record, he wasn't.

From what I'd observed, he and Gaby had a thing going on, nothing serious but definitely flirting during free periods and having lunch together. Not that I cared. The campus was just too small to avoid noticing such things. Especially when you ate lunch alone.

He narrowed his eyes as he approached us, focusing on me and giving me a look like I was the plague. Gaby seemed to stiffen beside me, as though just realizing who she'd been talking to. The class freak. Probably not so great for her otherwise sterling reputation.

As he drew closer, a smile spread across his lips. Not a real smile, but one that let me know I wouldn't like whatever he said next. "What are you doing back here with this loser? Are you guys friends now?"

Gaby seemed to freeze and I crossed my arms over my chest, glaring at Justin like the spineless worm he was. At least he had the sense to squirm under my scrutiny. Despite how much everyone hated me, I didn't usually get bullied. More ignored and avoided at all costs. Most of the people at this school thought I was crazy, the kind that would set them on fire if they messed with me too much. I wasn't, and I wouldn't. But they didn't need to know that.

Gaby looked from me to Justin. "Um."

Her skin managed to both pale and flush simultaneously as her mouth opened and closed like a fish sucking air. I'd just saved her butt and she couldn't even manage to say one nice thing about me. Typical.

"Nothing, and no, we're definitely not friends," I said, answering his questions for her. I hitched my old, threadbare backpack farther over my shoulder, turned on my heel, and stalked back toward the main campus.

"You're welcome for saving your butt, you ungrateful witch," I muttered under my breath as I drew farther away from them.

But before I could get too far, Gaby's voice rang out, stopping me in my tracks. "Jenna! Wait! You dropped this."

Justin let out a derisive scoff. "Who cares what she dropped, Gaby. She can get it herself. Let's go." His voice did that puberty squeak thing on the last word, and I suppressed a grin at having witnessed it.

As Gaby drew closer, her puffy jacket swished louder with her movements. She held a pen in her hand. A nice one. A purple jelly roll. Something my foster parents would never have bought for me. Way too pricey. She held it out, and I raised my brows. "That's not—"

But she interrupted me, her voice low enough that Justin couldn't hear it. "Meet me at La Fortuna Cocina tonight. Seven o'clock."

"Why?" I asked, eyeing her in confusion. She pressed the jelly roll into my hand, sacrificing her pen for the chance to talk to me without being overheard. Kind of a cowardly move, but what did I expect from someone like her? Then again, she had seen that demon. Maybe there was more to her than I thought.

"Because we need to talk." Her dark eyes burned with determination as she stared at me, pleading with me to say yes.

At last, I relented with a nod, taking her pen too. I had to get something out of this exchange, and the pen would do nicely. "Thanks. I'll be there."

Chapter 5

Sun creeped through my open window, shooting into my freshly squinted eye. I squeezed it shut and yawned, irritated. I'd managed to wrap my sheets around my legs like a boa constrictor in my sleep and I grumbled, taking a few moments to detangle myself. The night had turned into a restless one, full of fitful dreams that I couldn't quite remember. Memories of violent weirdness that I had zero intention of unpacking flashed through my mind.

Brain in a fog, I looked at the alarm clock on my nightstand and saw that it read eight a.m. Five hours of sleep sucked. I would need coffee if I was going to avoid murdering the innocent.

I shoved my body into a sitting position and pushed myself out of bed. Raising my arms over my head, I stretched and yawned before stumbling toward my bedroom door like a zombie. But instead of brains, I needed a caffeine fix. Reaching the kitchen, I turned on the coffee maker and began the process of filling the filter with grains.

Once it started brewing, I turned around and stared into the living room. Dimly, I registered that something was missing. Then in a rush of memory, I realized that it was Tara. Tara was missing. Adrenaline dumped into my system and my heart rate ratcheted to one hundred forty-five beats per minute in two seconds flat.

Without pausing to think, I ran to the couch. The blanket and sheets looked rumpled atop the cushions, but no sign of Tara. Hurrying to the bathroom, I shoved open the unlocked door and saw no one inside. Sweat sprang up along my hairline as I hurtled down the steps into the bar, hoping I'd find her nipping some liquor downstairs. Who knew? Maybe the chick had a habit.

"Tara! Are you down here?" My voice carried and echoed off the exposed rafters above me and the old-fashioned brick walls that surrounded me.

No response.

I rushed toward the back room, and into the office I used as JT Investigations' HQ. But still, no sign of Tara.

After I spent a frantic twenty minutes searching the bar, the storeroom, the parking lot out back, and everywhere I could think that she might have gone or hidden, a pit began to form in the bottom of my stomach. I called out her name over and over again, but she never responded and I found no hint of her presence anywhere. After I'd gone through every nook and cranny in the place, I'd come to one inescapable conclusion.

Tara had vanished.

Feeling sick to my stomach, I sprinted back up the stairs to my apartment and ripped my cell phone off the charger. I rang Gaby and hurried back into my family room, heart still hammering.

"Hello?" Gaby answered, her voice groggy with sleep.

"She's gone!" I yelled, my breath heaving. For some reason I couldn't explain, terror raced through my veins. Tara could have gone anywhere, left on her own, and I could have been having the overreaction of the century. But I knew on a bone-deep, visceral level that she hadn't. Something had happened to her. Call it another hunch.

"Who?" Gaby asked, still coming out of the fog of sleep.

"Tara! She's gone!"

"Holy fuck, JT! My ears!"

I ran a hand over my face, forcing my breathing to calm and trying to settle my racing heart. "I'm sorry. It's just, I woke up this morning and she isn't here."

"Maybe she left on her own."

"I don't think so."

"Are you sure about that?"

"No," I admitted, still trying to take calming breaths so I could think through the swell of panic.

"Well, did she take her purse? Maybe she went to get donuts or something."

I did a mental head slap at the simplicity of that suggestion and executed a quick search around the apartment. If she'd taken her purse with her and changed her clothes, then maybe that meant she'd left of her own volition.

As I looked, I found neither her purse nor her jeans and sweater from the night before. I breathed out a sigh of relief. That was a good sign. Maybe I'd overreacted. Maybe she'd just left to get something to eat.

"I don't see them."

"See? I'm sure everything is fine."

I exhaled, trying to force some of the tension out of my body. Moving to the couch, I slumped onto the familiar, well-worn seats, and as I did, I felt something hard and lumpy beneath me. I moved to the side and lifted the dark blankets, and what I saw there made my heart drop into my stomach.

Her purse and her clothes sat on the cushions beside me, lumped into a pile under the covers. And beneath them, a large dark stain spanned the length of the cushion. I couldn't mistake what that stain was, and I knew exactly what it meant.

Blood.

I gagged at the putrid metallic scent that filled my nostrils with a sudden rush, lunging from the couch and turning to stare at it. My phone slipped from my boneless fingers to thunk on the ground and I could hear Gaby's voice, but it felt far, far away. "JT, what? What is it? Are you okay? Goddammit, woman, answer me!"

But I couldn't bring myself to speak. Instead, I sank to my knees and stared in horror at Tara's blood.

A few hours later, I leaned against the railing of the grated fire escape connected to my bedroom window, staring out onto the street that adjoined the alley below me. The asphalt shone a glossy black with the recent rain and naked trees lined the streets of the main drag. A crisp breeze cut through my leather jacket and jeans as I raised a cigarette to my lips. I'd bummed it from one of the many cops who now occupied my humble abode.

I sucked in the calming smoke and felt the slight headrush I always got whenever I decided to imbibe in the cancer sticks, which I didn't do often. But everything about my current situation seemed like it warranted a damned cigarette.

In the moments since I'd awoken to find Tara missing, my home had become an active crime scene. The cops had questioned me ad nauseum about my affiliation with her. How did I know her? What was her address? What was her last name? Why did she stay here last night? Most of which they could have just gotten from her purse, rather than asking me. Oh, and let's not forget the crème de la crème of questions: Did I have an alibi for last night?

Strictly routine, you see.

Routine, my left ass cheek.

I took another drag and released the smoke through pursed lips before pinching the bridge of my nose with my free hand. I'd done the best I could to explain why Tara stayed at my home and even told them about the alleged stalker. When they pressed me further on it, I explained that she'd tried to file a report with the precinct a few times. That seemed to get me somewhere. Providing an alternative suspect always helped when the cops suspected you of potential murder. Or at minimum, aggravated assault.

A creak had me turning my attention toward my bedroom window as it opened and Luke appeared. Perfect. Of course, he just had to see me mixed up in one more suspicious situation. I felt pretty confident that if things kept up at this rate, he'd finger me as some sort of serial killer.

Deciding to ignore him, I turned my head to look out at the street. My tacit dismissal didn't seem to deter him. Instead, he pulled himself through the window and onto the fire escape, an impressive feat considering our height discrepancy and the small size of the aforementioned window. He stood on the fire escape with me, the heat from his body somewhat comforting, given the circumstances. It was cold outside, dammit, but that warmth only did so much, considering the coldness of his stare. I could feel it on the side of my face, burning with icy intentions. I almost cracked a grin at my mixed metaphors, realized how inappropriate that would look, and turned it into a grimace at the last minute.

Without saying anything, I offered him the cigarette, still staring at the street below. We'd gotten close before he caught me doing all that crazy shit. But now he probably found me suspicious as fuck, and who could blame him? I was suspicious as fuck. Or at least, if you didn't know that demons existed and you couldn't see them, I was. Because without that oh so critical context, I could see how I might seem like a danger to the community, or to myself at minimum.

To my surprise, he took the offered cigarette, his warm fingers brushing mine as he did. I turned to face him and watched as he wrapped his lips around it and inhaled. Maybe he didn't like me for Tara's disappearance after all, if he was willing to swap spit with me. One could hope.

He passed the cigarette back to me. "These will kill you, you know."

Despite myself, my lips tugged up at the corners.

"Thanks, kettle, I'll be sure to keep that in mind."

Luke let out a low chuckle and the sound vibrated through me, filling the small space we inhabited. He stared out at the street, seeming to follow my gaze as he shifted to lean on the railing. I could feel a sense of foreboding, like something bad was about to happen, right before he cleared his throat and fixed his attention on me. After a few beats, I turned my body toward him, squaring off against him for what felt like the hundredth time in the last month. "You have something you want to ask me?"

"I have a lot of things I want to ask you. Starting with what you were doing in your apartment with the woman you had tied up to that chair, and ending with how you got wrapped up in this fiasco."

"I've already answered the first one, and as for this one? I have no idea. Tara came here looking for a PI to help her. She tried to report a stalker to the police department, but she said you all blew her off. Thought she was tin-hat-level crazy."

Luke pressed his full lips together. "The first one was the worst lie I've ever heard in my police career. Which is saying something, considering that I'm a cop and criminals are usually pretty fucking stupid. But as for the missing girl—" He paused, slipping a small notebook out of his back pocket and flipping to a page. "Tara Bronsen—you had never met her before last night?"

I shook my head. "Look, I swear, if I knew anything about what happened aside from the stalker thing, I would tell you. She was my client, and I promised her my protection."

My back straightened as I let the truth of those words soak through me. I'd failed her and let someone or something get to her inside my fortress of solitude. Whatever had done this must have had enough power to break through Gaby's wards. I chewed on my lip as I tried to figure out what the hell kind of demon had been in that damn photograph.

He leveled a finger at me, pointing directly at my mouth. "It's that expression right there that makes me question everything you just said. That calculating look that tells me you know something you're holding back. I shouldn't have to remind you that your client is missing and she left a hell of a lot of blood on your couch. She could be injured, maybe even running out of time for us to find her, and keeping secrets won't help Tara."

I snapped my attention back to him, glaring as I heard Bud's rumbling voice inside my apartment, bossing the uniformed cops around. Taking a step closer to Luke, I glared up at him, realizing in that moment that I had to really crane my neck to do it. I wished I had a step stool or perhaps a small ladder so that I could look down my nose at him, but alas I didn't. So I'd just have to make due with good old-fashioned menace. "I'm not keeping anything from you, jackass. Did it ever occur to you that maybe I'm trying to figure out how they got into my apartment and into the bar? Someone broke in and hurt her while I slept in the next room. I was supposed to protect her. Me." I pressed a finger to my chest in emphasis. "So, excuse me if I'm not behaving exactly the way you want me to." Only half true, not that he needed to know that. Still, that time I tried not to let my mind wander again and not to give anything away.

He stepped closer and looked down his nose at me, which had my ire spiking, the challenge clear as he crossed his arms over his well-muscled chest. "Alright. Then I assume you wouldn't mind coming down to the station to answer some questions for me, in an official capacity."

I settled my hands on my hips and straightened my back, rising to the fullest of my less than impressive five feet seven inches. "Not. One. Bit."

"Good, I'll give you a ride now."

"Fine, I'll take it." As we stood there glaring at each other in a proverbial pissing match, I hadn't noticed Bud poke his head out from the window.

He cleared his throat. "You two definitely had sex."

I turned my attention on him and offered him the meanest of all my glares—my badass demon hunter glare. He turned red and coughed in discomfort before he moved back inside and wisely shut his mouth.

Chapter 6

After a solid hour of questioning and recording my answers via both video and notepad, Bud and Luke had released me from the police station and allowed me out into the world again. Gaby waited for me in the parking lot in her old Subaru Outback.

Her car was damn near the same age as us, and at just shy of twenty-six years old, the Sub had seen better days. Sadly, I had the sense it might be in better condition than me at the moment. Especially after the grilling Luke had just given me.

On the positive side, they didn't consider me an official suspect. Despite Luke's tough talk at the apartment, I knew I likely had him and Bud to thank for that small mercy, along with the dozens of other cops present during Tara's abrupt entrance into The Office the night before.

They could all attest to her apparent distress and how she'd come looking for a PI to help her. After I'd told them about the stalker thing, they'd moved on to greener, more sinister-looking pastures. Thank the Big Guy Upstairs. Though Luke did still seem to have his suspicions about me, despite my best efforts to convince him otherwise.

The man was like a dog with a fucking bone. He just wouldn't let it go already.

As I approached Gaby's car, I yanked open the back passenger door and chucked the backpack I'd stuffed with my clothes and laptop inside. They still considered my home an active crime scene, which meant that I couldn't stay there. A point that irked.

I slammed the back door shut and pulled open the front one, slumping into the seat like a dramatic teenager, the car wobbling from the impact of my body.

Glaring out the windshield, I ground my teeth, sensing Gaby's eyes on me, but I tried to ignore it. Useless anger swelled inside me at the monumental waste of time that Luke and Bud had just put me through. Time that I could have spent looking for my client. I dragged my nails over my scalp as Gaby pulled out of the parking space and edged onto Auburn Blvd, pointing us back toward the freeway and midtown.

The weather had turned gray and gloomy and rain spit at us in splattering drops from the sky. She flicked on her windshield wipers and cleared her throat. "So, what do you want to do, JT?" Gratitude warmed my blackened soul at her question. She understood me better than anyone. When I didn't answer right away, she continued. "I mean, obviously we aren't going to just let the cops take this one, right? This is our wheelhouse, not theirs. They'll be sitting around with their dicks in the wind or their thumbs up their asses or... you know... whatever. The point is that they'll never find Tara if we don't help."

I let out a begrudging snort of laughter. She had such a way with words. “You’re right, I won’t drop this one, and Luke seemed to know it too.”

“He did?”

“Yep. So I have a feeling my stalker won’t leave me the hell alone anytime soon.”

Her mouth twisted in annoyance as she mulled over that little nugget of information. “Well, damn. You know, he really needs to get a life.”

“Right? The man needs to get a girlfriend, someone to keep him nice and distracted and out of my damned business. Now about the case—” I turned in my seat to look at her so that she could fully understand the depth of my intensity. “I think we need a witchy solution.”

Her pretty face transformed with a grin. “You know I always like those. What’s your poison, amiga?”

She merged onto the freeway entrance and turned a tight circle as I reached into the inner pocket of my leather jacket and produced the photograph Tara had given me. The one with the demon. It was the only shred of evidence that I hadn’t handed over to the cops. In fact, I’d swiped it from Tara’s purse before they’d gotten there and hidden it inside my backpack. What use would they have for a picture of nothing, as far as they could tell, anyway? I set it on my lap and stared at the demon. “I figure we can start with a location spell.”

Energy all but buzzed from my witchy friend as she accelerated onto the freeway. “My specialty. You have something of hers we can use?”

“Yep, I got it right here.” I tapped the picture and Gaby flicked her eyes to it before looking back at the road. “Alright. Sounds like a plan. I’ll make a quick stop at Roger’s to get supplies.”

Roger was our friendly neighborhood magical supplier and our close friend. He ran a magic shop just two blocks from Gaby's townhome. The guy was legit in the magical world, which made him pretty much indispensable for Gaby and me.

Already focused on our plan, Gaby crossed three lanes, not bothering with a blinker, and I leaned back in my seat, feeling in control for the first time since I'd awoken that morning. We would find Tara, and I wouldn't allow for any other outcome. I couldn't.

I closed my eyes, thinking through our most logical next steps should we find the demon who'd kidnapped her. Because what the hell else could have happened? She'd come in looking for my help, needing protection from a demonic stalker. Her disappearance couldn't be a coincidence, right?

I didn't allow myself to consider the possibility Tara had presented when she'd first begged for my help. That her stalker wanted to kill her. No, I had zero hard evidence to make me believe that whoever had taken her had killed her. Though the bloodstain had soaked my couch, it didn't measure up to a lethal quantity. Or so Bud and Luke had assured me, after Luke's asshole posturing on my balcony.

Just then, we heard a loud bang and the car jerked upward, as though we'd run something over. "What the hell?" I cursed, turning in my seat instinctively and looking at the road behind us. The offending object caught my eye and my lips twitched in amusement.

Gaby grimaced. "So, was that what I think it was?"

I turned around in my seat and cleared my throat, trying not to laugh. "If you think it was your headlight, then yes."

She peered into her rearview. "Fuck me. That's the second one this month!" She gnawed on her lip and glanced over her shoulder. "Think I can go back and get it?"

I turned in my seat and looked out the back window just in time to see a huge black pickup truck run it over. Glass and plastic spewed like exploding guts all over I-90. I turned to face forward once more, and no matter how hard I tried, and believe me I did, a snort of laughter escaped.

Gaby glared at me from the corner of her eye. "Are you laughing?" She didn't so much ask as grind out the words with adept precision.

I snorted again, covering my mouth with my hand. "Me?" I asked, trying to effect innocence. Not really my strong suit. "I'd never."

She sighed. "Fine, laugh it up, asshole. I guess it's payback for the whole Idra thing."

I burst into laughter and didn't stop until my eyes burned with amusement. As I gave in to the levity of my friend's fucked-up car, some of the tension and the fear of failing my client eased. I swiped the tears from beneath my lashes as one thought permeated my mind.

At least I was in better shape than the Subaru.

Chapter 7

About twenty minutes later, Gaby flipped open her grimoire, a Lisa Frank notebook she'd carried around with her since elementary school. I still remembered the first time we met in the fourth grade. She'd had it even then, though I hadn't known what it contained inside its perky pages at the time.

I'd like to say that we'd become fast friends, but that would be a bald-faced lie. We'd started more as mortal enemies who hated each other with the passion of a thousand burning suns. A misunderstanding that we'd cleared up after two years of that aforementioned vitriolic hatred.

Gaby thumbed through the pages of trusty old Lisa as she pulled open the door to A Witch's Whimsy. A bell jingled overhead and we strolled inside. My boots left damp prints on the scarred wooden floor as Roger peered up at us from behind the counter.

His smile bloomed white and wide as his blue gaze settled on us. "Well, look what the cat dragged in."

He slid off the stool behind the glass counter, which displayed all kinds of stones and talismans, and moved to greet Gaby. They air-kissed each other's cheeks before he repeated the greeting with me.

After giving me a quick once-over, he pursed his lips. "Not to be a dick or anything, but you look like shit, hon. You should try sleeping. I hear that helps."

I rolled my eyes. "Thanks, Roger. That *is* super helpful."

He smiled wider and crossed his arms over his silky teal kimono. Roger had a thing for kimonos; no matter how hot or cold it got outside, he wore them indoors... always. "You know I jest! But seriously—" He turned to Gaby and hitched a thumb in my direction. "What happened to her?"

Before Gaby could open her mouth to answer, I beat her to it. "Bad night. That's why we're here. We need some supplies for a locator spell. And we're on a timetable. It's sort of a matter of life or death."

Well, assuming the demon hadn't already killed Tara. A thought I refused to utter aloud. Because again, I had no evidence or reason to believe that. At least not yet, and I wouldn't give up hope that I could bring her back safely so soon.

"Oh, dramatic," he said, widening his eyes, well, dramatically. "Don't you worry, Roger is on it. I've got everything you need for the basics, and if you're really in a hurry, we can set up in the back room. I don't have any contractors today."

Gaby wrapped an arm around Roger's waist and hugged him to her. "I'll take you up on the second offer. But as for the basics, I think we'll need something with some additional oomph. We'll also need to use a little of your mojo. We need a third for this spell, and—"

He raised a perfectly sculpted brow at us. "And since I'm a medium and an empath, you figure I fit the bill?"

Gaby grinned. "You got it."

Without warning, a gasp escaped him, and he turned wide eyes on me. It looked like his brain had just made the connection as to why we'd gone there asking for his help and what could constitute a life-or-death situation.

He crooked a finger in our direction and leaned closer, as though getting ready to tell us a big secret. No idea why since the shop had no one else in it except us. "Is it a *demon* thing?" He whispered the word *demon* as though someone might overhear it and get offended by his use of such a naughty slur. Again, no idea why.

I resisted the urge to roll my eyes once more. He'd aided and abetted our demon hunting gig for over three years now, but he still hadn't quite adjusted to it.

"I'm going to say all signs point to yes on that one," I replied, striding over to the wall next to the counter where Roger kept a vast array of enchanted items. I grabbed a magic eight ball, grinned at the readout which matched my previous sentiment, and tossed it to him. "See? Just like I said."

He caught it with a hiss, cradling it against his body as though it might shatter if handled improperly. "Be careful with that, you heathen. You break my enchanted eight balls, you buy them." He set it back in its place with extra care and I bit the inside of my cheek.

"Hey, man, no one wants to hear about your enchanted balls. Now, can you help Gaby find what she needs already? Like I said, timetable. Ticktock."

I tapped my nonexistent watch and he exhaled a bitchy sigh at my impatience. Turning on his heel, he strode toward Gaby. Before he made it two steps, he peered at me over his shoulder. "Just so you know, my balls are *exquisite.*"

I made a gagging sound and he grinned back at me before doing what I asked. I watched as he consulted with Gaby, grabbing objects off eclectic shelves and handing them to her, smiling despite myself. Having my dynamic duo nearby always cheered me up, even in my darkest hours.

I still remembered the first time we met Roger. Gaby and I had searched high and low for a legit magic shop after Charmed Boutique had gone out of business, and Roger was the only real action left in town. We hadn't realized he had supernatural talents of his own until he'd touched me during a good old-fashioned handshake. At which point, he'd collapsed while his eyes rolled into the back of his head, forcing me to catch him before he could face-plant on the floor.

He'd kind of flipped out when he realized that Gaby and I both had a few special talents of our own. But to my unending surprise, he hadn't let the fainting spell deter him from befriending us, but he had refused to touch me since.

My shit was dark. Or at least that's what he told me.

While Gaby and Roger continued grabbing supplies for our handy-dandy location spell, I played with the eight balls and other enchanted objects. A rabbit's foot and a horseshoe, both of which I rubbed for luck, and then I eyed a Ouija board, stroking my chin as I pondered its efficacy. But before I could open it up and give it a shot, Gaby called out from behind a display of Tarot cards. "JT, a little help here?"

After a single, longing stare at the Ouija board, I spun on my booted heel and joined Roger and Gaby. She handed me three candles, a large bronze goblet, and three small jars of oils. She carried a black velvet tablecloth and a few bundles of herbs that looked like she had just tied them together with twine.

Roger carried... well, nothing. That damned diva. Instead, he pulled a set of keys from the pocket of his kimono as he strode to the front door. He had one of those signs with a clock hanging in the door. He changed the clock's face to an hour from now before flipping it around so that the Be Back Soon side faced the street.

After that, he locked the bottom deadbolt and joined Gaby and me at the entrance to the back room. The door to it was set into an exposed brick wall, with racks of crystals and herbs set up against either side of it. He'd painted it teal and had it carved to look like some kind of fairy den resided on the other side. It added to the allure when he had contractors reading Tarot cards back there during the weekend.

Roger slid the key into the lock and opened the door to exactly what you'd expect a mystic room to look like. A large table dominated the center of the space with a deep burgundy crushed velvet tablecloth and crystal ball sitting on it. Three chairs surrounded the gaudy display while large tapestries of intensely colorful designs hung on the exposed brick walls. Along each of the back walls sat artistic tabletop displays of waxy candles in varying melted stages. The decor screamed *drama* as Gaby walked in and set the black tablecloth on a chair.

She and Roger moved the crystal ball onto a table littered with candles, shifting them around to make room. Once they finished, Gaby pulled off the burgundy cloth and replaced it with her black one. As she situated the cloth, I saw that it had a four-pronged star compass etched in silver in the middle. Once she'd arranged it to her liking, she snapped her fingers at me and waved her hand, indicating I should join her. Like a good pack mule, I obeyed, carting the goods to the table.

She snagged the candles from me while Roger grabbed the herbs, leaving me with the goblet. They placed the herbs on a bronze plate with Tara's picture and set the deep blue candles on the south, east, and west end of the star compass. Roger moved to the far edge of the room and lifted a purple tablecloth to display a mini fridge packed with water.

He grabbed a bottle and pointed to the north point of the compass. "Put the goblet there."

I approached the table and placed the goblet where Roger requested, feeling a little awkward, as I always did whenever we had to perform any kind of spell. My talents tended more toward the ass-kicking slash investigating arena and less toward the mystic one. But Gaby and Roger insisted that they needed three people with supernatural abilities to power most of our bigger spells. Apparently, my ability to see into the incorporeal realm, along with my other gifts, qualified me as a mystically powered entity.

So, I stood at the north edge of the table, feeling awkward as shit, while Gaby pulled a lighter from her oversized purse, along with her grimoire, which she had stowed away for convenience during her shopping spree. She set the grimoire on a chair open to the page she needed as she lit the three candles along the star compass. Roger filled the goblet about a quarter of the way with water and set the bottle aside.

From her purse, Gaby pulled out a map of Santa Sombra and the surrounding areas and smoothed it between the candles and goblet. I just hoped the demon hadn't gone too far with Tara and that this map would suffice. If not, we'd have to expand our search and figure out how the hell we'd manage to get her back with only two beat-to-hell cars and a moped at our disposal.

Once she'd arranged everything in its place, Gaby gestured for Roger and me to join her at the table. She cleared her throat and leveled her super-duper serious stare on me. Ruh-roh, I thought, as Roger and I exchanged a meaningful look. She took magic seriously, and that was probably a good thing. Reverence, from what I understood, was an important part of the process. Spells and the mystic arts required respect or else they could backfire and come back on the wielder.

"We need to talk about something before we do the spell." Since her eyebrows looked crazy serious, neither Roger nor I dared to interrupt. She filled Roger in on the full story of what had happened the night before, down to the bloodstain that remained on my couch. By the time she finished, Roger's face had grown pale, his bright-blue eyes and dark hair vibrant against his skin.

When Roger said nothing, she continued. "So, whatever happened to Jenna's client last night, we have to consider the possibility that a demon may have gotten through my wards at her apartment. And then there's the picture she showed Jenna of that demon... Jenna says that it looks fully human, aside from the aura and the hellfire." She jerked her chin toward the image. While Gaby and Roger couldn't see demons all the time, like me, they could for shorter spurts with some witchy intervention from Gaby. And Roger could sense them, their oppressive energy as he called it, but he still couldn't actually see them. As a result, Gaby's spells came in handy if I ever needed backup in a pinch. But for the moment, they'd just have to take my word for it.

Roger swallowed, the sound a loud gulp as he glanced between us. "What does that mean?"

I chose to remain silent, already knowing where Gaby was going with her sermon, but deciding to let her complete it. She had a much more soothing way about her than I did, which would increase the likelihood of getting Roger to help us.

Gaby licked her lips and slid a hand through her silky brown hair. "It means that what we're dealing with could be something stronger than we've ever encountered before. So this might be risky. I just want to make sure you guys know that." She tapped a finger to her temple. "You need to fortify your minds. Especially you, Roger. Make sure you have your mental walls up." Gaby reached for his hand and I watched as she pressed a piece of black tourmaline into his palm. "And this will help too, for protection."

As Roger's face grew even paler, a feat I hadn't thought possible, I wondered if maybe I should have told him about the case instead of her. She was totally freaking him out. "Rog," I said, pulling his attention back to me. "Can you please do this for me? For Tara, my client? It could be life or death for her. She needs us."

Roger blinked, refocusing his attention on me, and I could see a little of the terror subside. He stiffened his spine, straightening to his full height of five-eleven. "Of course, JT. If it's life or death, of course I'll do it."

I caught his eye, careful to pour all my gratitude into my expression, knowing he wouldn't want me to touch him at that moment. Alright, so he *never* wanted me to touch him, but that didn't matter. I still read the mood. "Thank you, Rog. I promise, it'll be okay. We'll keep you safe." It was a promise I didn't know if I could keep, but I had every intention of doing my damn best to.

Despite my resolve, a kernel of nervousness slithered in my belly, along with a dash of guilt. I hated to ask this of him when I didn't know what danger we might face next. But I didn't have a choice. Tara might not have much time left.

Gaby and I had both protected Roger at all costs, since the first moment we'd let him in on our little secret. He'd been through a lot, and having empathic abilities hadn't made his life an easy one. Knowing exactly how people felt every time you touched them really put a damper on one's interpersonal relationships. As a result, Roger had remained pretty much solo until he'd met us, and neither of us liked to see him hurt.

He looked at Gaby, who smiled at him in assurance. "We all agree, then? It's time?"

Roger nodded and so did I.

"Okay, let's get started," she said.

With everyone on board, Gaby produced a pocketknife from her jeans and pressed the tip onto the fleshy pad of her fingertip. She sucked in a sharp breath as the blade pierced her skin and a bead of bright-red blood appeared. She set the knife down and held her finger over the goblet of water, letting her blood drip into the cup.

From her purse, she grabbed a pack of wet wipes and swiped it over the blade. Then she passed the pack of wipes and the blade to me and I repeated the same process, letting my blood drip into the goblet. Roger went last, his gasp as the knife cut his finger a little more dramatic than either mine or Gaby's. Probably because he hadn't gotten his ass kicked quite as many times as we had. He did kind of owe us on that front. A thought that eased some of the guilt I still felt at talking him into doing this for us.

Once complete, Gaby snagged the three oils from the chair next to her and dropped those into the goblet. Then she pulled off the pointy lavender-colored crystal that dangled from a chain around her neck and dropped it into the oily, bloody water.

Gross.

Roger flicked off the lights and we all gathered around the table.

We reached out and hovered our hands over each other's as Gaby began to chant something in Spanish, enunciating the words so that I could follow her lead. Picking up her rhythm, I repeated them, along with Roger. After a few verses, the room turned staticky around us with power, the joining of our words and the focus on our purpose calling the magic to us like the north end of a magnet. The language didn't matter, Gaby had told me once, only the intent. She chose Spanish because it helped her focus her mind better, and I did my best to visualize our purpose as we chanted.

Despite our enclosure inside a windowless room with brick walls on all sides, an unseen wind whipped around us. It swirled like a cyclone, surrounding us in a cocoon, blocking the outside world with its dull roar but keeping our table and the spell intact. My hair slapped my face, whipping into my eyes and making them water, but I kept chanting, picturing Tara's face and focusing on my desire to find her.

The power around us intensified as the liquid inside the goblet began to boil, transforming from a thin, watery substance into something viscous and dark. I watched as the crystal rose from the goblet, floating up from the cup to levitate over the map as though possessed. We didn't stop chanting.

The lavender stone hovered over the city's streets and nearby towns, quivering as though trying to decide where to go next. It flicked from left to right before it settled on a spot. It dropped closer to the paper, the thickening fluid forming a perfect droplet on the end. I focused on it, waiting with bated breath for the liquid to drop onto the map, knowing that its blotch would mark the path we needed to follow to find Tara. We were so close, and I almost couldn't believe how simple it had been.

Just as the droplet fell from the stone, its journey to the map moving as though in slow motion, the goblet exploded.

Hot, gooey liquid splattered my face, burning as it hit me. The candles blew out and the crystal dropped like a dead weight, hitting the map with a thud. I sucked in a stunned breath and swiped at the moisture on my face, spitting it out of my mouth and resisting the urge to hurl.

The candles flickered before they blew out and the wind ceased, as a deafening silence swept through the room. All I could hear was my own coughing and Gaby's muffled curses. "What the hell happened?" I asked, realizing with horror that I'd just ingested Gaby and Roger's blood. We were close, but not *that* close.

Gaby sputtered and cursed a few times in Spanish. "I have no idea."

She cleared the goop from her eyes and stepped closer to the map, staring down at the crystal in the dimly lit room. I followed her lead, eyeing it warily. I had a bad feeling about this; the fear that it might shoot up from the map and impale my eyeball seemed all too possible. Hairs stood on the back of my neck right before the candles burst to life, fire skyrocketing up three feet in the air before settling back onto the wick. That was when I *knew* something was up. The danger Gaby had mentioned? I had the sickening feeling it had arrived.

I reached out, intending to grab Gaby's shoulder and pull her away and back toward the door, but before I could, a low guttural laugh echoed around us. I whipped my head to its source and saw Roger standing with his head down and his palms outstretched. He didn't have a single drop of the nasty goo on him. What the f—

"You will never find her." A smooth, cultured voice flowed from Roger's lips. It sounded too deep and emotionless for Roger's normal tone, and I knew right away something was off. His eyes snapped open, revealing pools of depthless black as he stared at us.

Dread coursed through me as I realized that the crystal Gaby had given Roger to use as protection hadn't worked, and we had an uninvited guest we needed to deal with.

"So you're the one who took Tara Bronsen, *demon*?" I asked, the malice in my voice unmistakable. It grinned at me, the shadow of its true face shuddering over Roger's handsome one. It rippled between Roger, someone more devastatingly gorgeous than even Roger, and back to the true monster I knew lurked beneath.

It pulled Roger's lips back in a horrifying, yet somehow stunning smile. A pure predator, the effect of that expression sending chills shivering up my spine. I squared my shoulders in response and tried not to let the fear I felt show. In a normal human, demons couldn't just possess them without a fight. They had to wear them down over months in order to break through the protection of their minds and bodies. But Roger's abilities made him an easier target, though it still shouldn't have been this easy to take full control of him. It confirmed our fears that whatever had stalked and taken Tara had serious power at its disposal.

"I've seen your face before, demon slayer. You're in way over your head, trust me. Walk away, leave Tara to me, and maybe I'll let you live." Fat chance. My client's life was on the line and I refused to walk away from this. Not now. Not ever.

I stepped closer to Roger's possessed body and assumed an intimidating air, my default demon hunter persona on full display. I closed my fists and narrowed my eyes. "So, she's still alive, then?"

The creature clicked its tongue in disapproval. *"You're not listening... Jenna Torrence."* It drew out my name, emphasizing every syllable as its smug gaze traveled the length of me. The demon beneath Roger's skin flickered, its dark essence visible to the naked eye for the briefest moment. I froze, my body tensing to the consistency of marble, not daring to react and give away how much its knowledge of my name startled me.

Demons and me, we didn't operate on a first-name basis. We didn't play frisbee golf and drink microbrews together on the weekend. I killed them and they went to hell, end of story. But before I could offer any kind of a response, it recited my address. My guts turned to acid in two seconds flat and though I tried to maintain my stoic demeanor, I could feel my whole body react.

"JT," Gaby whispered, and the breathy way she said my name made her fear palpable.

The creature snapped Roger's head toward her, as though just taking notice of the witch who'd inadvertently summoned him. *"Ah, Gaby Perez. 5544 N. 54th St. Shall I continue? Roger-boy's head here is full of useful information, a real treasure trove. I have to say, ladies, you made a big mistake searching for me. I can assure you, the last thing you want is my attention."*

I gritted my teeth, trying to twist my fear into anger, a much more useful emotion considering our circumstances. "If you're in Roger's head, then you know exactly who I am, and how many of your kind I've killed. Let Tara go now and I won't come after you. This is the only warning you'll get from me." I leaned forward, resting my palms on the table we'd used for the spell, the paper map rustling beneath my touch. "Because the last thing you want, demon, is *my* attention."

We sounded like two big swinging dicks, striving to see who could intimidate the other more. But when it laughed, tossing its head back in sheer delight, I knew I'd lost. *"You've never killed any of my kind. I'm not a bottom-dweller. I'm not like the others you've exterminated like the vermin they are. You've never faced anything like Beaseldorf before."*

Beaseldorf? What the fuck was a *Beaseldorf*? Then I realized the demon had just given us its name. I felt stunned for a second. First, because its name sounded too goddamned ridiculous for something so terrifying, but also because it had given it up with no fight whatsoever. Every demon I had ever encountered protected its name like a virgin did her virtue on prom night. Okay, maybe not the best analogy, but you get the picture. They didn't give it up for free.

Taking advantage of my surprise, it leaned over to match my posture, resting Roger's palms on the table and getting right in my face. Its breath fanned over me, the smell like hot honey and bone-deep rot. I tried not to recoil. *"Please, try to find your client. I look forward to the challenge. I can't wait to drain all of the blood from your body before I cut you limb from limb."* He twisted Roger's lips back into that horrifying grin. "*You can't stop what I've already set in motion. No one can.*"

With that Roger's body shuddered and convulsed right before he flew back into the brick wall, a cracking thud issuing from his impact. I sucked in a startled breath and sprinted toward him, fear pricking up my spine. He'd hit hard, his head smacking against the stone, and I remembered my promise to keep him safe, guilt dropping like a stone in my gut.

As I skidded to a halt, sinking to my knees at his side, Roger's mouth opened, his jaw stretching wide while his head angled up to the sky. I watched with a sickening kind of horror as black primordial ooze ejected from his mouth. It spewed out of him like sticky vomit and splattered on the ceiling, undulating and rancid. Within the space between heartbeats, it curled together, like a sentient sludge before it disappeared into a thin veil of smoke.

And just like that, Beaseldorf was gone.

La Fortuna Cocina, Downtown Santa Sombra, Fourteen Years Ago

I paced back and forth outside of La Fortuna Cocina for about ten minutes before I decided to walk through the glass door that led inside. It was a small Mexican restaurant in downtown Santa Sombra, nestled between two high-rise buildings on K street—one of the main drags in the city.

As I walked in, a bell chimed and the scent of sauteed bell peppers, cooking meat, and fresh cilantro hit me. My mouth watered involuntarily, the humming, conversational sounds of the near-full restaurant buzzing in my ears.

I'd had yet another night of scanty food at ye old foster home. Erin and Dave's fridge only boasted a few remaining frozen french fries. They didn't even have any ketchup left for dipping. If I had any hope of getting placed into a new home, I knew I'd need to run away soon. But I'd just have to save that problem for another day. For now, I needed to focus on the one right in front of me. I needed to figure out how in the heck Gaby Perez could see demons and what that meant for me.

Or, well, us.

As I stepped farther into the restaurant, I admired the Dia De Los Muertos mural that spanned the walls, sugar skulls and elaborate costumed dancers decorating every inch.

After a brief moment, I heard someone call my name nearby. "Jenna! There you are!" Gaby popped up from behind the counter, her face flushed. I blinked, a little surprised to see her behind the service counter situated just in front of the kitchen. As she stepped around it, she untied a green apron and set it on the counter. Thick wooden tables sat in the center of the restaurant, and comfortable-looking six-seater booths lined the outer walls.

"Mama! My friend's here. I'm going to take my break!" I heard some vague shouting from behind two swinging doors that I assumed blocked the kitchen from view. A moment later, the doors burst open and a woman who looked like Gaby, but about twenty-five years older, came out.

She wiped her hands on a towel as her gaze swept from me to her daughter. "Mija, it's great to have friends, but you need to do your homework."

"Don't worry, Mama. I'll make sure it's done before we go home. I promise."

She looked from Gaby to me once more, and I could see her surveying me, eyeing me from head to toe. Only, I couldn't tell what she was thinking behind her mask of courtesy.

Normally, adults didn't love their kids hanging out with me. I had nearly black hair, sported dark eye makeup, and also wore a lot of blacks and grays. I didn't do the goth thing; I just didn't like bright colors. I wanted to fade into the background and avoid notice as much as possible, and bright colors didn't aid in my efforts. It also didn't help that most of my clothes looked old and not in a cute vintage way. But in a legitimate hand-me-down way, which made sense since I bought them at thrift stores.

Rather than turn her nose up at me though, Gaby's mom stepped around the counter too and extended her hand to me. "Hi, I'm Sandra, Gaby's mom."

I only hesitated for a moment before I returned the gesture, her warm, calloused fingers sliding around mine. "Hi, Mrs. Perez. I'm Jenna, Jenna Torrence."

Surprise crossed her features, and I knew that she'd heard about me. Probably from that time I tripped Gaby and she face-planted in the mud.

"Jenna," she said, drawing my name out and looking at Gaby in confusion, who seemed to plead with her eyes for her mom to say nothing. "It's nice to meet you. I see you have your backpack. Do you also have homework?"

Gaby groaned before rolling her eyes. "Moommm."

"I do, actually."

Sandra smiled. "Perfect. You can do homework while you visit together. Are you hungry?"

"Oh, that's alright, I—" and then my stomach betrayed me. It growled. Loudly.

She let out a soft laugh. "Alright, I'll make you both a quick dinner. Are fajitas okay?"

My mouth watered once more. "Yes, but you really don't have to, I don't have any—" I swallowed. "I didn't bring any money with me."

She grinned warmly, her eyes sparkling against her tanned skin as she waved me away with the towel. "No, chica, you don't need to worry about it. It's on the house."

Before I could protest, she turned, walking back into the kitchen. Loud mariachi music blasted out from behind the doors as she opened them. "Ernesto! Turn that down!" I heard her yell before the doors closed and the sound disappeared.

I turned my attention back to Gaby, and I could see her embarrassment, but I couldn't understand why. "Sorry about my mom. She can be a little con-

trolling." Gaby stepped away from me and moved back toward the counter before bending down and disappearing from view. When she rose again, she had her backpack slung over her shoulder.

Gaby led me to a booth far from the counter, and I frowned at her back. "Your mom seems nice to me."

She scoffed as we slid into the seats across from each other. "You should try living with her."

It took every ounce of self-control I had not to let the emotions I felt in that moment show. I wondered for the millionth time what it would be like to have a real mother of my own. Honestly, I would kill to know what it felt like to have a mom who gave a crap about me doing my homework. Instead of Erin, who was so drunk on the couch right now that she hadn't even realized I'd left after dark on a weeknight.

Rather than say any of that aloud, I settled into the booth across from Gaby, the red vinyl cushions just as comfortable as they looked. "So, do you work here?"

"Yeah. My mom and dad own this place. It's our family's restaurant, so I help out after school."

"That's cool." Mexican food on demand sounded pretty awesome to me. We opened our backpacks and placed our books and notebooks on the table. I took out her purple jelly roll pen, looking at it a little longingly. It was way nicer than any of the pens I had. But it didn't belong to me and I knew that I couldn't keep it, so I bit the bullet and held it out to her. "Here, you can have this back."

"Oh," she said, looking at it. A second later, she shook her head. "No, you keep it. Consider it a thank-you gift for saving my butt earlier." So she had

noticed, I thought, smiling a little despite myself as I looked down at my new pen.

I could feel her eyes boring into me, and when I looked up, she stared right at me. "You know, I don't think I've ever seen you do that."

"What?" I asked, hand going to my hair automatically. No idea why.

"Smile," she said, looking down at her papers and reading what looked like a printed assignment. "It's actually kind of nice, and it makes you look a lot less scary. You should do it more often."

It was hard to smile when you had no friends and the people who played the role of your parents didn't give a shit about you. But I didn't bother saying any of that aloud. It sounded a little too pathetic, and I neither needed nor wanted Gaby's pity. "I'll take that under advisement."

She snorted a laugh, shaking her head at me. "Under advisement? You're so weird."

I cracked another grin, shrugging. "Yeah, I read a lot."

"Really?"

"Well, I kind of had to in order to figure things out. You know, the kind of things we saw earlier today."

She stilled, her eyes rising to meet mine just as the kitchen doors popped open. I heard sizzling as Gaby's mom strolled over, carrying two plates of food and a basket of chips and salsa. My stomach growled again, but this time it was overshadowed by the sound of still cooking steak and chicken.

She reached us a few seconds later, handling the plates with ease. Setting the food down in front of us, she offered us both a smile as she gestured at our open books on the table. "Good girls. I'll bring you some drinks." We waited in silence as she filled two glasses from a pitcher of water at the counter and brought them back to us.

"Thank you, Mrs. Perez. This looks delicious," I said, all but drooling at the spread she'd laid out before us. Sauteed vegetables, meat, refried beans, Mexican rice, and all the usual fajita fixings.

She beamed. "You're welcome. Enjoy." Turning on her heel, she headed back into the kitchen, and I noticed the place had filled up even more since my arrival. Every single table was full and the sound of talking and the clinking of silverware surrounded us as we piled food on our plates.

Gaby cleared her throat as I took my first bite of fajita. It was heavenly, and I made an effort not to groan at how delicious it tasted. She set her own fajita down and leaned forward, looking at me with intensity. "So, what did we see today? What was that thing?"

I hesitated, chewing more slowly as I set my tortilla down. "You mean, you still don't know?"

She shook her head, her eyes going a little distant as though slipping into deep thought. "I'm not sure. Not exactly, at least."

Taking advantage of the silence, I grabbed a chip and scooped up some salsa. I bit into it, the sweet spice of the salsa and the saltiness of the chip a delicious combination. "This is good."

"Right? My dad makes it. It's his secret recipe."

When I finished chewing, I rubbed my hands on the napkin in my lap. I'd read somewhere that napkins sat in your lap when you ate at a restaurant, and it seemed like good advice because everyone had theirs in the same spot.

But as for Gaby's question, what could I say that wouldn't freak her out? Then again, did I care if I scared her? She'd seen a wrath demon, and I doubted she'd believe a milk-toast lie that didn't add up with the horror of that thing.

"What you saw earlier, it's a demon." Better to just get it out there, I decided. She could freak out for a few and we could move on to other things, like how the heck she managed to see it in the first place.

Gaby's eyes widened, her fajita apparently forgotten as she stared at me. "No way! Uno demonio? Are you sure?"

"Unfortunately, yes. It's a wrath one too. Real nasty buggers." I took another bite of fajita. She may have decided she wasn't hungry, but I didn't feel the same. Hunger rumbled through my empty stomach, and this was the best meal I'd had in... well ever. I spoke through a full mouth, doing my best to conceal my food with my hand. "I take it you've never seen one before?"

Gaby shook her head. "No, I haven't. My abuela has told me about them, so I knew they existed, but I just never expected to come face-to-face with one. She's una bruja, a good one too, and she's taken me under her wing. She's teaching me." She leaned in, her voice dropping to a whisper. "My mama doesn't know and she wouldn't approve, so please don't say anything. She doesn't like me messing with that stuff. Mama thinks my abuela is kooky." She twirled her finger around her ear. "And I used to think it was mostly just coincidence and kind of a game we played together, but lately I'm not so sure. We've been able to make things happen that I can't explain otherwise. And we, um—" She broke off, looking down at her tortilla once more, as though debating whether or not she wanted it. She refocused her attention on me without touching it. "We did a spell last night. It was meant to help me find my spirit guide. Ever since then, I've seen the strangest things. Really weird things, and I thought maybe the spell had just gone bad on me. I've been waiting for it to wear off, but then you saw it too, the demonio. So, how did you see it?"

I shrugged my shoulders. "I just see them."

She paused, considering what I said. "So, you see demons like... all the time?" I couldn't tell if she was shocked, horrified, or something else. She didn't seem as terrified as I thought she should, and that definitely struck me as weird. Maybe it just hadn't sunk in yet.

I tilted my head from side to side and wiped my hand on my napkin. "Yeah, I mean not like all the time. They aren't around all the time, you know. Only sometimes."

She continued to stare at me and shivered. "That thing was terrifying, and I only saw one this one time. How do you deal with seeing them all the time? And oh my gosh, when no one else can see them? Or do you know other people who can, like your mom or dad? Can they too?"

I didn't know what to say, so I hesitated for a few beats. "I, um, no. I've never met anyone else who can see them. At least, not until now. Why aren't you more scared?" I asked, genuinely curious.

Most kids our age would have been terrified, shaking in her boots, peeing in their pants level afraid. The demon had almost targeted her today and used its power to pour its rage into her. She'd come this close to it, but then she probably didn't realize the true scope of the danger. And I didn't plan to tell her. Not yet at least.

She shrugged. "I am scared, I just—I don't know. Like I said, I've always known demonios exist. Just because I hadn't seen one before didn't mean that they weren't already there. It's scary, but not like earth-shattering or anything. And by the way, what did you mean earlier, about it being a wrath demon?"

I cleared my throat, launching into a short explanation, feeling a little emboldened by her curiosity. "Well, from what I can tell there are seven types of demons, at least that I've seen so far. They are all harbingers of the seven deadly sins. That one was wrath." I sighed. "I hate the wrath ones. They're the hardest breed to fight, and they always seem to cause carnage wherever they go."

Her eyes went wide. "You fight them?" And that was when I realized I'd probably said too much. I'd let her soften me up with delicious food and conversation with another human my age. Then the gift of the jelly roll pen. Stupid, stupid, stupid.

"Erm, yeah."

"Wait, what do you mean carnage?"

I let out another long sigh, as though debating how much more I should tell her. I'd already let her in too much. It was probably best to stop while I was already behind. Before I got further behind. Before I shoved my foot so far in my mouth that my toes came out of my nose.

Seeming to sense my hesitation, she wagged a finger at me. "No, no, no. You don't get to clam up on me now. I saw that thing, same as you did. I go to that school too, and so do my friends, and you said that wrath demons cause carnage. What do you mean? How bad?"

I tried to brush it off with a shoulder shrug. "Don't worry about it. I'm going to take care of it before anything like that can happen."

"By yourself? No way. I'm not going to let you fight that thing alone. I can help you. You and I can confront it together."

My back stiffened. "No," I said, my voice louder than I'd intended. A few customers looked in our direction, and Gaby snapped her mouth shut, clearly surprised at my refusal. I waited until the other patrons looked away before I continued. "We are not going to confront anything. That demon can't know that you know about it. I've made that mistake before, and I'm immune to their influence. Other people aren't. Which probably means you aren't either.

It's safe to assume that the only reason you could see it was that spell. So again, no, it's too dangerous."

"So it's too dangerous for me, but not for you?"

"It's different for me, alright? I'm different."

"Right, because you're so much better than everyone else." She rolled her eyes, an expression she seemed to enjoy a lot since she kept doing it.

Suddenly, I felt like she'd slapped me, the shock of those words seeping into my very bones. "Better than everyone else? You really believe that I think I'm better than everyone else?"

"Don't you?"

A deep pit formed in the bottom of my gut. "No. I think I'm cursed." The words hung between us for a moment before I pushed my plate away from me. "Well, thanks for the dinner, but I better get going." I started to pull the books and notebooks together in a pile, preparing to put them in my backpack when I felt a warm hand press over mine. I stilled, looking down at it like it was a venomous spider.

"What are you doing?" I asked, still staring at it.

But she didn't move, and instead, she just kept it there. "I'm sorry, Jenna. Please don't go yet. I didn't mean that."

"Pretty sure you did."

"Maybe I did, but I was obviously wrong." She waited and I released my books as I looked back up at her.

I sighed. "Look, I just don't want to be responsible for someone else getting hurt. I'm still learning how to fight them myself, and no offense, but you don't look like the fighting type. You take notes in a Lisa Frank notebook for Pete's sake. I mean, who still does that anyway?" I gave a pointed look at that very notebook sitting on the table next to her and raised my brows.

She pointed at it in question before letting out an amused laugh. "This? This isn't for school notes. It's my grimoire, my spell book. My abuela gave it to me when I turned ten. Lisa Frank was still kind of big back then, and she went a little overboard, so I'm stuck with it now. And I know you think I'll just get hurt, but I won't. I can help. We can fight this one together."

I stared at her notebook before I returned my attention to her, my once mortal enemy. I shouldn't have let her wear me down so easily. But deep down, I wanted to accept her help. The comfort of having someone else to share my life with, to share the burden of fighting the demons I saw overwhelmed my better judgment.

Because what would happen if she got hurt? The guilt would eat me alive, I knew. But at that moment, I couldn't stand the idea of doing everything alone for another second. Not when I finally had the chance to change that. I'd been alone for so long, I just wanted to have someone else to talk to. For someone else to give a shit about me, and maybe even have my back. Did it make me selfish to let Gaby get involved? Maybe.

But she had abilities of her own, just like me. Maybe together, we could find a better way to fight off this demon. To fight demons in general. Because even I had to admit, my current method consisted of me getting my butt kicked nine times out of ten before I managed to send them back to hell. And I knew that sooner or later, I wouldn't make it out alive.

So I stared at her, her eyes eager as she waited for my response. "Okay. We can try to fight this one together. But first, we need a plan."

Gaby's grin spread wide, and I wondered if I'd gotten myself into serious trouble. Or if maybe, just maybe, I'd found the friend I'd wished for my whole life.

Chapter 8

Roger collapsed and I lunged forward, catching him under the arms just before his head hit the floor like a ton of shit. I lowered him slowly and prayed that Beaseldorf hadn't done any permanent damage. Hope flooded me at the knowledge that the whole demon hadn't possessed his body. Instead, only a piece of its essence had made its way into my friend. Or at least I assumed that small puddle of sludge didn't encompass the entire demon. Especially not with the level of cockiness Beaseldorf had exuded.

Gaby rushed forward too, falling to her knees next to us. We patted Roger's face with gentle taps as we tried to wake him. Finally, after a few minutes of effort with no effect, I hauled back my hand and slapped the ever-loving crap out of him.

He sucked in a stunned breath and jolted upright. Noting his position on the floor and the state of his back room, sticky with dark, bloody goop from the goblet, his mouth gaped open. “What the hell happened?” He patted his chest and face as though to make sure his head remained attached to his body. Thankfully, it did. “Did I pass out?”

I cleared my throat and looked at Gaby, brows raised. She offered him her softest, most maternal expression. “You don’t remember anything?”

He shook his head, a little bewildered. “Did the spell work?” He brushed off his kimono and scowled at the goop he’d picked up from the wall and floor. “Well, this will never come out.”

I offered him a wry smile. If he’d already shifted gears to concern for his wardrobe, then I felt confident that Beaseldorf hadn’t damaged anything critical, like his brain. Or his glorious balls, or whatever he’d called them.

Chuckling softly in relief, I rose to my feet and walked over to the crystal, which still lay undisturbed atop the map on the table. I’d taken care not to touch it and had made a mental note of its position earlier, when I’d leaned over to threaten Beaseldorf. Though I had wanted to intimidate him when I’d squared off against him, the move also disguised my secondary goal. I’d wanted to see where the crystal landed before Beaseldorf did something crazy like set the map on fire. To my surprise, he hadn’t.

However, the fact that he had managed to possess Roger so thoroughly made me believe Beaseldorf couldn’t be far away. Mostly likely, he was holding Tara somewhere in Santa Sombra and maybe the stone had fallen close to that very spot. I didn’t know if that was just wishful thinking or not. But we had to start somewhere.

With Roger out of harm's way, I peered down at the map and gestured for them to join me. Once Roger sidled up beside me, I offered him an apologetic grimace, deciding I best get the explanation out sooner rather than later. "A demon possessed you and blew up the ritual, but I'm hoping the crystal homed in on Tara's location before the bad guy intervened." I stared at where the crystal had dropped and stroked my chin, Gaby's shoulder nearly brushing mine on my other side.

I spared her a glance as her brows knitted together in confusion. "Do you really think the spell pinpointed her location before Beaseldorf screwed it all up? Maybe it's a trap."

I shrugged. She had a point. "Well, we better get geared up—"

"I'm sorry… WHAT? I was POSSESSED? Who the— What the—" Roger yelled, seemingly unable to finish a thought. Maybe Beaseldorf *had* damaged his brain, and I turned to check him over again as he stared at us, his mouth agape.

"Yeah, Beaseldorf," I answered, shifting my attention from my kimono'd buddy to Gaby's purse and snagging a pen from it.

Roger stared at us, aghast. "What the fuck is a Beaseldorf? It sounds like some kind of German Wiener schnitzel. And oh my gosh, ow! My head is killing me!" He rubbed at the back of his skull, as though just now noticing the pain from smacking into the wall.

I half laughed, half winced, which happened more often in my business than you might think. The man had a point about Beaseldorf's name, and I also felt a little bad about the lump I knew he'd have on his head. Ignoring that for the moment, I used Gaby's pen to trace an area around the stone and then picked it up and handed it to her.

Refocusing on Roger, I patted his shoulder, careful not to touch any bare skin. I didn't want yet another reason to feel like a dirtbag today. "You're right, it does sound like a wiener, but it's not. It's the name of the demon who possessed you."

Roger crossed his arms over his chest and sighed. "Fat load of good this crystal did." He grumbled a few choice curses under his breath before chucking the black tourmaline onto the table. "I'm not going to get any sympathy from you two, am I?" When we didn't answer right away, he plowed on. "You know, being a medium sucks the big one. The big fat juicy one. Demons and ghosts can just ride shotgun whenever they want and take over the steering wheel like I'm a Ferrari in the ghetto with a flashing sign that says *Free Ride Baby, I'm Yours!*"

"Uh-huh," I said, no longer paying attention. I knew this line all too well. Though we tried our best to protect Roger, we couldn't save him from everything nefarious in our lives, and we'd gone through something like this a few times before. He could usually fight off any kind of possession on his own, but not Beaseldorf's. That knowledge did give me just the teensiest bit of pause, before I dismissed any caution I might have shown out of hand.

Honestly, though, I did feel bad for Roger. Being a medium sucked. It meant he was always open for business as a supernatural conduit. But it also had its perks. For example, I now knew the name of the demon we hunted and we had a rough location of where to start looking for Tara. Or maybe, where to go if I wanted to get extra specially unalived in some kind of an elaborate trap. I couldn't quite tell which way this would go yet.

But since we had a grand total of one lead, I planned to follow it. I pointed at my drawing. “I’ll start in this area. It’s about ten square miles. I can canvass it and look for her there. You guys stay here. If it’s a trap, I don’t want to drag you into it.”

Gaby shook her head gnawing on a lip as she stared at the map. “Jenna, I don’t know. First the picture, then Tara disappearing from your *warded* apartment, and now this? Roger didn’t even know he was possessed, and he can normally shake a demon on his own. But this one took him over completely, and now he has zero memory of it. Are you sure you want to do this?”

I looked at her and Roger and in both I could see the trepidation etched in the lines of their expressions. I recalled the conversation with Gaby the night before. About my lack of invincibility and my non-superhero status. But if we didn’t help Tara, then who would? Luke and Bud couldn’t find her alone, and even if they did somehow catch up with Beaseldorf? Well, human weapons didn’t work on demons, and something told me that Beaseldorf didn’t play by the same rules as the demons I usually hunted. He could put their lives in actual danger, and perhaps not just their souls.

“What are you asking me to do here, Gabs? This is our only lead. If I don’t follow it, I may as well just let Beaseldorf have his way with her. Maybe even kill her. And you know I can’t do that.” I’d taken her in, promised to keep her safe in my apartment, and Beaseldorf had stolen her right out from under my nose.

When Gaby didn’t respond right away, I pressed on. “And what about what Beaseldorf said about us not being able to *stop what’s already in motion*? That sounded bad, like big picture kind of bad. Do you really think we should just walk away and pretend none of this ever happened? Who else can do what we do? Look guys, I'd gladly farm this one out, delegate it to Joe-Schmo demon hunter, but oh yeah, we've never met another one like me, and I highly doubt I'd find a legit hunter to take my place on such short notice. So, it's just me, and you guys."

Gaby sucked in a breath before she released it, shaking her head. "I'm sorry, you're right." I felt a little bad coming down on them so hard, but they needed to think with their heads and not their fear for me, or for us. I'd be fine, so would they. I had gifts, we all did. And we could use them to stop whatever plan Beaseldorf had set into motion and save Tara. I couldn't let this go. That thing had come into *my* home and attacked *my* client, possessed Roger, and recited our addresses on cue. The demon had made this personal.

I nodded. "Good. I'll canvass the area and report back to you every ten minutes. That way if I disappear, you'll know where to start looking."

Gaby crossed her arms over her chest, clearly unimpressed by my plans. But I pushed forward. "I've got his scent now. For all his talk about how I shouldn't have gone looking for him, well, I've got news for you guys, he shouldn't have goaded me. Knowing him, knowing *his essence*, will only make him easier to track." I had a pretty decent sense of supernatural smell. Once I came into contact with any demon, I could pick up its scent if I got within range. And my range seemed to span about a mile or two. So, I'd still need to get decently close in the large urban and suburban sprawl that comprised the greater Santa Sombra area.

Gaby turned to Roger, her eyes narrowed as though I'd said something deeply stupid. I racked my brain, trying to think of what I could have done, but came up blank.

Then she spoke to Roger, pointing at me like I'd lost the last marble I had in my sad little noggin. "Does she seriously think she's going alone? Like we'd let her go alone into a possible trap."

"Wait, we're not?" Roger asked, surprise plain in his expression.

Gaby rolled her eyes before she smacked his arm. "Seriously, Rog?"

Roger turned to me. "No, right. Of course. We're obviously coming with you, Jenna. Right?" He turned back to Gaby for confirmation.

"Right."

The column of Roger's throat bobbed as he crossed his arms over his chest and nodded. I could still see the discomfort that both he and Gaby felt for the whole situation, and I didn't blame them. But I couldn't let their fear dissuade me from doing what I had to do to find Tara. Something big was brewing. I could feel it. In fact, I think I felt it the moment I met Tara and saw that picture. And I intended to find out what that something was, preferably before Beaseldorf could rip me limb from limb.

CHAPTER 9

We spent the rest of the day and the early evening canvassing the area where the crystal had landed. Its position on the map had forced us to drive to the other end of town, farther east and outside the city limits. After what happened at the magic shop, Gaby and Roger refused to let us split up in any meaningful way. As a result, the process was taking longer than usual.

I looked at Gaby, who served as our designated driver. Her puffy white coat and furry hood made her look just a touch like the Stay Puf Marshmallow Man, but I refrained from commenting since I didn't have a death wish. We turned right, heading toward the Relics Loop and Old Willow Glen. We'd already canvassed most of Verde Heights, the other city where the crystal had dropped, and had come up empty.

As we edged closer to our fifth stop of the day, I had to admit, my Spidey senses emitted zero tingles. Not even a little one. Perhaps I'd overstated the matter of Beaseldorf's essence and my ability to trace it. My tracking capabilities had never failed me before, but as Beaseldorf said, I'd never faced anything like him before. Or maybe the crystal really had just dropped in a random spot and he wasn't lurking anywhere close to our search area. I had no way of knowing for sure.

Gaby took the Relics Loop at breakneck speed and we blew past Relics & Roots, a giant outdoor flea market, before we whipped into the visitor parking lot. Old Willow Glen consisted of a massive working railyard, narrow streets lined with older Craftsman style homes, and plenty of apartments. It had a functioning and busy old-town area with shops, bars, and restaurants, along with the Relics & Roots outdoor market, which meant we had a lot of ground to cover.

We pulled into a parking space, intending to walk as much of the area as we could with Relics & Roots as our starting point. Gaby yanked her purse off the floor by my feet and rummaged through it. I saw the metal gleam of her illegally concealed pistol just before she zipped up the bag and hauled it onto her shoulder. Apparently, she'd decided to take no chances either, should we run into Beaseldorf.

Though, I did have serious questions about the efficacy of her magic bullets, considering how little the wards had done to keep Beaseldorf out when he'd kidnapped Tara. I decided not to bring that up just yet. Nothing we could do about it at the moment anyway, and she needed the sense of security the gun provided.

Roger sat in the back seat and had exchanged his signature kimono in favor of something less conspicuous. He now sported a navy peacoat with a pair of skinny jeans and ankle-high lace-up boots. He looked like he'd stepped right off the cover of *GQ*, with his brown hair perfectly quaffed. As we all climbed out of the car, I considered taking him up on his offer to dress me and decided against it. I had my own style, and I didn't need him putting me in a pink wrap dress or something equally horrifying. I mean, where would I put my gun in something like that?

As we made our way to the entrance of the market, said gun felt heavy in the back of my waistband. I also illegally concealed it, so I adjusted my coat to better hide it. Even though I had a weapon for protection, my back felt naked without the scabbard of my katana. I would have brought one of my old faithfuls, but a sword had a way of drawing undo attention that a concealed firearm didn't.

Roger's voice broke through the silence we'd kept since our last stop. "Why are we going to Relics & Roots again? Do we really think Beaseldorf has Tara trussed up somewhere in a flea market? Like he's going to barter her soul away for some ghost pepper plants and a gently used dresser set?"

I shrugged helplessly, frustrated that my hunter's instincts hadn't bothered kicking in to offer any assistance. "I have no idea, Rog, but we check everything. And I mean everything. No stone left unturned, alright?" I scanned the parking lot and noted the massive lines of campers and RVs, thinking that those would make for a good place to hide a kidnapping victim.

We walked through rows of them, listening for anything out of the ordinary. Gaby and Roger remained quiet, understanding my process and my need for silence, while also tapping into their own supernatural senses. Roger reached out with his empath gifts, trying to read the area for any ominous energy. Gaby used her witchy crystals and charms, which she'd stuffed into her pockets, trying to sense anything unnatural nearby. By the time we'd walked the lot, all three of us had come up empty.

We decided to head into the market, with Roger citing the need for some fresh vegetables and a killer BBQ sauce.

I narrowed my eyes on him. "Focus, Rog. Don't get distracted."

"I'm multitasking, not getting distracted."

I frowned at him, and he gave me a pissy look that told me to drop it. So I did. But honestly, he needed BBQ sauce? I had no idea Roger even knew how to operate a grill. He'd been holding out on us, and I would definitely have a bone to pick with him over that later.

As we entered the market, we split up, each taking a row, but making a point to stick close together. Never out of earshot, just in case we happened upon something deadly.

I roamed through the throngs of people. Kids shouted and ran, gathering around a petting zoo with goats and other farm animals. Vendors offered their wares from open-aired booths—paintings, statues, furniture, jewelry, plants, and Tarot cards decorated the tables and the makeshift wooden walls alike.

The fresh aroma of funnel cakes and tamales filled my senses, and I realized that Gaby and I needed to come back for a non-business trip. It could be fun. I liked goats, deep fried cake, and authentic Mexican cuisine, and I'd bet my last dollar she did too.

Something tugged at me, nothing nefarious or demonic as far as I could tell, but I felt something pulling me toward the east end of the market. I followed that sensation, turning a corner right before I sucked in a surprised breath. The booth seemed to come from nowhere, jutting out from the end of a long row like a siren's song, its magnificence undeniable. The sun peeked out from behind the clouds as a beautiful ray of light shone upon it, a double rainbow forming in the sky.

Okay, so not really, but it felt that way as I stared at a collection of knives and swords unlike anything I'd ever seen. Their ornate beauty suggested skilled craftsmanship and lots of TLC. My eyes widened of their own accord as I resisted the urge to drool at the sheer radiance of the weapons before me.

Sparing a quick glance around, I stepped closer to Valhalla. Knives decorated a makeshift table encased in plexi-glass for safety, and behind the cobbled-together counter where the vendor stood hung swords of all makes and styles. Broadswords, shortswords, and best of all, katanas.

I leaned forward, peering at them with squinted eyes trying to make out the markings on the blades, thinking that this might just solve the katana problem Cheekybastard115 had subjected me to.

Within seconds, a booming voice rang out to greet me. "Hello there, welcome! What can I help you with today?" I turned to look at the seller, a little surprised that someone had spoken to me, so absorbed was I in the beauty of the swords that surrounded me.

His presence forced me out of my pretty weapon induced stupor. "Oh, hi." The man had ruddy brown hair, a large frame and a thick, Norse godlike beard. I pointed at the blades behind him. "Do you make these?"

I didn't bother to mask the awe in my tone and he beamed with obvious pride. "Most of them, yes. Some, though, are collectibles that I've picked up along the way. Bartered for one thing or another. Do you see something that interests you?"

"Um, all of it?"

He laughed, the sound contagious, and I cracked a smile in return right as I realized I should probably play it cool rather than salivate over his beautiful creations. Everything in Relics & Roots worked on a barter system, and if I came off too desperate, I'd probably end up signing over Gaby's car before I realized what I'd agreed to. He gestured at the swords behind him. "Do you have a collection?"

I sighed, looking forlorn. "Yes, but my most recent addition, a katana, had an unfortunate incident, and now I need a new one."

"Katana?" he asked, running fingers through his epic beard in thought. He had a nice way about him, and for some reason I found him oddly trustworthy. "May I ask why a katana?"

I rested my forearms on the counter and leaned forward, excited to talk to someone else who might actually understand my love of swords. "Well, it's thin, light, long, and fast. It's easy to handle and sharp as a motherfucker. They've never let me down before."

"What do you mean they've never let you down? Are you saying that you *fight* with these weapons?"

Oh crap. My mouth had gotten away from me again. I needed to remember that normal people didn't use swords for their intended purposes, at least not anymore. I always seemed to forget that. "Oh yeah—um—you know—tournaments. I'm a karate master." Were karate masters even a thing? I had a silent, internal debate about that, wincing a little at how capital C *crazy* I sounded.

The suspicious look left his eyes, thank God, and he nodded in understanding. "Right, well, if you want another katana, they're along this wall to your left. Would you like to get a closer look?"

I nodded, but this time with less feverish enthusiasm.

He stepped aside, gesturing for me to enter the confines of the booth, and I moved closer to the amazing display of blades he had available. "Are they genuine or replicas?" I asked as I examined the four katanas that hung one below the other on the far wall.

"All genuine. I have papers to prove it, if you're interested in purchasing one."

I nodded and moved closer, but as I did, something made me hesitate. A hum or a buzz or... something. It was hard to explain, but my blood felt like it had started to electrify in my veins and something clawed for my attention. I halted and turned my head to the right, searching for whatever it was that had me lit up like a bong at a frat party.

It caught my attention instantly, a sword unlike any I'd ever seen before. It wasn't a katana, a broadsword, or a shortsword, or at least not exactly. Instead, its wide, long, and ultra-thin blade gleamed a silvery gold, and the hilt... well, the hilt took my breath away. Intricate carvings of demons and angels spanned the full length of it, a representation of battles fought and won. As I dragged my eyes over it in reverence, they settled at the very top of the hilt. I squinted to examine a woven symbol unlike anything I'd ever seen before.

I stepped closer, the blade calling to my soul like a song on the wind that only I could hear. This sword was no ordinary weapon and it seemed to want... *me.* It was responsible for the pull I felt earlier, I realized, the one that had drawn me directly to this spot. I couldn't explain other than to say that it had a soul and that soul called to my own. I reached up and ran my fingers along the writing carved into the metal of the blade, a stunning set of feathered wings at the top of it.

"Where did you get this one?" I asked

"That one I won in a hell of a lucky card game many years ago. You're the first person to ever ask me about it, despite its obvious beauty. Never did understand why. Are you interested? I can make you a good deal."

As my heart hammered in my ears, I turned back to him, the act of looking away from the weapon almost painful. "I'm interested." I tried to keep my tone casual and hide just how much I wanted that damn blade. I may have desired the weapon more than I wanted my next breath, but I couldn't let him know that.

We haggled back and forth for a few beats before we settled on an acceptable price. I might have to forgo any food that didn't come from a can for a little while, but it would be worth it. Or at least that's what I told myself as he slid the sword into its sheath and handed it to me.

I slipped the carved leather over my shoulder and felt elation spike inside me, a sense of homecoming that seemed foreign for a serial foster kid like me.

As I stepped away from the booth and back into the market, my phone rang. I jumped, remembering the *actual* reason we'd come to Relics & Roots in the first place as I dug into my back pocket and pulled out the device. Roger's name appeared on the screen and I swiped to answer. "Yo, Rog, you got anything?"

"Yeah! Some amazing-looking root veggies, but on the Tara front, I got nada. Gabs and I are waiting for you at the entrance. She struck out too, though she did get some pretty fabulous crystals we can use to amp up our warding. She's a little jumpy after the whole Beaseldorf incident."

Who could blame her? I was jumpy too, though I'd never admit that out loud. At least she had plans to reinforce our digs, though. I just needed to remind her about the bullets and probably my sword collection too. Something told me they'd also need a little amplification.

"Alright, I'll meet you there in a few," I said before hanging up and striding back to the entrance. I could feel the weight of my new sword on my back and wondered if Gaby and Roger could use their abilities to tell me more about it. It didn't seem like your garden-variety blade. It had a presence about it, something I couldn't quite explain. Maybe Roger could do a reading on it, and as I considered that possibility, I wondered if he'd even entertain doing me another favor after that whole possession fiasco earlier.

Somehow, I doubted it.

When I caught sight of my two partners in crime nearing the exit, I hurried to catch up with them, still having zero tingles on the demon front. I knew we had a lot more ground to cover in Old Willow Glen and that it could take another couple of hours. Maybe we would pick something up then. I could manifest a Spidey tingle, couldn't I? Put it out in the universe and make it happen?

Because I had to admit the pit in my stomach that had formed the moment I'd seen Tara's picture of her demon stalker was growing by the second. Beaseldorf's ominous statement about whatever he'd set in motion didn't help either. Not one bit.

Just then, a hand gripped my wrist, yanking hard. Startled, I skidded to a stop, my feet scraping on concrete. I spun, trying to break free from the viselike grip, my free arm driving down on instinct to disable my attacker. But I froze in midair when I saw who held me. Gnarled fingers riddled with arthritis and spotted with age clung to my forearm like a life raft, and when I dragged my gaze up to hers, I saw milky-white eyes spotted over with cataracts. The old woman stared into my eyes, as though she looked through me and straight into my soul.

Discomfort swam through my gut and I looked away, noting the Tarot card booth behind her, and a startled-looking young woman sitting in a chair before it. "Excuse me?" she said, confusion clear in her expression.

A chill slithered up my spine, and I looked away, back toward the exit where I'd seen my friends only moments ago. Gaby and Roger hadn't noticed me and kept walking farther away, back toward the car.

The woman tightened her grip on my arm, drawing my attention back to her. White hair floated on an ethereal breeze around her face, and the intensity in that milky stare had everything inside me bracing. When her mouth opened to speak, the voice sounded unnatural, inhuman. "Finish what she started. You must finish what she started."

As much as I wanted to break her grip on me, I forced myself to stay rooted to the spot, knowing what this was—a premonition—and recognizing the potential importance of it. I stepped closer. "What are you talking about?"

"What happened before happens now. She couldn't stop it. It has come full circle. You must— You must finish what she started."

People stopped, turning to look at us, staring. I cleared my throat and lowered my voice low enough that only she could hear me. "Finish what?" I asked, pressing my luck. Premonitions like this happened to me more often than I cared to admit, and I knew the spirit world never entertained my Q&A desires, but I figured I'd at least give it a shot. As though on cue, the woman blinked away the milkiness in her eyes, and they cleared, the cataracts evaporating like morning fog from the river. She seemed to realize all at once how close she'd pulled me and that she'd put her hands on me too. She released my arm, shaking her head.

Decades of age melted away from her as she took a step away from me, putting distance between us. "I'm so sorry." She lost twenty years in the space between seconds as I blinked in shock. At first blush, she'd looked at least eighty-five to me. Now? She couldn't have been more than fifty. "Umm, I don't know what—" she said, backing away from me, but it was my turn to grab her.

"Wait, what the hell did that mean?"

She looked at me with such genuine confusion that I knew she didn't remember anything that had just happened. She must be a conduit, sort of like Roger, but not. If I had to guess, she couldn't read emotions or energies like he could. Mostly because she didn't recoil at my touch, but also because she seemed truly befuddled. She must be a medium, and someone or something had decided to hitch a ride to deliver a message to me. But who? Why? And what the hell had it meant?

Releasing her arm, I backed away, holding up my hands to show her I meant no harm. "Sorry about that. Never mind."

She nodded, her brows knitting together as though trying to piece together how she'd ended up next to me and not in her seat across from her client. Rather than stick around to watch that play out, I turned on my heel as I repeated her words in my mind. A few minutes later,

Gaby and Roger came into view, both leaning against the driver's side of Gaby's car.

Gaby grinned at me as I approached and she saw what I carried on my back. "Replacement for that eBay debacle?"

"Yep," I replied, still dazed by both super strange experiences, unsure what it all meant. "I just had the weirdest thing happen to me." I pointed back toward the flea market before launching into an explanation and repeating verbatim what the woman said to me.

Roger shivered. "Ugh, because that's not creepy at all."

Gaby chewed on her lip, arms crossed as she seemed to think it over. "Yeah, and it's not helpful either."

"Not yet at least," I corrected. "But maybe it'll come in handy later. You know how it is with spirits."

"They do seem drawn to you," Gaby said, surveying me from head to toe. "You get more messages from the great beyond than anyone I know, and that's saying something."

She had a point. They did seem to like talking to me. Unfortunately for me, they often inserted themselves into my investigations in ways that boggled the mind. Their messages either came too early or too late, almost as if they didn't exist on the same timeline as us. They always seemed to pop in at the wrong point to deliver a premonition that would fuck everything up until it suddenly all made sense.

It irked.

Nodding in agreement, Gaby unlocked the car and popped the trunk. She and Roger strode toward it and deposited their hauls inside, apparently moving on from my revelation. Fair enough. It wouldn't be useful until it was. So we'd file it away for a later date.

As I locked the memory down in ye old memory vault, I pulled the sword and its scabbard from my back and hesitated. I stood there, gripping the leather strap as Gaby slid into her spot in the driver's seat and Roger folded his tall, slim frame into the back seat. Something felt wrong about leaving him—the sword—there. So I closed the trunk and moved to the front passenger side door, resting him on the floorboard and against my leg as I settled in my chair.

Gaby offered me a raised, disapproving eyebrow. "Oh, no, no, no. You know the rules. All large pointy objects go in the trunk while I'm driving."

I frowned, looking down at him. I didn't know why I called the sword *him* in my mind, but it felt right. I tried to make myself obey her rule, to get off my ass and put him into the trunk, but I couldn't bring myself to stand up. All I knew was that he *really* didn't want to go in there.

"Can we make an exception?" I asked, unsure how to explain my inexplicable dilemma. What was I going to say? *The sword doesn't want to ride in the boot?* And where the hell did *boot* come from? When did I suddenly become English?

Gaby squinted, confused by my refusal. "My car, my rules."

"He doesn't want to ride in the boot, Gabs! Cut him some slack, alright?"

Gaby shook her head at the desperation in my voice, blinking once and then twice as she tried to process the boatload of crazy I'd just dumped on her. "Who— What? It's a sword, Jenna. What are you talking about? And *boot*? Since when are you English?"

Roger's low chuckle rolled from the back seat before I could reply, and he leaned down as though concentrating on the scabbard resting on my lap.

"My, my, my, you did have an eventful day at the flea market," Roger said, his amusement plain on his face as he pointed at my new blade. "That's not just any sword, is it, honey?" He leaned forward between our two seats, head popping between the cushions as he strained to listen. "JT's right. He *does not* want to sit in the trunk, and he's not going to let her put him back there. So you should just drop this one, Gabs."

Gaby and I swiveled our heads back to stare at him as he settled back into the center of the bench seat. I gaped at him. "You can *hear* him? I mean, it. Or whatever the fuck, I don't know! The sword!"

Roger smiled, nodding as though supremely entertained. "Yeah, he's actually pretty funny when I can make out what he's saying, but it's all sort of jumbled." He flicked his gaze back up to me. "Why? Can't you?"

I frowned, eyes pinned on the glinting silver handle. "I don't know. I can *feel* what he wants, but I can't hear anything."

"Huh, that's funny. Because he's talking to you, not me."

I looked down at the sword, wondering what the hell I'd gotten myself into this time. Maybe today just wasn't my day. Maybe I should have stayed home and eaten Ben and Jerry's on the couch, whittling away the hours watching *Supernatural* reruns so that I could drool over Dean. Now that guy could take a punch.

"So, you don't even have to touch him to hear him?" I asked, a little surprised by this revelation. Roger's medium and empathic abilities usually required tactile stimulation to work.

"What can I say? He's loud."

"I wonder what you'd hear if you did make contact," I mused, picking up the sword and shifting it to Roger. "Want to give it a try? Maybe it would help you understand him better since it's jumbled and all."

Roger bolted upright and held up his hands in surrender. "Oh no, not right now. Did you forget that a demon possessed me like five minutes ago? I'm not going to let some kind of magic sword into this baby too." He tapped his temple for emphasis. "Roger needs at least a few hours of break time before you drag him into any more crazy today, okay?"

Gaby let out a long sigh. "Great, we go to a flea market to look for our kidnapped client and the demon who's holding her captive, and JT brings back a possessed sword and a useless premonition. This all sounds about right. Let's just hope that sword doesn't end up impaling any of us on the drive home."

That didn't seem fair.

She threw the car into gear and sped out of the parking lot, hopping off the entry curb with a shrill tire squeak. Roger propped his boots on the center console. "It's not possessed, not exactly. It's more... I don't know how to describe it..." Gaby looked at him in the rearview as I spared a curious look at him from over my shoulder. We waited for a long beat as he seemed to search for the right words. "It's more *alive* than possessed, if that makes sense."

"It's an inanimate object! How can it possibly be alive?" Gaby grumbled, whipping into the inside lane to pass a minivan.

"Shh, you'll hurt his feelings," Roger admonished, giving Gaby a reprimanding glare. To be fair though, it was a good question. One that none of us had the answer to. We all fell silent, unsure what to say about the sentient sword. I shook my head at all the insane and terrible impossibilities the day had dealt us, thinking that this epic level of insanity could only happen to us. Well, to me.

We spent the next few hours driving up and down the streets of Old Willow Glen, canvassing every nook and cranny of the town we could find. We even got out to walk most blocks, trying to pick up any sense of demonic presence. But we found nothing. For our last attempt before we called it a night, we hit downtown Old Willow Glen, walking the streets like tourists, not that we got too many of those here. Still, we pointed and gestured in different directions, trying to catch a break, but came up empty.

The sun hung low in the sky by the time we got into Gaby's car and drove home. We dropped Roger at A Witch's Whimsy, and promised we'd come back to help clean up the back room tomorrow, which he insisted upon under pain of death. Honestly, it was the least we could do after the whole Beaseldorf sludge vomit thing.

As we pulled away from the curb, that feeling in the pit of my stomach, the bad one that had appeared with Tara's entrance into my life the night before, grew yet again. Something felt off, like a disturbance in the matrix or the force or whatever. And after everything that had happened today, I had no doubts that I needed to get to the bottom of it fast. Too bad my only lead had just dried up like a California creek in summer.

The inexplicable picture of Tara's stalker, my new sword, Beaseldorf's arrival onto the scene, and the mysterious appearance of my card at Tara's house. Then what that old woman had said to me at the market? It all felt connected somehow. I just didn't know how to knit the pieces together into a cohesive whole.

Gaby parked her small car on the side of the road and we each got out, slamming the doors after I grabbed my backpack and sword.

We walked up the few steps to her complex, each distracted by our thoughts.

"So, what's next?" she asked, knowing that this one setback wouldn't deter me. Our friendship so rocked. We opened the small iron gate that protected the white stucco collection of townhomes from outside interference, and she reached for her key. Striding through the small courtyard, I noticed that the rose bushes had gone dormant and the trees had lost all their leaves, depositing them onto the brick pathway like slippery, wet death traps. We followed the leafy path to the back of the building, where her bottom-floor home dwelled.

I thought about how we could best use our time and knew we couldn't afford to take any more shortcuts. The location spell should have sped up our ability to find Tara without going through the normal process of a missing person case. Now, though? Magic seemed like a dangerous idea and an unnecessary risk. I sighed as she unlocked the door and flicked on the lights. We had to go back to the basics and work the case the traditional way.

In response to her inquiry, I pulled my phone from my pocket and scrolled through images. Before I'd called the cops to report Tara missing, I'd used my rubber cleaning gloves to keep my prints from leaving any smudges and rifled through all of her belongings. I took pictures of her ID and all the contents in her wallet and purse. Even then, I knew I wouldn't let this case go to the cops alone, not when it involved a demon.

I set the phone on the table, pictures pulled up and visible on the glowing screen. "We work the case the old-fashioned way."

Chapter 10

I went to work on my laptop right away while Gaby heated up a frozen pizza for dinner. Once the timer beeped, she took it out of the oven and left it on the counter for us to enjoy.

We both ate and worked. Gaby used her new crystals and some other questionable substances to double down on the anti-demon warding on her townhome and to amplify our weapons cache, which we'd decided to keep at her place after Luke's undue investigation into my life. Considering our run-in with Beaseldorf, both actions seemed like the smart thing to do. While she worked her magic, I started a background search on Tara.

As a PI, I paid for memberships to a couple of web services that offered comprehensive background searches. They would give me a lot of information to look over, including social media accounts, and criminal and financial records. She didn't strike me as the criminal type, but I couldn't afford to overlook anything that might give us a clue as to where Beaseldorf was keeping her.

After a few hours of pouring through social media and picking out any close relationships or odd interactions from Tara's feeds, I had a small list of follow-ups to make in the morning. From there, I analyzed her finances and her criminal background, neither of which yielded anything remotely resembling fruit.

At about four a.m., a couple of hours after Gaby went to bed, I'd compiled about half a page of notes and to-dos for the next day. Not a lot to go on, unfortunately. I could only hope I'd find something to sink my teeth into tomorrow. With that thought, I set my phone's alarm clock to seven a.m. and landed face-first on the couch, hoping to catch a few zzz's before the sun came up. I didn't question the fact that I settled the sword next to me and wrapped my fingers around it, feeling unable to part with it.

Just as my eyes drifted shut and the fuzzy warmth of sleep invaded my limbs, the carved hilt vibrated beneath my fingers. Unwilling to open my eyes, the blessed escape of near-sleep too blissful to disrupt, I felt it vibrate again. Grogginess swam through my mind. "No. Not right now."

It vibrated one more time and my legs twitched, prompting me to snuggle further into the throw blanket. "Mmm-mmmm," I groaned. Then it decided to amp up its game. The damned sword sent a jolt of electricity through my arm that had me leaping up from the couch and jumping onto my feet.

"Holy f—" I started, dropping my voice, realizing that if I screamed at the thing I would not only look insane, but I'd wake up Gaby as well.

So, instead, I shook out my hand as a sharp, residual pain shot up and down my arm. I looked down at the offending object and glared. "What the hell was that for?"

Something about the blade looked different, and I squatted down to pick it up, unsheathing it to get a better look. As I did, I realized that the blade glowed a soft gold in the pitch-dark of Gaby's living room. I'd never seen a sword do *that* before. My mouth dropped open right before it tugged me. I jerked forward, stumbling a few steps, as though pulled along by a magnet, and I frowned down at the blade. With another yank, it forced me an additional few steps forward.

My hands tightened on the hilt and I dug my bare feet into the rug to stop any new forward progress. "What the hell? Stop."

But it kept going, pulling me forward, my feet stumbling over each other in the thing's haste to get to the front door.

"Wait—hold on—I need—" But we'd already reached the entryway to Gaby's townhouse. The hilt jerked down, thunking my hand on the knob as though demanding that I open it and take him outside. "I don't have pants or shoes on," I argued, trying to let go of the hilt to grab something to wear so that I could avoid frostbite. No one liked black toes. But he wouldn't let me. My hand stayed glued to the hilt and my feet wouldn't move back into the house no matter how hard I tried to force them to. I stood at the door for a second, dumbfounded that this stupid sword had woken me out of blissful near-sleep and now demanded I take him outside.

What was he? A fucking dog? Did he need to tinkle in the middle of the night like a golden retriever puppy? If I'd known he had so many needs, I never would have bought him! He sent another jolt through my hand, as though in reprimand for that thought, and I hissed. Forcing myself to drop him, I almost had my fingers uncurled when a bolt of electricity rocketed through me again. Wait a minute, could the damn sword actually *hear my thoughts*?

Letting out the most monumental sigh I could manage, I cracked open the door to avoid another jolt. Without even a fraction of hesitation, the sword yanked me outside, and I sucked in a stunned breath at the feel of cold concrete and damp leaves beneath my bare feet. An icy breeze smelling of rain pierced through my thin clothing and seeped into my skin. I shivered, the whole of my body convulsing in protest, but the sword tugged me along, uncaring of my discomfort. It led me around the winding pathway between the small stucco buildings and toward what served as a tiny shared backyard.

When I stepped off the path, the soggy grass soaked my feet in seconds flat and they promptly went numb. But before I could mutter a curse at the damn sword, a pulse of awareness swept through me. Hairs rose on the back of my neck and my skin hummed with apprehension. Suddenly, I understood why the sword pulled me outside and what it wanted me to find.

A demon.

Beaseldorf or something else?

A kernel of fear mingled with anticipation traced a line down my back as I allowed the sword to lead me, moving in unison with its desires. This could be the big break I needed to find Tara. Or it could be the exact thing that got me killed.

Hard to tell.

With my senses on high alert, we crept along the narrow gap between the back fence and the condo buildings, the sword's light flicking on and off as though in urgency. And at last, I saw what the sword wanted me to find.

A figure stood in the dark, shadowy and hooded, and I watched in mute shock as it slipped around the second building in Gaby's complex with unnaturally quick movements. I broke out into a hurried run to follow it, my footsteps masked by the soft ground.

As I reached the end of the building and hurtled my body around it, the figure slammed into me. My breath went out of my lungs in a whoosh and I felt a grip like iron wrap around the wrist of my sword hand, the other covering my mouth. In a rush of momentum, the demon shoved me against the back fence and a hard, steely body pressed against me.

I gasped in reaction and found myself unable to take a full breath. Which made sense, considering how hard he pressed his rock-solid chest against mine. Giving in to my instincts, I fought, struggling to get free, using every technique I'd mastered in my time as a hunter, but to no effect. As I squirmed, yanking at my hands trying to free them, the sword dropped to the ground in a soft thump.

When every effort I made to buck free failed, panic stole through me. I felt helpless, like a child struggling beneath the iron grip of a full-grown monster, and fear blossomed in my chest without my permission. The more I struggled, the harder whoever held me pressed into my body, pushing a muscular thigh between my legs and pinning me with so little effort that I wanted to scream.

I'd never encountered anyone or anything, demon or otherwise, who could hold me captive. The bottom-dwellers, as Beaseldorf had called them, couldn't keep me contained for long. And regular non-supernatural humans? They didn't stand a chance against me. But this creature merely pressed himself closer to me, cutting off my air supply entirely with what seemed like no effort at all.

Terror flooded my nerves for the first time since the sword had awoken me. I wanted to scream, to bite the hand that covered my mouth and get free. My muscles burned with the effort to move, but I gained no ground. The demon leaned closer and I closed my eyes, sure that this was the end. The demon would kill me. Damn this fucking sword. Damn him right to hell.

Gaby would find my body in the morning, and my heart wrenched at the horror she'd feel, the terror of knowing I'd died just feet away from her while she slept. I could only hope she'd be okay, that she'd move forward with her life and keep fighting the good fight.

But to my astonishment, no pain came. Instead, the heat of sweet-smelling breath, the scent reminiscent of cinnamon and vanilla and something much, much smokier and darker, brushed over my ear. The words that followed came in a voice that was undeniably male, as I'd suspected. "I'm going to take my hand off your mouth, but you have to promise not to scream." The deep timbre of his voice rolled through my body, straight to my core. My eyes widened in complete shock. He didn't want to kill me? I tried to think through the blaze of terror that assaulted me, not to mention the lack of oxygen, but before I could muster any kind of a response, he forced my gaze to meet his. "Nod if you agree."

I hesitated for the briefest moment, but when black circles started to dance at the edges of my vision, I nodded. The hand dropped from my mouth and he moved back just enough for me to suck in air, the puffs of my breath visible in the dark, cold night.

Before I could get my bearings, he grabbed my other hand and yanked it up, pinning both arms above my head in a single, unbreakable grip. He leaned back, giving us a little more space, though his leg remained pressed between my thighs. Cool air swirled between us and I tried not to convulse in reaction to the freezing bite of it.

As he moved, his hood shifted back to expose his face, and I could see the outline of features in the dim streetlights. But even in the dark, I could tell that he was gorgeous. No, not just gorgeous, but the most intensely beautiful being I'd ever seen. My body hummed in reaction to him, and my mouth went dry.

He had full lips, a strong chiseled jaw, and when my eyes traveled up to his, my mouth parted as I took in the sheer beauty of them. His irises glowed golden in the dim streetlights around us, the frame of dark lashes enviable. Without warning, desire pooled in my belly and I became painfully aware of his leg between mine. The pressure felt far too good, too delicious, too indecent.

I swallowed hard, my mind a jumble of thoughts and arousal as I tried to think through the haze of it all. Only one thought made it to the forefront—he looked *human*. Just like the demon who'd watched from Tara's house. Like how demons looked when they possessed a human body. But somehow, I knew that he hadn't stolen this body. It belonged to him.

Power emanated from him, an aura so potent I could taste it. And to my profound disbelief, it tasted good. Smoky but sweet, a drug unlike anything I'd ever experienced before.

A low burning, sweet and sharp, formed deep in my center. My blood heated and I trailed my tongue over my parted lips, my mind shifting in a different direction, one I'd never experienced before.

At least not with a demon.

My gaze trailed from his soft, sensuous mouth, back up to those arresting eyes. The golden depths scanned up and down the length of my body, and I felt my nipples go hard from his lazy perusal, my mind painfully aware of how little clothing separated us. And how little we'd have to take off to do the very thing I wanted most in that moment.

And what did I want, exactly? His hands roaming over every inch of my body, his mouth exploring my bare skin. As I imagined what that might feel like, an ache pounded between my legs, and I knew he'd find me wet. If only he'd slip his fingers beneath my boxers and find out.

Somewhere in the dark recesses of my mind, a niggle of awareness told me that I should be embarrassed, maybe even full-scale humiliated at the thoughts that dominated my mind. But I couldn't muster it, couldn't even think beyond the haze of arousal that he seemed to elicit with every single move he made.

His eyes traveled downward, and my gaze followed, locking on the sword which I'd dropped to the ground.

Shit, get a hold of yourself, Jenna. Some semblance of brain function forced its way to the surface and I shook my head to clear away the lust sweeping through my blood like a raging river. When the demon's gaze flicked back to mine, one side of his mouth tilted upward. Pleasure and amusement warmed his gaze and I clamped my teeth shut, fighting with everything I had against the pulsing waves of desire that I was beginning to understand he commanded.

What the fuck kind of demon was he? Even incubuses, the most potent of the lust demons I'd encountered, didn't have this effect on me. His voice broke through the daze of my jumbled thoughts. "Good. You got my message and found the sword. Didn't know if my plan worked after your locator spell went sideways."

"Your message?" My voice came out breathy, and oh my God, was I panting? Yep, I was fucking panting. A combination of humiliation and desire flamed my cheeks.

His grip remained ironclad around my wrists and his features hardened. "Yes, Jenna. I've sent you quite a few messages lately, with Tara as the first."

His knowledge of my name struck me, but he didn't seem to notice. I sucked in a breath, inhaling the elixir of his aura once more. The ache at the apex of my thighs turned downright painful and I tried to fight against it. I needed to stay alert, but the effort to concentrate seemed impossible with him standing so close. With him touching me.

Oh, he was definitely something different, something new, and I forced my gaze on his eyes. I needed to focus on what he said, not how he made me feel. "You sent Tara to me? You're the one who gave her my card?"

He inclined his head a mere fraction of an inch in acknowledgment. "I did. You know so little, and you must figure it out fast. So I decided to help."

"Help with what?" I asked, barely managing to keep my thoughts together as I tried to muddle through why a demon would want to help me.

"With what comes next." The words flowed with a casual air from his sensuous lips, as though they didn't have the distinct impression of impending doom laced through them. "He may want you in the dark, but you can't remain there anymore. Not if you're going to help me."

I shook my head to clear it. "Who's *he*? And why would I help you, demon?"

A cool breeze brushed across my cheeks and allowed me the first breath of fresh air I'd had free of his aura since he'd pinned me. My head cleared from the onslaught of pure lust, and I prayed it would stay that way, even if just for a moment.

A low chuckle rumbled through him. "You met *him* earlier, and you'll help me because what's coming is bigger than either of us, and we don't have much time left to stop it."

"Beaseldorf," I guessed, and he offered me a pleased grin in confirmation. "But stop what? What's coming?" I asked, growing tired of the cryptic bullshit.

"I've already intervened too much. If I do more than this, he'll know it's me. So, one last message, Jenna, and you're on your own."

He paused, and my mind raced, trying to make sense of this interaction, of him. Was a demon really trying to lend me a hand? Or was this just a trap? I couldn't know for sure, but if I had to put money on it? Trap. One hundred percent for sure—trap.

"Why should I trust you?"

"So many questions." Despite the rebuke of his words, amusement danced in his eyes, as though he found me entertaining. "You don't need to trust me. You just need to do your job."

He moved closer, and I watched with rapt attention as he slipped one hand off my wrists and slid his fingers into the pocket of his fitted jeans, eyes still trained on me. I tried not to squirm, for an entirely different reason than the desire to escape, as he pulled a small slip of white paper out.

Holding it between two fingers, he let me see it. "This should be enough to get you there." His hand started moving again, and I shivered with reaction as he slid the slip of paper inside the waistband of my boxers. When his warm, calloused fingers brushed my skin, I had to bite my lip to keep from moaning. Once he'd secured the paper, he withdrew his fingers from my flesh and leaned closer, his mouth a mere fraction from the shell of my ear. His warm scent heated me from the inside out, scorching me with his nearness. "Work fast, Jenna."

He spared me one more smoldering stare before he released me and vaulted over the fence, clearing my body and the eight-foot-tall structure behind me with no effort whatsoever. I slumped to my knees, gasping for breath. I felt woozy, delirious, and unsure about what the fuck had just happened.

The cold had me dragging myself and the damn sword up from the ground and making my way back to Gaby's door. I checked over my shoulder, careful not to run into anything else in the dark. I didn't know what to make of everything that had just happened as I walked back into Gaby's home, the sword tight in my grip, its light no longer glowing.

Sitting down on the couch, I wrapped my shivering body in the throw blanket and stared at the wall for a few minutes before I remembered the paper. I slipped it out of my waistband, glad it had remained in place, and grabbed my phone, using the light from my screen to illuminate it. A list of names had been scrawled on it in apparent haste. It included city, state, and country along with the names, and they hailed from all over the United States, some even abroad.

I licked my lips, setting the paper on the table, and lay back down on the lumpy couch cushions. My body still seemed to hum from... whatever the hell that demon had done to me. I'd never felt anything like it before and knew it couldn't be normal, not even by supernatural demon standards. Fuck, he'd almost made me come from a single touch to my waist.

Lust demons didn't have the same effect on me as they had on other humans. They couldn't reduce me to a simmering pool of desire, not like he did. And it didn't help that since he'd left, I felt edgy and dissatisfied.

Alright, I could admit it, he'd made me horny as fuck.

I set the sword on the coffee table and glared at it, banishing it from the bed. "I'm holding you responsible for that debacle."

Giving it one last, good glower, I settled back onto the cushions, closed my eyes, and let sleep take over.

CHAPTER 11

A hot mouth, skilled hands, and a well-muscled body overwhelmed my senses, filling me with unspeakable pleasure. I saw no face, only eyes, molten gold and intense as they bored into mine.

Scalding, sumptuous lips trailed over the column of my neck and along my collarbone before they covered the peak of my breast. His tongue swirled in expert motions over my tight nipple, and I groaned in pleasure, my back arching. My fingers wound into thick black hair, soft as feathers, and I pulled him closer, wanting more from the man who damn near brought me to climax from just his tongue on my breast.

The rock-hard column of his erection pressed into my thigh and I shifted beneath him, inviting him inside. I had no idea who he was, but I knew I wanted him to fill me, to give himself to me so that this intense, unimaginable pleasure would never stop.

His mouth broke away from my nipple, and he slid his tongue between my breasts and up my sternum. I writhed beneath him, moaning and begging him for more. No one had ever made me feel like this before. I panted and dug my nails into the smooth muscles of his back as I tried to draw him closer, to get more of him.

His tongue stopped its journey along my skin as he lifted his head and looked into my eyes once more. Perfection, I thought, unable to break our locked gazes as he opened his mouth. "Dude, what are you doing?"

I started, surprised. Blinking, I looked up at him in confusion. What did it look like we were doing? Annoyance speared through my body at the abrupt question. His lips moved again, but somehow, the voice didn't seem to belong to him this time. "Ummm...Jenna? This is getting awkward. You're humping my throw pillow."

At that, his stunning face blurred and I felt the cozy bliss of sleep and near sexual gratification fall away. I blinked and shook my head, the real world coming into focus around me. Gaby stood above me, looking down at my place on the couch as she blew on two mugs of steaming hot coffee.

Well, that was awkward. I threw a hand over my eyes and groaned in mortification. Refusing to let her see it, I yanked the throw pillow from the death grip of my inner thighs and chucked it on the ground. I rubbed my face, my eyes feeling grainy as I tried to get my bearings. It seemed last night's encounter had longer-lasting side effects than I'd expected.

I glared at the sword on the coffee table, still bitter over its role in the whole travesty. "Sorry."

Gaby passed me a cup of coffee, keeping one for herself, and I rose to a sitting position to accept it. "Don't apologize on my account. Sounds like you two were having a great time. Happy dreams?" She wriggled her brows and made kissy faces at me and I cleared my throat, my cheeks flaming in embarrassment.

I had to remember that this entire situation wasn't my fault. It was that guy, that demon, that whatever last night. He had residual side effects. Sexy ones. I couldn't be blamed for that, now could I? I decided that, no, I could not be as I swallowed my first sip of coffee.

Gaby eyed me with interest. "You gonna answer there, Spawk? You've got that thousand-yard stare going."

"Right, erm, sorry. I had a weird night, actually." Dragging a hand down my face, I did my best to shake off my humiliation and launched into an explanation of everything that had happened, gesturing toward the paper on the table and relaying the conversation I'd had with the guy—well, the demon—word for word. After that, I explained his *other* qualities. The ones that made me want to strip my panties off, stuff them in his mouth, and have my way with him.

"So... the demon who assaulted you and stuck that list in your pants? *That's* who you were dreaming about?"

I leaned back on the cushions, throwing my arm over my face in mortification. "Unfortunately, yes." Yep, I had a sex dream about a freaking demon. That was just ten thousand shades of wrong.

She raised her brows, the judgment in her gaze evident. Thankfully, she refrained from commenting on that little nugget of horror and instead held out her hand. "Can I see the list?"

"Have at it. It's on the coffee table."

Bending down, she picked it up and scanned the names, dates, and locations listed. "What are we supposed to be digging for with these, exactly? And why is a demon helping us? Because that would be a first."

I shrugged my shoulders, every bit as clueless as her. Maybe even more so considering the number he'd done on my brain last night. "I have no idea. He says he's the one who gave Tara my card and sent her to me. But he didn't get into any specifics on why or what I'm supposed to do about it. He also failed to elaborate on those names. He just said that I needed to do my job and work fast. Vague and cryptic pretty much sums it up. Oh, and weirdly lusty, of course."

Gaby took a sip of her coffee as she continued to stare at the list. "Huh."

"Can you run point on researching those names today? Full background checks, searches for newspaper articles, social media accounts, and mentions? The usual workup? May as well see if anything useful turns up," I said. I had zero faith that a demon wanted to help me out of the goodness of his heart. But that didn't mean I wouldn't look into every lead I received, no matter how untrustworthy the source might be. Taking another sip of my coffee, I looked around the room for my backpack. I needed pants and a jacket.

"Sure," Gaby replied, setting the list down on the coffee table again, next to my laptop. She had full access to everything on it, including my PI services. She'd gotten pretty damn good at research, so I knew I could count on her to find whatever we needed to on those names. "Where are you heading off to?"

"I've got my own to-do list today." I pulled my research notes from the front pocket of my backpack and held them up as evidence. "Interviews to conduct."

"You think you'll get anything helpful from that?"

I pulled on my pants and buttoned them. "One thing I've learned in this business is people always know more than they think they do. Sure, Tara said no one believed her about the stalker, but that doesn't mean she never told them anything useful. I might get something that helps tie together those names quicker or gives me a direction to go in faster. And besides, it's best we divide and conquer."

"Plus, you can't sit still for more than a minute when you're on a case."

I leveled a finger gun on her. "Also true. Keep me posted on what you find. And just, I don't know, be careful. The lead did come from a demon, after all."

"I always am. You watch your back too, okay? The last twenty-four hours have been far too coincidental for my taste. And knowing that demon gave Tara your card and sent you to find that sword? I don't like it. Not one bit."

"You and me both, sister."

Fifteen minutes later, and I was walking away from Gaby's townhouse with the keys to the Subaru and my newly purchased sword in hand. Before I left, I took a picture of the list the hot demon guy had given me and texted it to myself, leaving the original with Gaby. Couldn't hurt to have the names handy, should I need them. After that, I texted Tony and asked him to cover my shift for the evening. He agreed, not bothering to ask why. I loved that about him. No questions, no curiosity, just a mediocre work ethic and a strong desire for tips.

As I settled into the well-loved seat of Gaby's Sub, I pulled the list of names and addresses I'd gathered from my pocket and punched them into my phone's GPS. First stop, Tara's next of kin—her sister. I dialed her phone number from my list. It rang twice before someone picked up. A soft female voice filled my ears and I promptly hung up. *Good, she's home.* I felt like a bit of a dick for prank-calling her. But I didn't want to go into what I had to ask or say over the phone.

I started the Subaru and put the car into gear, sucking in a long breath, praying that Luke and Bud had already spoken to her. I didn't want to be the one to break the news of Tara's disappearance. They, after all, didn't have the option of a potential locator spell shortcut like I had. Surely, they'd have gotten at least one step ahead of me on the interviewing friends and family front.

Navigating through the streets of east Santa Sombra, I turned onto Falcon Blvd and headed toward 66th Street and the Highway 70 on-ramp. It appeared that Bethany, Tara's sister, lived farther east at the base of the Sierra Nevada foothills in Sombra Hills. It would take me a while to get up that way, so I settled in for the ride, casting a sidelong glance at the sword. I'd settled him into the front seat, and for some reason I didn't dare to explain, even to myself, I'd buckled him in. Sure, he had put me in a very awkward and humiliating position the night before, and yet I still couldn't seem to part with him.

Refusing to unpack that at the moment, I turned up the radio and zoned out, focusing on the drive, climbing ever closer to my destination with each passing mile. As I did, I thought about the questions I needed to ask, running through them in my mind. Thirty minutes later, I took the Sombra Hills exit and followed the GPS instructions. Ten minutes after that, I pulled up to a large house. Not unusual for this part of town. Sombra Hills tended toward fancy.

It had a whole suburb meets wilderness vibe that I kind of dug, despite my preference toward city life. Large pine and oak trees, the latter barren, lined the streets and dominated the front yards. Manicured lawns and other, less natural but equally pretty, plants added some variety.

A drizzle had started during my drive, a light rain that I couldn't seem to shake and it soaked the streets, turning them slick and black. Zipping my jacket, I opened the glove box and rummaged through it, finding the spare notebook we kept in Gaby's car, along with a pen. I took a deep breath, sent up yet another prayer that Luke and Bud had already informed her about her sister, and checked the rearview mirror.

As I did, I saw a black Crown Vic pull in behind me and an all too familiar face came into focus. I clenched my jaw, my teeth grinding. Handsome features, dark-blond hair, and a wry smile that lifted the side of his mouth as he surveyed me. Luke opened the car door and pulled himself out in a smooth move, already striding toward me. Shit. My eyes darted to the sword strapped into the front seat next to me. I leaned over to unbuckle it, unsnapping the seat belt just as a knock sounded on my window.

Fuck, fuck, fuckity, fuck.

I froze, forcing myself to move with less urgency so as not to seem like I wanted to hide something. Using my body to block his view, I lay the sword on his side on the front seat, praying that maybe Luke wouldn't see him. Why couldn't he just ride in the trunk like a normal inanimate object? And why did I care what the goddamn sword wanted anyway? In response to that rhetorical question, said object sent a jolt up my arm. I jumped, my head colliding with the ceiling as I launched out of my seat.

He rapped on the window again, and I turned to address him, Luke's face appearing in my window as he rested his forearms on the roof to peer inside. "Everything alright in there?" he asked, eyeing me with more suspicion than I would have liked. Then his gaze landed on the sword, and he lifted a brow in question.

Expression grim, I opened the car door. As I did, I made a valiant effort and managed to resist the urge to hit him with it. Instead, I opened it slowly, allowing him the opportunity to move out of the way, which he did. As I exited the car, a cool wind hit me and I did my best to compose my face into something a little less bitchy.

I cleared my throat. "Yes, everything is fine."

"You sure about that?" He didn't believe me. I could tell.

"Yep. Leg cramp," I lied.

He leveled a finger at the sword still sitting in my front seat. "Another collector's item?"

"Sure is. Want to take a look? He's a real beaut."

Luke stared at the sword, shaking his head. "Nope, I'll take your word for it." As I followed his gaze, I could make out the intricate carvings on the hilt and the smooth leather of the scabbard, decorated with markings of its own. It was another sword, but at least he might actually buy this one as a collector's item. So I had that going for me.

"So, JT, what are you doing here?" To my surprise, I didn't see anger or animosity in his expression. Only curiosity.

"She was my client, and she went missing on my watch. You didn't think I would actually let this one go, did you?"

He shrugged. "I hadn't given it all that much thought, to be honest. Too busy doing legwork and making phone calls. On that topic, though, do you have an appointment here? Because if you do, then she double-booked us."

I stared at the house in question, refusing to meet his eye. "Nope, I sure don't."

We stood in silence for a moment and I could feel his eyes boring into the side of my face. I turned my gaze to his, offering him a semi-irritated glare. He grinned at me. Luke always seemed to find my irritation amusing, which irked.

"Tell you what," he said, unfolding his arms as he rummaged through his jacket pocket. He pulled out a wallet, opened it, and withdrew a dollar, holding it between his fingers. "You want in on this? I could use a consultant. We're short-staffed and Bud got pulled into a homicide, so I'm riding solo today. I wouldn't say no to a second set of eyes and ears." Given how many demons and other sorts of nefarious entities Santa Sombra seemed to draw within its borders, murders and other crimes happened frequently, which left the police department shorthanded more often than not.

My mouth dropped open as I gaped up at him, unsure what to make of his offer. What in the motherfuck? "You want me to consult? Me?"

"Sure, but on an informal basis." He extended the dollar, and I just stared at it, stunned. He let out a long sigh and dropped his hand to his side. "The way I figure it, you aren't going to drop this case, and you're not a bad PI. You've helped me on cases before, and I'd rather work together on this one than against each other. So..." He held up the dollar again. "Are you in?"

"Yep." Not giving him a chance to rethink his offer, I snatched the dollar from his hand and stuffed it into my jeans pocket. As a paying client, it provided him the benefits of the confidentiality agreement I gave to all my clients. Which meant I would keep our findings internal and not go to the press or talk about it outside of our investigative capacity. "But just so we're clear, what's the catch?"

He leaned forward, eyeing me with a seriousness that let me know he meant business. "No secrets. You find something, you tell me. Got it?"

I gave him a look like he might not have all his marbles. "All that for a dollar?"

"No, I'll afford you the same professional courtesy. I'll even give you eyes on everything we've got so far. Agreed?"

He held out a hand to shake, a way to forge our agreement. I thought about it for all of one second before I clasped his hand in mine. With that settled, he pulled out a notepad from the pocket of his long wool coat and started toward Tara's sister's not-so-humble abode. I followed his lead, falling into step beside him. The rain had slowed and only misted us while we walked up the driveway.

As we drew closer to the house itself, I whistled through my teeth, impressed. It was massive, a sprawling Spanish style villa with a little courtyard in front.

Luke leaned across me and rang the doorbell, leveling a serious expression on me. "Let me ask a few questions to get them started, then you can jump in. Does that work for you?"

"Don't worry, I'll do my best to restrain myself."

A woman damn near Tara's mirror image minus the red hair opened the door. Her locks shone a pampered honey gold, long and soft as they fell in perfectly quaffed waves down her back. This was what Tara would have looked like, if she hadn't been wet and terrified the night she'd come into the bar. Careful to keep my expression sympathetic, I watched as two more women appeared behind her and I could tell that they'd all been crying.

Red lined their eyes and the tips of their noses burned a bright, irritated pink. The other two had light-brown hair and looked like they belonged on the front page of *Homes & Gardens* magazine. One wore a headband and a sweater vest combo while the other wore a set of pearls and a prim, collared shirt. Total Stepford wife vibes.

"Hi, Bethany. I'm Detective Luke Parsons with the Santa Sombra Sheriff's Department and this is Jenna Torrence, a private investigator assisting with your sister's case. You spoke with my partner, Bud, last night at the station and he mentioned I'd be coming by today. Is this still an okay time to talk? We'd like to ask you a few more questions about Tara."

His face shifted from the casual handsomeness with a hint of amusement and suspicion that I'd grown accustomed to into a mask of concern and sympathy.

Bethany's eyes watered, but she blinked to stave off the tears and stood aside to let us in. "Of course."

We walked through the doorway and into a dramatic entryway. Large pillars lined the separation between the foyer and the formal living space, while a massive spiral staircase dominated the other side. Intricate wrought iron railings swirled down the steps, their beauty impressive.

Yep, Tara's sister was loaded.

Bethany wrung her hands as she led us inside and I noticed the massive rock on her left ring finger. So, she had a husband, and that made me wonder where he was at that moment. Working, I guessed, thinking that any schmuck worth his salt would have taken the day off for his wife, considering the circumstances.

As we moved out of the entryway and into a sprawling chef's kitchen with stainless steel appliances so shiny that I could have plucked my eyebrows in them, I resisted the urge to gape. I needed something like this in my life. This kitchen just made me feel all warm and fuzzy inside. Too bad I was broke and couldn't cook.

My attention jerked away from my imaginings as Bethany's voice filled the space. "The police hire private investigators to help with missing person cases?"

Luke rubbed his free hand over his jaw, a dark stubble I hadn't noticed before just barely visible in this lighting. "Sometimes, but this is a special circumstance. Your sister hired her the night of her disappearance, so we've decided to let her help with the case."

Bethany's lips turned down. "She hired an investigator?"

I nodded, doing my best to project the sympathy I felt for her. "Yes, she came to me asking for my help with a stalker."

Bethany's lips pressed into a thin line of disapproval. Apparently, she didn't like that. The other two ladies, Margaret and Primrose, judging by the Facebook profiles I'd poured through the night before, shared a look that I couldn't quite translate into non-bitch speak.

Luke's face remained impassive. He must have followed up on my tip with his department, and I wondered what he made of Tara's complaints. As for Bethany, I didn't need to guess. From that single expression, I knew exactly where this was going.

Bethany gestured to an arrangement of comfortable-looking armchairs and two plush love seats in a den just off the kitchen. "Please, let's have a seat."

Following her lead, Luke and I sat down in two of the creamy white armchairs while the three ladies piled onto the love seat closest to us. "Would you like anything to drink?" Bethany asked, and I could tell that we—well, probably just me—made her uncomfortable.

Luke looked professional, clean-cut, and I had to admit pretty damn good. I, on the other hand, wore a rumpled gray flannel with the front tucked into boot cut jeans and steel-toe boots. I hadn't thought to pack anything nicer when I'd grabbed clothes from my closet before our trip down to the station.

"No, but thank you," Luke said as I shook my head in answer too.

Bethany nodded, fiddling with the massive diamond ring on her finger. "I'm sorry I couldn't answer more of your partner's questions last night. I really should have explained better, but it's just been—" She pressed her forefinger under her nose as she sniffed out a quiet sob. "You see, Tara isn't... she's not... Tara isn't *well*. And hearing what your partner said last night? I just couldn't bear it." The other two women reached out and grabbed Bethany's hands to comfort her as a sob escaped her lips.

Luke kept his tone level and soothing. "That's alright. Everyone grieves in their own way. Now, what did you mean by Tara wasn't well? Was she sick?"

Bethany looked between Margaret and Primrose, as though consulting them before she refocused on us, her eyes filling with even more tears. "Tara had mental health issues. She had what the doctors thought was schizophrenia. Paranoid delusions. She saw things that weren't there, heard voices, and she thought someone was stalking her."

Primrose spoke up then, her face drawn and sad as she fingered the pearls at her neck. "We tried to get her to check into a mental health facility, to get help, but she wouldn't listen."

Bethany locked her gaze on Luke. "So when you had us come down to the station and told us that she'd gone missing under suspicious circumstances, we just assumed—"

As Bethany started to falter, Margaret stepped in. "Tara had a... failed suicide attempt about eight months back. They put her on a mandatory seventy-two-hour hold for observation at a mental health facility after that. She seemed to do better then. The doctors gave her meds and she stopped seeing and hearing things."

Bethany nodded eagerly. "She improved so much after that, but then she stopped taking her meds about a month ago. I don't know why, but she said they made her weak, that they made her mind foggy and confused. She said that she needed to keep her strength if she had any chance of surviving him. I didn't know what she meant by that. I was just so worried about her."

Primrose leaned forward, as though to appeal to us. "We all were. She went off the rails after that. She saw her stalker everywhere. At night, at her house. That's when it was the worst for her. She would take pictures and show them to us."

"But the pictures had nothing in them!" Margaret said, shaking her head as her eyes welled up with tears. "She kept insisting that he was there, but no one else ever saw *anything*. So, when we heard about what happened, Beth and the rest of us, we just assumed she'd gone somewhere to try again. To take her own life."

Bethany sniffed, the force of it making her body hop up from the seat a little. Her friends wrapped an arm around either side of her for comfort as she shook her head, tears falling freely now. "I know your partner said that you suspect foul play, but I'm just so afraid that with the blood? I'm afraid that maybe—she just might have been successful this time." Tears dropped onto her pressed pants as Margaret and Primrose did their best to soothe her.

We waited until she settled and her breathing grew regulated once more. She sniffed before leveling a desperate, pleading gaze on us. "Please, promise me you'll find her, no matter what happened to her. Whether she did this to herself or someone else did something to her. Our parents died about five years ago, and we're all that's left of our family. I just... I just need to know if she's alright."

I recognized the sound of someone who'd given up hope a long time ago. My heart cracked just a little for Tara. I couldn't imagine how alone she must have felt, how terrified. It surprised me that she hadn't given in to everyone's insistence that she was crazy a long time ago. She had to be strong to withstand that influence, and I knew that strength would serve her well now. Until I could find her.

Luke's voice interrupted my thoughts. "Is there anything else you ladies can think of that might help us? A place she'd go? Somewhere special that she'd want to see one last time, if this was, in fact, a suicide attempt?"

"So, you still think it's possible she did this to herself? Even with what you told Bethany yesterday?" Margaret said, her brows furrowing in confusion.

"Given the scene, foul play is more likely, but I'm inclined to rule out all possibilities."

All three women on the couch across from us seemed to pause, each thinking. After a brief moment, Bethany gave a determined nod. "Rattlesnake Bar, on Falcon Lake. We used to go out there as kids. It's secluded, especially during the winter. We liked to play in the water, climb on the rocks. She always loved it. After her divorce, she used to go to the lake to think. But she stopped talking to me as much after I tried to check her into the last facility, so I don't know—" She broke off, her lips wobbling as a clear wave of guilt seemed to wash over her. We gave her a moment to compose herself while she sniffed, slim fingers covering her mouth as her friends closed ranks around her to offer their comfort.

Luke waited for a long time, each of us silent, until her sobs quieted. "We'll take a look at Rattlesnake Bar and let you know if we find anything. Now, about Tara's ex-husband," Luke said, flipping through his notepad before he landed on the name. "Taylor. Does he still live at 1863 Stewart Lane?"

Bethany nodded, a bewildered expression on her face. "Taylor's a good man and a friend of the family. He'll help you in any way he can. But they haven't been together in over three years, and her erratic behavior started long after their divorce. I really don't think he had anything to do with this."

Luke nodded, scribbling something else in his notepad. He rose to his feet, and I joined him, a little surprised that he wanted to leave already. But then again, it did seem like we'd gotten everything we could from Bethany and her friends.

Settling his gaze on the three grieving women, Luke offered them a reassuring smile. "Thank you, ladies. You've all been very helpful. We'll be in touch if we have any further questions or if we find anything." They nodded, each grabbing a tissue from a decorative copper box on the side table. "We can show ourselves out if that's alright?"

Bethany hiccupped and agreed, turning to her friends and speaking with them in a hushed tone. Giving them their privacy to grieve, Luke and I strode from the sitting room back over to the kitchen and through the formal living space and foyer. As we opened the door to leave, a deep, quiet voice caught our attention.

"Are you with the police?" Clearly surprised, Luke dropped his hand from the doorknob and peered into a room off the foyer. It looked like an office, though I hadn't noticed it when we first arrived. The door must have been closed, but now it stood open, as though waiting for us.

Luke and I eased toward it, unsure what to expect as we stepped inside where a man stood next to a large carved desk that must have cost a fortune. A monitor sat on one side and a large window that overlooked a sprawling, gorgeously manicured yard dominated the space behind him. He walked over to his chair and sat down, his whole body seeming to exhale as he did so.

"Yes, I'm Detective Luke Parsons with the Santa Sombra Sheriff's Department and this is Jenna Torrence, a consultant working with us on the case."

He pursed his lips and nodded, as though debating what to say next. Rather than interrupt, Luke and I waited for him to make the next move. "Did my wife tell you about Tara's *mental illness*?" he asked. The skepticism laced through his last two words let me know that maybe he had something else to add. Something that, for me, might actually prove relevant.

I stepped forward. "She did."

He nodded, spun to the side in his chair, and looked out the window before letting out a long sigh.

When he didn't say anything else, I decided to press him. "Do you have a different opinion on that?"

His dark salt-and-pepper hair gleamed in the streaming sunlight. He had a handsome face, if not a little weathered. Definitely older than his wife but still appealing. "I don't know."

Luke and I exchanged a look as alarm bells went off in my mind. "What do you mean?"

I hadn't asked Bethany any questions because I knew she'd already made up her mind. I could tell within one millisecond that I would never get anything useful from her. She dismissed her sister long ago as crazy, and people didn't listen to crazy. But her husband, on the other hand? He looked up at me, as though uncertain if he wanted to divulge whatever it was he knew.

"You can tell me," I encouraged, trying to make my voice as soothing as I could. "I'll believe you and I promise, we'll take it seriously in our investigation."

Luke's face remained impassive and I couldn't tell if he agreed or disagreed with that sentiment. At last, the man relented. "My name's Arthur, and for the record, I'm Tara's brother-in-law." He rose from his chair and moved to a large cabinet to his right, reaching for a crystal decanter of what looked like whiskey. He poured himself two fingers and knocked it back before he continued. "I've always liked Tara, loved her like my own sister really. She and Bethany were close when we married and she always supported us, even when my family didn't. They couldn't understand why someone as young and beautiful as Bethany would want a guy like me." He shook his head, a sad smile spreading across his lips. "They all thought it was about the money, but it never was, not for Bethany. Tara knew that as well as I did."

He poured another drink, his eyes growing sadder with each passing second. "Bethany was only twenty-two when we got married. We eloped to Jamaica, and Tara was the only person from either of our families who came with us, along with her ex-husband, Taylor. She was always so vibrant, so alive, smart too. Both she and Bethany were, so when she got sick, I wanted to believe her. About the stalker, about the voices, about everything. I couldn't accept that this woman, whom I'd grown to care for so much, had lost her grip on reality."

He took a small sip of his drink this time before he moved back to his chair, settling into it. "One night, about a week ago, Bethany sent me to check on Tara. She'd gotten this crazy phone call from her and Bethany was at her breaking point; she couldn't handle it anymore. Tara was hysterical, claiming that some man was watching her from her front yard. I went over there, and at this point, I'm long past thinking that maybe there's something to this stalker thing. I believed that Tara was having another episode. I planned to talk her into getting help, into letting me drive her to the hospital. But when I got there, I saw something."

He pulled his bottom lip through his teeth and shook his head, his eyes distant, as though lost in thought. "A man stood outside her window, staring inside, right where she always said she saw him. I ran up to him, yelling, furious that he was doing this to my sister. He turned and started walking away, around the back side of the house. I don't know what I was thinking, this guy could have been anyone. He could have had a gun for God's sake, but I was so angry that I chased him anyway, and I rounded the corner, intending to beat him to a bloody pulp, but he disappeared. I don't mean like he just walked away. I mean he had vanished into thin air. I hunted around for a while, trying to find any trace of him, but I never found anything. No footprints, no scuff marks in the grass, nothing.

"By the time I'd walked inside, my heart was hammering so hard in my chest I thought I might keel over. I didn't know what to tell Tara. I thought I must have imagined it. I felt crazy, and I didn't want to feed her delusions, so I lied. I never said a word about it. Not to her, not to anyone."

His eyes filled up with tears as he rubbed his forehead with his hand. "But now... I can't help but wonder... did I see him? Was he real? Was she being stalked all this time and did we just let it happen? Is that the reason she's gone? Did he take her?" Tears spilled over his lids and he sniffed hard, just as broken up about Tara's disappearance as Bethany. I'd been wrong earlier. He wasn't a schmuck and his grief for Tara consumed him just as much as his wife's did. Maybe even more so. He clearly felt responsible, and my heart squeezed in sympathy. It hadn't been his fault. He couldn't have done anything to stop what had happened to Tara.

We left Arthur a few minutes later, after he'd calmed down a bit and answered some routine questions for Luke. Unfortunately, he hadn't seen the guy's face or anything useful to help us identify him. But it still seemed encouraging that someone other than Tara had seen the stalker. At the very least, it kept Luke searching in the right direction and on the same page as me. Though, it begged the question, how had he seen him? Had the demon just let his guard down? Or did Arthur have a supernatural gift of his own?

As I walked away from the house, my heart felt heavy in my chest. This demon had done a number on these people, turning them against each other, making them think that Tara was crazy. I knew it had to be Beaseldorf or someone he controlled. Maybe even the sexy demon guy had done it. The picture had been of a very attractive guy who looked human, I thought, as we approached our cars, noting that the rain had stopped at some point during our visit.

Luke paused at the end of the driveway and reached out to grasp my elbow to stop me. "So, what did you make of that?"

I eyed him, deciding whether or not to tell him the truth, unsure what he might think. In the end, I decided to give him my honest opinion this time. "I think Arthur was telling the truth. I think something happened to Tara that night. She—" I broke off trying to choose the right words. This might be my only chance to convince Luke to see my side of things and I couldn't lead with *Beaseldorf*. If I did, he'd sign me up for the first available padded room, and I didn't think I could pull off the whole straitjacket look. "She didn't seem like she wanted to die the night I met her. In fact, she came to me because she wanted to *live*. She told me so. So, why would she go and off herself a couple of hours later?"

He sucked his bottom lip through his teeth in thought. "You know, I followed up with the officers who took Tara's complaints. They said they never found evidence of a stalker. That's why they wrote it off as paranoia. So what makes you so certain it's true and that this is foul play? Mentally ill people do not always behave rationally."

I debated what to say next, wondering why I wanted Luke aligned with me so badly on this one. Perhaps because the more people looking for Tara, the better. I needed to give her the best shot at survival I could, and at this point, that meant having the resources of Santa Sombra PD searching in the right direction.

At last, I settled on the simplest explanation. "She showed me his picture. I saw him plain as day."

"Was the picture on her phone?"

I nodded, the lie flowing easily. I wished again that I'd asked her to send me the original that night. That I hadn't waited until the following morning. If I had, perhaps I would have seen something else within the image. Something I could use to find the damned demon in the image. To track him.

Luke gave me a determined nod. “Good. We have some officers sifting through everything on it at the station now. Maybe we can locate him that way.”

My throat tightened, knowing they wouldn’t. There was nothing I could do about that, though. All I could do was make sure I kept them hunting in the right direction. For now, at least.

Chapter 12

After departing Bethany and Arthur's house, we decided to leave the Subaru behind and take Luke's Crown Vic instead. He'd gotten the keys to Tara's house from Bethany the day before, and she'd given him permission to go through it without a warrant. After that, he had an interview scheduled with Tara's ex-husband. Man, did having a cop on your side make things easier or what? I'd planned to ask Bethany if she had a key to Tara's house and I'd also intended to swing by the ex's house too, but Luke had already done all the pesky administrative legwork for me. Nice.

As we settled into the comfortable leather of the police-issue seats and got on the road, I tapped my fingers on the file folder that Luke had left sitting on the front seat when I'd entered. It now rested on my lap and it had Tara's name on it. I pursed my lips as I surveyed it. It was thin. Much thinner than he led me to believe when we'd made that deal earlier. But then I had a grand total of one piece of paper's worth of information, so who was getting the better end of the bargain? Me. Definitely me. My lips twitched as he flipped on the blinker and merged onto the main drag.

I tapped the folder in question once more, this time loudly, and broke the silence between us. "So, this is your file on Tara?"

"Yep," he said, glancing in my direction for a brief moment to grin at me before refocusing on the road. "That's everything we've got so far. You can look it over if you want." I recognized the gesture for the olive branch it was, doing a mental fist pump as I opened it and scanned through everything they had on the case. I read and Luke drove, his pace leisurely and his methods comfortable, nothing like Gaby's death-defying antics. To be honest, not needing to grab the oh-shit handle a few dozen times on our ten-minute ride to Tara's place left me feeling a little bored.

As far as the case went though, it looked pretty thin on the evidentiary front, which didn't surprise me. They hadn't had much time to compile everything or to interview possible witnesses. So far, they'd briefly spoken to Bethany during the next of kin notification and had helped her file an official missing person report. But according to their notes, Bud hadn't gotten much out of her when they tried to question her the first time. She'd become hysterical when she'd heard about the blood on my couch. Ergo the secondary interview today.

Other than that, they had fingerprints and blood that still needed to be processed for DNA, but they'd only found two sets of prints. Which meant that one probably belonged to me and the other to Tara, so it didn't look too promising. It also said a lot about the amount of visitors I had in my apartment.

I scanned through the docs, noting the list of Tara's close contacts. It covered the same people I'd put together: A sister, two friends, Primrose and Margaret, and an ex-husband, which felt heartening. At least we had the same agenda for today. I flipped deeper into the file, trying to tie some of the names back to the list the hot demon guy had given me. I didn't see anything that rang a bell though, and once I'd skimmed everything Luke and Bud had to offer, I flicked the folder shut.

Leaning back in my seat, I propped my boots on the dashboard. "Looks like we're on the same track."

Luke's eyes moved to the dash and my feet for a brief moment, but he declined to comment. Probably because he didn't want to ruin our newfound camaraderie. "Come on JT, I showed you mine. Now it's your turn."

I gnawed on my lip, trying to figure out how I could dress up my lack of investigatory findings in a way that might impress him. I came up blank and decided that the truth would have to do. "I'd planned to talk to friends and family today." I did my best to project nonchalance as I lifted a shoulder. "Same as you. I wanted to see if they might have seen or heard anything out of the ordinary. Also, I wanted to visit her house to see if her stalker may have left any traces behind. So, like I said, same track."

Luke pressed his lips together, and I could tell he didn't believe me, at least not fully. He opened his mouth, but my phone rang. I pulled it out of my pocket and saw Gaby's name on the display. I swiped to answer and she started talking the second the line made a connection.

"You won't believe this."

"Sure, I will. Try me." Before Gaby could answer me, I maneuvered my pointer finger to turn down the volume on my cell. I didn't need Luke overhearing every word she had to say.

"I ran those names you gave me and... guess what."

She paused and I waited with bated breath for her to continue. After an irritatingly long pause, she said, "You're supposed to say *what* when someone asks you to guess what."

"Oh, for the love of all things holy, Gaby, WHAT?" I enunciated the last word carefully, just so she could understand the depth of my annoyance at her stalling.

"They're all missing. Every single one of them."

I sat up straighter in my seat and looked at Luke from beneath my lashes—all covert-like. Though he stared straight ahead at the road, I could tell he was straining to listen to every word she said.

"You're kidding."

"Nope, and guess what? They all disappeared within the last week."

I ran my tongue over my teeth as my mind worked to try and piece this together. A pattern certainly, but that list had over two dozen people on it. I'd never witnessed corruption attempts en masse before, like a coordinated effort. Demons tended to be solitary creatures, with more of a territorial rivalry among their own kind than anything.

"Okay," I said, trying to think through our next steps. Kidnapping over twenty-five people and doing all of them perfectly? Demon or not, I doubted anyone could pull that off. Someone must have screwed up somewhere along the line. Surely some kind of evidence got left behind in a chain that tangled. "Are any of them local? Or driving distance at least?"

I could almost feel Gaby's energy coming through the phone. Not that she was happy to learn that people had gone missing, but because we had a lead. A clue that could help us find Tara, and in the process maybe even the rest of the people on that list. "Actually, one is," she said, and I could hear her typing and clicking on a keyboard as she searched for the name.

I flipped open my notebook and pulled Gaby's pen from the page, clicking it open.

"Elias Hunter," she said, and I propped the phone on my shoulder so I could use both hands to write steadily. "He has an address in Silverwood. According to the police record, he went missing from a saloon on Main Street there two days ago. He went for a post-shift beer with a couple of friends, but he never made it home. His sister found his truck the next day with the keys still in the ignition and the gas tank empty."

"Really? It was running all night, then?"

"I guess so," she answered before she recited the address to me. As she did, I could feel Luke's stare boring into me and I knew I would have to give him some kind of an explanation once I hung up. The question remained, what kind?

What was I supposed to tell him? Some guy assaulted me and made me hornier than a nineteen-year-old dude in a strip club, before he gave me a list of names to investigate? Then, funny story, we just found out they all went missing this week. Call me pessimistic, but I didn't think that wouldn't go over too well.

"So, are you going to check it out?" Gaby asked, and I hesitated.

"Well, I'm with Luke right now, so—"

"You're what?!" she whisper-yelled into the phone.

"With Luke," I supplied again, on the off chance that she actually hadn't heard me.

"Shit, Jenna. What are you going to tell him?"

"I dunno. The options feel pretty limited," I replied, trying to keep things as vague as possible.

"Well, good luck with that. You should probably make something up, though, you know, to avoid possible jail time. They did find Tara's blood in your apartment after all."

"Thanks, that's real helpful."

I ended the call and looked out the front windshield to focus my attention back on the road. A red light hung overhead and Luke leaned over, snagging my notebook before I could react. Though, honestly, I didn't think a strong reaction would have done me much good. A move that obvious probably would have made even him more curious and then suspicious. It would also have been a pretty clear breach of our earlier agreement to share intel, and knowing him, he'd have stonewalled me in retaliation.

He held the notebook up to his face, one hand resting on the steering wheel with it while he read. "Who's Elias Hunter from Silverwood?"

I swallowed, trying to think of a plausible lie before deciding the best option was to throw him off the scent until I figured out what the hell was going on. "I got a tip this morning, but it's for another case we're working on. Elias Hunter is one of the many guys we suspect that the wife is... you know... doing the nasty with." I could almost feel my nose growing and hoped that they didn't reserve a special place in hell for liars like me.

But I couldn't explain how I got the intel and I couldn't have him there with me during the interview, at least not right away. Add to that, if I blew this into a multiple missing persons case that crossed state lines, then the FBI might get involved and I'd lose any shot I had at finding Tara before Beaseldorf finished his grand plan. Whatever that might be.

The light turned green and Luke's brows cinched together, the car not moving. His eyes bored into mine and I had to double down with every ounce of my limited self-control not to look away. "Are you sure about that?"

"Yep." We continued staring at each other for an uncomfortably long moment.

If I broke eye contact now, it would out me as a big fat liar, and that would put me in some serious hot water. Boiling hot.

Someone honked behind us. "It's green, you know?" I observed, hoping I appeared more collected than I felt.

His eyes stayed locked on mine for a beat before he refocused on the road and hit the accelerator, the car jerking quicker than I expected. A much more Gaby-esque move than his usual fare. Without warning, he whipped us to the right and maneuvered with deft precision into a parking spot in a strip mall off the main drag. If I hadn't been so worried about getting caught in a lie, I might've taken a moment to admire his driving skills.

Slamming the car into park, he clicked his seat belt free, turning wholly in his seat to face me. But rather than the anger I expected to see on his face, I saw frustration and maybe even a hint of betrayal. "Why are you lying to me, JT? We had a deal, and when have I ever given you any reason not to trust me?"

I licked my lips, uncertainty crawling through me as his blue eyes all but seared mine, making my stomach lurch. I opened my mouth to reply, to say something smart-ass, but then stopped myself. Sincerity burned through his eyes and though I intended to lie, to evade and divert his questions, something in the way he looked at me made me hesitate.

This was Luke. Yes, he was investigating me, poking around in my life, and being a general pain in my ass. But before all the bullshit had happened between us, he'd come by the bar after hours on more than one occasion, needing company and friendship, and stupidly, I'd obliged. I clamped my eyes shut to try and clear my thoughts. I needed to focus on the issue at hand and not let any of those cozy memories seep in to confuse things.

But Luke didn't give me even a second to recover my thoughts. "After what happened at your apartment with your friends, you know most people, *most cops*, would have reported that. But I didn't, even though I knew you were lying. And I decided not to say anything about it afterward because you're important to me, Jenna, and I chose to trust you. Just like I am choosing to trust you right now." When I didn't say anything, he swore, and his hand tightened on the steering wheel, knuckles whitening. "Dammit, Jenna. You can trust me. I want to find Tara, too."

After what felt like a long moment, I lifted my eyes from his clenched fingers and refocused my attention on him. "Of course I trust you." To my surprise, I wasn't lying. Somehow, I did trust him. At least, when it came to this case, I did.

It was just that I didn't tell anyone about the other part of my life. And much to my dismay, my two worlds had come crashing together in Tara's case, and I had no idea how to deal with it. Luke didn't deserve to get wrapped up in the far too dangerous and patently insane supernatural world I dealt with every day. Nor did I love the idea of finding myself in a mental institution when I came clean with the full truth and he didn't believe me.

"Then be honest with me. Who is Elias Hunter?"

I let out a long breath, trying to figure out how best to answer him. At last, I decided on the truth because, despite everything, he hadn't given me any reason to believe he wouldn't have my back on this case. "He's another missing person. He went missing the day before Tara did."

Luke's eyes hardened. "And you decided to hide this because...?"

I shifted, uncomfortable under his scrutiny. "It's out of your jurisdiction, in Silverwood, and I have no idea if the cases are actually related." Another lie, but I couldn't explain how I got the information about Elias, now could I? "I planned to check it out on my own, and if it turned out to be relevant, I would have looped in you and Bud." Yet another lie, but I sold it harder that time. Damn near made myself believe it.

He arched a brow as he surveyed me. "See? Was that so hard?"

"Yes."

He shook his head, his lips twitching as he turned to face forward and buckled his seat belt. "Go check out your lead, if that's what it turns out to be. Bud and I will go to Rattlesnake Bar and follow up with her doctors at the psychiatric facility. Just let us know if you find anything that would make it worth going through the red tape of working with Silverwood PD. Sound fair?"

I nodded, feeling like a bigger jerk than usual. I'd still lied. I just did a far better job of it the second time around. Guilt coiled in my belly, but I pushed it aside. I needed to remember that I liked having Luke alive and with a pulse. Plus, I didn't want to ruin his life with my crazy, fucked-up world. I couldn't tell him everything, not like I could with Gaby and Roger. It was different for them and for me. We belonged in the whole supernatural world, and Luke didn't. Simple as that.

As we turned onto the freeway, I tried to remind myself that I was only doing what was best for him. Bud had been off the mark about the sex part. Luke was the only person I knew who kept the same strange hours I did. And we'd developed a sort of camaraderie when he'd come by after I closed down The Office. We used to shoot darts, drink shots, and talk mad shit to each other.

Despite my best attempts to keep him at arm's length, he'd wormed his way into my *people I gave a shit about* column. But it had been that extra attention into my life that had caused him to witness just a fraction of my crazy. I reminded myself for the hundredth time that pushing him away kept him safe. And I would need to tell some lies to keep him out of the crosshairs of whatever the hell Beaseldorf had planned.

Gaby's House, East Santa Sombra, Fourteen Years Ago

Gaby laughed as she threw a fistful of popcorn at me. "You're ridiculous!"

In response, I caught at least half of it in my mouth, which only made her giggle harder. It was Friday, Gaby's only day off at the restaurant, and we'd agreed to meet at her place to iron out the details of our plan to confront the wrath demon.

We hadn't gotten the chance to do much in the way of plotting at La Fortuna Cocina before Gaby's mom interrupted us. Instead, we'd spent over two hours talking about all kinds of things—school, Gaby's friends, her family, homework, and boys, too. As an aside, Gaby had terrible taste in boys.

Just as we'd started to work through the beginnings of a plan, Gaby's mom insisted I go home. She hadn't wanted my parents to worry, especially with me having arrived there on foot. Walking at night in downtown Santa Sombra wasn't safe for a young girl like me, according to Mrs. Perez at least. Little did she know, Erin and Dave couldn't have cared less about my whereabouts, as long as the foster care checks arrived on time.

Two days had passed since then, and we had Gaby's house to ourselves. It was a small two-bedroom, one bathroom place in East Santa Sombra near Saint Augustine High School. The cozily decorated house came with a Latin flair that I had to admire. The bright colors and beautiful artwork made me wish I had a place like it to call home. It was something I couldn't help, the longing I felt whenever I hung around Gaby. She had such a close family, and aunts and uncles and cousins too, and she talked about them all the time. I wondered if one day I'd get to meet them.

As for school, we'd spent the last couple of days passing notes and trying to keep our fresh alliance under wraps. Mostly for her benefit, but also for mine. I couldn't afford to lose my reputation as a terrifying, unapproachable freak, now could I? So we'd dropped notes into each other's lockers between periods and came up with this plan.

Justin and her other lame friends had gone to a movie and Cold Stone that night, but she'd decided to spend her time with me instead. Apparently, she'd determined that defeating a demon who could terrorize the school and wreak untold havoc and carnage mattered more than a fun night with her bros. I had to admit, she had more brains than I'd given her credit for.

As she searched Netflix for something to watch, I grabbed my backpack and pulled out some of the demon-fighting supplies I'd acquired over the past few months. I emptied them onto her pink and teal bedspread that burned my eyes a little from its brightness and set my backpack on the chair of her small white desk on the other side of her room.

She came back to sit at the base of her bed and pressed play on a movie I didn't recognize. "Have you seen this one yet?"

"Oh, no. Erin and Dave don't really let me watch anything I want on TV. They have that pretty locked down."

"Erin and Dave?" Gaby asked.

"Yeah, my foster parents."

"You're in foster care?" she asked, and I waited for the judgment I thought I'd see, but it didn't come. Neither did the pity.

"Yep." I sat on the edge of her bed and started to rearrange the holy water and wooden crucifixes, careful not to meet her eye.

She swallowed, her throat bobbing as she picked at a loose thread on her ultra vibrant bedspread. "That must be tough. Do you know your parents? I mean, your real parents?"

"Nope, I know as much about them as you do. So nada."

"Hmm, I wonder if they're like you. Do you think when you grow up, you'll try to find them?"

I slipped my hands into the pockets of my charcoal-gray hoodie. "I don't know. Maybe. But they abandoned me as a baby, so I'm not sure they want to be found." We sat in silence for a long moment. My life tended to be a mood killer, so I didn't usually talk about it. At last, I decided to break the uncomfortable silence. "Can you do me a favor?"

"Sure."

"Can you promise not to tell anyone that I'm in foster care? I don't usually talk about it. It's sort of—private."

"Of course, I promise." She held out her pinky to me, and I hesitated for a minute. Though I understood the concept of pinky promises, I'd never made one before. After a brief moment, I grasped her pinky with mine. "Alright, so why don't you show me the weapons and tell me how they work?"

I spent a few minutes explaining the nuances of demon fighting that I'd gathered as the TV hummed in the background.

"So, you're telling me that regular weapons, like knives or baseball bats or whatever, don't work on demons? And that demons can't touch regular humans, but you can touch them and they can touch you too? How does any of that make sense?" She stared at me, completely baffled. Her carefully curled dark hair swayed as she shook her head.

"I don't know, because I didn't make the rules. I'm just learning them as I go."

"But wait—if they can't touch regular people, then how do they cause carnage?"

I swallowed. Honestly, I'd wondered when she was going to ask me for more specifics. She hadn't so far and had just taken me at my word. I wiped my hands on my torn jeans. "They don't have to touch you. They influence you. They draw out anything that makes you mad, and they... like... amplify it. I've also seen them possess someone, but that was just once."

Gaby's eyes went as wide as saucers. "Wait, what? Possess? Who was it? When?"

"Do you remember Brittany Walker?"

"No!" she gasped.

"It happened just before she moved. I saw the demon take over her body in the hall during class. We both had bathroom passes and I—didn't know what to do. I froze, and I just watched." I squeezed my eyes shut, the image of that awful day flooding my mind without my permission. Her body frozen in an arc, as though suspended by a rope, her toes scraping against the ground, her mouth open so wide that I could hear her jaw cracking. The smoky aura of the demon pouring into it, consuming her. I shivered as goosebumps trailed up my arms.

Gaby reached out and gripped my hand, the firmness of it surprising me. "It wasn't your fault that you froze. We were barely even ten yet when she moved away. We were little kids." I stayed quiet as I waited for her to make the connection, knowing she would. "Wait, didn't her little sister drown in their pool right before they left town?"

Everything inside me tensed as I nodded, guilt burning my stomach like acid.

"You don't think—" She broke off, staring at me with a horror I completely understood because I felt it too.

"I don't know for sure, but I don't think it was a coincidence. That's when I decided I had to fight them. I froze that day, and maybe I could have saved Brittany or her little sister if I'd just done something. Did you know her sister

was only four? Four years old?" My heart squeezed in my chest at the thought of her small body, all alone in that pool. At the pain and agony her parents must have felt at losing her. I shuddered. "I should have done something, anything I could have to stop it. But I didn't, and I promised myself I'd never make that mistake again."

Better me, I told myself, than an innocent little kid. I might have been a kid too, but someone had given me this curse for a reason. I would have to make the best of it and do what I could to make sure nothing like that happened when I could stop it.

Gaby watched me, her hand still squeezing mine, keeping me anchored. I wondered if this was what it felt like to have a friend. Someone you could tell your darkest secrets to, someone who would hold your hand through it and support you.

"Don't worry," she said. "We'll make sure we don't let this demon get that far. We'll stop it, together.

CHAPTER 13

I pulled up to the street parking in front of Gaby's community an hour or so after Luke and I had gone through Tara's place with a fine-toothed comb. We'd come up empty, unless you counted a medicine cabinet that would have put any local pharmacy to shame. It seemed that Tara liked to self-medicate on top of all the prescription drugs her doctors had given her. Or perhaps it had been in lieu of them.

After her house, we'd done the obligatory ex-husband interview. As Bethany had warned, he knew little of Tara's condition and hadn't spoken to her since her discharge from the mental health facility several months ago. He knew about her mental health struggles but had nothing else of interest to add. After that, Luke dropped me back at my car and we went our separate ways.

I couldn't help but feel like I'd wasted the day, yet again, and having Luke there as my partner instead of Gaby or Roger didn't exactly help matters. I needed Roger to touch things and tell me what he felt or saw. Maybe I could convince him to come back with me later, when we could sneak into Tara's house without the ever-watchful, far too perceptive eye of Luke.

As I opened the gate and walked down the narrow path to Gaby's door, a shiver rolled down my back, the hairs on my neck rising. The sun had set and darkness cloaked the street around me, but a single streetlight glowed about fifteen feet away and my eyes fixed on a shadowy figure standing beneath it. He leaned his tall, powerful body against the post, arms crossed over his chest and one booted foot propped up behind him. Though his form appeared in silhouette under the bright light, I knew without understanding how, that he was staring at me. And my instincts told me that his stare would be a golden one.

My feet moved, seemingly of their own accord, ushering me toward him without question or hesitation. Because apparently, my feet had a death wish. Or maybe just an orgasm-wish? When only a few feet remained between us, I saw those golden eyes almost glowing beneath the streetlight and anticipation fluttered low in my belly.

Still, I moved closer, trying to get a better look at him, wondering what the hell I was thinking. I had my new sword looped over my chest and slung across my back, but I hadn't bothered to either grab or unsheathe him, and I couldn't bring myself to care. I just wanted to see the demon again.

I had questions about the case, about Tara, and I told myself that was my primary motivation for running to him like a moth to a flame. It had nothing to do with the dream or our encounter the night before and how it had made me feel.

If only I believed that.

His low voice, like sensuous smoke, filled the air around me. "Did you look into the names I gave you?" He stared straight ahead, as though he couldn't be bothered to register my presence.

I swallowed as I stepped into the light of the streetlamp, close enough to him that I could feel the sensuality rolling off him in waves, threatening to pull me under.

"What are you?" My words felt breathy as they steamed in the cold night air.

His eyes fixed on me then and it took every fiber of control I had not to gasp beneath their scrutiny. Their golden depths seemed to move with intensity as his gaze perused my body with a seductive leisure that made my knees wobble. "You already know the answer to that."

"A demon, sure. But same question, what are you?" I watched him in amazement and couldn't help but feel the sex pouring off him. Clearly, lust was his preferred seven deadly, but the raw power of it? That was unlike anything I'd ever experienced. No demon had ever tempted me before. But with him? I struggled to keep control of my mind, my thoughts, and my body. His power felt like an all-out assault on my senses.

"That's not important and we don't have a lot of time. The names, Jenna." He stepped closer and his scent enveloped me, making my mouth water. He smelled like pure sin and sex, all wrapped into one sculpted, scrumptious body. My eyes locked on his lips as he spoke, his voice sounding far away as his mouth moved. "Did you look into the names or did you spend all day wasting your time with that *cop*?"

At the bite in his last word, the logical part of my mind crawled up from the depths of where he'd banished it, finally registering the rest of what he'd said. I shook my head to clear it and took a step back, away from him and his sex-on-a-stick aura. When he got close to me, it was all I could do to keep from leaping on him and ripping his clothes off like some lust-crazed animal. What was I thinking? He was a demon for fuck's sake!

I took a breath of fresh air and felt my senses clear a bit, relieved to discover that away from his pheromones, I could think clearer. As my brain and body recovered, I looked up and glared at him. "Gaby looked into the names today; they're all missing."

The corner of his mouth tilted upward, as though pleased with my answer. I didn't know why, but warmth pooled in my belly at his approval. Why would I care what this demon thought about me? My logical brain knew that his opinion of me didn't matter, but my feral one, the one that seemed to take control whenever he drew too close? That one didn't mind one bit. Rather, it seemed to purr and preen in response to his approval. I really needed to work on that, if he was going to keep popping in like this. I should probably just kill him and call it good, but something deep in my gut told me that would be a mistake. And I always listened to my gut.

He stepped back to lean against the post again. "Good."

It seemed like he wanted to keep his distance from me, and I wondered, did he know what kind of effect his nearness had on people? He must, and putting space between us seemed to combat it. I couldn't decide if I felt relieved or disappointed by the cool air that rushed over me and cleared my head.

"Have you found the connection yet?" he asked, his voice low enough that I could barely make it out.

I shook my head in confusion. "Connection? What connection? I mean, they're all missing, and they all disappeared within the last week."

He opened his mouth to answer before he snapped it shut, turning his head away to stare off into the distance once more. His hood slipped back just a bit and graced me with a view of his sculpted jawline, the perfect arch of it clenching in apparent frustration. After a brief pause, he turned back to me, his liquid eyes skimming the length of my body before he spoke. "Yes, but that's not what I mean. You need to find the tether that connects them all."

Surprised, my eyes widened without my permission. "I thought I had. They're all missing." I felt a little like a broken record and he shook his head, as though disappointed in me.

My mood somersaulted, plummeting into something like despair at his disapproval, and the logical part of my brain wondered again—what the fuck? Why did I care what some random demon thought of me?

His voice filled the air once more. "But why, Jenna. Why did they all go missing this week? What ties it together? You need to make the connection and do it fast. We're running out of time." His head jerked away from me again, as though he heard something I didn't. "I need to leave. I shouldn't have come back here." He dragged his gaze away from whatever he'd sensed in the distance and fixed it back on me.

"Why did you?" I asked, and through the haze of last night's... interaction... I remembered something he'd told me. "You said you couldn't interfere any more than you already had, so what changed?"

The demon's gaze bored into mine, and he smirked at me, the expression making him even more breathtaking. "I'm surprised you remembered that. Just shake the cop. He's only going to slow you down. He isn't part of our world." The way he said *our* made something warm tug in my belly, another sensation I couldn't understand because his world and my world didn't get cozy together. I hunted his kind and sent them back to hell, end of story. And yet he had a point. We did both exist in a world full of supernatural craziness, and Luke didn't.

The logical part of my brain fought its way through the haze of semi-arousal he exuded, even at a distance. "The cop isn't the problem, you are. If you want me to help you, then you should tell me what the hell is going on."

His smirk deepened, and I could've sworn I saw a flicker of desire slide over his features, which seemed strange considering that he was the apex sex predator and I couldn't hold a candle to him. "You have quite a mouth on you, don't you? It's not what I was expecting from someone like you."

He prowled a little closer to me but seemed careful not to invade my space bubble this time, and I wondered what he meant by that comment. *Someone like you*. I knew how people saw me, so I knew that I looked like the exact type of woman who said all kinds of insane shit.

"But like I said before, I can't get more involved than I already am, at least not yet. It's not a matter of choice."

I sighed, looking up into the darkened sky above me in exasperation. Stars twinkled behind thick fluffy clouds, visible in the moonlight. Why did he insist on being so damned vague? If he wanted me to stop whatever was coming, then why didn't he just tell me what I needed to do to stop it? That'd sure make things easier.

When I dropped my head and tried to return my attention to him, he no longer stood before me. I turned a few quick circles, searching through the darkness before I saw someone turn the corner just a block ahead. I took off at a dead run. I didn't question what I expected to happen, I just knew that I wanted more from him. My muscles burned as I tried to follow, icy air filling my lungs and stinging my throat.

The street in front of Gaby's complex had minimal streetlights and after running for a few heart-pounding moments, the darkness swallowed me. I spun another quick circle, pulling my phone out of my pocket and clicking on the flashlight, looking for him.

I had every intention of tracking him down and forcing his secrets out of him. I just didn't know if I'd manage to get close enough to beat it out of him without losing my shit. More likely if I got within touching distance of him, I'd end up tossing my bra at him instead. Though, considering the massive pit of concern that had formed in my stomach with his warning, I was willing to take that chance. I aimed my flashlight around me in the darkness, feeling useless as my breaths puffed out in aggravated wheezes. When nothing appeared in the darkness, I realized I'd lost him.

He'd disappeared on me again.

CHAPTER 14

Feeling sexually frustrated, disturbed, and more confused than ever, I made my way back to Gaby's house. Everything about this case seemed to throw me off my game. I had too many people in my ear and too many things happening all at once. I needed to take a step back and get some perspective, finish the research Gaby had started, and interview Elias Hunter. As I approached Gaby's front door, I pulled it open and a flood of warm air and lights hit me, along with two voices I knew all too well.

A smile tugged on my lips when I spotted Roger, decked out in a vibrant red kimono, a gold scarf, and skinny jeans. He sat at the kitchen table just off the family room. "Hey, hon. Gaby called and told me about what happened last night."

"Did she now?" I asked, striding over to the table and dropping my notebook on top of it. From the corner of my eye, I saw Gaby moving around in the kitchen. It looked like she was heating up soup for us, which made me happy. I was cold and hungry, dammit, and also, I couldn't cook. As I returned my attention to Roger, a sudden rush of horror flooded my veins. Gaby wouldn't have mentioned the throw pillow incident, would she? I narrowed my eyes. "What did she say?"

"Enough to know that I need to do a reading on that sword, you know, before it gets you into any more trouble." Vague enough. Perhaps she had let me off the hook on the aforementioned pillow ordeal.

In response to his offer, I pulled the sword off my back and set it in the center of the table. He sat there, looking innocuous and far too pretty for his own good. I didn't trust him. Not one bit. The sword, not Roger. I could feel him beckoning me to pick him up, but instead of listening, I pulled a chair out with my boot and slumped into it.

I returned my attention to Roger, his handsome face neutral as he sipped from a mug of his signature black tea. "You sure you're up for this?" I asked. He'd seemed so dead set against it when I'd brought it up yesterday.

"Not really, but I'm getting the sense that it's probably important, right? Besides, Beaseldorf was *so* yesterday. I've since slept, showered, and drank a nice little revitalization tonic that Gaby gave me. I feel like a new man."

"Speaking of Beaseldorf," Gaby called over her shoulder. "Did you get anything from him, you know, when he was up there kicking around?" She tapped her temple to further demonstrate her meaning with one hand while she stirred our sustenance with the other.

Roger frowned as he tried to think about it. He usually needed a little time after an experience like that one to decompress before he could come up with any useful information. After a few beats he shivered, shaking out his shoulders and the red fabric of his kimono rippled like water with the motion. "Nothing, like really *nothing*. Just cold, dark emptiness. Oh, and evil. Lots of evil with a touch of insanity and full-on rage. It still gives me the creeps just thinking about it."

My eyes softened as I realized that the incident may have traumatized him more than he'd originally led us to believe. "Are you sure you're okay? You really don't have to do this tonight. It can wait."

Even though the words left my lips, I knew I needed his help with the sword or else it might put me into an even more dangerous situation next time it decided we had to go for a midnight romp. But I also didn't want to force the issue either and risk hurting Roger. He'd done enough for me already.

Roger shook his head and set his mug down, cracking his knuckles. "No, I've got this. I mean, after having Beaseldorf in my head, how bad can it be?" Gaby moved over to us, setting bowls of steaming hot chicken soup from a can in front of us.

I stared up at her in appreciation. "You know I love you, right?"

"Uh-huh, you're only saying that cause I feed you."

"Obviously."

She moved back to the kitchen to snag spoons and napkins for us. Oh yeah, and a bottle of Rose. Say what you want about us, but we were classy ladies and we always drank wine with our chicken soup.

I watched the sword while she poured our wine, unsure if I really wanted to touch or unsheathe him. Admittedly, I did feel a kind of bond with him. Like he might want to kill demons and send them straight to hell as much as I did, but after the danger he'd put me in the night before, I didn't know if he had my best interests at heart. Plus, hot demon guy had claimed that he'd sent me to find the sword in the first place. So, whose side was the sword actually on anyway?

I leveled a finger and an accusing glare on him, his leather scabbard and carved hilt elaborate under the stark light of the chandelier. "No shocking me this time, mister, or I swear to all that's holy, I'll throw you in the dumpster and never look back." I'd been careful not to touch his hilt today, just in case he decided to electrocute me again. And as I stared at him, I did my best to morph into my surly demon hunting persona. But instead, I felt like the mother of a toddler making empty threats I'd never live up to. Who was I kidding? I was more connected to this sword than I had been to my virginity. Not that that was saying much, but still, you get the point.

With a scowl of warning on my face, I waited for a response. After Roger and Gaby snickered, I realized the fruitlessness of that expectation and pulled him off the table and unsheathed him, revealing a silvery-gold blade more beautiful than any I'd seen before. I closed my eyes and held my breath, but the dreaded electrocution never came. Not even the slightest zing of static electricity.

I smiled, the taste of victory sweet on my tongue, as I set the scabbard down on the empty seat beside me. My tough-gal speech must have worked wonders. Just as I moved to set his blade down on the table between the three of our bowls, electricity zinged up my arm and caused my hand to spasm and I dropped the sword right onto my soup bowl.

Liquid splattered onto my jeans before the bowl righted itself, wobbled, and remained otherwise intact. "That was so uncalled for."

I swiped at my jeans and glared at the inanimate object, wondering if he really qualified as inanimate anymore. I mean, he did animate with electricity and he did glow sometimes. He also spoke, or at least according to Roger he did.

Gaby slurped her soup from across the table. "Did he shock you?"

I sat down and picked the sword off my bowl with as few fingers as possible. To my immense relief, not too much had spilled and I could still salvage most of the meal.

"Sure did. I don't know what his problem is. It's not like I go around abusing *him*."

Roger chuckled between sips of soup. "Actually, that was payback for leaving him behind in your car today and for threatening to throw him in the dumpster. He doesn't care much for threats."

"You can hear him again?" I asked.

Roger nodded. "He's quiet, unless we're talking about him. Then he turns into a chatty Cathy. Again, most of it is hard to make out. He's very pissy and demanding, though. I kind of like him."

"Well, that sounds about right," I muttered, taking a few cautious slurps of my remaining soup, concerned that he'd somehow electrified it. Thankfully, he hadn't.

While we ate the rest of our meal, I filled them in on my most recent rendezvous with the suspiciously helpful, sexy demon guy.

"You didn't get anything else from him? Anything specific we can work with about that tether or tie or whatever he alluded to?" Gaby asked, her eyes locked on me as her spoon hovered halfway to her mouth.

I shook my head, feeling like a failure yet again. Deciding to let that whole interlude with that suspicious AF demon lie for a while, we discussed the case and what we needed to do next. Interviewing Elias's family and friends in Silverwood was the obvious next step. Gaby had found three other people close enough to our location to drive, but the travel time would take all day to visit any one of their families. We couldn't afford to waste that kind of time, so we decided to push that to the backburner in the hopes that maybe we'd find the connection between Tara and Elias in Silverwood. The other next step? We needed to get back into my apartment.

The cops had opened the bar, but my apartment on the other hand, not so much. I'd already looked through all of Tara's things and had read through Luke's files. But maybe Roger or Gaby could sense something I couldn't. If the cops didn't relinquish control before we found our next lead, we might have to resort to breaking a crime scene seal to enter it. Illegal? Yes. Ill-advised? Yes. Necessary? Hopefully not.

That left us with an interesting conundrum. How would we break into my apartment with a bar full of cops downstairs? Nighttime was out of the question, so it would have to be early morning after closing. And after several minutes of bickering over the best way to do it, we figured we could make that little nugget of joy a future us kind of problem. The interview with Elias's family in Silverwood took priority anyway and better to wait it out as long as possible before we did anything rash.

I poured myself a third glass of Rose, then topped off Gaby's and Roger's glasses too, thus polishing off our second bottle. We'd all finished our soup and had spent our time deftly avoiding the elephant in the room.

The sword.

Gaby and I both knew without him having to tell us, that Roger wasn't looking forward to the reading. As one may recall, my shit was dark, remember? Anything tied up with me was likely to have similar undertones. Or maybe even overtones.

Yet, despite our best efforts to ignore him, the sword still sat at the center of the table, his beautifully carved leather scabbard smelling like a new high-end handbag in the seat next to me. We all grew silent, each of our attention fixing on him in a single breath. I wondered how much of that he influenced and how much had to do with us running out of excuses to procrastinate.

"Are you ready?" Gaby asked, staring at Roger, whose eyes seemed to look straight through the sword lying before him.

He downed the last of his wine, which he drank in tandem with his tea, and nodded, his confidence unwavering. "Yep. Let's do this."

At that, Gaby rose from the table and dimmed both the kitchen lights and the chandelier overhead, leaving us in a soft glow. Roger's abilities worked better with less visual stimulation. Bright lights either distracted or agitated him whenever he did a reading. He could do it, sure, but the fewer distractions, the better.

He offered his gratitude as she sat down and folded her hands in front of her. We required no magic this time, no ritual or spell. Just a simple connection forged through touch. Time seemed to slow and my anticipation grew as Roger reached out and brushed the tips of his fingers over the sword, like a hesitant lover, unsure of the mutual desire for his touch.

His brow furrowed, his face morphing into a mask of confusion right before he gripped the sword so hard his knuckles whitened. "You can't be serious," he breathed, right before his eyes rolled back into his head and whatever he saw took him under.

Chapter 15

I'd never had a family.

Some parents give their kids up willingly, others are taken by CPS, but then there are kids like me, who never knew where they came from in the first place. I can't explain the listlessness of what it feels like to have no heritage. To have no idea what race or ethnicity you belong to, let alone to have no origin story.

I didn't even have a name when someone dropped me off at Fire Station #13 in downtown Santa Sombra. A baby, only a few days old, surrendered with nothing more than a blanket, the clothes on my back, and a bottle of formula. Or at least, that was what the well-meaning social workers had told me my whole life.

As a result, I'd always felt different, like I never quite belonged with anyone. If I thought about it long enough, I supposed that's why I'd become a runner—one of the many kids who always ran away from their foster homes. It didn't matter how well, or not well, they treated me, I never fit in with them.

I'd tried too. Hell, I'd tried harder than I would dare admit to anyone, but I could never seem to make it work. My abilities, what I could see, what I could do, they branded me an outsider.

A freak.

So, what Roger said next shocked me so deep to my core that it sucked the air from my lungs. "The sword... he says, you look just like your mother."

Once the words registered, my heart started to pound so hard I could feel it in my throat. I tried to get a breath, but I couldn't, the utter insanity of his statement so complete that he'd overloaded my system. When I finally did manage to suck in some air, I stuttered under the onslaught of unfamiliar emotions.

"M—my mother? What the hell does he know about my mother? I don't even know my mother."

I froze, everything inside me going quiet and furious with emotion at the same time—a raging tempest and a frozen tundra. I had no idea how to react, what to think, or what to feel. The only thing I knew for sure was that he couldn't have said anything that would have stunned me more.

Roger's eyes rolled back to center and he held up a finger, giving me a pleading look for patience as he closed his eyes in apparent concentration. I looked at Gaby, my mouth agape, and realized that she'd gone pale as well. She knew everything about me. All the little details, the good, the bad, and the ugly. So she would understand just how deeply this kind of revelation would rock me.

Roger's voice drew me back to him. "I see a battle. A woman. She's fighting with the sword, this sword, I mean. She's incredible, and he's right, JT, she does look like you. Dark hair, olive skin that seems to glow in the moonlight—" He cut off, shaking his head and cinching his eyes shut tighter. "But there are too many of them. They're dark, like mist, insubstantial. I can't *see* them. It's too dark where we are, but I know they're bad... they're demons, and they want her dead. They want the sword, he's the key. He'll free them somehow."

Roger sucked in a pained breath. His hand gripped the blade instead of the hilt that time, knuckles whitening even further. Without warning, he threw his head back and his lids fluttered like rapid wingbeats, only the whites of his eyes visible. His hand tightened, his palm gripping the blade. It was too tight, and I saw blood trickle as he cut his flesh on the sword.

I lunged forward without hesitation. "Holy shit, Roger!"

As much as I wanted to know what was going to happen next, I didn't want to risk him. I started to wrap my fingers around his and Gaby reached for the hilt of the sword, each of us intending to pry it out of his grip, to end the reading. But when I touched him, heat scalded my fingertips and I heard Gaby yelp too, each of us letting go. Both Roger and the sword had turned burning hot, like molten lava. Fuck, I hated magic.

"If you kill Roger, sword, I swear to God—"

Roger's voice cut me off, still his own despite the trance he seemed enthralled within. "She's running now. Through the forest, away from the demons. They're chasing her, but she's killing them. She's able to stay one step ahead. She's strong, she's so strong. Fast too, it's not—" His body jerked again, and I dropped into a crouch in front of him, unsure what to do with my hands. I wanted to help, to pry him away from that damned sword, but my palms stung from where I'd touched him just moments before.

I felt helpless to stop him, to stop this. I had the terrible feeling that his skin would melt the flesh off my damn bones if I tried again and held on any longer. Gaby knelt beside me, her face white as a sheet as we both rode the wave and waited for it to end. It was all we could do. We had no choice.

"She's there now, at the edge of a cliff. They have her surrounded. I can hear water, a river rushing below and a waterfall across the cliff. It's so far down. Rocks crumble beneath her feet and she presses as close as she can to the edge. No escape. No escape."

Tears formed at the edges of Roger's eyes and rolled down his face and I prayed it would be over soon. I promised myself I'd never ask him to do something like this again. How could I have let him hurt himself like this? Blood seeped from his palm and another red droplet formed at his nostril, a third sliding from his ear. The connection was hurting him. I should have known better. My shit was dark. He'd told me that so many times. Why hadn't I refused his help?

He gasped, another shudder racking his body, once then twice. "He's there now. The darkness. It swallows everything. It's night, so dark. So dark. He eats the moonlight and it's all gone. Hopelessness, despair, wrath, it oozes out of him like a noxious fog. He's bigger than the rest, more deadly, more dangerous. She knows it. She can't kill him on her own. She knows what she must do."

Roger's head jerked to the right, and a voice, sinister and dark but smooth as chocolate, came from his throat. "Give him to me now and I'll let you live."

Then a voice that didn't belong to him, feminine, determined flowed from his lips. "Never. What kind of life would that be, Beaseldorf, if I handed him over to you?"

I pressed my hands to my mouth as I realized who that deep voice belonged to. Who threatened my mother, the same creature we faced down now. Did Beaseldorf know who I was? Did he remember her? Or was this some kind of massive coincidence? I felt like I might choke on the air around me as I tried to suck in a breath. My mind flew to the apex sex demon, and knew it had to be him. He'd pulled me into this for a reason. Was it because of her?

The dark voice permeated again. "You'll rule by my side, Celia. One of *your kind* would prove useful for me." *Your kind*, the words boomed through my mind, as my memory dragged me back to my moment with hot demon guy just a couple of hours earlier. He'd said something similar. Then the name rang like a bell in my mind—Celia. My mother's name, and one I thought I'd never hear.

Roger started whispering low in the voice of my mother, in another language, one I didn't know and didn't recognize. It sounded other-worldly, ethereal almost.

Suddenly, his voice shifted back to his own, narrating the scene once more. "She throws the sword off the cliff. It disappears into thin air, its light gone, and then she—" His eyes snapped open and the sword leaped from his hand, popping a few inches into the air before landing back with a thud on the table, severing the connection.

I inched forward, desperate for him to finish the vision. “She what, Roger? She *what*?”

Caught between fear for his safety and for my unknown mother’s life, my stomach lurched and my heart raced. I’d never met my mother. Never touched, hugged, loved, or held her hand, and yet I still had to know. Was she alive? Had Beaseldorf killed her? Did she manage to get away? What happened to her?

Roger’s eyes grew wide, before sympathy filled them, and something inside me cracked. “I’m sorry, JT. She jumped.”

Chapter 16

My chest tightened painfully as I stared at the sword sitting on the table. It looked like the inanimate object it should have been all along, harmless, as it lay there. But I knew better. It carried secrets. Earth-shattering ones that had my mind and heart doing somersaults as I tried and failed to process it all.

On the positive side, Roger had come out of his trance, wiping the blood from his nose and ears, and though Gaby had reached for his hand—when she'd turned it palm up to inspect it, we found no wound there. It had healed, leaving only a trail of sticky blood as evidence that it had ever existed at all. None of us could explain that phenomenon, and as Roger pulled himself together, he promised us that the vision hadn't hurt him, despite the blood that slid from his nose and ears.

The way he explained it? The sword's consciousness had grabbed him by the balls and held them like two glass orbs that it would cradle and not crush, as long as he recited everything he saw verbatim. As for the healing afterward? He said the consciousness that resided within the blade had promised him he'd remained unharmed while he relayed its critical information, and the sword kept his promises.

Which brought me back to the contents of that damn vision—my mother. My heart lurched as it stuttered in my chest. Sure, I knew that my parents had been out there somewhere. That they'd existed at some point in the time space continuum. Otherwise, how else would I be alive right now? But the reality of knowing that I'd had a real mother and that she'd been like me? A fighter, likely even a hunter? I felt like my heart had grown eighteen sizes in ten seconds flat, only to have it ripped from my chest when I learned that she had jumped to her death who knew how long ago. I'd never get to know her, never see her face for myself. Even though I hated to admit it, that truth damn near gutted me.

Gaby pulled herself together a little faster than me. "So, the sword used to belong to JT's mom?"

My mouth opened and closed, and I shook my head, at a loss. Thankfully, Roger saved me from making a blubbering idiot out of myself. "The sword has a name, actually. He says that JT's family line has passed him down for a couple of generations."

I took a deep breath as I settled my gaze on Roger while he drank a sip of tea, as though nothing had just happened. As though he hadn't just blown my entire life to cinders with his vision. Granted, it hadn't been his fault, but still. I needed time to process, to think. Could I even handle more?

I waited for him to answer for what felt like forever until I got impatient. "Spit it out, man! The name!"

Roger gathered his kimono protectively around him. "It's *Remus*, alright? For the love of french fries, Jenna, I'm still decompressing here. It's a process, alright?"

I slumped down in the chair and rested my elbows on the table, hands dragging through my hair as I tried to relax, a feat that was becoming more impossible by the second. Taking a deep breath, I did my best to steady my emotions. "You're right. I'm sorry, Rog. It's just... holy shit! Of all the things I expected to hear tonight, *my mom* wasn't on the list. And Beaseldorf? She fought against Beaseldorf? He's the reason she's dead?"

Gaby nudged her chair closer to me and gripped my hand. My mind whirled as I remembered the psychic at Relics & Roots and what she'd said about things coming full circle. I'd known that premonition would end up making sense at some point, but I hadn't expected her to mean my mother.

Gaby's words felt like a soothing stroke down my ragged nerves. "It seems like she stopped whatever he had planned back then, but she couldn't defeat him. Do you think this is what that psychic's premonition meant?" Her thoughts tracked exactly where mine had, and I rubbed at my temples as I nodded in confirmation.

Leaving that aside for the moment, I started to wonder why the hell helpful hot demon guy had led me to Remus in the first place. Why send me to find a demon-slaying sword when I could tell that Remus wanted him, and all demons for that matter, dead?

"Rog, did Remus tell you what Beaseldorf was planning back then? Did he mention *how* the sword is the key? And what the hell Tara and the other missing people have to do with any of this? Or maybe anything about the goddamn demon who led me to him?"

Roger pursed his lips before he shook his head. "No, he didn't. I'm not sure if he even knows the answer to that, but Remus did want me to tell you that he belongs to you." He cleared his throat and fidgeted in his seat. It looked like he had more to say, but it seemed like he didn't want to chance it, afraid I might bite his head off again.

I gave him a come-hither gesture. "What aren't you telling me? Out with it."

"He says you belong to him too. The minute you picked him up at the market, the bond was forged. Remus is *your* weapon and you're *his* wielder. Whatever significance that holds." He shrugged as though at a loss. "But it seemed very important to him that you know that."

"What the hell does that mean?" I asked, having no idea what that might mean outside of the fact that I happened to have Remus in my possession for the moment. Roger offered me a confused grimace, and I knew only time would tell, but I had the sickening feeling that it would turn into some kind of a catch-22. Something that would come back to bite me in the ass later, because that was the kind of luck I had.

Pinching the bridge of my nose, I forced my thoughts into submission, needing to glean something I could action rather than wallowing in this newfound knowledge of my mother. If I stopped moving, stopped working this case, I knew we'd fail, and I couldn't let that happen. "About Beaseldorf... what did he look like? Did you get any features or anything unique about him that could help us track him?"

"I'm sorry, JT, but he looked like pure blackness. It was just so dark in the forest. All I know for sure is how he felt. And that was absolutely terrifying. His size filled all the space around your mom and she knew she couldn't win. From what I was able to make out, she hid the sword from him with a spell right before she jumped. She cloaked it so that he couldn't find it. Until now at least."

My mom was a witch and a hunter? I shook my head in shock and my mouth opened and closed like a fish sucking air. It seemed impossible, but then again, I had always been a third in Gaby and Roger's spells.

"Did you see why Beaseldorf is back now? If it's all full circle, he still doesn't have the sword, so... what's changed?" Realization hit me like a punch in the gut as my questions earlier pulled to the forefront of my mind. Hot demon guy had sent me directly to Remus, which meant he'd known the location. Did he want me to have it to stop whatever came next? Or did he want me to have it so that Beaseldorf could complete whatever he'd started with my mother? But if he wanted Beaseldorf to have it, why not just give it to him? Why let me have it at all?

I explained my line of thinking to Gaby and Roger, who both seemed to agree with my logic, but Gaby took it one step further. "You know, JT, that demon keeps saying that someone will find out if he helps you too much and that you know who he means. It has to be Beaseldorf, right? Do we all agree on that? I mean, who else would scare him enough to force him to stay in the shadows, considering how powerful you say he is?"

I nodded, having decided that right off the bat. "Definitely. He's wrapped up in whatever Beaseldorf is planning. I just don't know how." I chewed on my lip as I thought about the unnatural draw he had, the immense sexuality that pulled me in without my permission. The way his voice rolled over me like silk over bare skin, and I blinked, forcing back the alluring aftereffects of his presence with some effort. "I don't know if he's playing both sides or if he's somehow priming me for whatever Beaseldorf is planning. It's literally impossible to tell. He's a damned demon, and hot or not, we definitely can't trust him. But he's something more too, something other than a normal run-of-the-mill demon."

As I thought back to the involuntary reaction he'd pulled from my body, it almost felt like an incubus on steroids. But I had immunity to that particular species' charms. One prickly little fucker had learned that the hard way when I shoved my boot up its well-formed ass after its ill-advised attempt to seduce and kill me. So I knew there had to be another explanation.

Pinching the bridge of my nose, I fought through my racing thoughts and tried to pull the pieces together. The problem was that I didn't have enough of them. Something important was missing, something big, and without it, I knew I couldn't make sense of the full picture just yet. Why did he need the sword? What was it the key to? And he wanted to free the demons, how, exactly? Was Beaseldorf trying to get them all out of hell? But why would he need the sword for that, if so many of them already walked among us?

Giving up for the moment, I cleared my throat and looked at the sword. "Did Remus happen to mention to you... what my family's name is—or was, I guess?" I had no idea if any of them were even alive anymore. If everyone in my family did, in fact, share my abilities, then I doubted many of them had made it very long with a pulse. That didn't matter, though. I still wanted to know just the same. It seemed too coincidental that I'd ended up killing demons, just as my mother had, even without knowing where I'd come from.

"It's Bellator. Remus says it's Latin and that it means *warrior*."

"Like Latin from ancient Rome?" I asked, brows furrowing as Roger nodded. I supposed Italian made sense, given my olive skin, dark hair, and brown eyes. My family name even meant warrior, which felt a little on the nose, but also made sense considering what I did for a living. And what my mother apparently did too. Celia Bellator, I thought, rolling her full name over in my mind.

A name I thought I'd never learn, and I started to wonder. Did she die, really? Could I find her or maybe others in my family like me? No, I needed to focus. That would waste precious time on a hope that I had no business feeling. She'd jumped, she was gone, and I had a job to do.

My pointless, stupid grief didn't matter. But some small part of me wondered, had she given me up for a reason? To protect me? What would I do if I got pregnant right now? Discomfort swept through me as my world, along with everything I thought I knew about myself and my parents, shifted again.

I dragged my hands down my face before I rose to my feet, meandering to the kitchen to open another bottle of wine. Because I needed a goddamn drink, obviously. I poured the three of us another glass and stared at Remus. I felt that odd connection once more, that sense of homecoming I'd felt at the market taking on a whole new meaning.

The silence stretched for a few beats, all of us seeming unsure of what to say or do until, at last, I broke it. "Did you get a reference to a timeline of when all this was happening? Like a month? Or the year? Or even a decade?" My mind whirred, trying to fixate on what we needed to know right now. And what I needed was a fucking clue to find my client. I didn't need to fixate on my mom and answers that we didn't have. She wouldn't just appear and start giving me a rundown of all her life choices, including me. Which made fretting over it a pointless waste of my time.

Roger squinted, as though running back through the vision, trying to recall. At last he shook his head. "I'm sorry, I didn't see anything to give me any kind of a hint to the timeline. Even her clothes were just like, monochrome and black. So, nothing to go on there either."

"Damn."

Why did Beaseldorf want the sword so badly? Why was it so special? And what did he have planned for it that would make life not worth living, according to Celia Bellator? According to my mother?

Chapter 17

Roger left Gaby and me to our own devices a few hours after the jaw-dropping revelations from Remus's reading. Agitation nipped at the edges of my mind, frustration that we hadn't gleaned more information about Beaseldorf's plans from Remus dogging me. I chose to direct that frustration at my newfound weapon, not Roger. Roger was a fucking saint.

But honestly, what good did a sentient sword do for us if he failed to get any useful details from my mother's last case? I glared at him as he sat on the desk next to me at The Office. I left Gaby's house a couple of hours ago when I realized that sleep would evade me yet again, and despite my annoyance with him, I couldn't seem to leave Remus behind.

Evening had turned into about two a.m., and I still couldn't manage to relax my mind enough to sleep. Next to Remus sat the bottle of

Jack Daniels I kept in my desk as part of my private stash. I'd polished off roughly half of it, or maybe it was two-thirds. Not that I bothered counting.

I hiccupped as I began to question my life choices. Always a dangerous thing to do when you were me. I shook my head to clear it, my body already beginning to metabolize the booze and kick it from my system. That was one thing that really sucked about being a demon hunter—all the random supernatural abilities. I had to drink stupid fast to keep a buzz going. On the bright side, though, I never had a hangover for long.

As my vision started to clear one tiny fraction at a time, I refocused on the computer screen in front of me and pinched the bridge of my nose, squinting. The Jack was probably a bad decision. But all the revelations about my mom had screwed with my head big-time. No matter how hard I tried to tell myself that thinking about her was an epic waste of my very important time, I couldn't shake it. She'd jumped to her death. Killed herself to keep Beaseldorf from getting that sword. From finishing whatever he'd started back then.

Now I was in the same predicament. I'd spoken to Beaseldorf. He knew where I lived, and I had the thing he wanted most on the planet—Remus. Or at least, I assumed he wanted that most. Who knew? Maybe he'd prefer candy apple nipple tassels and an aggressive karma-sutra massage?

Nah, it was probably the sword.

As the little dots that indicated a report running kept blinking, I tapped my fingers on the smooth wood beneath them. Before I started drinking the hard stuff, I'd done some deeper digging into Tara and the other missing people's backgrounds. I'd attempted a few different paths, trying to find whatever damn connection that sexy helpful demon guy had alluded to.

When I came up blank on the individuals, I traced all the family lineage I could find on social media. From there, I looked back through the familial origins. Not as easy as you might think, considering what I searched for may not have been one hundred percent ethical. I didn't exactly have these people's permission. And that's where things stood for now—waiting for the results of some reports I'd paid for with my epic lack of money. So I'd used ye old trusty credit card. Another poor life choice. If things kept up at this rate, this case would not only break me mentally and emotionally, but it would also bankrupt me.

But that didn't matter. I needed to hurry the hell up or the clock would run out on whatever Beaseldorf had planned. As I waited for the relentless blinking of my Processing icon to finish, I resisted the insane urge to chuck the computer out the window in frustration. But that would count as an additional poor life choice resulting in yet another credit charge I couldn't afford.

Right as I decided to quell my irritation and let my saner head prevail, a knock sounded on the door of The Office and I sat up straighter, unsure if I'd actually heard something or if I'd just imagined it. A moment passed, and another soft knock sounded. I looked from side to side in confusion, as though I might be able to discern who came calling at this late hour from the cave that doubled as my office. Not likely.

Worry slid down my spine and I pulled Remus from his sheath. No glowy weirdness and no shocks. I could count that as a good sign. Yet suspicion still crawled through me and I frowned as I debated if I should answer that knock. After a couple of minutes of debate, I decided that my Spidey senses weren't tingling like they usually did when something bad was about to happen. So surely everything would be fine.

With that naive and cheery thought in my mind, I shoved back from my desk and stalked up to the front door. Darkness enveloped the normally busy streets of midtown, and rain splattered the glass door as a shadowy form shuffled from foot to foot, as though trying to stave off the cold.

When I drew closer, the form turned toward me, and I caught a full view of Luke's face. Every muscle in my body tensed. What the hell was he doing at my bar? He hadn't come back after hours since... well, since the exorcism incident.

I hesitated, staring at him from behind the glass pane on the top half of the door.

"Open the door," he said, pointing at the lock and then rubbing his hands together. He wore a thick pair of leather gloves, and I could see his breath fogging the air.

"Why?" I asked, sobriety winning the battle over the booze as I tried to figure out what he might want from me at nearly three in the morning.

"Just open the damn door, JT. I'm freezing my ass off out here." My mouth twisted as I eyed him with suspicion. But just when I decided to tell him to get lost, I thought about our deal and realized that maybe he'd found a lead. Perhaps sobriety wasn't winning quite as handily as I'd thought, considering that it had taken me far too long to put that mensa-level puzzle together.

With hope in my heart, I turned the bolt and opened the door. Cool, wet air assaulted me. He hurried inside and I locked the door behind him. "Damn, it's cold out there," he said, still rubbing his hands together.

I arched an annoyed brow and stared at him in expectation. "I assume your presence at nearly three in the morning means you found something on our girl?"

"You smell like whiskey," he observed, moving past me and farther into the bar, the scent of a faint cologne, sandalwood and something spicy, trailing in his wake. It smelled good and reminded me of better times. Times when things had been less tense between us. The events of our shared day had done something toward mending our once cozy relationship. But I didn't qualify our friendship as repaired. Not even close.

"What I do on my time is my business."

Luke turned to face me, that charming, crooked smirk on his face. "No one said it wasn't."

When I continued to glare at him, he sighed, the sound long and exhausted as he ran a hand through his dark-blond hair, and I really looked at him for the first time since he'd entered. A little sheen of his usual polish had worn off and I could see the deepening shadow of a beard along his jaw. His normally groomed hair looked tousled like he'd been trying to sleep and failed. It fell over his brow, brushing over his eye while the back stood on end. It looked ridiculous.

"Alright then," I said, not moving from my spot near the door and doing my level best not to mock his do. "Do you have news on Tara? Is that why you're here?"

He cleared his throat and looked at the bar again. The dark rings under his eyes seemed to darken even further as he turned into the light. "No, it's just been a long day. I could use a drink."

I stared at him, careful to keep the surprise from my expression. Did he seriously think that one moment of semi-truth in the car and a deal to share information on our case erased the past few months of police harassment he'd put me through? Because as far as I was concerned, we still had a long way to go before we mended the very broken fence between us on a personal level. I may trust him with the case, but I needed baby steps for anything else. I needed time. Maybe even some groveling apologies.

I kept my expression neutral. "Sorry, we stopped serving over an hour ago. I can't pour anything for you."

To his credit, my cool demeanor didn't seem to deter him. Unfortunately, it never did. Instead of scurrying out of the bar with his tail between his legs, the smirk turned into a full-fledged grin. "Well, I was thinking we could do a drink between friends, not in an official bar capacity. What do you think? For old times' sake?"

I pressed my lips together as I considered his offer. No, not an offer, but a request. Another olive branch. "Why the about-face?"

"I'm sorry?" he replied, a question in his eyes as he slipped his hands into the pockets of his wool coat.

"Two nights ago, you swore you'd get to the bottom of whatever I was hiding, and now you want to have a drink and chat like we're buddies again. Not only that, but you want to work a case together too. What changed?"

He shrugged, and suddenly, it dawned on me. Keep your friends close, but your enemies closer. “You’re still investigating me, aren't you? You’re just using this case as an opportunity to get closer.” When his whole body stilled, I knew I’d hit the nail on the head. “You’re a piece of work. Tell you what, Luke, I’ll work this case with you because it suits me. But as for the friend stuff? No thank you. You can leave now.”

I went to unlock the door and show him out, but he moved quickly, his hand pressing on the door and keeping it closed. “Maybe I am, but not tonight.”

I jerked my head up to glare at him, but his expression was so earnest, so raw that I softened. I couldn’t help it. He looked wounded somehow, and it made me hesitate. “Please, JT, have a drink with me? I need a truce tonight. You’re the only other person I know who sleeps as little as I do, and I need someone to talk to.”

Hesitation filled me, and I thought about all the reasons I should kick his ass out the door. The most critical one being that, aside from his determination to help me find Tara, I couldn’t trust him. He was running a secret, off-the-books investigation on me. And he always poked around where he didn’t belong, catching me on the edges of my crazy supernatural world. A world I had no business bringing him into and that I should do everything in my power to shield him from. Yet, as all those thoughts flowed through my mind, another did too. Maybe I wanted someone to talk to tonight too—a distraction. Maybe I wanted company, and maybe after everything that had happened to me that night, I needed a friend too.

Against my better judgment, I relocked the door. The sigh of relief he released was so intense that I could have sworn I felt it in my bones. "Thank you. I know I've been a shitty friend lately, but thank you."

"I'll go get my private stash. Don would kill me if I stole from the bar." Don King owned The Office. He was a pretty chill guy, and he trusted me to manage the place. So I took that trust seriously, and I never stole from him. I actually didn't steal from anyone, period. Personal rule.

I sauntered back to my office to grab the bottle of Jack I'd been nursing all night. Only about half of it remained, but it should be enough to get the job done. As I grabbed it from the desk, I heard a barstool creak and knew that Luke had sat down and that I'd find him waiting for me when I returned.

I strolled back to the front, eyes locking on his as I kicked the stool out next to him and sat down. I hopped up almost immediately when I remembered we needed glasses. No way I would drink straight from the bottle with him watching. So, rather than walk around to the passthrough, I leaned over the bar, giving him a full view of my ass while I grabbed a couple of shot glasses. Oh well, it couldn't be helped.

I poured one for each of us and held mine up. "Cheers."

He clinked his glass to mine and tossed back the shot.

"So, tell me, Luke, what is it that you wanted to talk about at three a.m.?"

He poured himself another shot immediately and swirled the honey-colored liquor in the glass, the low light catching the liquid and making it shine just a little. "To be honest, I don't feel like being alone tonight."

I let that sink in, thinking about the many times he'd come here for that same reason. Right before he started witnessing all my weird-ass shit and had gotten suspicious.

Earlier in the car was the closest we'd ever gotten to broaching the subject of our fizzling friendship, and while I knew I mattered to him, I just didn't know how much. It begged the question, if he found out the truth about me, would he believe me? Or would he be like Tara's family and try to have me committed? I didn't know for sure. I simply didn't trust him enough to let down my guard around him and find out.

So, rather than relent and give him what he wanted, I put up my walls. "Am I really the only person you know who isn't sleeping right now? You strike me as the kind of guy who has lots of options. Lots of friends."

He pointed a finger at me. "You know, you make a lot of assumptions about the kind of guy I am."

I scoffed, rolling my eyes. "Like it's not true."

"If you knew anything about me, then you'd know it's not." He slammed back the shot and placed the glass on the bar. "You know, I'm new to town, and you're one of the only friends I've made since I've been here. You and Bud."

"I'm one of your only two friends, and you're investigating me? You have a real interesting way of making friends."

"Yeah, I'm aware," he said, swirling the glass on the scuffed bartop. "It's just... I don't trust people all that easily." He grabbed the bottle and poured another round for each of us before lifting the glass to cheers me. "Don't take it personally. I tend to think the worst of people. Occupational hazard."

I snorted, clinking our glasses together. "Hard not to take it personally when you think I'm some kind of a criminal."

Genuine surprise flitted over his features as his brows rose. "Criminal? You think that I think you're a criminal?"

"Don't you?"

He laughed, like really laughed. The sound was rich and contagious, as always. Shaking his head, he leveled his intense blue eyes on me. "JT, I don't think you're a criminal. I never have."

I stared at him for a minute, my shock complete. My mouth opened and closed as I thought of something to say. "Then why are you investigating me? Why are you following me around and showing up at odd hours, poking your nose into my life where it doesn't belong? Why does it matter what I do, if you don't think I'm doing anything illegal?"

"Because you're a mystery, and that's what I do. I solve mysteries. And if I'm being really honest, I think you're wrapped up in something dangerous, and I want to know what it is." His eyes locked with mine and his expression looked so earnest and raw that I couldn't help but hold his gaze. He pressed a finger to the bartop for emphasis as he spoke. "You see, I'm involved now. Like it or not, you're one of my only two friends in town. If you're mixed up in something risky, then I want to know what it is."

The intensity of his stare and his words had my muscles tensing, and I broke eye contact in favor of pouring us another round. "Has anyone ever told you that you should really learn to mind your own business? And besides, you and me? We're not involved."

He laughed again, shaking his head as he swirled the booze. "You see, that's what I like about you. You don't beat around the bush. You just say whatever you're thinking. Except when you don't. It's a total mindfuck."

"And you like mindfucks?"

"Yet another of my many personality flaws." He took the shot, swallowing it in one swig yet again. And while my body could handle large amounts of liquor, I couldn't imagine he had that same ability. He must have been getting tipsy, if not outright drunk.

"Maybe you should slow down there, cowboy," I said, taking the cap and screwing the bottle shut.

But before I could get it totally closed, he rested his hand on top of mine, stopping me. "Why do you do that?" he asked, the warmth of his hand enveloping mine beneath it. He pulled away from me, his eyes watching me as though assessing me for truth.

"What? Cut people off? I'm a bartender, Luke. It's sort of my thing."

"No, not that. Why do you always keep people at arm's length?"

"I don't know what you're talking about."

"Yes, you do."

I opened my mouth, unsure what to say. Instead of giving him the explanation he sought, I unscrewed the top, poured myself a shot, and tossed it back. "It's just who I am."

It wasn't a lie. And besides, how could I ever explain to him that letting people in was a little more complicated for me than for other people. I came with strings attached, deadly, life-altering, terrible ones. Something told me that he wouldn't enjoy the answer to my mystery if he ever managed to solve it.

He pressed his lips together and nodded. "Well, we are who we are, right?" Taking the bottle, he poured us both another shot, and that time, I let him do it. "Can't fight nature."

I nodded, thinking about my family. My heritage. He had no idea how much that statement resonated with me after today. Deciding to move us on to safer ground, I changed the subject. "So, are you gonna tell me what kept you up tonight?"

He let out a long sigh. "It's this case. Nothing adds up. Her sister thinks she killed herself, and I'm starting to wonder if she isn't right. That blood on the couch? That could have been self-inflicted. There was zero evidence of a struggle aside from that blood. But then there's you."

"What about me?"

"You seem so sure about the stalker, even though we still haven't found a single image on her phone of him. I don't know what you saw, but it's not there now. And then there's that insane story from her brother-in-law. It has me turning in circles. I don't know what to think."

I grasped the bottle, fiddling with it as I thought about what to say. It would probably be safer for him, for me even, if I lied to him and told him I'd changed my mind. That I'd come around to the idea that she'd killed herself. Intentionally keeping him out of our path would be the smart move, the best move for him and Bud and me, too.

But did I really want to lie to him again? He'd said I could trust him in the car, and after everything that happened today, I just felt ragged and raw. And what if I did lie again, and he found out? I'd promised him the truth, made a pact, and given him my word. If I went back on it and sent him on a wild goose chase and he found out, what would he do?

He was a cop for Pete's sake. He could charge me with obstruction of justice or something. And then I thought of Tara. What would be best for her?

Despite knowing that Tara's situation was one hundred percent supernatural, the fact remained that it couldn't hurt to have a cop, with access to resources I didn't have, helping me with the case. Cases, supernatural or not, required hunting down leads in the normie world. The human world. I could use him on my side should I need to make use of his police assets, even if I did have to keep him one step behind us.

I let out a breath and leveled a serious stare at him, decision made. "She didn't kill herself, Luke. She was too scared of her stalker. I don't know what happened to the picture, but I saw him, and I believe her. I swear it."

Tara deserved to have more people than just me looking for her as a missing person, instead of as a possible runaway suicide. After all, Luke might find something I didn't during the course of his investigation. Though I might have supernatural abilities, I couldn't be everywhere and do everything. I would just need to tread very carefully with this one. Having him involved and potentially underfoot might screw me over royally later, but we would cross that bridge if, or when, we came to it.

His eyes searched mine as though looking for truth in them and he let out a long breath before snagging the bottle and pouring himself another drink. "I think you're right. I'm just coming up blank." That was probably for the best, at least for the moment. And I felt like a real shithead for hiding information from him. But how was I supposed to share everything I knew with him? How would I explain the spell gone awry with Gaby, Roger, and Beaseldorf, the reading with the sword, and hot demon guy without sounding batshit crazy? I'd given him everything I could, and I refused to feel guilty about it.

Luke scrubbed his hand over the back of his head, smoothing down his hair at last. "You want to play a round of darts and talk about whatever's bothering you? You listened to me, the least I can do is return the favor."

"Who says anything's bothering me?"

"That expression on your face. You look, I don't know, upset? Mad? Sad? I can't quite tell. You aren't the easiest person to read."

The question and its offer lingered in his gaze, another olive branch. I remained still for a moment, contemplating my next move. Should I crack open the vault? Let him get to know me, even if just a little? It wasn't like I could tell him everything. I didn't tell regular, normie humans about my life. Period. But something about the way he looked at me, it made me wonder if he could handle it. Truth, though? I didn't want to find out. I couldn't deal with the rejection if he decided I was a nutjob and tried to fit me for a straitjacket.

Instead, I grabbed the Jack bottle and screwed its top into place. "It's really late. You should probably get going."

Luke sighed, the sound long-suffering before he rose to his feet. "Like I said, arm's length."

"We are who we are, no?"

He cracked a grin, his teeth white and straight, except for a canine that tilted a little too far to the side. "Using my own words against me, huh? Well played, Ms. Torrence. Well played."

I shoved out from my seat and led him back to the front door. I could feel him moving behind me. "I can't believe you're kicking me out," he teased, and I snorted a laugh.

"Some of us need sleep. Besides, if I let you play darts in this state, you're as likely to hit me as the target. And I have no interest in digging a dart out of my ass before bed."

He pffted me. "Yeah, right. I did a semester abroad in Ireland. I can hold my liquor."

I didn't miss the slur in his voice. "Riiight." I unlocked the door, opening it for him, and an ice-cold breeze swept over me.

He chuckled and slid his hands into his coat as he leveled hooded eyes on me. "Thank you for the conversation. Let me know if you ever need me to return the favor. My friends tell me I'm an excellent listener." Oh yeah, he was definitely still investigating me.

"Uh-huh, I bet Bud's a real chatty guy."

"You'd be surprised," he said through a laugh.

Though I jested, I still eyed him with suspicion, knowing the veiled insinuation there. He wanted me to tell him things. He wanted to get to know the real me without all the snooping into my life and having to investigate me, and I felt the wall I'd erected since early childhood drop into place between us like an anvil. An involuntary reaction to anyone inviting me to spill my guts.

"Good night, Luke," I said, hearing the coldness in my own voice and hating myself a little for it. I closed the door and bolted it shut, sparing him a quick glance as he walked along the sidewalk toward his apartment.

Before I could so much as turn on my heel, a voice sounded from behind me that made everything inside my body freeze.

"I thought I told you to ditch the cop."

CHAPTER 18

I whirled, my heart in my throat as my gaze locked on hot demon guy. He sat at the far end of the bar, at a table steeped in shadow. He had his legs kicked up, heavy boots on the scarred surface of the table, and muscular arms crossed over a broad chest. A casual air permeated him, but I could sense the tension rolling off him as he stared at me beneath his thick hooded jacket.

"Holy shit," I hissed, pressing a hand to my chest as the adrenaline rush from his sudden appearance slid over me. "What the hell? How long have you been sitting there?"

"Long enough."

I narrowed my eyes into my best glare. "Were you watching me?"

"I have a vested interest in your survival."

"So, that's a yes?" He didn't deign to answer me and booze swam in my head, my body processing it a little slower considering how much of it I'd just imbibed. Maybe, if I had better survival instincts and less alcohol in my system, I would have appreciated the danger of him showing up uninvited in my bar. The fact that he'd managed to get through Gaby's amplified wards alone should have given me pause. But instead, anger and irritation rose within me. It didn't help that a steady stream of seductive heat rolled from his direction to mine, making my senses just a little hazy.

"Why do you bother with that cop? It's like I told you before, he doesn't belong in our world."

His voice sounded short and impatient. It made me bristle, irritation slithering inside me. "He's looking for Tara, same as me. And my friends are none of your concern." Despite the issues Luke and I had on a personal level, I had no interest in a demon telling me who I could and couldn't associate with. Even if I did agree with him on principle.

He shifted and the hood of his jacket slid over his head, revealing his face to me for the first time. My throat tightened, his perfection utterly devastating, leaving me at a loss for words. "Friends? With a *human cop?*" He scoffed as though he found the idea ludicrous. "Laughable for someone like you. Their laws don't apply to people like us."

Those words sobered me. What the hell did he mean by—their laws didn't apply to us? I might have supernatural abilities, but I still operated within the human world, and I could still get arrested and thrown in jail just the same as anyone else. But I suppose a demon like him would think they were above something as petty as human rules. As my mind tried to fight through the roll of lusty power he exuded, I realized dimly that he'd grouped me together with him again and had eluded to *my kind* for a second time. I also didn't miss that Beaseldorf had said something similar to my mother before she jumped.

My mind latched on to that point, unable to let it pass this time. "What the hell is that supposed to mean? *My kind*?"

He rose to his feet, boots landing on the floor with a solid thunk, his body unfolding with the grace of a true predator. As he stalked toward me, eyes laser-focused on mine, everything inside me went hot. Waves of intense desire slid over me, growing more potent with each step he took. He rolled his eyes. "For fuck's sake, you're so untrained. It's unbelievable you've survived this long."

My body trembled as he drew close enough for me to reach out and touch him, which distracted me from his last comment. I didn't move an inch, my tongue thick in my mouth, and I didn't dare get any closer. Instead, I held my ground and waited for my body to adjust to his nearness.

As the humming tingle beneath my skin subsided just a fraction, my mind whirled as I considered everything he'd told me since we'd met. He'd been the one to lead me to Remus. Had he known the connection to my family? To my mother? "Did you know about the sword? About who it belonged to?" The words slipped out before I could stop them, but I wouldn't take them back even if I could.

My heart beat a steady rhythm in my chest, and my legs felt weak with him so close to me. My body trembled and my fingertips burned with the urge to touch him. His lips were a fucking work of art, and I wanted to trace them with my tongue, explore them with my teeth.

"Remus told you about Celia, I take it?"

"My mother." The words came out as a breathy whisper and my heart ached. "Did you know her?" I didn't know why I bothered asking, but with everything that had happened that night, I just wanted to know something with some level of clarity. I wanted some honesty.

"I did."

He kept his eyes trained on me, as though no one and nothing else mattered. The intensity of his attention sent pulsing waves of lust sizzling over me, sweeping beneath my skin and making me wet my lips as I breathed through it. It felt good, too fucking good, and a tortuous ache pulsed between my legs. God, how did he do this to me? Turn me into a puddle of needy want every time he came around? Closing my eyes, I tried to push the thoughts of him and his body out of my mind and focus on what I needed to know.

"Is she really dead?" I didn't know why he was bothering to answer my questions, but I felt starved for them, and I didn't want him to stop.

My eyes found his again, and the gold of his irises burned with intensity, the moving liquid of them unlike anything I'd ever seen before. Something like regret washed through his features and he dragged his long, clever fingers through his dark hair, strands breaking free to hang loosely over his forehead.

"No one has seen Celia Bellator in twenty-five years." I didn't miss that he didn't really answer me. But that didn't matter. It was enough, and I did the math. I would have been almost two years old when she disappeared. Some small part of me had hoped that maybe what happened with Beaseldorf had happened before my birth. Which would mean she survived that jump. But with his tacit confirmation of the timeline, all my hopes deflated. And if no one had seen her for that long, what was the likelihood she still lived? My chest caved in, my stomach twisting and the sexual energy that radiated from him made everything more confusing.

I wanted him, but I didn't. It was his power that told me I did, not my real desires. I needed to remember the difference. But with him standing just an arm's length away from me, that was easier said than done.

His brows furrowed and he stepped closer, pulling me deeper into his seductive aura, the burning ache of lust outweighing my pain and anger, dulling everything but his presence. "You're hurt that she's gone?"

I breathed through it, inhaling the intoxicating scent of him—vanilla, cinnamon, and smoke—a combination that made my mouth water. "Why did you come here?" I asked, not wanting to discuss my complicated feelings about my mother with a demon of all people. He wouldn't care if a hunter died, and I doubted he gave a shit about my heartbreak, my grief. More likely, he was working some kind of angle. He had some alternate agenda for helping me or he needed something from me that he wanted to manipulate me into giving him.

Seeming to sense that I'd shut that topic down, he slid his hands into his jacket pockets, the innocuous move ridiculously sexy. "We got interrupted earlier, and I needed to deliver a message."

"And you just decided to break into my bar at three in the morning?"

"I didn't think I'd find you awake."

"So you planned to deliver a message to me in my sleep?" I gave him a look like he might not have all his precious little marbles, and he smirked at me. That time, both sides of his mouth curved upward and everything inside me shivered in reaction. He looked even more unbearably gorgeous when he smiled, and I wondered how devastating he'd be with a full grin. Though he still felt potent, powerful, and hot as fucking hell, I found that if I fought hard enough, gave myself a moment to breathe through the haze, that I could at least form coherent thoughts and words. I just didn't know if that would hold up if he ever decided to touch me again. And God, did I want him to touch me.

"Not all messages are verbal." His gaze flicked to my lips, and I saw a ghost of something that looked a lot like desire shadow his eyes before he took a step back. The intensity of his power ebbed, and I let out a sigh of relief. Or maybe it was regret. I didn't know which. "Ditch the cop, Jenna. He'll only slow you down or get himself killed."

My eyes hardened, my body stiffening as I stared up at him. "Is that a threat?"

He snorted a derisive laugh, as though he found Luke little more than an irritant. Not worth his time or concern. "Consider it a warning. A byproduct of our world." I opened my mouth to say something, but he held up his hand to stop me. For some horrifying reason, I did. My body hummed, my muscles locking, and my breaths hitching as waves of his magic flowed through me and it took every ounce of focus I could muster to listen to what he said next. "You must understand the gravity of what we face. Figure out the tether, just like I told you, and do it fast."

"You could just tell me."

That earned me another smirk, and I all but purred in reaction to it. "Everything balances on a razor's edge, and I must walk that line with care."

My eyes narrowed, fighting through the swell of want burning low in my belly. "What does that mean?"

"That we're playing a dangerous game, and I've already spent too much time in your company tonight."

"You keep telling me you can't come back or stick around. That helping me is dangerous. So why do you keep showing up?" I'd never asked for his help, though even I could admit I'd needed it. He'd given me my only leads I'd gotten so far, and without him, I would have jack all on this case. But I knew without question that he was leaving out critical information. He would only tell me what suited him, and we both knew it. Demons didn't have an altruistic side.

His lip quirked up before rubbing his hand over the stubble along his jaw. "A question even I can't seem to answer."

He stepped back, putting even more distance between us, and his body, the one that looked utterly human, dematerialized before my eyes. He went from solid and there to shadow and mist in the blink of an eye. Heat brushed over my skin in a caress that left me breathless as his power left the bar, and I sucked in fresh, clean air, free of his influence. My body still buzzed with awareness, my nipples peaked and my panties soaked. But at least, with him gone, I could breathe without that pulsing ache.

With my head clear, I ran through our conversation, trying to piece together any information from it. He'd given me precious little, but he'd said he wanted to deliver a message. That he'd meant to leave it for me while I slept. So, had he left me a note? Or something? My brows knit together in curiosity and confusion as I strode from the door toward the table where he'd been sitting. Body humming with muted need, the aftereffects of his magic growing familiar, I peered down at the chipped wood surface and my brows rose. A crucifix lay atop it, and I recognized it right away—Tara's necklace. The one she couldn't stop touching the night she'd hired me.

I reached down to pick it up, and when my flesh made contact with it, I heard a voice so faint, I almost couldn't make it out. And then recognition hit me. "Tara?"

Elliott Grove Middle School, East Santa Sombra, Fourteen Years Ago

"I'm scared," Gaby whispered, standing next to me, our breath foggy in the early spring air. Nighttime in Santa Sombra was always somewhat chilly, but in March? It was downright icy.

"You'd be crazy not to be," I whispered back, my heart thrumming as I tried to control my own fear. The last few times I'd fought a demon I'd won, sure, but I'd also gotten my butt kicked. I didn't relish the idea of getting another beatdown. But maybe, just maybe it would be different this time. I had backup, so surely that would count for something.

"That's not reassuring," she muttered as we each rubbed our hands together and blew into them. Silence settled around us and I could hear the soft hum of traffic coming from the road nearby while the scent of burning wood stung my nostrils. Standing under the streetlights on the sidewalk, we surveyed the

looming brick building of Elliott Grove Middle School in the light of the full moon. We'd gone to school there for two and a half years, and while I may not have loved the people or the place, I definitely didn't want a demon working its dark influence on them. Neither did Gaby.

Before making the trek to campus in the middle of the night, we'd scoured Gaby's grandmother's grimoire in secret, looking for the spell they'd used that had allowed her to see the demon in the first place. We'd found it and had already completed the ritual. It allowed her to see into the spirit realm, and we discovered that with that ritual, she could see a heck of a lot more than me. As a result, she'd been a bit on edge since we'd left her house and taken the light rail to school.

But we'd made it to our destination, and we could no longer afford to drag our feet. We needed to act. I could sense the presence of the demon inside, and during our preparations over the past few days, I'd done some recon, trying to find out where it went after school hours. For the most part, it seemed to stick around campus, as though it hadn't picked someone to fixate on just yet. Which meant, we still had time. We'd acted fast enough, and for that, gratitude and relief had taken up residence in my chest.

We locked eyes, and I could see the nerves that seemed to vibrate from Gaby. They mirrored my own, and I took a deep breath to settle them. "Let's go."

We creeped forward slowly at first, each of us dressed in full black and sneaking on tiptoe toward the fence that surrounded the school. I could scale it no problem and had spent a couple of evenings teaching Gaby how to do the same.

We each dropped our backpacks, which carried all our weapons, on the ground, knowing that if we got caught during our mission, we'd have a hard time explaining the contraband. It would bring us into expulsion level territory, but we had to take that risk if we wanted to prevent whatever terrible havoc that demon would bring. We both knew that.

Gripping my hands together, I dropped onto a knee and formed a step for Gaby to use. She placed her foot into it and I boosted her up until she grasped the top of the fence and used her momentum to swing over it. I watched through the black aluminum rails as she dangled for a moment before dropping onto the other side with a soft crunch of gravel. I grabbed my backpack and then hers, throwing them up one at a time while I held the strap and maneuvered them down so Gaby could catch them on the other side.

Once she had the backpacks in hand, I took a few steps back and sucked in a deep breath, then broke into a sprint. I bolted toward the fence, jumping as I reached it. I grasped the top of the aluminum cross-rail easily, kicking my feet against the bars and vaulting over the top. I landed on the other side in a smooth motion, dropping to one knee in an epic superhero pose.

Gaby hitched her backpack higher and handed mine to me. "Show-off."

The school had four main rectangular-shaped buildings and a larger rectangular building across from the play yard, which housed the gym. All of the structures combined made an odd-shaped square around the center quad, with breezeways between buildings. We had mobile classrooms across the soccer fields that dealt with the overflow of students that came when Kinnley Park Middle School shut down about a year before.

We hurried out of sight of the fence, just in case anyone happened by, and rushed to the first building, turning the corner to hide at the main office. We stopped, each of us breathing heavily. I felt the familiar fear and the rush of adrenaline I always got before a fight, and I concentrated to push them aside, searching for that dead calm I needed if I wanted to have any chance at surviving the night.

I pointed toward the far end of the play yard. "We need to head to the gym now. Move fast and keep close to the buildings so we can blend in with the shadows. Got it?" Gaby nodded, and I could see her face well in the bright moonlight, her eyes wide and skin paler than usual. "When we get to our rendezvous point, we'll prep our weapons and once they're ready, I'll draw the demon out while you stay hidden."

"I know, Jenna. We've gone over this plan a hundred times. I've got it. I'll take care of my end; you take care of yours. Just make sure you make it back here in one piece."

"Okay," I said, letting out a long sigh. I sent up a small prayer, hoping against hope that we didn't get killed. Or at least that Gaby didn't get killed. I didn't think I'd ever get past the guilt if she died because of me. She was my only friend, and the very thought of that was enough to make me choke. To make me freeze up and demand she go home. But I didn't. Instead, I signaled for her to follow me, and we took off along the building walls.

As we hurried, I scanned our surroundings, looking for any threats that might surprise us. We couldn't afford to let the demon see us yet, not before Gaby had a chance to work her magic. Because we had a plan. A plan that involved a way to prevent me from getting a full-scale beatdown for a change. After all our research, after everything we'd scoured in her grandmother's grimoire, we'd found something. Something that I hadn't realized was even possible.

We'd found a way to trap a demon.

Chapter 19

Voices filled my head, Tara's louder than the rest but still too quiet to make out clearly. My fist tightened around her necklace, the pungent, staticky feel of magic raising the hairs on my arms. Though I didn't perform my own spells, I'd participated in enough of them to know what their power felt like. And I knew with total certainty that Tara's jewelry had been altered with magic somehow. Wind swept around me, my hair blowing right as a thread drew tight in my chest. It felt strange, like the necklace wanted to pull me apart and take my spirit inside it.

The voices grew louder, and I heard a panicked cry. "No! Please! Don't!"

My heart galloped. That sounded too much like Tara for me to even consider giving the sensation threatening to tear me in two an ounce of caution. I threw myself toward that shriek of terror, letting the magic within the necklace rip me apart as I plummeted from my body and into a dark, dank place.

My knees hit the ground, and I winced in pain as I blinked, trying to focus. Why had they brought me here? I clutched my wounded arm to my chest, the stinging pain of it enough to make me gasp. A man I didn't recognize, whose face I couldn't see, locked chains around my wrists, right around the jagged gash. I groaned in pain, tears blurring my eyes. It hurt so fucking bad, but he didn't seem to care.

Why was I here? My stalker, I knew. He'd taken me while I slept at Jenna's apartment, and when I tried to fight back, he'd cut me. Cut me so deep, the blood loss had made me woozy and I'd had to stop struggling.

Wait—that thought—it made no sense. It didn't belong to me. My mind went fuzzy, trying to push its way through a sudden rush of confusion. But before I could, the scene changed again.

More people surrounded me, all chained, their tears and despair silent as they huddled together for warmth. None of us knew each other, and our captors didn't like it when we talked. They wanted us isolated and alone, and I knew why. The dreams told me everything, invading my mind even when I tried to force my body to go without sleep. I was never strong enough to win that battle.

They had an advantage because my blood—it was defiled, and I wish I could say they'd defiled it. That they'd ruined me in their effort to own me, to force their way into my body, to take over my soul.

But I came tainted.

It was why they wanted me in the first place. And I'd started to realize, it's why they wanted all of us.

Flashes flew through my mind then, and something felt wrong, like I couldn't control the direction of my thoughts. It seemed like these memories, these thoughts? They belonged to someone else. I fought with every ounce of will I had to separate myself from that consciousness, but she pulled me under again with no effort, forcing me to see through her eyes.

Lapping water, a strange, woven symbol painted black on concrete, cold air, and bolted chains. A man made of blackened smoke, humanoid and massive, his features indiscernible and his power utterly terrifying. A demon, my stalker. Feelings that didn't belong to me crawled up my throat. I loathed him more than the rest, and that was saying something. The others wore fake human masks, but they blurred to dark, smoky terrors at night, when they let their disguises slip. They fed on us, weakening us whenever they got the chance, preparing us to host them.

They were close to their goal, too. I could feel my body weakening, the barriers of my mind collapsing. And I knew what the future looked like for me. The image blurred and I saw a face I recognized, as though in a mirror—red hair, eyes cold and aura black with demonic possession. I saw the others, dozens of them, their faces blurry and unclear, but they had that same aura. And I realized whose thoughts or memories or consciousness I'd invaded. It was Tara.

One final, desperate thought rushed through my mind, right before the necklace released its choke hold on me.

Someone please, kill me. I don't want to turn into one of them. And I can't let them use me for what they have planned next.

My spirit slammed back into my body with a force unlike anything I'd ever felt before, and I awoke gasping. When I'd thrown myself down the magical connection, my body had collapsed to the floor, and my hip ached as I pushed up into a sitting position and groaned.

"Ow." My head felt fuzzy, but the static of the magic had dissipated, and I frowned down at the golden necklace still clutched in my grasp.

Was this how Roger felt every time he did a reading? No, I decided, rubbing my hip and wincing at the bruise I found there. That was a wholly different experience. I'd been *inside* Tara's head, hearing and feeling her thoughts and emotions. I'd been *her*, my own consciousness erased while I lived her experiences as though they belonged to me.

That was one hell of a message.

Though my head pounded and my stomach lurched with nausea, I rose to my feet, knowing I needed to write down everything I saw before the images cleared and the memories started to blur. Limping a little, I hurried to my office in the back room and lowered myself onto my chair with a wince. Flipping open my notebook, I wrote down everything I could remember, drawing out the symbol and noting any unique characteristics about the place I'd seen.

Lapping water against a grassy bank and concrete. A river, a bay, or a delta of some kind? I gnawed on my lip, trying to think if I'd seen anything remotely discernible about the place. But I'd witnessed nothing aside from a dank, dark building, chains, water, and concrete. That could describe dozens of places in Santa Sombra alone, and that didn't include private residences. And if I broadened out my search to California or farther, in case they hadn't brought everyone here, there was too many to count. I had no idea where to even start looking.

But something told me, mostly my common sense, that hot demon guy was up to his neck in whatever Beaseldorf had planned. And if he kept popping in uninvited? Then my gut told me they held them somewhere close, if not in Santa Sombra itself.

That made a disturbing sort of sense. We did have a lot of supernatural activity here, and demons always seemed to gravitate toward my home. Though I hadn't experienced many other cities, this place was different. I understood that on a gut level. And it was what kept me flush with clientele and what made me certain I could never leave.

When I finished writing down everything I remembered, I stared at my notes, an intense resolve taking hold of me. I inhaled and exhaled deeply to steady myself and tried to approach what had just happened with calm rationality. I had so many questions, even more than I had before I'd received hot demon guy's message. And by the way, how did I manage not to get his name again? Annoyance flashed, but I pushed that aside, swearing I'd deal with that on his next unwelcomed visit.

Instead, I focused all my attention on what I'd seen through Tara's eyes. As I struggled to find something I could use, anything that could point me in the right direction, I thought about what she'd said again. About her defiled blood, and when she'd said *I came tainted.*

As I considered that, I remembered that she'd said they all had it. Did she mean every kidnapping victim on that list had the same defiled blood? She must. That was the only explanation that made sense. Who else would Beaseldorf have with her, if not the other kidnapping victims? Was their blood the tether that hot demon guy wanted me to find? Or perhaps a part of it?

Yes, absolutely, it had to be. But part of the story, not the whole enchilada. I knew that without question because he never seemed to give me the full truth, only the pieces I needed to uncover it myself.

Almost like he wanted to hold me back from learning everything and keep me balanced on a razor's edge of knowledge. I would just have to be better than him. Faster than he expected to make the connections he dangled in front of me like carrots. Beat him at his own game, if only I knew which one he was playing.

I rose from my desk once more and started pacing, the chair creaking as it rolled back and knocked into the wall behind me. What about their tainted blood made them so damn special to Beaseldorf? What did the demons want to do with them, aside from possess them?

I had no way of knowing if they'd already succumbed to the demonic invasion or if I still had time to save them that suffering. How long ago had hot demon guy taken that necklace from her? How had he stored her memories in it and passed it to me? No, I would figure that out later. I knew witchcraft when I felt it, and Gaby and Roger could help me there.

I needed to focus on Tara and the others and what I'd learned from her. The demons wanted the kidnapping victims for their defiled blood, they wanted to possess them, and they wanted to do some kind of a ritual or something once they achieved that goal. Those painted symbols looked ritualistic, from what I could tell, and I said an internal thank you to Gaby for forcing me into her witchy business. Otherwise, I didn't know if I could have put that together from the quick flash I'd seen.

But that begged the question, what kind of ritual? Tara's thoughts had made it clear that she'd rather die than take part in whatever they had planned next. I peered down at the symbol on my desk and knew I'd give it to Roger and Gaby, but something about the sweeping lines of it made me frown. It looked familiar, even if I'd only gotten a partial look. Picking it up, I rubbed a finger over it, and recognition struck me.

My head whipped toward Remus, who sat on the storage cabinet behind my desk and I charged over to him. Gripping his hilt, I flipped him so his pointy end hit the floor, and I frowned as I took in the winding twists of the symbol at the top of his hilt. It matched my drawing damn near exactly.

Throat tightening, my stomach hollowed out. "Holy shit." I didn't know why I was so surprised. Beaseldorf had said he needed the sword for what came next, and I'd just received confirmation of that fact. If I'd needed any at all. But the part that made me most nauseous was how confident Beaseldorf seemed that he'd find Remus. If he needed him for the ritual, along with Tara, Elias, and the others, and he'd already started the possession process? He must have at least a plan to locate Remus.

Fear pricked my neck, and I set Remus down again and dragged a hand through my hair, trying to think without twisting myself into knots. No, I wouldn't let him find the sword. Remus was my weapon, and I was his wielder. It made sense to keep him with me, where I could keep an eye on him. Even if hot demon guy knew about him, he hadn't given Remus to Beaseldorf. He'd given him to me. So I'd keep one eye on the sword at all times and make sure neither of those demon pricks ever laid a finger on him.

Which brought me back to Tara and the others—I needed to confirm my suspicions about their blood. If Tara's blood was defiled, did that mean her family's would be too? Would Bethany share those same characteristics? Same with Elias Hunter. Based on some additional research I'd done, he had a sister as well. Did she share his allegedly defiled blood?

There was no evidence that either sibling had endured the same demonic assault as Tara or Elias had. But why? Why wouldn't the demons have come after them too? I searched my memory, going back through all my research and my background checks, and the only thing I came up with was that Tara and Elias were both firstborn children. But that just didn't feel like enough. It felt like there had to be more to it.

At a loss, I tried not to fixate on what she'd begged me, or someone, to do.

To kill her.

Would she take matters into her own hands? Would the demons let her? I could only hope they wouldn't and that I could work fast enough to save her. If she wanted to die rather than see through Beaseldorf's plans, just like my mom, then I knew I couldn't afford to fuck this up.

She needed my help. They all did, and I knew what I had to do next and who I needed to do it with. When I looked up and saw the time—four thirty a.m.—I groaned in frustration. I couldn't do anything at this god-awful hour, and with the adrenaline buzzing through my system, I knew I couldn't sleep. But when my gaze slid to my screen, I noticed the processing icon had stopped, and I knew just how to pass the time.

Chapter 20

After two hours of research, I'd run out of patience. I unlocked my cell and dialed just the person I wanted to talk to. I could only hope he didn't maim me for calling at such an ungodly hour.

A few rings went through before he picked up and offered a groggy, "It's early. Call back later."

"Roger, don't you dare hang up on me."

"JT?"

"The one and only."

"It's six thirty a.m." He sounded cranky about that.

"You owe me."

"No, you owe me, remember?"

Well, damn. He had a point, but I didn't care. "No, I don't. I saved your life that time, remember?"

"Are you talking about that time your eyebrows got burned off? Because if you are, you only saved it after you put me in danger. So that doesn't count."

I growled in frustration. "Dammit, Roger, people's lives are on the line and you want to argue semantics?"

He let out a super bitchy sigh that let me know just how annoyed he was by the moral quandary I presented him with.

"Fine. What do you need?"

"It's time for that trip to Silverwood and Sombra Hills. I need you to do that reading on Elias's family and Tara's sister stat."

"But it's so early. Why do you hate me?"

"Lives. At. Stake. Roger."

"Ugh. Alright, fine. I'll call Gaby. She can cover for me at A Witch's Whimsy. When are we going?"

"I'll be at your place in ten and *no kimonos*. I need you to look, I don't know, presentable? They can't be afraid to let you touch them."

"Do you ever think that maybe you should take your own advice?" I gave him a dry, rueful laugh before I spared a quick glance at the mirror that hung in the hall outside my office door and winced. Maybe he had a point.

"Speaking of that, I'm gonna need to borrow some clothes."

"Ugh, I hate it when you do that. Your giant lady boobs always stretch out my sweaters."

"Again—"

"Yeah, yeah, yeah, I know, lives at stake and all that. See you in ten."

I clicked Print on the rest of the files I had to review and waited a few minutes for the reams of pages to finish getting inked. Once completed,

I snatched them up, put them in a file folder to keep them dry, and tucked them under my arm. I also pocketed the crucifix, knowing I wanted Roger to take a look at it. Though he didn't have the right kind of magic for spells, he did run a magic shop, and he knew his stuff like the back of his hand. I felt pretty confident that he could give me some answers. And if not him, then Gaby could.

A few seconds later, I jetted out of the bar with Remus in tow, looking less than presentable as I locked up behind me. I texted Tony, who offered to cover for me once again. Rent was going to get a little tight this month, especially since I'd only been paid one dollar on this case from Luke. Cheap bastard. Add to that, I was missing shifts like a senior in May missed final period.

But what was I supposed to do? From that reading Roger had done on Remus, it sounded like we couldn't let Beaseldorf get his way. My mother had jumped off a cliff to keep him from completing whatever the hell he had planned, and Tara wanted to die rather than help him. The images of that symbol flashed in my mind, and I wondered what the hell they wanted to accomplish with it. Free the demons, sure, but what the hell from? And what demons, exactly?

Shit, if Beaseldorf had managed to gather that many possessed or soon-to-be possessed people in one place, I knew deep in the pit of my stomach that nothing good would come from it.

I stomped out into the parking lot and sighed as I looked at the thing I hated most on this planet. The old rust bucket sat in the parking lot, looking like it would have fit in better at the dump instead. God, I hated being poor. I sulked as I made my way to the 1989 Honda Civic I drove when I couldn't borrow Gaby's Subaru. Since she would need her car to cover Roger today, I decided to bite the bullet and take my hunk of junk.

Jessabelle, as I'd named her when I bought her after high school, had served me well and reliably, but I still hated her. She had a red driver's side door while the rest of her body maintained the original white. Someday, I would save up enough to get her a new paint job, or maybe just a new car. But sadly, today was not that day.

I unlocked her door and slumped into her seat, my breath steaming in her chilly interior. I started her up, and she purred to life with ease, like always. Maybe someday she'd die and thus force me to get another car. But then I remembered that she liked to torment me.

I pulled out of the parking lot behind the bar and drove over to Roger's home above A Witch's Whimsy. Remus, strapped into the back seat like a passenger, seemed to pulse with urgency as I scrolled my phone to find the address Gaby had sent me on Elias Hunter. He lived with his mom and sister, from what I could tell. After that, I figured we could swing back by Tara's sister's house and see if Roger got anything new from Bethany there.

As my car rambled down the road, I blew into my fisted hands at alternating intervals trying to warm them and realized that I would need to call ahead for Tara's sister. After meeting her, she definitely seemed like the type who needed appointments scheduled and shit. Besides, she hadn't exactly "taken" to me, so I wasn't sure how dropping by even with an appointment would go. Probably not so great. I would just have to turn on that charm I didn't possess, which annoyed me almost as much as Jessabelle's heater's lack of heat.

By the time I rolled up to A Witch's Whimsy and the vents still blew only icy air, I'd resigned myself to the fact that no heat would come. I shoved open the driver's side door and walked up the front stoop to Roger's small home. He owned a one-bedroom, one-bath single-family in East Santa Sombra. It dated back to the early twentieth century and probably had lead pipes, paint, and loads of asbestos, but at least it was trendy and in a happening part of town.

I hammered my fist on the door, yelling that he better not have fallen back to sleep loud enough to wake the dead. A few seconds later the door clicked open. "Impatient much?" he muttered, fully dressed and styled, to my utter astonishment. He must have felt really bad for not caring about Tara's life-or-death situation amid the fog of sleep.

"Yep." Without waiting for a response, I breezed past him and back to his only bathroom. I yanked off my clothes and jumped in the shower, tugging the rubber ducky curtain closed. I didn't bother to close the door, knowing that Roger wouldn't want to sneak a peek at me naked anyway. Since, you know, I lacked a penis.

A few seconds later, I was washing my hair while he set clothes on the vanity countertop for me. "You hungry?" he asked, and I could sense him hovering on the other side of the curtain.

"I could eat." It was the truth. The last thing I'd shoved down my throat was Gaby's soup the night before.

"Come on out when you're done. I'm making omelets. You smell like a barroom floor, so I'm guessing you could use a meal."

"To be fair, I am in the shower which combats the smell," I grumbled, soaping up my body while the conditioner soaked into my hair. "But I wouldn't say no to breakfast." Man, I loved that my friends cooked for me. If they didn't, I would probably just forget to eat altogether. Especially during a case like this one. The kind that absorbed me, mind, body, and soul. But then again, I'd never worked a case quite like Tara's before.

I heard Roger shut the door quietly as he left the room, the absence of his presence removing all distractions from my mind. I ran through everything that had happened since Tara walked through my door. Meeting her had launched me into a past I'd known precious little about. My mother, Remus, and not to mention Beaseldorf. I couldn't help but marvel at the fact that everything really had come full circle.

After all, there I was, in possession of the very thing my mother had died to protect. Hiding it from the very demon she'd died to protect it from. Did Beaseldorf know who I was? Not just my name, but who my mother was too? I wondered about that as I rinsed my hair and body.

Demons could read most humans like an open book. They knew their stories from start to finish, especially if they wanted to possess them. But I'd never met one who could glean a single piece of information off me that I didn't want to give, and that fact gave me hope that maybe he hadn't pieced it together yet. And that I could keep the sword safe and tucked away from him.

Sure, he'd known my name and address, but that didn't mean he knew about my mother or about my connection to Remus. From what he'd alluded to that day, he'd gotten that information from Roger's mind, not mine. But demons lied all the time, even when the truth would make more sense.

I reached outside the curtain and snagged a soft towel from the cupboard next to the shower. I dried off and scrunched my hair to create some kind of natural wave. Roger didn't have a blow dryer, which was so not ideal. Especially considering Jessabelle's lack of a functioning heater.

After wriggling into Roger's snug dark jeans and a soft, dark-green thermal sweater that fit like a glove, I surveyed myself in the mirror. Not bad. At least semi-respectable. Still scrunching my hair with the towel, I crouched down to the floor and rifled through the front pocket of my jeans to grab Tara's necklace. A few seconds later, I strolled out of the bathroom and toward Roger's kitchen.

I watched in just a tad too much excitement as he opened the fridge and pulled out a carton of eggs, a bag of cheese, ham, and some of the veggies he'd picked up at Relics & Roots the day before. He deposited them on the counter, moving to the oven-stove combo and snagging a pan from one of the hooks overhead. The kitchen was smaller, with a square island in the middle and minimal cabinet space.

The size of the kitchen didn't surprise me, since most people sacrificed space for location when they bought in East Santa Sombra. Walkability, cool shops and restaurants everywhere, pretty parks and trees, and itty-bitty living space were all part of the package. I meandered to the two-seater table set against the wall opposite the stove and looked out the window and down into the small side yard next to his shop.

He had cut back the rose bushes for the winter and removed all of his usual herbs for the shop. I knew I'd find about a million little bundles of the last harvest hang-drying in the back room downstairs. Witches loved that shit. Or at least Gaby did.

As Roger cooked, I let out a long breath and checked my phone for the time—six fifty a.m. I tried not to let my anxiety get the better of me. As much as I wanted to get on the road, I knew I couldn't very well go knocking on the door of a missing guy's family before eight a.m. That would be rude. Hell, eight a.m. might even stretch the limits of propriety, but I needed to confirm my suspicions or move on to a new theory as quickly as possible.

Roger finished chopping the veggies and meat, then dropped them into the pan to cook together. I heard them sizzle and a few moments later, the scent of cooking onion and peppers as well as bacon wafted toward me. My stomach growled again.

Roger chuckled in reaction to my rude gut, stirring as he turned to face me. His bright-blue eyes fixed on me, his perfect hair quaffed into the epitome of the cool, sexy guy style you'd see in *GQ*. "So, why don't you tell me what freaked you out so bad that you called me at the crack of dawn and insisted we drive to Silverwood to do a secret reading on a missing guy's family members? I mean, I know we planned to talk to them at some point today, but you seem much pushier than you did last night."

I pursed my lips and considered his question. As much as Roger liked to help Gaby and me, he also hated it when I told him shit that prevented him from sleeping like a baby at night. I had a feeling that if I told him about the possibility of over a dozen possessed humans somewhere nearby, that might just give him nightmares. Or a panic attack. Despite that, I did need to ask him about the necklace, and it didn't hurt to give him fair warning that he may not like what I had to say. "You sure you want to know?"

He turned back to the food and continued to stir. "Not really. But if I'm doing a reading, I'd rather prepare myself in advance for what I might see." Just then, the coffee pot dinged and he pulled two mugs down from his oak cabinets. He poured a serving into each cup and sauntered over to me, handing me the one that said *World's Okayest Worker* and I chuckled as I took a sip. He moved back to the stove and dumped the veggie and meat mixture into a bowl before adding the beaten eggs into the warm pan.

I licked my lips. "You know how all those people went missing at the same time as Tara?"

He nodded, adding the innards to the eggs, and waiting for the magic to happen. "Yeah."

"Well, I'm pretty sure that they're all either possessed or on their way to getting possessed."

Roger turned back to me, the quick movement betraying his shock, and I launched into an explanation of my vision and the necklace. I also ran through my latest interlude with hot demon guy, emphasizing his insistence that all of the kidnappees had some kind of connection between them.

"The only lead I have right now is that Tara believes her blood is defiled along with the rest of the kidnapping victims. I'm hoping maybe Bethany, her sister, has something similar in her blood to give us something to go on. Also, Elias Hunter has a sister." At Roger's confused look, I elaborated. "Elias is the other kidnapping victim I mentioned, the one in Silverwood."

"Alright, that all sounds batshit crazy, but what else is new?" He passed me a finished omelet and a fork, taking the seat across from me before giving me a come-hither gesture. "Let me see the necklace."

Pulling it out of my pocket, I set it on the table between us.

Taking a deep breath and eyeing it with suspicion, he seemed to gird his loins as he reached out a hand and touched it. Nothing happened. No reaction. He frowned, peering down at the delicate gold chain, and lifted it into his palms to examine it. I took a bite of my omelet as I watched him, the delicious flavor exploding on my tongue. Man, we should really just let Roger cook from now on. Screw Gaby's canned soup and frozen pizza.

Roger's eyes lit up. "Oh my."

"What is it?" I asked through a mouthful, leaning closer as he rubbed the crucifix between his thumb and forefinger.

"It's something I've only read about. A rare magic—a Crypta Cogitationis."

"A Crypta what?"

"A Crypta Cogitationis. That's the formal name for it, but we call it Cogitato Crypta for short."

"That's not very short," I mused, trying to roll the pronunciation around on my tongue and falling short.

"It's a memory holder, like a supernatural diary. It records the wearer's thoughts, feelings, and even what they see too." He waved a hand as though to encompass all those things. "Most witches don't bother with them anymore, now that we have cell phones." His ice-blue eyes flicked up to mine. "This is Tara's?"

I nodded, thinking about what he said. Tara hadn't known whether or not she possessed supernatural abilities, so why would she wear something so clearly witchy in nature? "Are you sure that's a Crypta whatever?"

"One hundred percent." Roger held his hand out toward me. "See the crystal there?"

Embedded in the gold crucifix was a pale stone. It looked more like an opal than anything. But as I watched it, the swirls of color seemed to come alive, to move and sway, and I sucked in a surprised breath.

"Once that stone is imbued with power, which this one has been, it records the wearer's memories and thoughts."

I marveled at the beauty of it, smiling. "How long does it last?"

He shrugged. "For as long as the magic does. Stronger witches can imbue the stone with decades worth of power, while others can only manage a few days at a time. Truly a lost art." He handed it back to me and I pocketed it, a frown knitting my brows together as I started to think through his explanation.

"Why could I see it, but you couldn't?"

"The wearer, or someone who controls the stone, can designate who can read the Cogitato Crypta. It seems this one was calibrated for you, not me. Honestly, thank God for small favors. I don't think I would've much enjoyed Tara's thoughts."

"Probably not," I agreed, a frown still drawing my lips down.

"What's wrong? I mean, aside from the whole defiled blood and suicidal ideation thing. I get the feeling something else is eating at you."

"It's just, how clear are the memories? And how many should I have been able to access? If it records everything, and Tara wore it all the time, which judging by her social media images, she did, then why did I only see bits and pieces? Small fragments of the recent past? Why not more?"

Roger frowned too, considering my question. "I can't say for sure, but you want the most likely reason?"

"Why not? Hit me with it."

"Someone altered the memories. Not changed the general content of them, because that's not possible. But you can select what memories can be accessed from the Crypta or shade certain aspects of them. Think of it like parental guidance, almost."

My teeth clenched. "Hot demon guy." I really needed to get his name so I could curse it properly.

"If I had to hazard a guess, yeah, he seems like the most likely culprit. I know you think he's been helpful, but I don't know if we should trust him."

I rolled my eyes, taking another bite of my food. "I'm using him, not trusting him. There's a difference. I'm not suicidal, you know."

"Good. Now, about the trip to Silverwood."

"What about it?" I still shoveled my breakfast down my throat with gusto, and only hoped Roger wouldn't judge me too harshly.

"I know you've got this lead about the blood and all, but you know my visions don't always cooperate on command. I'm as likely to get a flash of their most personal bedroom interests as any other dark secrets."

I finished chewing the last of my food and followed it up with a sip of hot coffee. "I know, but I literally have nothing else. Well, except for some possible leads that I haven't had a chance to review yet waiting for me in a folder on Jessabelle's front seat. Which means, you're driving so I can peruse while en route."

He scrunched up his face. "Ugh, we're taking your car? Are you sure we're going to make it all the way to Silverwood and back?"

I rolled my eyes. "Unfortunately. She always seems to make it."

"You make it sound like that's a bad thing."

"Do you think I *want* to keep driving her?"

"You could get a new car, you know."

"Excuse me, no thank you. I'm not throwing away a perfectly good car."

"You and I have very different definitions of perfectly good."

An hour later, we approached the city limits of Silverwood, California. I'd burned through my research and background checks, unable to find anything of particular interest. They all looked like regular people, with normal lives, until a creepy demon started stalking them all and they went a little crazy. But then, who wouldn't go crazy if they had a demon stalker? The disappointment stung a little as I realized that my costly research hadn't proven more fruitful.

But after processing everything last night with my mother, and all the research this morning, a thought had occurred to me. An idea, and a possible connection that might just get us our next lead. I tugged my cell from my pocket and dialed Gaby's number, clicking on the speakerphone so Roger could hear her too. She answered on the third ring.

"What's up?"

"Just on the road to Silverwood in Jessabelle—send prayers that we make it home tonight."

Roger glared at me over his shoulder. "I thought you said Jessabelle always makes it?"

I offered him a devilish grin. "Well, there is a first time for everything." Roger's grip on the wheel tightened, making his knuckles turn white, and I bit my lip to keep from laughing.

"Don't worry, Rog, Jessabelle stays alive out of spite," Gaby said through a laugh, and I lifted my shoulder in agreement. "Now, why are you calling me?"

"Dang, can't I just call to talk to my bestie?"

"You can, but you don't. At least, not during a case."

"Alright, fair enough. I do have something I need you to do for me today."

"I'm shocked. What is it?" Funny, she didn't sound shocked. I filled her in on everything that had happened the night before, and she listened in silence, soaking in all the insanity.

"That's a lot. I don't even know where to start."

"Everything that's happened with Remus, hot demon guy, the Cogitato Crypta, and all my research, it gave me an idea. Remember that premonition at Relics & Roots?"

"Sure."

"Well, I think this is all connected. My mother, Tara's defiled blood—everything's coming full circle. And if it is, maybe something like this happened before, when my mom fought Beaseldorf. If I'm right, then maybe there was another mass-kidnapping around the same time in January. The timing could be significant, since everyone went missing within a few days of each other this time around." I chewed on my lip as another thought occurred to me. "Maybe even the names, too. If Tara's blood is defiled, maybe someone related to her or one of the others on hot demon guy's list was taken back then too. I know it's thin, probably even a shot in the dark, but—"

"I think you're onto something. It might be hard to pin down, but if anyone can do it, it's me. Do you have any idea of where to look? Or when? Like Santa Sombra, twenty years ago? California? Or do I need to go farther away or search further back in time? I mean, since whatever Beaseldorf had planned failed last time, maybe any possible victims showed up in the place he ultimately took them."

"We think hot demon guy censored some of the memories, so I didn't get a clear location. But I still think they're keeping them local. That suspiciously helpful demon seems to show up whenever the fancy strikes him, and I can't shake the feeling that whatever is happening, it's happening here." Santa Sombra always seemed to attract the supernatural, like the flow of magic that emanated through the city made me and every other paranormal entity stronger. So, why not here? My throat tightened as I remembered what else he'd said about my mother and the last time anyone saw her, and I did my best to keep my voice free of emotion. "And I think you should start with twenty-five years ago."

"Alright, I'll start with January around that time, search for surnames and family of the current missing people, and check for similar crimes committed, branching out if I need to. It might be a long shot, but maybe something will pop."

"God, I hope so. Whatever Beaseldorf has planned, it's big, Gabs, but I'm missing too many pieces to solve it. Maybe this will tie it all together."

"I know what you mean. I have this unshakeable feeling that we're running out of time. I can't explain why, but we need to figure this out and soon."

"That sounds ominous," I replied, pinching my bottom lip between my thumb and forefinger. "Is that a witchy feeling?"

"I think so. You need to hurry. Something is just... off. Like off in the time-space continuum. I can sense it."

"Well, fuck me, not the time-space continuum," I said, unable to stop the sarcasm despite the seriousness of our situation.

"Hilarious. But seriously, something's wrong."

"I know, I promise, I'm taking it seriously." Shutting my eyes, I said a quick prayer to the big guy upstairs that we'd get to the bottom of whatever Beaseldorf had planned. Preferably before it was too late.

"Good. Just let me know what happens in Silverwood, alright?"

"Of course." Roger pressed a little harder on the accelerator and Jessabelle groaned but obliged. "We'll keep you posted, I promise. You'll give me a call if you find anything?"

"Yep. I'm already logging in now. I'll work on it while I hold down the fort at the magic shop."

"Thanks, Gabs. Oh, and one other thing, since hot demon guy got into the bar—"

"The enhanced wards didn't work."

"Exactly."

"Alright, I'll research a solution. But I'm honestly not sure what else to do." I didn't miss the concern in her voice, and I felt the same. If he could breach her wards without any effort whatsoever, what the hell did we expect to do against Beaseldorf?

"You'll figure it out." I sounded more certain than I felt.

"I'll do everything I can, but it might take me a little while to work something out. You'll need to be careful until then."

"Alright, understood."

We hung up as we took the Silverwood Road exit, and I blew out a breath. My Spidey senses tingled, and I hoped that Gaby's research prowess would come through for us. I really needed a break, one not provided by hot demon guy.

And maybe, if my hunch proved correct, we'd find something about her—Celia Bellator. Something about her death. My heart skipped and my gut twisted. Would I be ready for that? Could I ever really be ready for that?

CHAPTER 21

As we pulled into Silverwood and cruised down the main drag, a semi-restored relic of the Gold Rush, my heart pounded a little harder in my chest. Tall, green grass covered the ground and bare trees dotted the landscaping. Winter was sort of a catch-22 in the northern Central Valley of California. The usual golden grass turned green, but then the normally green trees lost their leaves and stayed bare. The only time of year when all the foliage could agree on a color scheme was spring. During that time, the trees had fresh green leaves while the wildflowers bloomed within the lush, grassy hills. Alas, that didn't happen in January.

Instead, a persistent drizzle pelted our windows, though I didn't dare complain. Maybe someday we'd get enough rain to beat the damned statewide drought. But then again, probably not. As Roger turned right off the main drag and into a collection of older homes, I checked the navigation on his phone. Three minutes until arrival.

"So, how are we going to do this?" he asked, and I realized just how infrequently he'd done interviews with me.

"We're going to flash them my PI license and we are going to ask Elias Hunter's mom and sister about his disappearance. I'm going to stick mostly to the truth. Another woman hired me and I believe their disappearances might be connected. I'm going to mention the stalker, because from all my research so far, it seems that Elias had one too. Then you are going to shake their hands only when we say goodbye, after we get all of the information we can because you have a total lack of brain to mouth filter when you do readings and I don't want you freaking them out too soon. Better to leave that for when we can make a quick escape. Sound good?"

Roger nodded before pulling up to a small Craftsman home that looked worse for wear. Brown paint chipped a little on the siding and the wraparound porch slanted a bit to the right. The whole house, in fact, seemed to lean just a bit to the right. Roger and I both tilted our heads involuntarily when we looked at it. "That can't be a good sign," Roger observed through a grimace. "Probably termites."

"Not really our problem, Rog," I reminded him, opening my door and closing it. It was eight thirty a.m. and I clocked two cars in their driveway. One old Ford Ranger and a small Civic hatchback, both white. So, they were definitely home. A good sign, considering that in my haste to get out here, I hadn't bothered to call ahead to confirm that. Sometimes luck was on my side. Or at least that's what I liked to tell myself.

As we walked up the front walkway, which consisted of an uneven path of old bricks, I pulled my license from my wallet. The front porch groaned and titled beneath our weight and I tried not to wince as I knocked on the door. The whole house felt sad and somehow ominous. I didn't have a chance to question why before I heard a deadbolt slide and the door creaked open.

On the other side stood a woman, tall and thin, her gray hair tied into a bun atop her head. Gray-blue eyes, hard as steel, surveyed us. "I'm not interested. Didn't you read the sign?" She pointed to said sign, nestled in a pot of dead plants next to the door. "No solicitors."

She moved to slam the door in our faces, but I stuck my boot between the frame and the door before she could manage it. Her eyes snapped down to my foot and back up to glare at my face and I lifted my hands in surrender. "Sorry, Ms. Hunter, I don't mean to intrude, but we are not solicitors. I'm actually a private investigator." I held up my ID for her inspection, and she opened the door a little farther, her eyes narrowing. "I'm here because of a case I'm working on, and I think it might be connected to the disappearance of your son, Elias. I'm very sorry to hear that he's missing." I did my best to show the empathy I felt in my expression, and she softened ever so slightly.

Opening the door a little wider, she ducked her chin. "Thank you." She wore a pale-pink V-neck shirt with a flannel jacket that had seen better days and a worn pair of jeans. Her fuzzy house slippers let me know she hadn't been expecting company. But then who did at eight thirty a.m. on a Saturday?

Probably sadists.

"My name is Jenna Torrence and this is my colleague, Roger Pierce. We're here to ask you some questions. You see, my client went missing on the same day as your son, and the circumstances are too similar to ignore. May we come in and ask you a few questions?"

A sudden eagerness seemed to wash over her expression. "Please. Come in. No one has stopped by since the day he disappeared at that bar. I've called a dozen times, but they have no leads. Damn useless small-town cops."

She ushered us inside and led us to a small sitting room. The furniture looked well worn but cared for and the warmth inside felt homey. It reminded me of one of my better foster care homes. Though, I still felt a pervasive sense of sadness as we moved to a floral-printed couch in the living room. She gestured for us to sit on the love seat as she took a spot in the armchair across from us.

"Would either of you like anything to drink?" she asked, as though just remembering the normal duties of a hostess when company arrived.

I shook my head. "No, thank you."

And then she eyed Roger, as though hovering at the edge of her seat, waiting for his response. "I'm okay, but thank you for the offer," he said, his formality and general air of courtesy a little surprising. He never bothered with niceties with me. We'd need to talk about that.

Rather than dwell on it, I turned back to her and focused on her face. I could see the tight lines of anxiety pulling across her features, a clear sign of the desperation that a mother who'd lost her son would feel. Before I could get started, a voice called from the hall to our right. "Mom! Who's here?"

A young woman with pale-blond hair of the natural variety popped out from behind the wall and turned to stare at us. "Hey, Sarah, this is—I'm sorry, honey, what was your name again?"

"I'm Jenna Torrence," I said, standing and extending my hand to the newcomer. Elias's sister, based on my research. "I'm a private investigator. I'm working on a case I believe might be linked to your brother, Elias's, disappearance." I gestured to Roger, "And this is my associate, Roger Pierce." She crossed her arms and shifted her stance a little, eyeing me with no small amount of suspicion.

"How do you know he's my brother? How do you know about his case at all?"

I smiled reassuringly. "I'm thorough and I wouldn't have come here or bothered either of you if I didn't think it was important. I'm trying to find my client. She hired me the day before she disappeared. She was scared. She had a stalker." A flash of recognition crossed their faces, and I knew that Elias had told them about his unseen stalker. I sent a small prayer of thanks to the big guy upstairs before I continued. "I have reason to believe that she might be with Elias and that they may have been abducted by the same person."

The young woman's face crumpled with sadness and she stepped closer, moving to stand behind her mother. "What reason is that?"

I leaned forward to rest my elbows on my knees, and I watched as Roger tried to mirror the posture. Careful not to snicker at his awkwardness, because it was inappropriate, I refocused on the two women before me. "First, I want to say I'm really sorry that your family is going through this."

A cocoon of despair enveloped them like an invisible shroud. Elias's sister rested her hand on her mother's shoulder, and her mother reached up to squeeze it. "Thank you, Jenna. I'm Marie, and this is my daughter, Sarah. It's been hard, not knowing anything about what happened."

"I can't imagine what you both must be going through."

"You said that your client had a stalker?" Sarah asked, before I could say more.

"She did, and that's part of the reason I think their cases are connected." Then I hit them with the thing that I knew would be most likely to get them talking. "But the other part is that no one ever saw her stalker."

A shared glance between mother and daughter let me know that I'd touched on a similarity they both found compelling. Good. My hunches about this case may have finally borne some fruit. Sarah spoke first, her pale-blue eyes burning into mine. "Elias said he had a stalker. But we could never find any trace of him. We thought—" Her voice broke, as though her throat tightened too much to force the words out.

Marie rubbed her hand down her worn jeans. "We thought he was sick. Like, in the head."

A little pang of pain jolted through me. The same situation as Tara. No one had believed him. I couldn't imagine how isolating and terrifying that must have felt for either of them. Having a demon stalk you and no one to confide in.

"Eventually, he stopped talking about it," Sarah said. "We thought he was getting better. I mean, he seemed better, but then he disappeared." A small tear slid down her freckled cheek. She was tall and thin like her mom, and she had a certain grace about her that surprised me, even in her grief.

"You guys never saw anything? Never had a hint of this stalker?" I asked, and I could feel Roger leaning closer, his uncomfortable silence leaking into the space around me. I'd need to talk to him about his bedside manner if he was going to come with me on an interview again.

Sarah shook her head, but Marie's eyes fixed on the picture window behind Roger and me. She stared out at the dreary morning rain and her face seemed to pale a little. "There was that one time."

Sarah whipped her head back and forth in denial. "Mom, that was nothing. We agreed. It was just your imagination."

Marie's expression looked resigned, and she turned her attention to her daughter. "Honey, I know we thought that then, but given all that's happened, I think we have to consider that maybe it was real."

"I'm sorry, but what do you mean?" I asked.

Sarah pressed her lips together and removed her hand from her mother's shoulder. She clearly disapproved, but Marie ignored her and turned her attention to me.

"There was one night last week. I sensed something—no, someone—in the house. I woke up and came to the kitchen to get some water. I swear every single hair rose on the back of my neck. Chills went down my spine. Then I heard a loud thump coming from Elias's room. I ran back there like the devil himself was on my heels. I don't know what made me do it, but my heart was pounding out of my chest and I just knew something was wrong. When I went into the room, I swore I could see this dark figure standing over him. I screamed something like *what are you doing?* I don't know exactly. I was terrified, and when I flipped the light switch on, he, um... the figure disappeared." She shook her head and pressed her fist to her chest.

Relenting a bit as she saw her mother's apparent distress, Sarah sank onto the arm of the chair and hugged Marie's shoulders. Elias's mother's eyes watered. "I thought I'd imagined it. Elias woke up right as the lights switched on, and he had no idea why I was so panicked."

"I understand," I said, piecing this chance sighting together with the one experienced by Tara's brother-in-law. I couldn't say why they'd managed to see the demons, unless the demon's dark magic had allowed it. Maybe they'd been caught off guard and hadn't cloaked themselves? I chewed on my lip as I considered the possible causes.

"My client's family had a similar experience. I know that must have been terrifying."

Marie nodded, her eyes still watery and red-rimmed. "It was."

"Did Elias ever mention the reason he thought he was being stalked? Did he have any inkling what may have caused it?" I asked, hoping maybe this would give me something resembling an answer. Something that could help me stop Beaseldorf's plan.

Sarah blanched a little, her throat bobbing as Marie shook her head and stared out the window. "He never told us anything, other than that he had a stalker. And we didn't exactly believe him. So it's probably my fault we don't know more."

From the tight expression on her face, I realized that Sarah knew something. And after a long moment, she cleared her throat. "That's not exactly true, Mom."

Marie jolted slightly, turning her head to peer at her daughter. "What do you mean? You know something?"

Sarah nodded, swallowing hard again.

"Why didn't you say anything to the police?"

"I just thought he was having one of his episodes. I didn't want to worry you more, and I didn't think it'd help the cops any more than the stuff we did tell them."

I leaned forward, pulling their attention to me. "What did he say, Sarah?"

She cleared her throat, worry pinching at her fine-featured face. "He said they wanted his blood, and they wouldn't stop until they got it. I asked Elias who they were, and he called them the shadow people. Like I said, I thought he was having an episode."

Marie paled even further, her hand swiping down her face. "The only evidence left at the scene was blood. It soaked through the driver's seat of his pickup truck. They haven't determined whether the wound had been self-inflicted or the result of foul play, given his mental health history."

I nodded, another striking similarity to Tara's case. "I know this may seem like an odd question, but did he ever say why they wanted his blood?"

Sarah shrugged and shook her head, but it looked more like a confused gesture than a negative one. "When I asked him that, he started rambling incoherently. Something about our bloodline and how he had the gene they wanted and that it was active in him, but not me and I'd be safe. But that's crazy talk, right? It doesn't make any sense."

A thrill of connection raced down my spine, another piece of the puzzle clicking into place. So, according to Elias, he had the active gene the demons wanted, but not Sarah. Maybe it was the same for Bethany and Tara. I needed to talk to the other families and see if anyone else had said something similar. I felt damn certain that this gene, this blood was the tie that bound them together. But I wanted more data points to make sure I hadn't missed something. And I also wanted to know what the hell made the blood defiled in the first place and what that meant exactly.

I had all the phone numbers in my car and knew the instant we started back on the road, I'd make calls to everyone I could. "I'm not sure what that means," I said, hedging. Something about their blood was the key, and I knew that, but key to what? What made them important to the demons? Keeping myself grounded in the moment, I continued. "But I promise you, I will get to the bottom of it, one way or another."

I rose to my feet, wiping my hands on Roger's borrowed jeans, uncertain if I'd just wasted his time. If Sarah didn't share the gene or the reason for the tainted blood, I didn't know if he'd see anything relevant during a reading. Either way, it was still worth a shot. "Is there anything else you think I should know about?"

Marie and Sarah exchanged a look, each rising to their feet in turn. They shook their heads and stared at me, hope evident on their faces. My stomach knotted, hating that look, but knowing it all too well. I knew our conversation had given them that pesky feeling, and I would have to do my best to deliver on it. "Thank you both for your time today." I pulled a card out of my pocket and handed it to them. "Please call if you think of anything else. Also..." I pulled another card out of my pocket, along with a pen. "Can you please write down the best number to contact you, should I find anything or need to ask any further questions?"

As Marie wrote down her number, I looked over at Roger who stood silently next to me, hovering like my shadow. I gave him a squinty-eyed look and twitched my head toward the two women. I could only hope he knew it was the signal, telling him to work his magic.

When Marie finished writing and handed the card back to me, Roger stepped forward. He held out his hand and spoke for the first time since he'd politely turned down a beverage. "Thank you both for your time today. We're very sorry that Elias is missing. We'll do everything we can to find him."

Marie reached out and grasped his hand, and I waited for a reaction. I surveyed his face but saw nothing. Damn, I thought, as he let go and turned to Sarah. One down, one to go. Maybe this special, tainted blood tie came from the father's side. Too bad he'd passed away a few years back and we couldn't speak to him too. Turning away from Marie, Roger's fingers wrapped around Sarah's extended hand.

I watched carefully as his sympathetic smile stayed in place. Just when I thought we'd struck out, Roger's eyes rolled back in his head and he slumped to his knees, fingers locked on Sarah's hand, dragging her down with him.

Chapter 22

I stared down at Roger, who panted through clenched teeth on his knees. Sweat sprang up along his hairline in an instant and he let go of Sarah's hand, dropping it like he would have a scalding hot poker. She knelt beside him, her eyes wide with shock, which made sense considering he'd hauled her to the ground.

"Are you alright?" she asked, looking no worse for wear, thank goodness.

Roger waved a hand, as though wiping away the entire awkward episode, and I frowned at him. "My mistake. Low blood sugar. I get dizzy spells sometimes." He cut me a look that said Sarah's shit might just rival my level of darkness and I winced. On the tally of who owed who more, I knew this case would put Roger well ahead of me in that department. I could only imagine the level of future favors he'd call in once we defeated Beaseldorf. Alright, *if* we defeated him, though

I didn't dare voice that concern aloud. At least Roger hadn't gotten possessed or started bleeding this time or I would have felt like the biggest dirtbag on the damned planet.

Sarah rose to her feet, Marie helping her, and they each eyed Roger with concern. "Do you need anything to eat or drink?" Marie asked.

Roger shook his head. "Oh, I'm alright. We have snacks in the car. Again, it was nice to meet you both." He turned on his heel and walked out the door, leaving me to follow in his wake. Well, shit.

I turned to Sarah and Marie. "Thanks again for agreeing to speak with me today, and please call me if you think of anything else." They each agreed, and I hurried after Roger, who made a beeline for our car. Honestly, I'd never seen him move so fast. When I reached my dusty rust bucket, we each settled inside, him in the passenger seat this time and me on the driver's side.

Alone at last, I turned my focus on Roger. "What the hell happened? Are you okay? What did you see?"

He shook his head and pressed his fingers to his forehead, gritting his teeth as though in pain. "I don't— It's hard to— I need—" He coughed a little and reached for the water bottle he'd brought with him. He took a swig. "I need some time to collect my thoughts. Can you please just drive?" He closed his eyes and massaged the bridge of his nose, and I knew something had him shaken.

Rather than press the issue, I put the car in gear and flipped a U-turn, taking us out the same way we'd come in. After about fifteen minutes of driving, I let out a long sigh. "I know I'm leaning on you a lot more than usual with this case, and I'm sorry. I know that reading upset you. You have the same look you had when you touched me that time."

He shook his head and held up a hand. "I'm not a fragile baby bird, JT. Something big is going down, and I know that. So if I can help, I want to. Stop feeling guilty already; it's eating up all the air in the car." He cracked a window to demonstrate just how much I sucked.

Before I could reply, my phone vibrated. I pulled it out of my jacket pocket and stared down at the screen. Gaby. I swiped to answer and put it on speaker as I navigated a turn at high speed. "What's up?"

"So, your hunch about the date was right. I looked twenty-five years ago and found a rash of similar kidnappings committed on January eighteenth. The surnames helped me narrow it down. Not all of them matched, but there are enough similarities that this can't be a coincidence. Tyler Bronsen, Ken Hunter, Alexandra Baulm..."

"No shit. Do you have any information on what happened to them yet?"

Gaby swallowed and I could hear her typing, keys clicking rapidly in the background. "Jenna, they—" She broke off, the silence almost deafening.

"What, Gaby? Don't leave me hanging here."

"They all died. There's an article about it. Some kind of mass suicide event."

Panic slid through me. "What do you mean?"

"They said it was some kind of a cult thing, like that Halley's Comet situation. But the families they interviewed said none of their loved ones had any involvement in a cult and that none of this made sense to them. It talks about the mental health issues they suffered leading up to their deaths and there are a couple of mentions of alleged stalkers, too. But here, listen, 'The families involved have too many lingering questions in this brutal, tragic case. Why did twenty-five people kill themselves, with no obvious connections to each other until now? Why did all of them say they were being stalked in the days leading up to their deaths? Why could no one corroborate their claims? The authorities have no answers. They, and we as a community, may need to come to terms with the fact that we'll never know what really happened to these people.'"

My knuckles whitened as I tightened my grip on the steering wheel. "They all died?"

"Yeah, every last one of them." Gaby's voice sounded distant, haunted, and I swallowed hard.

I turned a side-eyed look on Roger, who also listened in rapt attention. "Roger, we need to know what you saw."

"Wait. Roger already saw something? What was it?"

He waved a hand at us, no idea why he thought Gaby would see him. He was obviously still a little shaken up from the Sarah-induced vision. "Okay, but can we go home first? I need to get my thoughts together. It's—" He broke off, sucking his teeth in thought. "It's hard to describe."

"I take it you don't want to go to Tara's sister's house?"

He shot me a glare, like I'd kicked his puppy or something. "What? One fucked-up vision isn't enough for you, JT? You want to make extra sure I get brain damage today?"

"Fucked up, how, exactly? And why does Roger think you want him to get brain damage?" Gaby asked, and I could all but taste the accusation in her tone despite the distance between us.

Rather than answer her, I dodged the point. “We’ll meet you at A Witch’s Whimsy in an hour, and Roger will give us both the rundown then. See you soon!”

“Oh no! You’re not getting out of this that—” she said, right before I hung up on her.

Whoops.

I looked at Roger. “You know I don’t want you to get brain damage, right? And I thought you said you weren’t mad at me.”

He looked glum as he stared straight ahead. “I’m not, and sorry for snapping at you. We just don’t need to go anywhere else today. I got everything we’re going to get from Sarah Hunter. Trust me. You’ll understand what I mean when we get to the shop.”

Chapter 23

An hour and six phone calls later, we pulled up in front of the magic shop. I turned down the small alleyway that led to Roger's private car port, where he kept his moped. I threw Jessabelle into park and looked at Roger. "See, I told you she'd make it. Say what you will about old Jessabelle, but she is reliable."

He grumbled something about freezing his ass off and hating that he didn't have his own car before he pushed out of Jessabelle and slammed the door shut behind him. I followed suit, a little more careful with my own door. Her engine may be reliable, but I didn't have faith that her noncritical parts would survive too much bashing about. With my luck, the door would fall off and I'd have to drive around all winter without one.

During our ride back from Silverwood, I'd directed Roger to call the families of anyone who'd gone missing in our time zone. He'd done so, holding the phone up to my mouth on speaker, and while three of them had hung up on me, I had gotten the other three to talk. Same weird situation, same stalker, and one of them had also mentioned something about his wife saying that the shadow people wanted her blood in the days leading up to her disappearance.

No chance we could write that off as a coincidence, not without sounding delusional. Roger hurried to his shop ahead of me, his pace still a bit brisker than normal, while I opened the back door and pulled Remus from the back seat. I gripped his hilt, the fit more comfortable than it had any right to be, and jogged to catch up with my agitated friend. The bell chimed as I swung the door open and I took a quick moment to survey the shop. No one but Gaby and Roger lingered inside, and Roger moved to the door and flipped the sign to Closed.

My eyes landed on Gaby and I strode over to the glass checkout counter where she sat with Roger's computer. "So, you got anything else?"

She shook her head, eyes intent on the laptop. "Nothing yet, though I may have asked for some help from my psycho ex. You know, the hacker guy you hate."

"No, not that guy. He sucks. Every time you talk to him, you guys end up back together. And then he does something fucking terrible to you, per the usual arrangement, and you end up crying at my apartment, guzzling ice cream and wine like there's no tomorrow. But there is a tomorrow, Gaby, there is, and during that tomorrow, I always end up holding your hair while you throw up."

She glared at me. "Look, desperate times, alright? Those people killed themselves on January twenty-ninth. That's only two days from now, and in order to get any more information on that case, I need to hack into the police database. I don't know how to do that, so we need him."

"Shit! Two days? We have two days to figure this out?" I let out a string of hissing curses that would have made any decent Christian blush because I knew she was right. Desperate times called for desperate measures, and I could feel urgency pulling me forward. "Fine, but tell Cliff to hurry his ass up, please."

"He said he'd start right away, but it'll take him a little while to get it done. So it's a waiting game for now."

I nodded, as we turned our attention to Roger who paced, muttering to himself, in front of us.

Gaby's face softened with concern. "Are you okay, Rog?"

The words died on his lips and he grimaced before running a hand through his perfectly tousled hair, even after he'd spent half the drive dragging his fingers through it. The guy had serious hair talent, and I decided that I should have him teach me his ways, as he gestured to the back room for us to follow him.

Gaby and I fell into step behind him, exchanging concerned looks. The complete change in his demeanor since we'd left the Hunters' house had me worried. I had no idea what he was going to say or what had him so rattled. He hadn't even looked this horrified after he'd touched me that first time, which was saying something.

As he opened the door to the room where our locator spell went awry, I could see that he and Gaby had cleaned the place well. They'd removed all the black goo and the tablecloths, and only a small wooden table with chairs sat in the center of the room, devoid of everything but the rows of candles and rectangular tables along the walls. I felt a little crummy for not helping, but I'd had a rough week. Surely, they'd forgive me just this once.

Thankfully, neither of them mentioned it as we strode deeper inside, and Roger slumped into one of the chairs and rubbed his temples.

"Roger, you're starting to freak me out. Can you please tell us what you saw?" Gaby asked.

He blew out a breath. "That's just it, I don't really know how to explain the vision in non-crazy speak. I thought maybe if I had a chance to piece it together logically, it might make more sense. But no dice. So, I'll start from the beginning and maybe it'll just work itself out if I say it aloud." He sucked in a long, long breath, shaking his head as though at a loss. "It was like a giant demon, porno montage."

I squinted my eyes. Knitted my brows. Tilted my head to the side. That was not at all what I expected him to say. "I'm sorry, but what in the actual fuck?" You could have knocked me over with a feather. Demon porn? Nope, that subverted all my darkest expectations. Murder? Mayhem? Sure. But demon porn?

Gaby also looked confused, her brown eyes wide with surprise.

He blew out a breath and shook his head. "It's hard to explain, and when I first touched Sarah, I didn't see anything. I had to press past what felt like an invisible curtain, deeper inside her psyche. Once I forced my way beyond it, it was like a barrage slamming into my skull. A very, um... spicy barrage. And I can't explain how I know this, but the sex was wrong somehow. I think maybe because it was always the same guy in every single one of them. I'm talking hundreds of images rushing through my mind all at once, and he always looked the same, spanning back decades, centuries even, and no aging. Then, as he screwed them all, I could feel the dark power rippling off him, but he didn't look demonic or anything. I could just sense it, like I always can whenever a demon's nearby. I felt his energy, like a disturbance in the force. After the very explicit montage ended, I saw really vivid images of childbirth, which I could only assume came from those encounters and maybe their descendants, too? Super horrifying by the way, since you all know how I feel about vaginas. Anyway, all the babies had the same mark on their chest, a birthmark. It was a strange, woven symbol, the same one that's on Remus's hilt. I even saw Elias at birth, with Marie holding him and stroking his hair, and he had the symbol, too."

I stared at him in utter stupefaction, though at least I was in good company, because Gaby's stunned silence mirrored my own. Fortunately, she recovered faster. "But Remus is a good guy. Anti-demon, remember? Why would demon offspring, if that's really what we're talking about here, have his mark on their flesh at birth?"

"Oh, it's definitely what we're talking about. That guy was a demon, no doubt about it, no matter how different he looked from others I've seen—"

"What did he look like?" I interrupted, my heart beating harder in my chest as a question formed in my mind. I knew a demon who looked different too. One who kept popping up at the strangest times and one who wreaked of lust and sex.

Roger paled, dragging a hand down his face and blowing out a breath. "He had the most intense gold eyes I've ever seen, tan skin, black hair. Honestly, he was absolutely gorgeous and also utterly terrifying. Somehow during the vision, his eyes locked with mine, and it almost felt like he could see me watching him in the past. It freaked me the fuck out, and that's when I broke the connection with Sarah."

I stared at him in disbelief, that question booming louder in my mind. I swore under my breath. "Gold eyes? Hot demon guy has vivid, intense gold eyes. You know, the demon who keeps popping in and claiming that he wants to help us."

Gaby's mouth dropped open. "You think it's him?"

I shrugged. "Gold eyes aren't exactly a common feature for a demon, Gabs. So I'd be willing to bet my last dollar it's him."

We all sat in stunned silence for a moment, letting that sink in. I had so many questions, and I pinched the bridge of my nose as I began to pace. Had hot demon guy banged all of those people, back from stone-age times? I thought about the babies and how many people he must have done the dirty with and gagged a little. It had probably been in the millions, if he was as old as Roger had described.

Mind moving away from that horrifying imagery, I wondered about Marie's baby. Elias and that symbol he'd been born with on his chest. The very same one on top of Remus's hilt and the one Tara's memories had revealed to me, too. Tara's words about defiled blood echoed through my mind. It had always been defiled, she said.

Always.

I knew my instincts were screaming at me to listen to Roger, but I just couldn't seem to force my brain to believe it. Never in all my time as a demon hunter had I imagined that demons could reproduce, and with humans no less. They couldn't have children. They couldn't even touch humans. It was absurd. Insane. Not possible.

Or was it?

I chewed on my thumbnail in thought as I looked at Gaby. "Rog, are you sure that the babies from your vision are half-demon, half-human spawn?"

He nodded. "That's what the reading showed me."

"But how?" I asked, shaking my head, unwilling to believe it. Because if demons could breed with humans, then humanity was in way more trouble than we could have ever thought possible. "Demons can't have kids with humans, can they?"

Gaby sucked her lips through her teeth. "I don't know. I didn't think so either. But—" She broke off, as though lost in her thoughts. "Didn't you say there was something different about that demon guy? More powerful and unusual? Maybe it's something that he can do and others can't?" He was different. So much different than any other demon I'd encountered. If he didn't radiate sex like the world's most powerful aphrodisiac, then I could have mistaken him for someone like me. Someone like us.

I shook my head, dragging my nails over my scalp. "This is absolutely insane. How many demonic children are there? If he's been getting down with humans for centuries, how many are we talking about here?" And they would all have tainted blood, always, from birth. If they shared the gene, that was.

If Roger's vision was true, then every last kidnappee, all of them, had some kind of demon lineage. That could explain Beaseldorf's interest in them, but why would he want hot demon guy's demon babies?

We were still missing something, an important piece to the puzzle, and I all but growled in frustration as I stalked out the door and to the front desk. Ripping a piece of paper out of the printer that sat under the front counter, I pulled open a drawer, a little on the violent side due to my testiness, and grabbed a pencil. We were running out of time to solve this mystery, I could feel it in my gut, and I hated being left in the dark. I needed some light, some certainty, and I needed it right now or I would lose my shit.

Stomping back toward Gaby and Roger, I pulled open the door and stormed over to them. I slammed the paper on the table where Roger sat. "Draw him, Roger. I can't assume anymore. I need to know. So, put that six-month sabbatical you took in France to study art to good use and sketch the demon you saw screwing the entire damn world. And we'll find out once and for all if it's who we think it is."

CHAPTER 24

Twenty minutes later, and the three of us stared down at an uncanny likeness of that seductive motherfucker—hot demon guy. Man, I really needed his name so I could stop calling him that.

"It's him," I said, snagging Remus from the table beside me. I stormed to the door, yelling over my shoulder as I did. "I have some things I need to look into. I'll be in touch." I closed the door on any protest they might have had and left A Witch's Whimsy. The door jingled as I opened it and stepped into the chilly Santa Sombra afternoon.

I'd said I had things to look into, but really, I just needed to get some air. I still couldn't wrap my mind around the idea that demons, even smoking hot demon guy, could procreate. And if all those babies had demon lineage, demon blood, then... what? What did it all mean?

When no answers came immediately to mind, I unlocked my phone, my finger hovering over Luke's contact before I hesitated. Hot demon guy's words rang in my ears, his warning—or threat. I still hadn't decided which. What did I think Luke could do? But I had made a promise to him for this case, and the time had come where I could use his resources. So, no matter what intrusive hot demon guy thought, I dialed.

He answered on the third ring. "Hey, what's going on, JT?" Professional, aloof, and oddly, he didn't sound hungover. Maybe he really could handle his liquor, but I couldn't afford to dwell on that. Something big was brewing. Twenty-five people were missing, all of them with possible demon lineage.

Not to mention the fact that my mom killed herself to prevent whatever Beaseldorf had planned twenty-five years earlier, and it had come full circle now. Bottom line? I needed more people looking for Tara and for the others, even if it meant inviting normie humans into supernatural territory. Cops had procedures and bureaucracy, but that didn't mean they didn't have resources. They just couldn't move as quickly as I could on any information they might glean.

I started talking before I could second-guess myself. "Remember Elias Hunter, in Silverwood? Well, I just interviewed his family and he's definitely worth looking into. He disappeared the same week as Tara, with the same MO. Unseen stalker and blood left behind at the scene."

He paused, and I could hear him shuffling papers. Probably looking for a pen to take down notes. "Slow down. Can you repeat that?"

I did as he asked, mentioning the bar where Elias disappeared, along with Marie and Sarah's names and address, just in case he wanted to pay them a visit and see for himself. Though I gave him the full rundown of my morning interview with them, I left out the demon orgy vision. Seemed wise given the circumstances.

"Alright, we'll look into this. Thanks for doing the legwork. Anything else I need to know?" I paused for a moment, debating how much to tell him. Seeming to pick up on that, Luke pressed. "You know, withholding evidence would be considered obstruction of justice."

"You think I don't know that?" I snapped, pinching the bridge of my nose once more to calm my nerves. I hated bringing him into this any more than I had to, but I was well past the *throw shit at the wall to see what sticks* stage of desperation.

"Just thought you could use the reminder. So, anything else you need to tell me?"

On a sigh of irritation, I pulled the list of names hot demon guy had given me from my pocket. "Fuck me, Luke, I'm telling you everything I know." I was such a despicable liar, but what else could I do? We were running out of time. We had less than two days to figure this whole thing out before the world went to hell in a handbasket. Or at least, I assumed that's what would happen based on what my mother had done and what Tara's thoughts had conveyed to me in the Cogitato Crypta. "Take these names down too," I commanded, right before I listed off the ones within driving distance. I decided to keep it semi-local, since that would probably give us the best shot at keeping Luke and Bud on the case and the FBI out of it. For that same reason, I kept the link to the mass suicide that happened a couple of decades ago under wraps too. No reason to overcomplicate things on their end by throwing that into the mix.

We needed them looking for Tara and Elias, same as me. But that didn't mean I wanted the full force of the US security state coming down on our case too. Call me stingy, but I had a feeling that the red tape would get brutal as all hell once the Feds caught wind of what was happening, and we didn't have time for that. I needed to give Luke enough to be dangerous, but not enough to blow up my entire case.

"Where did you get those names?" he asked, his voice full of suspicion yet again.

"Disappearances within one hundred fifty square miles in the last week with similar circumstances." I gave him the three names whose family members had answered the phone and confirmed my suspicions. I'd let him deal with the rest. Who knew, maybe one of the demon stalkers had left a clue behind at one of the kidnapping scenes. Something more than a pool of the victim's blood and a mysterious stalker no one else could see. Something that would lead us right to them. It seemed unlikely, but a girl could dream, and besides, I couldn't work every single crime scene. I didn't have enough time. But the cops? They had connections between departments and contacts. I could only hope that they'd tip me off if they found anything big.

"Thanks, JT, this is really thorough. I almost feel bad that I only paid you a dollar."

I scoffed. "No, you don't. Uncle Sam is as cheap as they come, and we both know it. But I'll tell you how you can repay me. You call me the minute you find something. I want to be there when you go in after her—after all of them."

A silent pause as he considered my request. "I'll let you know what I find."

"Same here."

"Before you go, I was actually about to call you when the phone rang."

"What for?"

"Your apartment is no longer a crime scene. They're done processing it. You can move back in anytime you want."

Sweet. I let out a sigh of relief that we wouldn't need to break in to look for evidence. Sometimes patience did pay off. "Oh, good. Thanks." We hung up and I drove Jessabelle back to The Office by rote memory, my mind running through scenario after scenario on why Beaseldorf needed twenty-five demon offspring and my newfound sword. My best assumption was that he wanted the power the blade contained for the ritual Tara had shown me, but I didn't know what that meant exactly. Or what that ritual would free the demons from. I should probably hide the sword, make it disappear just like my mother had. But then again, hot demon guy had found it, so what would stop Beaseldorf from doing the same thing? At least with Remus by my side, I could protect him.

My mind raced as I thought about the mass suicide from all those years ago and knew we'd have more detailed—as in not public—information on that soon. Once Cliff did his super illegal digging. If he got caught, I would totally throw him under the bus. I hated that douchebag, like a lot, and I would lose zero sleep over him.

Still, I couldn't help but hope that the intel on the old crime scene would bring it all together, give me at least some of the answers we needed, if not all of them. But something in the pit of my stomach told me I was missing something. Some integral part of the whole picture.

Like, for example, why was hot demon guy helping me, if he'd sired all of those demon babies?

There was one thought that occurred to me, and it made me sick with dread. Was hot demon guy actually Beaseldorf? Had he been toying with me this entire time? Trying to lure me into the creepy ritual, the way he'd tried to lure my mother in? My stomach clenched as I looked at Remus, who sat innocently on the passenger seat next to me.

I pulled into the parking lot next to The Office and threw Jessabelle into park. Grabbing Remus, I stomped to the entrance of the bar. And as I did, I really should have looked at Remus. Should have noticed the glowing golden sheen peeking through the top of the sheath. I should have felt the tingle of alarm that always preceded the presence of a demon nearby.

But I didn't. I was too distracted by the mystery in front of me and the urgency with which I needed to act to solve it. And as I opened the door to the bar and turned to lock it, a smoky fist slammed into the side of my head and stars exploded behind my eyelids.

Elliott Grove Middle School, East Santa Sombra, Fourteen Years Ago

"Hurry," I hissed, rubbing my arms as I watched Gaby work. She drew a large symbol on the ground with stark white sidewalk chalk. We stood in

the quad, in a paved spot between four trees, weapons stashed in each of the raised garden beds. As Gaby drew, anxiety churned in my stomach. I wished we'd had the guts to use something more permanent, but both of us feared getting caught too much to chance it. We didn't want to get tossed into juvie for vandalism, which was something that had happened to one of my foster brothers a few years back. It left an impression.

I checked the perimeter once more and made sure we'd placed the weapons within easy grasp. Gaby had found a blessing to help me translate the effects of holy water onto a bunch of random stuff we'd found around her house and Erin and Dave's place too. A baseball bat, three large knives, a hammer, a sledgehammer, and a nail gun. We planned to test them all that night, but I still brought full bottles of holy water and crucifixes, just in case none of them worked.

"I'm ready," Gaby said, just as I finished my final check of our weapons stash. "It's done. Remember, be careful not to smudge it, alright? You need to lead the demon to it and not scuff it up with your shoes." Demons didn't have the ability to permanently manipulate the physical world, only influence it. So, I felt pretty confident the chalk would hold up once we got it inside the symbol. Gaby and I would just need to be careful where we stepped.

I nodded, rubbing my hands together and exhaling a long breath. "Okay, make sure you stay hidden. I don't want that thing getting a look at you while I'm fighting it. We don't know if your ability to see it will also make it able to touch you, okay? I've got this covered."

Gaby nodded, then she scurried behind the largest planting box a dozen or so paces away. "Good luck," she whisper-yelled just before I turned and ventured off into the night to find a demon.

My heart beat steady in my chest, a loud thump that I could hear in my ears, and I broke into a quick-step jog as I scanned the buildings, not worrying about being seen anymore. I wanted it gone, which meant I needed it to find me. I stepped away from the shadows and into the full light of the moon, head swiveling back and forth, feeling like a little bit of an idiot as I did. Bait for a demon maybe wasn't one of my best life choices to date, but I didn't let the possible consequences sink in more than that.

I'd promised Gaby I'd lure the demon, and I planned to keep that promise. I turned the corner and saw it—a dark cloud pulsating just across the breezeway near the gym, by the wall of lockers. It hovered over them, as though drinking it in, raking its nails along the lockers. It groaned, shrieking in the night, and I resisted the urge to cover my ears. A small cut carved into the blue metal surface of the lockers before it healed instantly, part of the oddity of their existence in our world, I knew. They couldn't change anything, their disturbances to our dimension only seemed to last for a fraction of a second before snapping back to its normal state. God, I really hoped the chalk would hold. I didn't want to get my ass kicked.

Sending up a prayer to the big guy upstairs, I settled my gaze on the demon, my eyes fixating on it as it hovered over Justin's locker, Gaby's douchebag friend. It sniffed deeply, as though enjoying the aroma, and my back stiffened. Its aura pulsed and the scent of sulfur made my nose pinch as I struggled to breathe through it. I couldn't afford to think about Justin and why the wrath demon thought his locker smelled so delicious. I would deal with that later. At the moment, I needed to get its attention and make halfway decent bait.

"Hey, dipshit!" I yelled. "You're in my school, and you need to leave or else!" My voice sounded steady, almost tough, and I felt pretty impressed with that.

But when the terrifying demon turned, the aura growing to twice its initial size and its red eyes flaring, my bravado fizzled.

Fear trickled down my spine, raising the hairs on the back of my neck. "Ah, so you can see me, little dove," it said, its voice almost feminine, high, shrill, and terrifying. "I thought you might be able to, but you've been so careful to pretend, haven't you?" It surged forward then, so fast that I blinked and it stood before me, mere inches from my face. It inhaled as though smelling me, and I couldn't help it, I froze. It was so cold, and its teeth were so sharp, its eyes so red. Anger sizzled inside me, pushing through my fear from the demon's influence, but I pushed it down, like I always did when I fought them.

As it surveyed me, I slipped my hand into the back pocket of my jeans, looking for the flask of holy water I kept there. Its disgusting scent surrounded me and I did my best not to gag as I unscrewed the top of the flask behind my back.

"Oh, little dove, it's been an age since I've encountered one of your kind. I think I'll enjoy ripping you limb from limb." It raised its long, sharp claw, clearly intending to cut me in half. Instead, I heaved the full flask of holy water I carried straight into its face. It burned like acid, the thing shrieking and hissing, the sound shrill and unnatural. It cut through me like a knife and turned my blood to ice in seconds, but I didn't let that affect me. Instead, I turned and ran.

I could still hear its essence crackling as it burned while I sprinted across the breezeway, back the way I'd come. It cursed, swearing, snarling, and spitting at me, but I kept going. It could outrun me any day of the week. I would just have to use every bit of the head start I could get. Gaby wasn't far away, I'd be there in just ten more seconds, but before I could turn the corner and see our symbol on the ground, I felt something cut into the toe of my sneakers—a razor-sharp claw.

It sliced into my foot, sliding into my flesh, and I tripped, coming down hard, my knees smacking onto the concrete. I let out a grunting cry of pain, pushing through the shock of the agony to reach into my sweatshirt pocket. I pulled out the wooden crucifix just as its unearthly weight pressed down on my back. I twisted and shoved the weapon up, right into its chest. It leaped off me, screaming and sizzling once more.

I scrambled back on my butt before I rolled and got onto my feet. Then I was up, running again, forcing my body to move through the pain in my foot. I turned the corner, saw the chalk, and prayed I'd make it to the trap before the thing recovered. Just five more seconds and I would be there.

My thighs and calves burned with effort and the big guy upstairs must have been listening because I made it, skidding to a halt just in front of the trap and turning, the crucifix raised in my fist. I looked from left to right, but I didn't see the demon. I didn't dare look in the direction I knew Gaby hid, afraid I might give away her position.

Sweat dripped down my back and my foot throbbed from where its nail had pierced through my skin. Warm liquid filled my shoe and coated my sock. Blood, I knew, but I ignored that. I needed to focus if I was going to get out of this fight alive. Then I saw it turn the corner, its eyes burning redder than I'd ever seen. The black of its aura was scored through with more veinlike red than before. I didn't know if that was because I'd hurt it or because it was pissed at me. Probably both. Crap.

I gritted my teeth as I prepared myself. "Come get me you evil prick!" Admittedly, I felt a little bad swearing while holding Jesus's image in my hand. But then again, I had a feeling he'd forgive me. I was slaying demons after all. That had to count for something. It drew closer, slowing down as it did, and I got the sense that it was toying with me.

My breath fogged in the icy air and my grip on the crucifix tightened. I just needed to lure the demon close enough to shove it into the chalk circle. But before it could get within spitting distance of me, a laugh rang out, echoing from the walls. Its teeth flashed, sharp and glinting in the moonlight, before it turned away from me and moved like lightning. It rushed past my position in a blur of motion, and my heart rate skyrocketed as worry made adrenaline shoot through me. I spun to follow, watching my footsteps so I didn't scuff up the chalk marks.

No, no, no, no, no.

My stomach bottomed out as I tried to locate where the hell it had gone, but deep down, I already knew the answer. As for all of our plans? They'd been shot straight to hell in a handbasket.

I didn't hesitate, sprinting in the direction where I knew Gaby hid, praying I wouldn't be too late. The shrill laugh erupted through the silent air once more as I cleared the quad, running harder than I'd ever run in my life, and I knew then that my instincts were right.

Oh God, Gaby.

My heart thundered and squeezed as I gripped the edge of a concrete planting bed and spun around it. And as I cleared it, I saw her. My throat restricted, my muscles locking as my mind flashed back into the past, to a similar situation. Dark power surrounded her, holding Gaby up, her toes scrabbling against the ground. Her back arched in a way that looked wholly unnatural, her head tossed back, mouth gaping open wide.

The demon stood beside her. Black and red smoke leached away from its essence and seeped into Gaby's mouth, the progression like a slow drip.

Terror bled through every cell in my body and in my mind, I saw Brittany, and I was suddenly nine years old again. My heart stopped in my chest, my locked muscles wobbled as I stared at the demon that held Gaby, trying not to piss my pants. Her eyes had gone totally white and I felt sick, my stomach churning. Then I saw Brittany's face when she'd come out from the comatose state the demon had put her in. Her eyes had gone totally cold. All of the warmth—the humanity in her expression—gone. I'd ducked behind the lockers before she could see me, terrified of what the demon would do to me if it knew that I'd seen them.

Not again. I squeezed my eyes shut and forced the courage I knew lived in my heart to the forefront of my mind. This wouldn't happen again, not if I could help it.

The demon laughed, that shrill sound forcing me to the present. "Little girl, do you think you and this little witch can trap me? Banish me?" Gaby's body lifted, her back popping with the motion, and my focus sharpened to a razor's edge.

"Don't! Stop!" I said, still gripping the crucifix at my side. The edges of the wood dug into my palm, the stinging pain helping me focus. I stepped closer, daring to get within striking distance, and edged my way next to the planter, where we'd stashed some of the weapons. I could just make out the outline of the baseball bat and a hammer.

It hissed at me, snarling and baring its teeth. Without warning, it surged forward and raised its nail to swing for me in a deadly arc. I raised the crucifix right as I grabbed for the hammer, dodging as fast as I could. The second I moved, its nail swung down, slicing down my side, cutting through my jeans, and scoring into my skin. Pain exploded behind my eyes but I didn't stop. I gripped the hammer in my palm as the black smoke continued to pour into

Gaby's mouth. Turning, I twisted away from the second slice of its other nail, the demon still too close to Gaby. Sweat slicked my skin, and though I wanted to get more distance between us and Gaby, I couldn't afford to hesitate even for a second while it did its level best to kill me. I cocked back my arm and launched the hammer as hard as I could at its head.

My breath caught as time seemed to slow, the hammer spinning head over handle right for the demon. I had no idea if it would work, and I could do nothing but pray that it did. I grabbed the bat just as the demon's mouth stretched wide in a triumphant smile, fearless as the sharp end of the hammer slammed home, right into its face. It stiffened for a moment, seeming to solidify as the hammer stuck in its head. The ground crackled with fire, opening up as it fell backward, right onto Gaby. The fire spread, flames dancing around her too, and I realized for one horrifying moment that it wasn't going to take just the demon. Hell would take Gaby as well.

"No!" I cried, charging forward, dropping the bat, and reaching out for Gaby. Her eyes cleared and her body went slack as she fell backward, the demon pinning her legs beneath its weight, and now we knew for sure. It was definitely able to touch her. Crap. The fire grew, and she looked down, realization flashing in her eyes.

"Jenna!" she cried, trying to pull herself out from under the demon. The fire that I could only assume was hell pulled at its limp body, fingers made of flame snatching and grasping, dragging Gaby with it. I reached her just as her legs fell into the pit and the demon dropped away from sight entirely.

Our fingers clasped, and I gripped her wrist with my other hand. She fought against the tug of gravity, pushing and yanking as she struggled to get free of the fire. The pit beneath us began to close and her fingers slipped down my palm, our skin slick with our sweat. Our eyes locked, and I could see the terror in hers. I shifted, sitting on my butt, and dug my heels into the ground, pain lancing through my injured foot and leg. Ignoring it, I pushed with all my strength.

"Don't let go!" Gaby said, her voice thin and terrified.

"I won't. Now push yourself out!" I shouted back over the whipping winds and screaming shrieks of hell. She did as I asked, gripping my hand and moving her legs kicking and striving for whatever purchase existed in the pit beneath her feet. We worked together and we gained an inch, then another and another. The pit closed faster with each passing second and I gave one final yank with all my strength. The hold it had on her released and I fell backward, Gaby sprawling onto the ground next to me. She coughed, sputtering and shaking as she rose to her knees and the pit closed, fire extinguishing as quickly as it had started.

Gaby gagged then, heaving as black smoke expelled from her mouth. She heaved again, her stomach repelling all of the remaining essence of the demon. I watched, unsure what to do, and crawled toward her, placing a hand on her back. The minute the smoke hit the cold air, it dissipated. I let out a long sigh of relief as her body settled and she sucked in clean, cold air.

When she stopped gasping for breath and fell onto her butt on the ground, I asked, "Are you okay?"

She coughed and I winced, thinking about how close we'd come to total and complete disaster. If her weapons hadn't worked—wait. Her weapons worked! A small spike of excitement raced through me, and I let out a small stunned laugh.

Gaby turned to look at me, wiping a small droplet of drool off her mouth. "You're laughing at a time like this? I almost got sucked into hell, and you're laughing? Are you crazy?"

My foot throbbed and the slice along my leg and side burned, but a wide grin spread across my face in spite of that. "Maybe. It's just, Gaby, your weapons... they worked!" I gave her a look full of meaning.

"Wait, they worked?" she asked, and I could see the same look of shock and excitement spreading across her features as mine.

I nodded, still grinning. Rising to my feet, I fought through the pain in my foot and reached a hand down to help her. She grabbed it and I pulled her up, wincing a bit, each of us breathing hard. I ran through the whole encounter in my head again, thinking through what went well and what didn't. I hadn't frozen up that time. I'd fought, and I'd managed to come out on top. In no small part thanks to Gaby.

Tapping my chin, I said, "I think, next time, we need to find a different spell for you. That spell did a heck of a lot more than let you see the demons. You almost got possessed or killed, and then you also almost got sucked into hell. Possession normally takes time and demons can't usually impact the physical human world. Meaning they can't kill humans physically. Only spiritually. Those are some pretty big side effects."

Gaby's eyes widened as she seemed to remember just how bad things had almost gone for us, and I worried she might buckle under the terror of it. I figured she'd tell me that she didn't want anything else to do with me and my special brand of crazy. Not that I would blame her. We spent one night fighting a demon together and I'd almost gotten her sucked into hell. But rather than the loathing and disgust I expected, something else settled across her features and her eyes cleared.

"You're right. That spell has way too many side effects. We'll need to find something better next time." She turned, striding for her backpack, grabbing the baseball bat off the ground and starting to gather our weapons. I watched

her in utter shock, chattering away about what she thought we could do to improve our odds next time. "We also need to do a better job of hiding that trap if we're going to use it again. We still don't even know if it works."

I limped forward to help her. "Yeah, it definitely seemed to know what that was. I'm not sure it's worth trying again."

Gaby shrugged, and I knew deep in the marrow of my bones that she had no intention of running away from me screaming. She didn't cringe away from the darkest parts of me or my world. She faced it head-on and wanted to fight it with me, shoulder to shoulder.

She was like me. More so than I could have ever imagined.

We finished gathering the weapons and the chalk, and I yawned broadly. "Why don't you come sleep over at my place?" Gaby asked, frowning at the slice on my leg and the blood seeping from my shoe. "We can take a look at those injuries, too. I bet my grandma has something that can help in her grimoire."

"You think?"

"Sure. Besides, we need to get you back to full health before we fight the next one."

"The next one?" I asked, arching a brow at her.

"Yeah. You think I didn't notice that creepy pale-gray thing on the light rail?"

"More that I hoped you hadn't."

She laughed, looping her arm under my shoulder to help me walk as I limped. "It's gonna take a little more than almost getting sucked into hell to keep me from doing this again. The rush is amazing."

Gaby looked at me with wide eyes, full of excitement and intrigue. And that's when I knew for sure, Gaby was the friend I always hoped I'd find but never believed I would.

CHAPTER 25

I jolted sideways, my brain erupting with searing pain as I lost my balance. My body hit the floor, slamming into it so hard my teeth cracked together. Remus lurched from my grip and skittered across the room, panic filling me as I heard him skid to a stop on the far side of the bar. I could just make out the sheen of gold beneath his sheath, a glow barely visible at the hilt, and cursed myself for my stupidity, my lack of awareness. For how distracted I'd let myself get.

Before I could berate myself further, a bare, unearthly foot shot out, aiming a kick straight at my face. I got my hands up just in time to block the brunt of it, though my fingers still smashed back into my nose with the force of the blow. My eyes watered, but I rolled away with the impact, using my momentum to swipe at the legs of my attacker. The demon grunted as it hit the ground beside me, the contact with my body solidifying it for a moment. I blinked away the tears from the hit to my nose, trying to clear my vision, and rolled forward.

A heartbeat later, I sprang to my feet and ran toward Remus. But before I could grab him, a dark figure appeared before me. A second dark figure, I realized, the full scene coming into focus as I surveyed the beast blocking the way to my weapon.

The demon stared back at me, its human mask off, and this demon was not like hot demon guy. Not at all. It was a rage demon, just like Idra, the misty black of its skin laced through with red as its smoky eyes bored into me. It had long deadly nails filed into razor-sharp points that scraped against the floor. Its eyes, pools of depthless smoke and glowing red, watched me as cracked earth scorched the ground beneath it. There were two, I realized, counting the one I'd just tripped, and I had no weapon. This was so not good since their reach with those nails far outdid my own.

I dodged to the right, just in time to avoid a slicing nail to the back of my skull—the one I'd laid out a second ago coming back for more. Damn, I wished I'd brought my gun. But I hadn't. I'd let myself get lulled into a false sense of security bringing Remus with me everywhere. I twisted to face both the demons right as a third emerged from the shadows behind them. Its pale-gray skin and sunken features looked horrifying in the low-lit barroom. Its ethereal, leathery flesh seemed to hang from nonexistent bones and even at this distance, I could feel it fighting to drain the energy from my body. A sloth demon, plus the two wrath demons? Shit. My spine stiffened as I shifted into a fighting stance.

That sloth demon couldn't lay a finger on me or it would drain the life and vitality from my body. There were times when I really hated being me and having my abilities. My eyes flicked between the three of them and Remus, trying to calculate the best path to my weapon, but they'd cut me off from him good and proper.

I'd need to fight my way through them first, so I bared my teeth. "You sure you want to do this with me? This isn't my first rodeo, you know." I kept my tone taunting, trying to feign bravado even as that first blow to my head still had me reeling. Warm, sticky blood dripped down my temple, but I ignored it.

Rather than participate in my pithy banter, they surged forward with unnatural speed, the wrath demons' nails lashing out at me as I dodged left and right. The sloth demon leaped for me like a fucking acrobatic monkey, arms splaying, trying to wrap itself around me to feed. Without hesitating for even a second, I reacted, rolling and ducking to avoid getting cut by those deadly nails and to keep the sloth demon from wrapping its energy-sucking limbs around me.

One of the wrath demon's nails cut straight through a chair as it struck for me and I jumped out of the way. The ruined wood landed in a crashing heap on the floor as I sprang to my feet, and I spared it less than a second of my attention while it knit back together as though nothing had happened at all. I dodged another swipe of a nail and kicked the wrath demon in the chest. It flew backward, crashing into more tables and chairs, the sound of wood cracking and fusing back together filling the bar.

Without warning, the second wrath demon stabbed with its nail, aiming right for my chest. I moved, but not fast enough, and it cut straight through Roger's sweater, scoring my upper arm damn near to the bone. The stinging pain brought bright-white flashes to my eyes, but I pushed through it, not stopping as the sloth demon lunged for me again. Nails and limbs came from all directions, and I did my best to dodge and weave and work my way closer to Remus. We'd started our fight with the bar at my back and I'd shifted so that Remus lay to my right, no longer fully obscured by the demons.

Just two more steps right, and I could chance a running dive to reach him. I could almost feel his hilt in my hand when a fist rammed into my cheek. My head whipped sideways, pain and a strange kind of listlessness filling me at once—the sloth demon had gotten a hit in. Before I could recover, a smoky black arm wrapped around my waist, and a hand with sickening long nails crushed over my mouth. The force of its grip against my momentum left me breathless and I kicked, rage coursing through me as I fought against the ironclad hold of one of the wrath demons.

I twisted and I bucked, and my eyes locked on the other two demons as they approached me, dark glee on both of their horrifying faces. The sloth demon reached Remus, kicking the blade behind them as they prowled closer. Anger boiled in my blood, fury that I thought would consume me. I tried to fight it, tried to channel it into something useful. I could always fight a demon's sway, but it was becoming clearer by the second that these were not the same kind of demons I was used to fighting. They may look damn similar, but they commanded stronger influence, their auras more potent somehow.

My resolve stiffened as a plan formed in my mind. When they drew close enough I could have reached out to touch them, I jumped up, kicking out as hard as I could. My boots slammed into their chests, and they staggered back, dazed by the strike. Without waiting for a reaction, I ran backward using all of the strength in my legs to catch the wrath demon holding me off guard.

My muscles burned as it tried to stop me, but I kept going until we crashed to a halt, the demon colliding with the brick wall behind us. I saw stars, despite the demon taking the brunt of the blow. It dropped to the ground and loosened its grip on my waist and mouth, and I took the opportunity to flip it over my back. It hit the floor with a crack, snarling at me with bared pointy teeth.

The rage dissipated as I put distance between us just before fear, unlike any I'd experienced before, trickled down my spine. Remus was still too far away for me to reach, and there were three demons between him and me yet again. I'd lost every inch of ground I'd gained in the fight. His blade had slipped a few inches free of the hilt and the brightness from its glow shone in the dull light in the bar. If I could just get to him, then maybe I could make it out of this fight in one piece.

Fatigue and injury dragged at me, the wounds on my head and arm bleeding freely, but I knew I would get no reprieve when the demons attacked again. Just as predicted, all three of them lunged at the same time, and it took every ounce of concentration I had to fend them off. But with the pain scoring through my body, I couldn't stop every cut nor every touch from the sloth demon. Wounds slit open over my skin, my blood dripping onto the ground as I forced my body to keep moving.

I'd never seen this many at once before, never witnessed them attack in such a coordinated effort, and I knew deep down that Beaseldorf must have sent them. He knew where I lived and he'd sent them to kill me. The worst part? If they succeeded, they'd have the sword, and we'd be well and truly screwed.

I sprinted to the side, dodging around the sloth demon, spinning out of its grasp as I tried to get to Remus. Leaping up onto the tabletops, I ran like my life depended on it, hopping from surface to surface across them as the demons' nails slammed down behind me. One caught my shin, slicing through skin deep enough that it made me cry out in pain, and I went down hard, chin hitting the edge of a tabletop before my face slammed onto the ground.

Pain exploded through me as one of the wrath demons dropped to its knees, pinning my legs. The sloth demon grabbed my arms, hauling them over my head. I fought, bucking hard, stunned at how strong they were and terrified as I could feel my energy, my very life force getting sucked away, fed on by that fucking sloth demon. These three demons were unlike any I'd faced before. I'd never encountered a demon I couldn't outmuscle or overpower... except for one. He had to be behind all of this. Hot demon guy had to be Beaseldorf. It was the only thing that made sense. But that didn't matter. My energy leached from my limbs, my mind frantic with fear.

I wriggled and writhed as one of the wrath demons stepped over the top of me. It dragged its black nail softly across my face, and I bucked, trying to escape. It spoke in a voice that was shrill and cool at the same time. "Beaseldorf sends his regards." It raised its arm, nail angled downward, pointed straight at my chest.

I screamed my fury, knowing this was the end. Knowing that I couldn't stop what happened next. Knowing that I had failed and that there was no one to carry on the torch. I shouldn't have come here alone. Beaseldorf knew where I lived, and Gaby hadn't revived the wards since hot demon guy dropped in on me. I should have been more careful, less arrogant in my ability to keep myself and Remus safe.

Fear, rage, and regret scored through me. But before the demon's blow could land, I saw a glowing gold light whip through the air above me, right by its neck. I blinked, unsure if I'd really seen it as the demon paused, its misty eyes turning a muted brown as its head fell to the floor next to me with a loud thump. The body landed on the other side of me and the ground crackled, hell coming back to claim its own. I scrambled away from it, desperate to avoid its scalding grip.

Before I could say or do anything more, the gold-eyed sex demon stepped into view, Remus clutched in his grip. He raised it in a death promise to the other demons, and they let me go. They dropped my limbs like they'd been made of holy water, scrambling backward and hissing.

"You?" The remaining wrath demon snarled. Not bothering to wait for a response, I sprang to my feet with what little energy I had left, putting distance between me and all the fucking demons in my bar, but I didn't miss the look of recognition and utter shock they bestowed upon him.

"You would defy your own brother? Your father?" The sloth demon hissed, clearly afraid, but also disbelieving.

Hot demon guy didn't bother with an answer. Instead, he attacked. He moved with a lethal grace unlike anything I'd seen before. The demons fought back, the wrath one swinging its razor-sharp nails with deadly precision and the sloth demon throwing punches and kicks with an elegance unbefitting its horrifying appearance.

But hot demon guy was faster. He dodged, weaving and swinging the sword in smooth, practiced motions. He wielded Remus as an extension of his own body, meant for his hand. With a sudden strike, he stabbed the wrath demon in the stomach and sliced upward, the death blow meant to inflict maximum damage and pain. The demon slumped to the floor as the ground crackled and absorbed him, leaving the lone sloth demon to contend with.

It shrieked a shrill snarl of fury, doubling its efforts. But it was no match for him. I would have stepped in to help if I thought he needed it, but I honestly had no idea why he'd shown up there. To save me?

Somehow, I doubted it. Just moments ago, I'd thought for certain that he was Beaseldorf's emissary or that he was Beaseldorf himself and that he'd been the one behind all of this. But then the sloth demon had said something about betraying his father and his brother. Did that mean he was on my side? Or did he have his own agenda? I knew I should probably run, but instead, I stayed rooted to the spot, unable to move even if I wanted to as I watched in morbid fascination while he killed that demon too, lobbing its head clean off its body.

Once finished, he twisted the sword a few times, obviously showing off his prowess before sheathing it. Grabbing the leather-bound blade, he angled the hilt toward me. I stared at him, utter disbelief and stupefaction enveloping me. Who the fuck was this guy? Friend? Or foe? I honestly had no idea. But if he was Beaseldorf, why did he save me? And why hadn't the demons simply laid down their weapons, metaphorically since they were, you know, attached to their hands.

When I didn't take the blade right away, he stepped closer, his aura pouring over me. "I believe this belongs to you, Jenna."

I felt so tired, drained, and exhausted, and I knew I bled from far too many places to count. It seemed as though I watched myself from outside my body, and I reached out a shaking hand to take the offered sword. A wash of seductive magic coated me and a moan escaped my lips before I could stop it. Our hands brushed as I took Remus from him. My fingers felt leaden and numb all at the same time, and before I could think or say anything else, my vision darkened at the edges, and the room went black.

CHAPTER 26

I awoke sometime later, a soft surface beneath me and confusion clouding my mind. But that didn't last long as memories crashed into me like a freight train.

Three demons attacking me at the bar and me almost losing my life to them before hot demon guy showed up and—wait a minute—had I fainted?

Jolting upright, I searched for a weapon. Thankfully, Remus lay next to me on my bed and I grabbed him, unsheathing him in a single move. My apartment came into focus around me, and I blinked, trying to push the fog from my brain. How the hell did I get up here?

Hot demon guy, I realized, answering my own question. He must have brought me home after he'd saved my life. Man, I really needed to get his actual name so I could stop calling him that. But why had he done it? Why the hell had he saved me? The memory of just how familiar those demons had been with him slid over my mind.

They'd called him a traitor, I remembered, and my heart thudded in my chest. Awareness shot through me as I scanned my bedroom looking for any sign of him.

But before I could locate him, a deep, smooth voice, seductive as silk on bare skin, filled the room. "How are you feeling?"

My head whipped to the side, locking on his large muscular body as he stepped into focus. He moved as though he hadn't a care in the world and leaned a broad shoulder against my doorframe while he peered into my room, his corded arms crossed over his chest. I jumped off my bed, landing on my feet with Remus raised in a clear threat. Or warning. Either way, I'd strike if he made one wrong move.

Ripples of red-hot lust wafted in from his direction, and I felt the undeniable allure of him despite my best efforts to shove it aside. Heat spread through my body, but a tightness around my head and upper arm distracted me from his usual pull. The strange feeling had me touching them both with my free hand. And as my fingers traced them, I realized that someone had tied bandages around my injuries. I could still feel a slight pound in both of the wounds through their wrappings. Though, compared to the pain they'd elicited earlier, I knew that they were already on the mend. Part of the whole demon hunter gig, though just how little they hurt surprised me.

My gaze never left his as I took stock of my wounds, the sword pointed right at his chest, given our height difference. "What are you still doing here? Who the hell are you and why do you keep showing up all the time to help me?"

He may have saved my life and all, but I couldn't help the suspicion that enveloped me like a cloak. He was a demon. So if he'd ridden in on his black horse to rescue me, I could only assume he had a motive. His own agenda. And I doubted he had something nice planned either. Most likely, he wanted to use me for something. Like fucking over his brother and father, whoever they were and whatever that meant. The demons had mentioned something to that effect, but what did that entail, exactly?

Pushing off from his spot against my doorframe, he prowled closer, but I stepped back, moving toward the fire escape outside my bedroom window. He paused, and sunlight swept over his face, and I got my first really good look at him. Strong jaw, sharp cheekbones, smooth, tanned skin, and those vivid, unwavering eyes. His dark hair was brushed over his brow and he wore a fitted black shirt and a dark-green canvas jacket with dark-wash fitted jeans. To the naked eye, he looked like a normal human, and I still marveled at the impossibility of that fact. If he kept his distance from me, would I have known his true nature? I couldn't be sure, because without the seductive magic that poured out of him like water, he seemed human.

"You were injured," he said, and the intensity in his gaze combined with the pulse of his magic made my head swim. "Those demons weren't the bottom-dwellers you're used to fighting. They're high up in Beaseldorf's ranks, and the sloth demon's effects plus the blood loss from the dozens of times they cut you caused you to lose consciousness. Rather than leave you to bleed out alone on the barroom floor, I decided to help you."

Confusion swallowed me right before it cleared. I knew they'd cut me a lot during that fight, but—

"Bleed out? Dozens of cuts?" I asked, feeling faint again. I pressed a hand to the wall beside me to keep myself steady, daring to look away from him for a moment to scan my bare arms and legs. As I searched my body, I saw zero evidence of those alleged cuts anywhere on my exposed flesh. And as I looked at my body, I realized that someone had changed me out of Roger's clothes and into boxers and a tank top. I didn't bother to dwell on who might have done that, since that was a whole other rabbit hole I had zero interest in going down.

"Yes. If I'd left you there, you would have died. Instead, I healed you and brought you up here to recover. Now, I'll ask again, how are you feeling?" He stepped closer once more, and this time I held my ground. I wanted to see what he would do. Maybe I had a death wish or maybe I just couldn't believe what I was hearing, but I let him approach me.

As he did, I felt the thread of attraction in my belly pull taut, the ache that he always seemed to elicit pulsing at my apex, my center. To distract myself as much as to gain further information, I decided to keep him talking. "Healed me? You know, I wouldn't call wrapping my wounds healing me."

His lips turned up into a smirk that made my knees wobble as he stopped mere inches from me. "I'm not. I wrapped those after I healed you." He lifted his fingers, reaching for my face, and I flinched backward before I could stop myself. His hand dropped to his side before he slid it into his pocket. "I've asked twice how you're feeling, and you've yet to answer me. So, do you mind if I take a look for myself? The deeper slices on your arm and calf and the gash along your forehead will take a little longer to close than the rest, but I want to make sure I got the dosage right."

I narrowed my eyes before ducking my chin, giving him permission for God knew what reason. The tension and attraction that swelled around him made it hard to think straight. And when his fingers brushed over the wrap around my head and his eyes stayed locked on me, everything inside me fucking melted.

I tried to ignore the undeniable draw of him as his intense and unnervingly gorgeous eyes traced every line of my face. Unwinding the bandages with surprising gentleness, he slipped the gauze dotted with dried blood into his back pocket before his fingers traced a line along my temple, the touch featherlight, and his full lips pressed into a stern line, all traces of that sexy as hell smirk gone.

God, I wanted to reach out and touch him. Those full, bitable lips. That powerful, ripped body. Fuuuck. I closed my eyes trying to break whatever spell he put on me whenever we got too close, but I didn't draw away. Not even when his fingers traced over mine, sending electricity skittering through my body as he lifted my arm up so he could tend to that wound as well. I knew that one had cut damn near to the bone, and I worried at what I'd see when he pulled the gauze away. But to my shock, nothing except a bright-pink scar remained.

"Holy shit." I moved my arm, angling it to see the wound better in the sunlight that streamed in from my window. My gaze flew up to his as I realized that even that initial throb had ebbed. "How?"

With his sexy smirk back in place, I tried to ignore the molten heat it scored through me. "Like I said, I healed you. And it looks like I judged the dosage just fine." He leaned closer, the warmth of his honeyed breath brushing over my ear and making me shiver. "I had a hard time making you swallow." His eyes locked me in their hypnotic pull, and I gulped at the insinuation in that last word, squeezing my thighs together to ease the pulse that had formed between them.

My mind went hazy, and I blinked, fighting through the lust so I could ask the question forcing its way to the surface of my thoughts. "So, do you just carry around a magical healing elixir wherever you go? I mean, I heal fast, but not this goddamn fast."

A low chuckle rolled through him, his body still far too close for comfort. Shivers slithered down my spine, and I had to force my legs to stay locked in place when he answered. "The magical elixir, as you called it, is my blood."

Surprise washed through me and I pressed a finger to my mouth, a little icked out, if I were honest. He'd made me drink his blood?

But all thoughts of grossness washed away as my eyes moved back to his. I felt as though I could get lost in them, swim in their depths and never even bother to come up for air. I imagined what kissing him might feel like, his tongue sliding over mine, his teeth nipping at my lips. This man, this demon was far more dangerous than any I'd ever met before. His magic paralyzed his victims with desire, and on some coherent level in my mind, I understood that. Yet I didn't dare break the spell.

"That's disgusting."

The smirk broadened into a devastating smile, and my heart stuttered. "Would you have preferred I left you there to die?"

"No, but maybe a hospital would have been a nice alternative."

The laugh came again, and I realized I would have done anything to hear it, and motherfucker, I needed some air! I needed some space and for him to get the hell away from me so I could think.

"Hospitals take too long, and I need you whole for what comes next, Jenna."

My name wrapped around his tongue like a lover's caress, and I'd had enough. I raised Remus again, though I could admit, I did it a little half-heartedly. "Step back. I can't think when you're this close."

He lifted his hands in surrender, obeying my command. "Really? You're doing better than most."

"What, do the other girls just throw their panties at you and swoon?"

He lifted a shoulder, like perhaps that had happened more than once in his day and a searing slice of jealousy ripped through me. What in the actual fuck? *Demon, Jenna.* He was a demon, and I needed to remember that. Not to mention all the illegitimate children and lovers he'd taken over the course of centuries.

"Well, no one's ever called me disgusting before, so I'd say you're doing fine."

"Not as fine as you might think." I moved to my window, one hand still holding Remus partially extended in his direction as I flipped open the lock and raised the window. Fresh air blew through the room, and my head instantly cleared.

He was a demon, likely father to thousands of demon-spawn, and I needed to remember that. It didn't matter that he'd stepped in and rescued me, that he'd kept Remus away from Beaseldorlf's minions and given him back to me. Or that he had betrayed his brother and father to help me. I could only assume that Beaseldorf was either his father or brother, since he had never bothered to tell me anything about himself. Though none of that mattered, not really, because I still had no idea who he was or why he'd bothered to help me. I still didn't even know if he was actually on my side or just using me.

"You're smart to put space between us. It'll clear your head. You have good instincts."

"Don't patronize me. And don't think I haven't noticed that you haven't answered my questions. So, I'll ask again—who and what the hell are you and why do you keep showing up all the time to help me? And why the hell did you father hundreds of babies spanning back centuries?"

"In my defense, you only asked two of those questions earlier."

I raised Remus higher, and he fought a grin, his amusement irksome. "Don't test me."

"Very well. My name is Khamden. And I'm glad to see you found the blood connection—the demon-born. However, your suspicion about my role in their parentage is inaccurate. That was my brothers' doing. Although, I suppose I can't blame you for thinking it could be me, considering what I am."

"And what are you, exactly?"

"A demon. Which you already knew. You knew that the first night we met."

"No shit. But you're not like any demon I've ever seen before. So, I ask again, what are you?"

"That doesn't matter. You're asking the wrong questions. The right one is the one you've been asking yourself all day. So ask me. I've dealt with my brother's minions, and I have a little time yet before he starts to miss me. It's the only opportunity you're going to get because we're running out of time for niceties."

"So your brother is Beaseldorf?" I asked, already making the connection. But it didn't hurt to be certain. I liked to live assumption free in my business.

He gave me a patient nod.

"That's an unfortunate name, you know," I said, unable to keep my smart mouth at bay. "It doesn't exactly scream supervillain."

His lips twitched in amusement, but his voice remained serious. "Again, in the interest of time, why don't you ask me what it is you want to ask."

I cleared my throat and thought through the myriad of questions I'd had racing through my head all day. After a brief pause, I settled on two. "What does he want with the demon-born and the sword? What is he planning to do that he failed to do twenty-five years ago?"

"And she did her homework. Well done." He applauded then, the sound low and thrumming in my silent apartment.

"Again. Stop patronizing me. I'm missing a piece, a piece that I can't figure out where to get. So I'm asking you. Is that the right question, Khamden?" His name on my lips felt insanely lewd, ridiculously hot, but I didn't dare let him see my reaction to it.

He didn't respond to my rebuke, instead answering me more directly than I could have ever expected. And what he said chilled me to the bone. "He wants to bring forth the First World, the one God splintered from this one when he created it a mere forty years ago. The one where Lucifer, my father, is trapped with his army of demons."

Chapter 27

"What in the ever-loving fuck did you just say? I mean, I know you said words, and yet I have no idea what they mean. Except for the Lucifer and an army of demons thing. I think I've got that covered, but aside from that, I've got nada."

I dropped Remus to my side, completely dumbfounded, unable to work up the brain processing power to unpack whatever the hell he'd just told me. Despite my clear astonishment, his gaze never wavered, the seriousness of it like that of a heart attack. Or perhaps an aneurysm.

"And this isn't a joke, is it? You're not kidding, are you?"

"Not even a little."

My lungs expanded as I sucked in fresh, cold air, easing closer to my window, feeling a little dizzy with shock. All of a sudden, my brain decided to join the party, kicking into high gear as it put together pieces I'd been toying with for days now. "Beaseldorf said he wants to free the demons, but I didn't know what he meant by that. So he wants to help them escape from—"

"Their prison... a place we call the First World."

"Which God, like *the* God, created forty years ago?"

"That's right."

"And you—you're Lucifer's son? The son of the actual devil?"

"One of six, actually."

"Six? There are six of you?" I asked, stunned, my heart picking up its pace beneath my ribs. No wonder he was so strong and different from the others. He wasn't just some demon. He was the fucking mother of all demons—well, not literally—but holy shit. What the hell had I gotten myself into? "And you're sure you're not kidding?"

"Yes, there are six of us. And no, unfortunately, I'm not."

I stared at him for a long moment, unable to believe it. At last, I decided it would be best to focus on the problem at hand, rather than his lineage. Dragging my mind away from that revelation, I forced my mouth to move. "But what do the demon-spawn or demon-born or whatever have to do with that?"

He dragged a hand through his dark hair, his arms flexing beneath his jacket. "That is a long story."

"You said we had time before Beaseldorf came looking for you, didn't you?"

"I also said we were running out of time for niceties. Besides, that's a story better told with a drink in hand."

"Good. Just so happens I stock a full bar in my kitchen. After you, Khamden," I said, gesturing for him to get the hell out of my room. With the window open, I could feel my mind clearing of the sensuality he radiated, but it didn't feel anywhere near clear enough. And with my bed right beside me and him less than three feet away, I couldn't imagine concentrating fully on anything he had to say if we remained there.

Taking the hint, he eased out of my personal space and turned his back on me despite the fact that I held a deadly weapon in my grasp. *Ballsy move, Khamden.* He moved toward my two-seater bistro table, which was nestled into a nook beside my tiny kitchen, and pulled out a seat, watching as I snagged two short glasses and pilfered a bottle of whiskey from the cabinet beside the sink.

Pouring two servings of the liquor, I passed one to him, not bothering to ask what he'd like to drink before I backed away and hopped up on the countertop. My position on my counter gave me a bit more space, and I'd chosen it carefully. I now had all of about four or so feet to work with.

"There, you have a drink in your hand. Now explain."

"The drink's not for me. It's for you." I arched a brow at him and he smirked again. "But I take your point. You want to know how the demon-born fit into this fucked-up jigsaw puzzle, don't you?"

"You're stalling. Why?"

He chuckled and took a sip of his drink, his lips wrapping around the rim of the glass and looking like pure sin. "I'm not. I just haven't had to tell this story before, since every single one of my kind knows it already. Let me make sure I have the right starting point."

I opened my mouth to argue and he lifted a finger, eyes locking on mine in warning. To my eternal mortification, I obeyed him, my teeth clicking together as my mouth closed.

"Alright, I guess we'll start with your question—Lucifer, and my brothers, including Beaseldorf, figured out a way to sire half-human, half-demon children."

"But Roger saw you in his vision when he touched Elias Hunter's sister." Though he'd denied it earlier, I still couldn't get past this one point.

Khamden clicked his tongue in disapproval. "No, you saw my brothers and Lucifer. The family resemblance is... strong. But if you looked close enough, you'd see the differences."

For some reason I didn't dare question, a little pool of relief filled my gut. He hadn't banged thousands of women and fathered just as many children with them. I doubted demons stuck around to deal with their offspring, which meant his brothers and father would have abandoned them and their mothers. The idea that Khamden hadn't done something that brutal and cruel eased the burning sensation that had taken up residence in my stomach since Roger had drawn that image.

"So, you didn't join in? Take part in the fun?"

"No, Jenna. Lust might be my seven deadly, but I have no interest in having sex with humans for the sake of power."

"Power? How did demon-born children equate to power?"

"They share our predilection for... well... you'd call it corruption, and the first generation always has some of our magic. They can influence others, make them revel in whatever sin they received as part of their birthright. And the subsequent generations often find themselves in a position where their sins overcome them. The important thing, though, is that they operate in the physical world, unlike the rest of us. Well, aside from my brothers, our father, and me, at least. As you've noticed, we have physical bodies and incorporeal ones too—a perk of our lineage."

So many questions sprang to mind, and I watched in rapt attention as Khamden took another swallow of liquor, his gaze fixed on the caramel liquid. So, Khamden and Beaseldorf were both sons of Lucifer himself? The son of Satan was literally sitting at my kitchen table, telling me an insane story about demon babies and prisons that held legions of demons, along with the devil himself while I drooled over how damn hot he looked doing it. My life was so fucked. Why did the weirdest shit always seem to happen to me?

Before I could voice any of that aloud, Khamden continued. "Given the demon-borns' natural proclivities, they seized power and started a massive conflict the likes of which humanity had never seen before. A bloody, unimaginably violent brutal war that no one from this world, the Second World, even remembers happening. The demon-born started the dominos falling, and they kept falling until everything fell to ruin around them.

"You see, with Lucifer's presence and the full force of our influence at our disposal, they gave in to their darker instincts. There were countless of them, and they rose to positions of power, allowing themselves to become corrupted before they yielded their humanity entirely. The demons fed on them, and grew ever more powerful, while the demon-born did their bidding without even realizing it."

My throat felt dry, my mouth following suit, and I took a sip of my drink. Everything about this story felt utterly implausible. But I could tell from the look on Khamden's face that he believed every word of it.

"So, to save what remained of humanity, God and His Angels created a dividing line, cutting off the First World and Lucifer along with his demons. Your God created this world, a second dimension and a mirror of the First World before everything had fallen apart, as a safe haven for those lucky enough to stand on the right side of the dividing line. I ended up on the wrong side of that line for my lineage, along with a small legion of demons, and Beaseldorf too. To confine us and keep us in our place, God created a true hell dimension. A second prison for any of us he missed when he sealed the line. One nearly impossible to traverse and make it back topside. He banished us all there, and most of us remain in hell to this day."

Again, I had no idea what to make of what he was telling me. It sounded batshit crazy. Like maybe he was the one in need of a strait-jacket instead of me for a change, and yet somehow I could see him managing to pull that look off. "How could any of that be true? Why would God do that?"

"Because the demon-born destroyed the old world, ruining it beyond repair, and the demons, along with Lucifer's human-hybrid spawn, ran free there. They'd won, and Lucifer had won. He'd corrupted, procreated with, and terrorized the humans until he'd decimated it all. And God doesn't like to lose. So he put us all in our place to save the humans—his favored creations."

"But if the hell He created is impossible to get out of, then how did you get here? And what about the demon-born? What happened to them?" I asked, his explanation still leaving me with just as many questions as answers. Could Beaseldorf really undo God's work? Could he break open this prison world that Khamden described? And what did Remus have to do with any of this? And again, what in the actual fuck?

Khamden continued. "Only the demons strong enough to make it out of hell did. Me, my brother, some of his highest generals in hell. A relative handful of bottom-feeders followed us out too, which are the creatures you've been fighting. The rest of us are smart enough to steer clear of the Nephilim. Or at least, everyone but me, clearly, since I'm sitting here with you, sharing a drink. And as for the demon-born, most got trapped over the line. But they are human too, so they didn't receive the same treatment my kind did. Many linger in this world today, as you've seen."

"Wait, did you say Nephilim?" The word sounded both familiar and foreign, and something about it tugged at me somewhere deep in my psyche.

"Yes, the divine-born humans that the angels sired upon the conception of the Second World. God wasn't going to let our demon-born spawn come to rule again. So he sent down the Archangel Michael, and his best warriors to create their own line of humans born of divine blood. The Nephilim—our precise opposites and our unbreakable enemies—sent on a mission to stop us should things ever go bad again. Your family, among others." He waved that away as though it were nothing and finished his drink. A second later, his eyes locked on mine, and for once, I didn't feel like I might die if he didn't start touching me. All the lust I usually dealt with in his presence had evaporated in favor of utter astonishment.

I opened my mouth and shut it before I slid off the counter with Remus still in hand, trudged over to my couch, and slumped onto it, careful to avoid the bloodstain. I'd need to flip that cushion, I thought idly. Or maybe just burn the couch. "If we're enemies, then why are you helping me? And why would Beaseldorf want a Nephilim sword?" I asked putting that together as my mind struggled to take in so much world-breaking information at once.

Khamden followed me, his powerful strides eating up the distance between the kitchen and living room, limited though that space might be. He settled onto the windowsill right across from me, leaning his perfect ass against it, careful to keep his distance. It seemed he wanted my head clear for this conversation, which was good, because I did too.

"Beaseldorf wants Remus because that sword is special. It belonged to Lucifer when he was an angel. Michael took it from him when he fell from grace and passed it down to his own human descendants. Probably amused him to think of his family killing Lucifer's children with his own blade. Michael has always been a cold bastard. But then, maybe I'm just projecting."

He cut me a devilish grin, and it hit me again that he was the literal son of the devil. My skin crawled at his nearness and I tried not to let the full weight of that sink in just yet because I needed him. He needed to tell me more, so I could help. So I could stop this from happening.

"That sword is powerful, Jenna. Dark and light merged into one, because both good and evil have wielded it. It can bridge the gap between our worlds, and then Lucifer's descendants, their blood, along with the blood of the divine will solidify that bridge. So, in short, yes. He can dissolve the line."

"But why do that at all, if the First World is such a disaster? And what do you mean by the blood of the divine?" I asked, my mouth going dry, and I knew what he was going to say before he said it, at least about the second part.

"As for the first question, he wants to dissolve it because Lucifer is our power source—the energy that keeps all demons flush with our magic. And the longer we're away from him, the weaker we get." Weaker? He overpowered me without even trying, and he was weakened? That did not bode well at all for humanity, if Beaseldorf succeeded.

He pushed off from the wall and strode closer to me. The move reminded me of a wildcat stalking his prey, and I tried not to stiffen as he settled onto the coffee table directly across from me. I tried to remember that he'd helped me and saved my life. Why go through all of that if he meant me harm? But still, I knew what he was. No, *who* he was. He must have a different motivation. Something that I wouldn't like, an agenda all his own.

"And as for the divine blood, that means your blood."

I swallowed hard, my hand tightening on the sword as he leaned forward, settling his forearms on his powerful thighs and bringing us so close to each other I could feel the heat of his body rolling over my skin. I wanted to lean into it, to bask in the scalding hotness of it. But I refrained, forcing my mind to clear through the effects of his magic as much as I possibly could.

"My blood?"

"Yes, your blood completes the ritual. As your mother's would have, along with Remus's magic, all those years ago." I could feel my hands begin to tremble but squeezed my fingers around Remus to stop them. If what he told me was true, and I had no reason to think overwise, I was a Nephilim. A direct descendant of the Archangel Michael—considering that I wielded his blade. What the hell did that even mean for me? How was I supposed to process that? Short answer? I wouldn't. I would focus on the task at hand and deal with that revelation later.

A sudden thought occurred to me as I tried to keep my mind off anything to do with just how close he was to me right then. "Does Tara know all this?"

He gave me a quizzical look. "Yes. But why is that relevant?"

"Because you altered the Cogitato Crypta you gave me. You blocked my ability to see certain demons, certain memories, and I want to know why."

Clasping his hands in front of him, he seemed to weigh his words carefully. "Seeing Beaseldorf would have given you the wrong impression, just like what happened with Roger's reading on Elias's family. And I showed you what you needed to know—"

"No, you showed me what you thought I needed to know. If you'd told me all of this right out of the gate, I could have already found Tara and taken down your brother."

The chastising smirk he offered me made me want to bitch-slap him. "Unlikely. If I'd shown you everything, you and your friends would have just ended up dead. And as you may have noticed, I need you alive."

Anger and frustration burned through my blood, lighting me up from the inside out. "That's bullshit. I did a damn good job keeping myself alive before you showed up."

"You've never faced anything like what we face now."

We glared at each other for a long moment, and I didn't miss the intensity in his gold eyes, the way they seemed to liquify and burn at once. I could tell he meant every word he spoke, and I knew I'd get nowhere with him on this point.

"Let's just agree to disagree and focus on the problem at hand. How do I stop Beaseldorf?" As I waited for his response, I tried to shut out all the insanity, uncertain what to do next. I wasn't sure how I was going to handle all of this earth-shattering information and turn it into a plan to save the world.

"You don't."

My eyes shot open and I jerked my head up to look him in the eyes right before a blast of sensual energy hit me so hard, it left me panting. My fingers relaxed on Remus's hilt without my permission, wetness flooding between my legs, throbbing to the point of painful bliss, and a moan escaped my lips.

"What—what are you doing?" I panted, writhing and trying to fight against the onslaught of pure power he threw at me, but I couldn't breathe through it. He rose to his feet, peering down at me, brows furrowed in what looked oddly like regret as his jaw ticked.

"I really am sorry about this. But you're just going to have to trust me."

Then a needle appeared in his grasp, followed by a prick along the column of my neck, and everything went black.

CHAPTER 28

My head swam as a long, hard body pressed against mine. I moaned when his mouth covered my own, and I ran my fingers through his soft hair and tugged him closer. His tongue slid over the seam of my lips before he parted them, tasting me with a guttural, feral groan. Heat flooded my body and I raked my fingers down an unyielding, muscular back. When I reached the firm curve of his ass, I slipped my hand between us and palmed the bulge in front instead. His erection pressed hard against his jeans, and I wanted to free it, to slip the full length of him inside me and feel that delicious ache and stretch I knew would follow.

But as I worked his buckle, he growled in warning and maneuvered to rest on his knees, putting himself out of my reach. When he peered down at me, I could see his uncanny eyes, smooth as liquid gold, and his dark hair tumbling over his brow. Some distant alarm bells went off in my head, warning me to be afraid. To run. But he pinned my arms to either side of my head with strong hands and commanded in a hoarse whisper, "Don't move."

The promise of pleasure in his voice made all those pesky warning thoughts leave my mind in a rush. The sheer anticipation of what might happen next speared me to the spot, and I did as he ordered. He trailed hot, devastating kisses between my breasts, down my navel, all the way to my jeans. He unzipped them with adept precision and pulled them down along with my silken panties. His gaze found mine again, eyes full of desire and promise, right before he pressed his mouth to my center. His tongue swirled around my clit, causing me to squirm, buck, and cry out in bliss, and when he spoke, the vibration of it over my tender flesh left me panting. "I said don't move."

He went back to licking, sucking, and nibbling softly, taking me ever closer to the shimmering peak of complete abandon I sought. When he pushed two fingers inside me, I erupted and arched on a scream of pleasure. I rode the wave, his fingers pumping and his tongue licking me with such expert precision that it felt like the orgasm might never stop. And I didn't want it to either.

Long before I was ready to give up the high he'd just given me, his voice pulled me from it. *"Jenna."* The word sounded somewhere between a plea, a prayer, and a command. His eyes found mine again and he slid his body over me, pressing against my sensitive flesh and bracketing his hands on either side of my face to focus me. *"I need you to trust me. Can you do that?"*

I shook my head, confusion taking hold. *'What—why—"*

"For what comes next. You must pretend you've never seen me before."

Exquisite pleasure still beat a pulse between my thighs, and a memory, one I couldn't quite grasp, tried to fight its way to surface from the intensity of my lust. I blinked, the world swimming around me, coming in and out of hazy focus.

Wait a minute, this was a dream. Another one of those sexy dreams brought on by—Khamden—the son of the fucking devil himself. That's who held me, his weight pressing over me, his hips between my legs. Oh God, why didn't I hate that? Why didn't I ask him to get the hell off me? Part of me wanted to, and yet I couldn't bring myself to do it. Those arresting, beautiful eyes held me captive like a dove in a cage.

But if this was a dream, then how had he spoken to me? I shook my head to clear it and his palm brushed against my face, thumb skating over my cheekbone as though he found me precious. But that didn't make sense, did it? His swollen lips looked utterly bitable, and I had to force myself to focus on the words he spoke next. *"I can't afford for anything to happen to you, and though you don't realize it yet, you need me, too. You must trust me. Don't say anything to Beaseldorf. He can't guess that you know me or this will end before it starts."*

Without warning, the world around me faded and consciousness came back with a vengeance. My head swam, reminiscent of the aftereffects of too much booze, and I remembered that pinprick along my neck. Khamden had drugged me. But why? My mind grasped at straws, trying to figure out what angle he was playing.

After a few moments of fogginess, my head cleared, a perk of my demon hunter—or maybe Nephilim—abilities. Good Lord, I had a lot of things to unpack, but I decided to put that on hold as my thoughts returned to Khamden and his possible motives.

Why save me, kill his demon allies, tell me all about his demon brother's master plan, attack me, and invade my dreams, begging me to trust him? None of it made sense. And I realized at that moment that all the sexual dreams I'd had over the past few days weren't an accident or a coincidence. He controlled them somehow. He must. But why all the sexy stuff, aside from the obvious fact that he wielded lust as his seven deadly of choice? And why on earth did he think I would ever trust him? He was the literal son of Satan, and he'd just hit me with the full force of his magic, only to drug me the minute I couldn't defend myself.

A scared, female voice broke through the angry, sex and drug induced haze of my mind. "Jenna? Is that you?"

Blinking, I tried to focus my eyes in the dark that surrounded me and turned in the direction of the voice. Rolling onto my stomach, I rose to my knees and swayed a little, confusion muddling my mind as I noticed metal shackles attached to a chain binding my wrists. Maybe I hadn't sobered quite as much as I'd thought. My hands dragged over my body to check for injuries, and I realized he'd put me through yet another wardrobe change. Jeans covered my legs, and a t-shirt clung to my body, along with a thin zippered hoodie and my steel toe boots. Hand to God, if I ever saw Khamden again, I'd punch him in the throat. And call it a hunch, but I had a feeling that would happen sooner rather than later.

Still squinting in the dim light, I saw red hair and a dirt-smudged face. "Tara?" My voice shook as recognition hit me, my stomach hollowing out. I was with the demon-born, chained to the damned floor like an animal. Khamden had brought me to Beaseldorf.

Oh fuck, fuck, fuckity, fuck.

This was not good. What had he said about my blood and its ability to dissolve the line? Beaseldorf needed me to complete his ritual, and Khamden had brought me right to him.

A scraping metal sliding over concrete sounded and Tara's face appeared before me. "Oh my gosh, Jenna, what are you doing here? How did you find me? What happened?"

My gaze raked over her face, doing my best to focus on her eyes, and when I saw them, clear of the telltale coldness of possession, my breath came out in a relieved whoosh. This wasn't exactly how I planned to find her, but that didn't matter. I had found her, and I had no intention of doing whatever it was that Khamden and Beaseldorf wanted from me.

I sank down onto my ass, the remnants of dizziness still plaguing me more than I'd have liked, and she moved to sit at my side. What the hell had Khamden given me, anyway?

"A traitorous asshole of a demon happened," I muttered, surveying her filthy face and clothes, her vibrant hair dulled down with grime. "Are you alright?"

Despite the desperation to rescue her I'd been running on over the past few days, uncertainty filled me. After everything Khamden had told me about the demon-born, it made me wonder, had she succumbed to corruption already, if not total possession? Though, he'd made it sound like they only went evil with the full force of the demons' influence in the First World, and he'd also said they had a human side to them, one I assumed could be nurtured.

In response to my question, Tara nodded, a tear slipping down her cheek. Her eyes flicked to the cuffs at my wrist which matched the ones she wore, and she choked back a pain-filled sob. "It looks like you haven't come here to rescue us."

I held up the shackles in question. "What, you mean these?" I rolled my eyes, feigning a casual glibness I didn't feel. "Don't worry about these. I've got that covered." For the record, I totally didn't, but she didn't need to know that. "They kidnapped the wrong bitch, you got it?"

Tara wiped her nose with the back of her hand. "You do? Have it covered, I mean?"

"Absolutely. I've got this." Fake it till you make it, my favorite mantra, played in my less than coherent mind. Because I had every intention of figuring this out and getting us free.

"Alright, what can I do to help?" Tara may have said she wanted to die rather than face possession and complicity in Beaseldorf's plan. But now that a chance to live had come knocking on her door, I could see her desire to reach out and take it. Hope spread over her features, and I had no idea if I could manage to live up to it. But I would do everything I could to set us all free.

"Who else is here? Is this everyone?" I asked, getting down to business. I gestured at the bodies and drawn faces I could just barely make out lingering along the walls. Despite the dim lighting, my eyesight had adjusted, making it easier to peer into the near-dark. Though, I could by no means make out the finer details of their features. Only the broad strokes of bodies and the dingy warehouse where they kept us.

High ceilings, aisled racking, and a metallic roof made the general ambience of the building a dead giveaway. Boxes, empty pallets, and crates were stacked around the majority of the space and a low clink issued from the roof above. The cool concrete beneath my knees stung when I crawled a little farther back toward the other demon-born. As I did, their faces came into focus and I confirmed that none of them had been possessed either. Not yet at least. Thank God.

The twenty-four other men and women inside the drafty, damp-smelling warehouse turned hopeful eyes on me, having apparently overheard my conversation with my client.

"This is everyone that I've seen," Tara said. "Though we haven't spoken much. They don't allow it."

Before I could say anything else, a garage-style dock door rolled upward, and a bright light streamed inside the dank building. Two men walked in, their faces obscured by shadow from the light streaming in behind them. When they stepped inside, they closed the door and fluorescent lights flickered to life overhead.

They hummed before they fully turned on, the brightness causing me to blink and refocus my vision yet again. When I did, I clenched my teeth at who I saw standing before me. Khamden. Then I turned my head as I saw someone who was damn near his replica at his side, only not. I balked, startled despite myself. He'd said that Beaseldorf bore a strong family resemblance to him, but despite Roger's drawing, I still hadn't expected it to be quite so exact.

The demon whom I could only assume was Beaseldorf had the same tall stature, the same lithe, muscular body, and the same gold eyes with dark hair as Khamden. Only, where Khamden's face was ruggedly handsome and a seductive kind of perfection, Beaseldorf's was cruelly stunning. Sharper and harsher, more polished than rugged. His skin was a creamy white as opposed to the bronzed tan that Khamden boasted. If I'd seen them separate, I didn't know if I would have been able to tell them apart. But with him standing beside Khamden, I could see the differences clearly enough.

When both of their eyes fixed on me, I swallowed, my mouth drying in an instant. A combination of terror and rage swam through me. The anger built to an immediate crescendo in my blood that seemed unhinged, almost a living thing, as it coiled through me. I wanted to gnash my teeth and snarl with the sheer wrath igniting in my veins as realization hit me.

Just as lust was Khamden's weapon to wield, wrath must be Beaseldorf's power. That had to be the reason that I'd noticed an uptick in both their kind in recent months—wrath demons and incubi. We always had more than our fair share of supernatural entities in Santa Sombra, but lately? I'd been fighting more demons than I could keep up with. Now I knew why. They'd been drawn to their masters.

Beaseldorf's cruel, beautiful smile tilted one side of his mouth upward as his focus landed on me. "The infamous Jenna Torrence fails where her mother did not. Celia would be so disappointed to see you now—caught like a rat in a cage." He held Remus up in front of his face and closed his eyes as though savoring the moment. Then he unsheathed the blade, the golden hue of Remus's warning alighting his face further.

Anger pulsed within me and I tried to harness it. Despite how furious his words made me, he had a point. I had failed. Self-loathing and hatred flared hot and bright, every shade of anger pulsing within me. "Go fuck yourself, Beaseldorf."

"Nice powers of deduction. At least your mother would be pleased to know you're not a total imbecile." He stalked closer to me and I tried not to glare at Khamden, who stood back, looking disinterested. And I debated whether or not I should out him to his brother. But if I did, then I risked the possibility of losing my only ally, if I could even call him that. Despite my raging desire to watch Beaseldorf behead the lusty asshole, I kept my mouth shut. Something about the way he'd pleaded with me in my dream and the way his eyes had bored into mine made me bite my tongue.

So, instead of focusing on him, I leveled a glare on Beaseldorf, whose brutal smile never wavered as he surveyed me. "Celia Bellator's daughter. Your blood sacrifice will make a fitting end to her tragic story." He turned back to look at his brother as my stomach churned with fury, his three-piece navy-blue suit fitted perfectly to his body. Khamden still wore the same canvas jacket and jeans from earlier, looking like the polar opposite of his brother. "Brother, you've done well bringing her to me."

Khamden inclined his head in acknowledgement of the compliment. "Thank you, B." His eyes slid to me and I slammed my mouth shut to keep from screaming at him. I didn't know if it was Beaseldorf's power that caused so much anger to boil like a raging torrent inside me or if I legitimately wanted to kill Khamden. Maybe a little of both, since he'd been the one to serve me up to my enemy. Khamden continued as though oblivious of my loathing glare. "Unfortunately, she killed Levianne, Khalune, and Istris before I could subdue her. I knew you preferred her alive or else I'd have killed her myself."

The lie surprised me, and I fought with every ounce of self-control I possessed not to let that shock show on my face. Was he on my side? Did he want the same thing I did? I had no idea, and I somehow doubted we aligned on every single point of our goals. However, at the moment, I didn't have a choice but to ride it out and wait for my opportunity.

"I said alive, but I never mentioned uninjured. Bloody and weakened would have been preferable," Beaseldorf observed, eyeing his brother. Khamden inclined his head in a show of deference. I guess that explained the near-stabbing the demons had almost given me before Khamden had killed them. My mouth dried out as I realized again just how close I'd come to getting skewered and brought here like a lamb to the slaughter, helpless to stop it.

Khamden's eyes found mine, his expression blank. "There's nothing to stop you from cutting her now." And then again, perhaps he did not have my best interest at heart. I didn't react, keeping my face blank as the fury in my blood heated it to an almost painful level.

Beaseldorf surveyed me, stepping closer to the hoard of kidnapped, chained people as he approached me. He prowled, as though a predator, his grace both unnerving and marvelous. As he drew near, I could feel the force of his power assaulting my senses. It clouded my mind, threatened to overtake me, and I bared my teeth at him. "Ah, you feel it, then? The wrath boiling your blood?" He grinned at me, as though he relished the knowledge of how much his power affected me.

I jerked against my chains, lunging for him so that I could claw his face to ribbons with my bare hands. I came within inches from his cheeks when my bindings went taut with a loud clang, snapping me backward with the force of my momentum. They'd given me a long leash, but still a leash nonetheless. The bolts in the concrete groaned as I strained against them, struggling to wrap my fingers around his neck, drag my nails down his face, drive my knee into his balls. I didn't care what, as long as I could inflict pain on him. He chuckled, actually fucking chuckled at me. "I see she's more susceptible to our power than most Nephilim. She hasn't been trained, has she?"

"No, brother, she hasn't."

He gave a curt nod, Remus still tight in his grip. "Good." Without warning, Beaseldorf swung, slicing the blade in a long arc. It cut through my skin like butter, starting at my arm before he dragged it down my stomach and stopped at the top of my thigh. I gasped, the shock of pain stealing the breath straight from my lungs.

My eyes widened in total astonishment before I dropped to my knees, gaze fixing on Khamden's face for just the briefest moment. The only reaction from him? A slight flex of his jaw. Burning pain lanced through me, and I could feel blood, warm and viscous sliding down my skin, soaking through my clothes.

"That's better," Beaseldorf purred in a voice like warm whiskey. He walked away, and I struggled to slow my galloping heart rate, to calm down as the anger dissipated with his withdrawal. "Call it payback for your bitch of a mother."

I heard a clanging and a shuffle across the concrete, and I turned my head to see Tara crawling toward me, her bound hands outstretched. "Jenna!"

I shook my head at her in warning and she froze, not daring to move another inch. I didn't need her comfort. The jagged slice would heal soon enough. It wasn't deep enough to kill, only wound, and I didn't need her drawing undo attention to herself. At least not yet.

Khamden turned his back on me like I didn't matter in the least to him and dropped a companionable arm around his brother's shoulders. "Feel better?"

"Much," Beaseldorf replied, craning his head from side to side to crack his neck. I tried not to let the sting of betrayal burn me along with the cut of the blade. I'd known that Khamden likely had an ulterior motive. It seemed I'd been right before and he had been playing me, keeping me compliant, and making me ripe for the slaughter.

After all, why wouldn't he have just let me in on his plan before he drugged me and brought me here? Dread and hopelessness crawled through me as I sank from my knees to my butt on the cold concrete, feeling weak and exhausted. A hopeless, terrifying thought hit me, and I knew without a shadow of a doubt that I had no way to get out of this.

I would die here.

Darkness clouded my vision, and I slumped onto my side. The cuts had to be deep, despite knowing they wouldn't kill me. They would be deadly for a regular human, but not someone like me.

Still, I could feel the blood leaving my system, pulsing out of me with every heartbeat and pooling onto the concrete floor. I trailed my fingers over my ruined skin and took comfort in knowing that the blade hadn't nicked any arteries or damaged anything critical. But that didn't mean I wasn't injured badly. Unable to take the agony any longer, I closed my eyes, felt my head rush with dizziness, and swallowed hard as the blackness enveloped me.

CHAPTER 29

My eyes fluttered open, and I awoke in complete darkness. Night enveloped me, the steady inhale and exhale of rhythmic breathing along with a chorus of soft snores cluing me in nicely.

Crickets chirped outside the metallic walls of my prison, their muted sounds barely audible as I shifted, trying to sit upright. My head swam with dizziness and my throat felt like it was made of flypaper. I swallowed hard, attempting to moisten my mouth and lips before gritting my teeth and forcing my body upright. The resulting clang of my chains caused some of the sleeping forms, the demon-born who remained captive with me, to stir.

A voice, soft and low whispered next to me. "Don't be afraid."

Recognizing who that voice belonged to, I startled, feet kicking out as I scrambled back and away from it.

From him.

The chains rattled again and I heard groans of frustration from the sleeping forms around me, followed by more shuffling and snoring as they settled back into their slumber.

I dropped my voice low, putting distance between me and the other sleeping prisoners. "What are you doing here? Did you come to gloat? Feel like stopping by to enjoy my misery?"

Khamden let out a long, hoarse sigh, and he sounded... exhausted. I blinked hard, trying to adjust my vision to the depth of the darkness around me, and when it finally decided to cooperate, I could just make out the outline of his body and the shape of his face. He sat next to me, his back pressed against the wall beside me, so close that his power should have been doing a number on my senses. I felt nothing, though. No bone-deep desire, no arousal, no lust.

He sat with his knees drawn up, forearms resting atop them, and he shook his head. "I can see why you'd think that. But you're wrong. I take no pleasure in your pain."

My accusing glare bored into the side of his face, wishing I could set him on fire with the intensity of my loathing alone. "Could have fooled me. You let him cut me. No, correction, you told him to cut me."

Anger spiked within me, followed by useless betrayal that made me hate myself, if only a little. Why should I waste that emotion for a demon—for the son of the devil? Without thinking, I dragged my fingers along the worst of the wound, along my shoulder and side. Only, I felt nothing but the raised puckering of freshly healed wounds. I healed fast, I knew, but I'd never healed that fast before.

"Beaseldorf would have done it anyway. And I made the mistake of bringing you to him uninjured. I couldn't let him think I cared."

"Do you? Care, I mean?" The words left my lips before I could even think them through, and I felt like a complete idiot for even bothering to ask. Why did it matter if he cared about me? That question was wholly fucking irrelevant. But before he answered, a wash of arousal tugged up from the depths of my center, pooling into my belly. I sighed in annoyance, trying to fight through it. I wasn't sure if it was something he could control or not, but it infuriated me all the same. He was the last person I wanted to feel any sort of warm feelings toward at that moment. Well, maybe the second to last person considering Beaseldorf was still breathing.

Rather than answer my question, he shrugged. "I knew you'd heal fast enough. My blood still lingers in your system. Add in your heritage, and I figured you'd make it through just fine. Seems I was right."

I shifted, holding my chains to keep from making any additional sound. He'd calculated correctly. The wounds had closed, and all that remained as evidence of the gash was the dried blood that soaked through my ruined t-shirt. And the scar, but even that would fade in time.

My teeth clenched, my anger still hot enough to scald, but we were getting nowhere with this conversation. I decided to change the subject to something more useful. My neck felt stiff from disuse and I rolled my head around to loosen it. "How long have I been out, and where are we anyway?"

From what Gaby had told me, we didn't have much time left and any time spent unconscious could waste the precious moments I had left to prevent Beaseldorf from ruining the world. It had been daytime, afternoon most likely, when Beaseldorf sliced into me, and now it was nighttime, so I knew at least several hours had passed.

"A little more than twenty-four hours. And you're at the port in West Santa Sombra."

I rubbed my face with my bound hands as dread slithered through me. Twenty-four hours? I'd been unconscious for an entire day? Which meant I'd slept away my last opportunity to plan an escape because today was January twenty-ninth, the day the last ritual had occurred twenty-five years ago.

"That's not good," I groaned, pulling my knees to my chest and dropping my head to them. Helplessness filled me and I felt the sting of inevitability pull at me. The only shred of hope I had rested in our location. Somehow and for some reason, he'd kept us in Santa Sombra, close enough to Gaby and Roger that maybe, just maybe they could find me. But what would they do about it once they did?

No, I had to take care of this. I couldn't let them get involved because if they did, they'd have to face Beaseldorf. And as highly as I thought of my friends, I knew they were no match for him.

"Can you do anything about these chains? Help me escape? We need to find a way to stop him, and I can't do that locked up in here."

"No."

His denial felt like a slap in the face. "No about the chains? Or—"

"No to all of it."

I bristled, frustration, hopelessness, and anger mixing with the latent lust in my system. "Why the hell are you even here, if you're not going to help me?"

"I am helping you. It's like I told you before. You need to trust me." His words echoed in my mind, and I thought about the dream, about his mouth between my legs and another question pushed to the surface, my anger rising once more. Thank God for that.

"So, you were in that dream with me? It wasn't just my imagination or something?"

He ducked his chin in acknowledgment, turning his gaze to face me fully. "Yes."

"What's with all the sex? You went down on me and I didn't exactly give you my permission. It's one thing to sneak into my head for a chat and it's another to—to—"

"Give you an orgasm that shook the foundations of your soul? To make you scream so loud with pleasure that you ripped your throat apart doing it?"

"I didn't—"

"To ruin you for all other men who come after me?"

Heat flooded my body at the seductive hotness of his words and also at the sheer humiliation they brought me. "I didn't give you my consent to do any of that."

He tsk'd me, the sound sexier than it had any right to be. "I don't control what we do together in your dreams, Jenna. You do. So if I ended up on my knees, worshipping your body like a fucking temple with my tongue, then that's where you wanted me."

Warmth raced over my cheeks, his words making me shiver with... what? Anticipation? If I wasn't mistaken, I saw lust fill his eyes as he seemed to remember exactly what my dream had entailed. Did he enjoy what he'd seen? Or did he just enjoy taunting me with it? "If you don't control them, then how the hell did you speak to me?"

"The blood connection. It forged the moment I healed you in the bar. It'll wear off soon enough. For now, it gives me direct access to your mind and your thoughts. A convenient way to communicate, given our circumstances. But I don't control you." A smirk slid over his lips that made my traitorous heart flutter. "I can't help it if you wanted me somewhere specific—"

"Shut up. Don't say another word. You know what your power does to people. It's hardly my fault that you go throwing it around like a drunk girl does her virtue on spring break."

He chuckled, the sound causing more grumbles from those sleeping nearby and he quieted.

Another thought occurred to me. "Why are you here? If you can just pop into my mind for coffee and a chat anytime you feel like it, why bother coming at all?"

"Just wanted to see for myself that you're alright."

"Aww, worried about me?" I didn't bother to hide my sarcasm.

He snorted a laugh, keeping the sound lower that time, and a wave of lust rolled off him. I gasped, clenching my hands into fists, fighting through it. "Can you please stop doing that?"

I refocused on him and he shrugged. "I am who I am. If you don't want to feel my power, then learn to block me out. Only someone like you can—only the Nephilim."

"I can?"

He lifted a shoulder. "If anyone had bothered to train you, sure."

"Do you know how?"

He arched a perfect brow at me. "Maybe, but why would I give up my advantage?"

"You're such an—"

"Asshole? Yeah, I got that."

A moment passed where I glared at him and he smirked at me, and then I let out a grumble of frustration. "I know you think you're helping me, but you're not. So why don't you just go?"

A long breath exhaled from his lips and he dragged a hand down his face. "Like I said, I am helping you, just not in the way you want. Look, I doubt this will mean anything to you, given your low opinion of my kind, but you have my word that when the time is right, we will stop my brother. Together."

I tried to read his tone for any sign of falsehood, any indication that he was bullshitting me. But even I had to admit, I could find nothing. "And when will that be?"

"Once the ritual is complete."

I heard the rustle of his clothes shifting and watched as he reached toward me. Long smooth, but calloused fingers traced a path over my arm, down my stomach, and to my thigh. I sucked in a breath, his body so close to mine I could feel the hum of desire that pulsed off him in waves. When he spoke, his voice was soft, regretful. "I'm sorry he hurt you, and I'm sorry I had to let him." He rose to his feet and peered down at me, eyes full of what I could have sworn was turmoil and regret, along with a scorching intensity I couldn't place. "I promise, he'll pay for it."

My heart seemed to stutter in my chest as my breath caught in my throat, and I couldn't understand why. He was a demon. Evil to the core, wasn't he? Why would he bother to feel any regret over what had happened to me or promise retribution for it? I grabbed my chains and rose with him, careful to stay as quiet as possible. He didn't move an inch, and I reached for him, hand gripping his arm, the muscles firm and corded beneath my fingertips. I didn't want him to leave, not until I said my piece.

"But if we wait until the ritual is complete—"

He cupped my cheek and brushed his thumb over my lips, the touch feather-soft, and painfully tender. "Rest, Jenna. I can't afford to linger any longer. All you need to know is that I gave you my word, and I intend to keep it." He turned, striding away from me, leaving nothing but cool, dank air in his wake.

As I settled back into a sitting position on the cold, hard ground, I knew I had no choice but to trust him. I would just have to hope that the Khamden who'd visited me tonight was the real one and not the one who'd allowed his brother to slice me damn near in two and smiled about it afterward.

CHAPTER 30

A loud clattering had me jolting, my body stiff and cold with discomfort. After Khamden's departure earlier that morning, sleep had evaded me. I'd spent the remainder of the wee hours, along with the next day, running through everything I'd learned over the past several days, trying to figure a way out of this situation.

They fed us sparingly and provided just enough water to keep us alive, and I wanted to scream in frustration because despite my best efforts, I couldn't think of anything I could do to stop what came next. I arrived at one inescapable, unappealing conclusion. I'd just have to put a heavy dose of very reluctant trust in Khamden's word.

With that thought in mind, I jerked my head in the direction of the ruckus, which I quickly realized was the raising of the dock door. Startled whispers and cries chimed around me, the demon-born awakening from their slumber. Tara scooted closer to me, her eyes bleary with sleep as vivid floodlights from outside poured into the warehouse, casting those who'd opened the door in shadow. The sun had set a few hours earlier, and though I knew I needed to rest, I couldn't because I knew they'd come for us before midnight. Whatever would happen next, happened tonight.

"Good morning, my sons and daughters!" a voice I recognized as Beaseldorf's shouted, echoing off the high, metallic ceilings and making my ears ring. "Today is the day you fulfill your life's purpose! Your destiny!" My teeth clenched. Man, I wished he'd shut up and die already. But a random heart attack would probably be too much to ask for.

The fluorescents flickered on above us, bathing the room in harsh white light, and after a few seconds of furious blinking, I could see clearly. Beaseldorf stood at the head of a grouping of wrath demons. Dozens flanked him, including Khamden, whose eyes remained fixed on anything and anyone other than me.

I rose to my feet and caught Tara's gaze. She shook her head, reaching for my hand to try and pull me back down, but I didn't let her take it. Beaseldorf's attention whipped in my direction as I stood before him, ready to die on my feet. The rest of his prisoners cowered behind me, curled into terrified balls, hoping he wouldn't notice them. In response to my defiance, he flashed me his signature cruel smile, exposing too-white teeth. I hated how handsome he was, but then I remembered that Lucifer had been the most beautiful angel of them all. It shouldn't surprise me that his offspring would be gorgeous too.

"What purpose?" I asked, playing dumb, trying to maintain Khamden's cover just in case he actually happened to keep his word. Though

I wouldn't hold my breath on that, I refused to let myself give up on all hope just yet.

Beaseldorf prowled forward, the click of his well-shined shoes on the ground an ominous boom in the otherwise silent space. Anger, rageful and bitter, built with every step closer he took, and I tried to breathe through it. But by the time he stopped in front of me, I nearly vibrated with unspent fury. A soft scent of too-ripe fruit seemed to waft off him, and my nose puckered of its own accord. "I see you're looking well today, Ms. Torrence." His eyes trailed down the jagged slice of scar still visible beneath my ripped t-shirt and jeans.

"No thanks to you," I muttered, not sure why I felt the compelling need to run my mouth when he'd cut me down just a day earlier. Apparently, I would never learn. "You said it was time to fulfill their life's purpose. So then, what purpose are they going to fulfill?"

He rubbed a hand over his smooth jaw in thought. "You know. I did warn you to stop looking for Tara and that she belonged to me now. Only, I didn't realize who you were then. It wasn't until Khamden hunted you down and told me about your lineage that I fully appreciated my luck."

Those words landed like a physical blow and took everything in me not to balk in reaction. Khamden had told Beaseldorf about my heritage? About my connection to the sword and my mother? He hadn't just brought me here at Beaseldorf's order, but he'd been the reason Beaseldorf had even known to bother abducting me in the first place. Loathing combined with a useless kind of betrayal flooded my veins and I clenched my fingers into fists, refusing to look at Khamden.

It took everything inside me to school my expression, my reaction. I forced my jagged breaths into submission with more effort than I cared to admit. And rather than give in to my bitter anger at Khamden, I forced myself to focus all of it on Beaseldorf. I couldn't afford to lose my head and start swinging at the lust demon who plagued my dreams—my only possible ally in this death trap of a situation. Emphasis on the *possible* part.

I tried to remind myself that I'd known all along that Khamden had his own agenda and that he didn't have my best interest at heart. He was a fucking demon, and I didn't need to trust his every move. But I did need to bide my time before I made any rash decisions that could end up having deadly consequences for us both.

Beaseldorf watched me, as though gauging my reaction, clearly hoping that his magic might elicit some sort of unhinged response from me.

But I just stared him down, figuring it was about time I gave him a chance for a villain monologue. Villains really did love that shit. "You said I couldn't stop what was already in motion that day, during our location spell. What did you mean? What's the big reason you brought me here?"

"Ah, yes, well, may as well fill you in on the plan since you're a guest of honor. You see, Ms. Torrence, I created every last one of the humans you see before you. A little piece of me, my lineage, resides within them. They're the demon-born. And I'm going to use them and you, the blood sacrifice, to destroy the line, bring back the First World, and free my father."

"Your father? The First World? What the hell are you talking about?" I asked, feigning confusion. The fear, though? That I didn't have to fake.

He t'sked. "Celia has left you so untrained and so terribly uneducated. I guess it couldn't be helped since she's dead." He waved a hand as though her death didn't matter in the least, but pain lanced through my heart at his words. I may never have known her, but his callous declaration confirmed that she had died that day. I wanted to kill him in retribution for it. To cut him limb from limb.

But I couldn't, the chains weighing heavy on my hands as he continued. "The First World, the real world, where my father, Lucifer the Prince of Darkness, is trapped." I heard a hushed whisper rush through the people who surrounded me, and I turned toward them, spotting Elias easily among them. He sat cowering in the corner, rocking back and forth and my heart squeezed. Beaseldorf was going to kill all of them, and they'd done nothing to deserve it aside from being born with demonic blood. I had to stop him. I couldn't just let this all happen. "You see, not only is he my father, he's our power source. Without him, we weaken every day."

"Aw, B, you say that like it's a bad thing," I said, recalling the nickname I'd heard Khamden use the day before and saying it in my most smart-ass voice. Beaseldorf's hand snapped out so fast I didn't even register the slap until my cheek began to burn.

"Best keep your mouth shut, bitch," he snarled, leaning closer. His breath fanned across my face, smelling like rotted fruit, and I tried not to cringe backward. My cheek stung and the rage his presence caused within me grew damn near uncontrollable. But before I could snap and snarl with unbidden fury, he stepped away, heading back toward his demon entourage.

I took a deep breath, my senses clearing and my emotions stabilizing with the distance he put between us.

"All you need to know, Ms. Torrence, is that unlike twenty-five years ago, this time I have everything I need to succeed. No substitutions, no Hail Marys, as they say. So, let the festivities begin."

That horrific smile spread over his lips once more and he snapped his fingers. Wind immediately whipped through the building, twisting through my hair and shoving me forward. Only the shove, that wasn't wind. Instead, I felt someone press against my back and turned to see Tara there and realized she'd bumped into me.

"What's happening?" she yelled, her voice barely audible above the roar of the gusting wind.

"I don't know!"

That was when the screaming started.

My head whipped to the side, and I peered beyond her, my mouth dropping open. I watched in horror as the wrath demons surrounding Khamden and Beaseldorf dissolved, transforming into thick orbs filled with smoke.

Without warning, they lurched forward, moving so fast I could barely track them. The orbs smacked into the demon-borns' chests. Those who got hit fell to the ground, convulsing with such violence I thought their limbs and spines might break. The rest ran, screaming in terror as they pulled against their chains, desperate to escape. I grabbed Tara's hand and tugged her toward me before dropping to my knees, yanking as hard as I could on the bolted eye that secured her chains to the floor.

"Hurry!" she yelled, dropping down beside me and helping me pull. We had to get her out of there, but neither the bolts nor the chains would budge. More bodies hit the ground, and soon the sounds of grunts and convulsions overwhelmed the screaming. I looked at Tara and our eyes locked as bone-deep terror permeated every line of her face.

"Don't let them have me—" Then the smoke hit her.

She jolted, falling backward, and I lunged forward to catch her just before she hit the ground. She started shaking as a smoky aura flooded her body, swirling around her and through her. "Shit! Tara! No!"

After what felt like hours but couldn't have been more than seconds, she went still in my arms, her eyes flying open. Her gaze fixed on me and an eerie smile spread across her lips. "Mmm, it feels so good to be in a body again."

And I knew what lay burrowed beneath her pale, lovely skin. The demon inside her rose to her feet, grinning wider. Her bonds fell away, the chains unlinking of their own accord, and I jerked my head around, realizing all at once how silent the room had become. All of the demon-born stood around me, the smoky aura and cold stare of possession rolling off them in stifling waves.

Sheer panic filled me and I struggled to take in air, my throat constricting. I'd fought demons before, but I'd never faced anything like this. I remembered how I'd gotten my ass kicked by just three of the higher-up demons and how only Khamden's interference had saved me. What did I expect to do against him, Beaseldorf, and twenty-five possessed demon-born?

Cold dread coated my throat and I tried not to let panic overcome me. It didn't help that I'd been missing for over a day, which meant that Gaby and Roger would be looking for me. It was completely within the realm of possibility that they'd walk right into this situation, and I could only hope that they didn't find me. That I'd turn into just another missing person in the sea of people who went missing every year.

Only, I knew that wouldn't be possible. The world would end first, and everyone would know something had gone very wrong. Or at least the world as we knew it would end, and the First World would come back with a vengeance. I struggled through the panic, forcing my lungs to take in air and reminded myself that I would fight until the bitter end. With that knowledge, an eerie stillness settled over me—the calm before the battle. A sensation I knew all too well.

I would go down swinging, if it was the last thing I did, and I would start right now. I stepped forward, but before I could act on my newfound resolve, Khamden's deep, smoky voice filled my mind, and I struggled not to startle. *"Don't react. Now isn't the time."* I hesitated, stopping for a moment, my whole body shaking with adrenaline. *"I'll tell you when. You need to trust me."*

He spoke the words directly into my mind, and it took everything inside me not to flick my stare in his direction. Instead, I kept it leveled on Beaseldorf, whose smug and victorious expression filled me with more hatred than I'd ever imagined possible.

"Get out of my head."

"I will soon enough. For now, just remember, I gave you my word."

"You're a fucking traitor and a demon, how the hell am I supposed to trust anything that comes out of your mouth?"

"Yes, I am a traitor, but not your traitor." His eyes met mine for a fraction of a moment, and I saw something in them—a burning hatred that mirrored my own—and I hesitated. *"If you try to fight now, you'll lose, and I won't help you."*

"Coward."

He looked away from me, the only sign of emotion a tick of his jaw. *"Think what you want, Jenna. But trust me when I say, the world can't afford for us to lose."*

His words reverberated in my mind and I wanted to snarl at him, to ignore him and fight like I wanted to, but I refrained. And when I held my ground rather than coming out swinging, I could feel his presence withdraw from my mind, leaving a small void in its wake. Maybe I'd gone crazy, but for some reason I couldn't pinpoint, something deep down kept telling me to trust him. I could only hope that my gut didn't get me killed, as it had almost done so many times before.

CHAPTER 31

Beaseldorf hauled me to my feet and gripped my upper arm, his fingers biting into my flesh hard enough to bruise. He yanked, ripping my chains from the concrete as though they were made of papier mache. Wrapping the links of metal around his free hand, he let go of my arm and gave them a tug. I stumbled forward, the strength of his pull on my bound hands making me lose my balance for a moment before I could right myself.

He didn't bother waiting, though, and pulled me forward like a fucking dog on a leash. Everything in me rebelled against that idea and I tried to dig my heels in to stop him, but he jerked at the chains again, forcing me forward.

Losing my balance again, I fell into him and he caught me with rough hands, as though that had been his intention. He leaned down, his breath hot on my ear, and it took every ounce of willpower I had not to cringe. "You know, I think I'm going to enjoy watching you suffer. Watching you die." The light of insanity and evil in his eyes was on full display. I bared my teeth at him and he laughed, stepping back and taking my leash with him. "Now walk."

He kept my leash in his hands as I walked ahead of him, whipping my back with the metal chains anytime I hesitated, making me hiss in pain. The possessed demon-born filed in behind us and the door to the warehouse rolled shut as we stepped into the cool night air. The sun had set, and the rain had stopped, complete darkness, aside from the bright lights of the port, surrounding us. He continued to force me to move forward and I tried the best I could to stay vigilant as we maneuvered around crates and containers toward the water's edge.

We stopped when we reached a small clearing near the dock, and I looked at the concrete beneath my feet and saw a black-painted symbol under them. I smelled iron and rot and knew without having to ask that the symbol had been painted in blood, but not of the human variety. It looked vaguely familiar, almost like the substance Roger had vomited onto the ceiling at A Witch's Whimsy. As I looked around me, I could see the scene clearly—the marking from Tara's memory and so many others coated the ground like an omen. Everything had come to fruition all at once, with me helpless to stop it.

It was happening right now, and Khamden had begged me to wait. But wait for what? For the First World to come crashing into ours? For Beaseldorf to set Lucifer and his legions of demons free? I was out of time, and I knew it. The tentative trust I'd given him thus far had run out. Even though my gut screamed at me to wait, I couldn't do that. I couldn't give a demon my full trust. Not now, not ever. So Khamden be damned, I had to act and hope I didn't fuck up.

Without warning, I pulled hard on my chains, catching Beaseldorf off guard. As he stumbled closer, I jabbed an elbow into his stomach before I flung my head back to hit him in the face. He sputtered, eyes watering, and I leaped, twisting around and landing on his back. I stretched my chains across his throat and squeezed. The other demons rushed forward to stop me, but Beaseldorf halted them with a raised hand. Concern registered just before he grabbed my wrists. He yanked hard, snapping the chains before he tossed me over his back.

I hit the concrete with an agonizing crack, my head smacking against it, and I gasped for air. He knelt down and slammed his fist into my face. I heard as much as I felt the crunch and my eyes watered. But rather than stop, I swept out my leg, catching him at the knee. He went down with me and I wrapped my thighs around his neck this time, squeezing. He pressed his palms to either knee and pushed out, meeting resistance as I tightened my hold, impressing even myself at my ability to keep him pinned. He growled, gripping my ankle in both hands, preparing to break it, and I let him go, rolling free. He couldn't do the ritual without me. The thought pulsed in my brain with reckless abandon as I landed in a crouch, then sprang to my feet.

If I could just get to the water, I could hide beneath its black surface and the docks jutting out into the delta. I didn't need to win, I just needed to get free. To keep him from finishing the ritual, but before I could take three steps in that direction, a hand curled into my hair and yanked hard. I ricocheted backward, crying out in pain despite myself, and landed on the ground by Beaseldorf's feet. He dropped a knee to my chest and I felt a rib crack beneath his weight. I gasped in pure agony as he wrapped his fingers around my throat. “Fight, and I’ll make this even more painful for you, Ms. Torrence.” He pressed harder and another rib cracked. I cried out, swinging with my hands, trying to rake his face with my nails to no avail. His skin felt like iron beneath my pathetic attempts to claw him.

A hand appeared on his shoulder just as black dots danced in my vision, my breath completely cut off, and Khamden’s voice filled the space between us. “Brother, we need to finish the ritual when the moon is at its apex. It’s time. I’ll manage her.”

Beaseldorf stared down at me, his cruel gaze enjoying every moment of my suffering, and then he moved, his weight lifting from my chest and his hand leaving my throat. I coughed, winced, and tried not to groan in agony. Every breath I took caused sharp shots of anguish to rocket through me, and I wondered if I’d just lost my only chance at saving our world as we knew it.

“Very well then, get her up and hold her,” Beaseldorf replied, his air of command unmistakable. He peered down at me with utter disdain and I sucked in precious air before Khamden wrapped a hand around my arm and pulled me to my feet. His touch was far gentler than I expected, though he made a show of wrapping an arm around my neck to hold me and pressing my body against his chest. Every movement, every rough tug and shove caused sharp, brutal pain to slice through my body. I did everything I could to push through it, to stay conscious and alert. I’d had my ass kicked enough times to know how to compartmentalize physical pain, and I used every ounce of my concentration to do that now.

Beaseldorf turned his back to us, moving toward the water and spreading his arms wide, as though welcoming a large crowd.

"I told you you'd lose."

"Fuck you."

His chest rumbled behind me, and I didn't know if he growled in irritation or laughed at my expense. *"We must wait until the ritual starts. It's the only way to rid ourselves of him. I'll tell you when it's time to fight."*

"He's so much stronger than me." The thought slipped out before I could stop it, and hopelessness crashed through me right as the shame did too. I couldn't beat him. Not in a million years. Not hand-to-hand, at least.

"Don't worry, I've got that covered."

Before I could ask what the hell he meant by that, Beaseldorf's voice rose above the one in my head. "Welcome, everyone!" He lifted his arms at his sides and twirled around like a demented showman, his shining, dark hair blowing in the wind, black suit blending with the night. I questioned who the hell he was talking to, but I didn't have to wonder for long.

As though summoned by his greeting, demons, the usual bottom-dwellers I fought, materialized from the shadows. They drifted closer on insubstantial legs, scampering up the containers to stand atop them. They hadn't bothered with their human masks, and I didn't see only wrath demons in their ranks either.

The demons of all seven deadlies had come for the show, and my stomach lurched as I surveyed the growing crowd forming around us. Elongated nails scraped against metal crates, hisses and snarls as well as gurgling rumbles filled the air around us. The resulting sounds made me wince as dozens of them poured in, ready to watch Beaseldorf's fucked-up ritual.

I'd never seen so many demons in one place and my neck prickled with sweat. I could take on a lot of the bottom-dwellers, I knew, but dozens? Along with higher-level demons and Beaseldorf himself? The odds didn't seem all that great, despite my usual delusions of grandeur. I didn't think I had a real chance of winning, not with how outnumbered we were and not with the steady beat of pain throbbing from my injuries. But that didn't mean I wouldn't give it my best damn shot. That I wouldn't die trying.

Beaseldorf waited until they all found a place on the containers or surrounding the clearing where the demon-born and I stood among the blood symbols. "Today is the day we've anticipated for nearly fifty years. Today is the day we free my father! The day we bring back the First World, where we ruled and roamed free. Powerful and strong as any Nephilim and stronger than any human!"

Shrieking roars filled the air, demonstrating the excitement they all felt at the prospect of reuniting with Lucifer himself. At bringing back a world that had died long ago to everyone on our side of the line. A world that had never truly happened, according to everyone I knew and loved. Gaby and Roger flashed through my mind, Luke and Bud, too. What would happen to them when the First World came crashing into ours? Would they survive? My eyes burned, and I had to force back the worry that flowed through my limbs like water. They would make it. They had to. Even if I didn't.

Khamden moved, tugging my back tighter against his chest, his hand covering my mouth, and I felt the urge to bite his palm. *"Don't even think about it. Now, drink."*

My brows furrowed in confusion right before I registered the warm sticky liquid that coated my lips. It smelled of iron and honeydew, sweet and acrid at the same time—his blood. I cringed, shaking my head. *"Absolutely not."*

"Do you want to have the strength you need to defeat my brother?"

"What does drinking your blood have to do with that?" I could all but feel the impatience rolling off him, but I wouldn't open my mouth until he explained why I should.

"My blood enhances both healing and strength, temporarily. Your last dose was too long ago, and if we have any shot at stopping this, you must drink." Horror filled me at the prospect of lapping his blood off his palm like a deranged mosquito, and I hesitated. Beaseldorf still droned on in the background, but my attention was wholly fixed on Khamden with his body flush to mine and his blood soaking my lips. *"If you want to live, you'll do as I ask. I can feel how bad your ribs and nose hurt through our connection. And like I said, you can't defeat him without my help."*

"You can feel my pain?" I asked, incredulous.

"That's beside the point, Jenna. We're wasting time. Now drink."

I cringed but opened my mouth and did as he asked. Nose pinched in disgust, I sucked the blood from his palm, wondering if I'd lost my mind. But when the warm liquid hit my tongue, it tasted sweet. No, correction, it tasted like pure sex. I groaned, sucking harder, my hands trailing up to grip his wrist and hold him steady. I all but moaned into his touch before he wrenched it from me, spinning me around and grabbing me by the nape of the neck, looking for all the world like a reprimand. *"That's enough. Now lick your lips before someone sees."*

I obeyed, and his eyes traced every movement of my tongue over my lips as though inspecting me for any lapse of cleanliness. And perhaps looking for something else too, but the brief moment of heat I saw in his gaze cleared as he gave me a quick nod. Apparently passing muster, he tugged me forward, pulling me into the center of the clearing, as the demon-born surrounded us formed a loose circle within the blood-painted markings.

I could feel the crack in my rib already beginning to heal, the throbbing lump on my head and the ache in my nose all but gone, too. I healed fast enough on my own, and I couldn't help but wonder, given the effects of his blood, how fast Khamden must heal.

Beaseldorf's voice shifted then, and his words flowed out in an unusual cadence I didn't recognize, drawing my attention to him. As I listened, I realized it was the same strange language Roger had spoken during his reading of Remus. It was all guttural grunts and twisted syllables. Khamden's hand came down on my shoulder to hold me in place. *"Don't move. We need to wait until the first part of the ritual is complete and the line begins to dissolve. Trust me. The instant it does, we attack."*

"But if the line starts to dissolve, won't we be out of time?" I hated that he only fed me bits and pieces of his plan, and yet he expected me to just trust him. How could I be effective when he only told me fragments of what I needed to know?

"No, we won't run out of time, and I feel your anger at being kept in the dark. I wish I could have divulged more, but I needed your fear to feel real.

Beaseldorf isn't easily fooled, and we will only get one shot at defeating him. And as long as you stay alive, the line will stay at least partially intact. So, don't die. Got it?"

"Easier said than done," I thought-grumbled, looking at all the demon minions surrounding us—dozens of them, correction, hundreds. I thought about Gaby and Roger again and felt nothing but relief that they hadn't found me and that they didn't have to witness this insanity. I could only hope that they stayed as far away from the ritual as possible.

Beaseldorf raised Remus, and I heard a low rumble of thunder as he unsheathed the blade, the sword seeming to roar with displeasure, its bright golden light nearly blinding despite the port's floodlights surrounding us.

He tossed Remus to the nearest possessed demon-born, and recognition hit me—Elias Hunter. With no hesitation whatsoever, he took the blade and slid it across his own throat. Blood spurted from the wound and I cried out in horror. "No! What are you doing?"

But I could do nothing to stop the inevitable as Elias slumped forward, his body hitting the ground with a dull thud and his blood draining all around him, all over those damned symbols. The next demon-born picked up the sword and followed suit. Around and around it went, my world spinning out of control.

"Stop! You have to make them stop!" I shouted, fighting against Khamden's unbreakable hold as they all repeated the horrible ritual. This must have been what happened the first time, the mass suicide with the strange circumstances. But why kill them all twenty-five years ago if they didn't have my mom? Didn't have Remus? Revenge? Rage?

No, my thoughts crystalized as I recalled Beaseldorf's words from just a few moments ago. He'd tried it without Remus, perhaps using another sword, a substitute, and had failed.

I struggled against Khamden's grip, trying to make the death happening all around me stop. I begged him in my mind to do something for them as the sword got closer and closer to Tara, the last one in the circle.

When her hands grasped the hilt, I tried to surge forward and wrench out of Khamden's grip. But he wrapped his arms around my waist, grunting with the effort as he held me firm. I kicked and bucked, snarling and screaming as I watched the blade slide across Tara's pale throat. Her gaze fixed on mine and I could see her human soul, which still resided beneath the demon, shine through her widened eyes. She coughed, blood pouring from her wound causing her to choke. A confused expression crossed her lovely features right before she slumped to her knees and fell to the ground.

Chapter 32

"No!" I screamed. "You bastard! No! Tara!" She'd been my charge, my client, and I'd let her down. I hadn't kept her safe as I'd promised the first night we met. Tears pooled in my eyes and I sank my teeth into Khamden's wrist and he hissed, letting go.

I charged forward without thinking of the danger and dropped to my knees before her, gathering her into my arms. Her body shook, jerky movements that told me death would claim her soon. Her blood soaked my jeans, but I didn't care. I wanted her to know that she wasn't alone. That she didn't have to die alone. Her eyes locked on mine and I could see the despair give way to a moment of relief as a calm stillness overcame her, and I could tell that her soul had left her body. She was gone.

Tears flowed down my cheeks as I realized that Khamden had lied. He knew that she would die, that they all would die, and he'd told me to trust him. To wait. Somewhere in the dim recesses of my mind, I could hear him talking to me. *"We couldn't save them, Jenna. I thought of every angle. No matter what you or I did, they were always going to die. You need to let go and focus now. I can't do what comes next without you."*

I felt his hands on me again, his rough touch hauling me to my feet. As Tara's blood soaked into the symbols, into the pavement, the ground beneath our feet began to rumble and quake. Khamden grabbed Remus by his hilt, moving him out of the way as the pavement cracked and fell away, a yawning hole appearing in the middle of the port.

I staggered backward, Khamden's arm around my waist, pulling me with him, and an explosion of white light erupted from the depthless crater. It hummed, spread, and pulsed, shooting hundreds of feet up into the sky. I gaped at the sight as I saw movement within it. Dark shadows, no, outlines of bodies moving toward us, and I knew on instinct that they were demons from the First World.

Beaseldorf yelled, the triumph in his voice unmistakable. "It's time to bring home back! Khamden, kill her! Kill her for our father! Kill her to bring the First World into this one! One world, full of demons, where we can roam free, our power unmatched!" I didn't miss the gleaming excitement in Beaseldorf's eyes as Khamden held Remus's shining blade to my throat for the briefest moment before letting go and stepping beside me.

Everything seemed to slow around us as Khamden's voice rang out, filled with conviction and power. "No."

The word reverberated through the clearing, despite the deafening hum of the light, the dividing line to the First World.

Confusion flashed over Beaseldorf's features right before realization clicked into place. "You'd betray me, brother? You'd betray our father?" He seemed to pulse with rage, his power billowing around him in a depthless black wave. The pure strength of it took my breath away.

I gasped in reaction as Khamden raised Remus, pointing him at Beaseldorf. "Are you really surprised, brother? This is what we were bred to do, after all."

A roar ripped from Beaseldorf's lips as he surged forward. He grabbed one of his nearby demon henchmen and ripped the long claw from its finger. It shrieked, the sound piercing and shrill as it dropped to its knees, screaming in agony. Beaseldorf gripped the severed nail with two hands and charged his brother.

Khamden moved, angling his body toward me ever so slightly. Seconds seemed to slow as a long blade slid from his sleeve and he gripped it in his free hand before he handed it to me. *"It's time. Take the blade and fight for all your worth. The demons can't come through the other side yet. Not until your blood is spent. But you can send demons that are in our world over the line to the First World. Push them over it as fast as you can. Don't waste time killing them if you get overrun."*

I gripped the sword he offered, a katana—my weapon of choice—and spun just as Khamden raised Remus to block Beaseldorf's blow. I had no time to spare before the rest of the demons descended upon us. Rage filled their terrifying faces as they hurtled toward me.

They scrabbled off the shipping containers, charging for me with bloodcurdling screams, ready to tear me limb from limb. I sliced through them with reckless abandon, moving faster than I ever imagined possible, and I knew I had Khamden's blood to thank for that.

My body felt stronger and totally at one with the sword I held as I cut through one after the other, and I wondered how Khamden had known about my preference for katanas.

I did my best to avoid any swordlike nails or the long claws and sharp teeth of the other types of demons who swarmed me. I parried and dodged, slicing and kicking, shoving them through the white light to the other side. The light hummed, buzzed, and flickered as they crossed into the First World, and I knew Khamden had told me the truth. Once through, they couldn't return.

At least not yet. I spared a glance in his direction and saw that he and Beaseldorf still fought. The speed and grace of their battle was unlike anything I'd ever witnessed before. They moved like dancers, violent ones who aimed to kill, but their movements were beautiful just the same. I tore my gaze away as more demons charged me. I fought harder than I ever had before, never letting my stride break, never stopping my movement as I ran, bobbed, weaved, and rolled. Feeling my body begin to tire, I wished for one of Gaby's spelled guns. Sweat dripped down my back, sliding in rivulets down my spine, and my breaths came in heavy pants, but the demons kept coming.

More than I'd ever seen before. More than I ever thought existed. It seemed they'd emptied hell of them, though I knew that couldn't be true. They had clearly expected victory, and I knew, deep down, that it could still happen if they managed to kill me. Just then I heard a crack of gunfire and I spun to see a demon, poised to stab me in the back with its deadly nail, go limp, the fiery ground absorbing him.

I spared a glance at the source of the sound and saw Gaby and Roger standing at the edge of the pier. They had weapons strapped to every part of their body, having unloaded our full arsenal from what I could see. And that arsenal was nothing to sneeze at. Fear and relief pooled through me as they started firing at will, dropping demons as they vaulted over the shipping containers, thinning the herd, giving me a chance to fight my way out. I couldn't believe they'd found me, that they'd come. I did my best to quell the fear I had for their safety, and I kept on fighting. We needed all the help we could get, and stopping what Beaseldorf had done here today mattered more than any one of our lives. I knew it, and I could only imagine that they did too, judging by the glowing ominous spectacle on full display in the sky.

They ran toward me and I cleared the path for them as they fired, gunning down as many demons as I cut down. When they reached me, they skidded to a halt and pressed their backs to mine, all of us covering each other. "What the hell are you guys doing here?" I shouted, stabbing a demon through the heart as Gaby shot one through the head.

"Saving your ass! You'd think that was obvious," Roger sniped, firing his gun with far more precision than I would have expected him capable of.

"How did you find me?"

"Cliff came through. This dock was where they all committed suicide last time. They withheld it in the article to protect the owner's privacy!" Gaby bellowed a warrior's cry, kicking out and gunning down another. She held out her hand and grunted with effort as a pulse of power streamed from her outstretched palm. A wave of demons fell back as though hit by an invisible forcefield, stunning them and giving us a moment to breathe and aim.

Before I had time to be shocked at the display of sheer power from her, she continued. "When we didn't hear from you, we went to The Office. We found bloodstains on the floor and more of them in your apartment. So once Cliff told us the location, and we confirmed that something big was going down here again, we tore apart my abuela's grimoire for useful spells, emptied our arsenal for weapons, and came as fast as we could. It took longer to prepare than we wanted, but it looks like we made it just in time!"

I cut down another demon, slicing my blade through its chest before tossing it over the line. "Thank you! For coming for me."

"We couldn't let you save the world alone. I ain't no biggity bitch," Roger yelled, dropping his magazine and reloading in one smooth move. Apparently, he'd been holding out on us.

"What he said!" Gaby shouted, releasing another pulse of power.

Warmth flooded me and I resisted the inappropriate urge to grin as I spun, blocking another blow from a gluttony demon, its gnashing teeth mere inches from my throat. After cutting through the top of his head, I caught sight of Khamden, who didn't seem to be making any real headway against Beaseldorf, and I knew what I had to do. I turned to Gaby and Roger, voice carrying above the mayhem. "Keep them back! If you can't kill them, push them through the white light! They can't come back through it!"

We'd already killed dozens, maybe even hundreds of the low-level demon hoard, and though they kept coming, they'd thinned now. But that didn't matter. They wouldn't stop, I knew, until we killed Beaseldorf and closed the line. I could only hope Gaby and Roger would be enough to hold them back, to keep them at bay while I went to fight the real threat. The leader of it all.

I rolled, dodging the razor-sharp claws of a sloth demon and the fang-tipped tongue of an incubus before taking off at a dead sprint toward the fight at the edge of the water. As I neared, I could hear Khamden growl, Remus singing as he whipped him through the air at breakneck speed. Beaseldorf blocked him easier than I'd have liked with his own makeshift blade. I jumped forward, swinging my katana down in a deadly arc, using every bit of my amplified strength.

Surprised, Beaseldorf barely had time to react, blocking the strike as we both went down to one knee from the force of it. Khamden didn't hesitate, slicing Remus across Beaseldorf's chest. Dark blood seeped from the wound and Beaseldorf roared, rising to his feet. But we didn't stop, each of us attacking with our full strength and speed.

To his credit, Beaseldorf blocked, parried, and struck, handling the two of us better than I imagined possible, and I realized that he was the stronger brother. That was why Khamden had needed me, needed the advantage of surprise. I continued fighting, the song of battle in my blood ringing through my ears. My calling, my purpose was clear in my mind. And no wonder, I was Nephilim. We were born enemies, and I'd been bred to kill demons.

I dropped to my knees and sliced my katana across Beaseldorf's thigh. He roared and lunged for me, his rage getting the better of him as he tackled me to the ground and drove his blade down toward my throat. I raised mine just in time to block it, fully aware that my death would erase the line we had to hold, and the two worlds would collide.

So I fought harder than I ever had before, pushing up as he pushed down, attempting to cut my throat. Or maybe even cut off my head, but I didn't want to think about that. I couldn't. I had to live. As the pressure increased, I removed one hand from the hilt of my sword and gripped the tip of the blade to stop his advance, the razor-sharp edge cutting into my flesh so deep, stars erupted behind my eyes. Through the haze of my agony, I watched as Khamden moved over us, and Remus's golden blade slid through Beaseldorf's back, the tip of it cutting out of his chest. Beaseldorf's hand relaxed for just a moment and I hit the makeshift blade out of it, sending it skittering to the side with a screeching thunk.

Beaseldorf sank down to his knees beside me, sputtering in confusion, his face white with shock as more bloody ooze seeped out of his chest. Then he was moving, Khamden hauling him up and into his arms as though Beaseldorf weighed nothing. "Stand up, Jenna. I know you're hurt, but I have to throw him over the line to stop the ritual. And you need to protect yourself while I do it!"

Without waiting to see if I obeyed, he bolted toward the light and I looked down at where I'd landed. The outer edges of the symbols that the ground hadn't swallowed pulsed beneath my palms. The blood from my wounded hand mixed with the blood drawn symbols, and staticky magic buzzed over my skin before my injury knit shut. Fuck.

On instinct, I jerked my head toward the light, noticing how the edges of it flickered before it expanded and alarm bells sounded in my mind. Suddenly, the light became a vacuum pulling everything toward it. Pushing to my feet, I looked toward the place where I'd left Gaby and Roger to fend for themselves, heart racing with fear. Their eyes were fixed on the light too, each beginning to stumble toward it. As though realizing what was happening, they spun on their heels and ran like hell away from it and toward the protection of the shipping containers behind them.

I breathed a sigh of relief that they hadn't been caught in its orbit as Khamden flew by them, running straight for the First World. His speed was unnatural, unearthly as he carried his brother. Shadows began to seep in from the other side of the line, crossing back over before disappearing, and I felt sick.

Demons were escaping back into our world or crossing into it for the first time. It was hard to know for certain. I rose to my feet and ran toward Khamden, unsure what I planned to do, but something in my gut told me it wasn't over yet.

As Khamden approached the line, the suction built. I could feel it pulling me in, as though trying to suck the world around us into its prison. Shipping containers creaked and groaned under the pressure, the crane swinging and leaning in the air above us, and Khamden stopped abruptly. He reared back, ready to throw his brother over into the First World. But before he could manage it, Beaseldorf lifted his hand and plunged a dagger into Khamden's chest.

"No!" I screamed, skidding forward in a controlled slide, hurrying to get to him.

I heard Beaseldorf shout, "If I'm going back to another prison, then you're coming with me, brother!"

Khamden roared in pain and fury, throwing Beaseldorf across the line, but before he could cross the threshold, Beaseldorf caught Khamden's shirt in his fist and held fast. I could see Khamden shake with the effort to remain on our side of the dividing line, reaching back and falling to the ground before his fingers clasped around a curb stop.

Khamden's muscles flexed, straining against his jacket in the effort to hold on. Beaseldorf's grip slipped, and he slid a few feet down Khamden's body before he caught his leg. The suction pulled them both toward the light, the intensity of it growing stronger with each passing second. I bolted toward them, skidding, trying to keep my footing as I ran. I just needed to separate them. Needed to get Beaseldorf over to the other side of the line and this would be over. Or at least, that's what Khamden had told me just moments before. I could only hope he was right.

More demons swarmed into our world, but they didn't seem keen to stick around for the party. They disappeared as quickly as they came and I didn't have time to wonder why. I could hear Khamden shouting in my head with his eyes locked on mine. *"Get back! Don't come here! It'll pull you over."*

"Like hell I'll get back!" My heart pounded in my chest, and I had no idea why it mattered so much to me that I got to him. He was a fucking demon. But the voice in my head, the same one in my gut, told me I had to stop Beaseldorf from dragging Khamden down with him. And I always listened to the voice in my gut, no matter how unreliable Gaby always claimed it was.

I took one last running skid and raised my knee as I jumped, crashing through Beaseldorf's hand and breaking his grip on Khamden's leg. His beautiful, unholy face gazed at me in utter shock as he flew back and crossed over the line. Only, the vacuum-like suction didn't stop right away and I started to slide.

Oh shit!

I was going in with him.

I dropped to my belly and dug my nails into the gravelly asphalt beneath me. But I kept sliding, the First World still trying to claim me. Fear washed through me, making my stomach lurch, right before a strong hand locked around my wrist.

I looked up into Khamden's eyes, his fingers wound tight around my arm.

Blood oozed down the wound in his chest—correction, his shoulder—and he looked pained. The insistent pull of the line dragged at me, but as he stared at me with those liquid gold eyes, I knew he wouldn't let go. He wouldn't let me fall into that terrible place full of demons and death.

At last a bright pulse of light burst from the ground, as though Beaseldorf's sacrifice had been the very thing needed to end the ritual, to stop it in its tracks. The suction stopped as suddenly as it had started and I let out a startled breath. Wind whipped around us, the bright light of the line still glowing in the darkness.

I gasped as Khamden's grip tightened and he pulled me to my feet with him. He wrapped his arms around me, holding me against his body as strong gusts of wind blew through my tangled hair and ruined clothing. He didn't loosen his grip as the dividing line roared in my ears, a beast defeated. The ground beneath us quaked and I would have stumbled, but Khamden's arms held me steady, not giving an inch. I turned my head, my cheek pressed against his chest, and watched in absolute amazement as the concrete reformed and the light shrank slowly until it at last winked out.

CHAPTER 33

My breathing heaved, my cheek still pressed to Khamden's chest, my eyes squeezed shut now. I could feel a hand in my hair and another on my waist and I tried not to shudder. Instead, I forced myself to release my hold on the terror and the bloodlust and everything else I'd felt throughout the battle. Khamden didn't move an inch as he held me flush to his body, almost like he was shielding me from the force of everything that had happened, and I didn't fight it. Truth was, I didn't want to.

He hadn't lied to me, at least not completely. And loath as I was to admit it, he'd been right. At the end of the day, he'd proven I could trust him. We'd saved the whole damn world, and had saved each other in the process too, and I couldn't help but wonder why? Why would a demon do that? Why would he want to keep the world as it was, and not go back to the way it had been when his kind had ruled it? To get back to his full strength? To see his father again?

As though sensing my questions through the blood link, he answered me. Pulling back, he brushed my hair aside and leaned close to whisper in my ear. "I have my reasons."

The answer sent a shiver down my spine and made me wonder if I shouldn't have just let his brother pull him over that line. If maybe the world wouldn't have been better off if he'd gone too. He pulled back to look at me, trailing a thumb across my cheek. A smile crept across his perfect, handsome face and I felt that familiar sense of lust and desire pool in my belly. "Don't worry, Jenna, like I told you before. You're not in any danger from me."

"And why don't I believe you?" He laughed, the sound throaty and growing familiar, given all the time we'd spent together lately. Before he could answer further, I heard Gaby shouting, and I turned to find her. Seeing her a second later, I stepped out of his arms and yelled back.

"Gaby! Over here!" I waved my arms, and relief flooded me as I saw Roger hurry out from behind a shipping container, hot on her heels. They hadn't been hurt, or at least not badly enough that they couldn't stand or walk. And more importantly, they hadn't gotten pulled over the line. They ran toward me, and my heart squeezed a little, happy to see them alive and grateful as all hell that they'd come for me.

I turned back to Khamden, ready to say something to him, but he was gone. I tried not to let the disappointment I felt show, and I wondered if I'd ever see him again. Before I had a chance to dwell on it further, Gaby tackle-hugged me to the ground and Roger piled on top of us. She kissed my cheek, tears streaming down her face, and I noticed that

Roger was touching me too. Apparently, my dark shit didn't matter at that moment. It was good to feel loved and appreciated, and I soaked it in. My two besties had come for me. It meant more than they could ever imagine.

"I can't believe you guys came. That you found me and you came," I said, shoving them off me because I needed to do frivolous things, like breathe.

Gaby's mouth gaped open in shock. "Of course we did. I told you, my witchy feelings were on high alert. I didn't know why, but I knew we couldn't lose. And that meant I couldn't leave you to face it alone. You needed us."

She was right. If they hadn't been there to fend off the demons, I could never have helped Khamden take down Beaseldorf. From the looks of them, they'd ditched their weapons behind the shipping crate, and I knew that meant that we didn't have to worry about more demons. Otherwise, they'd never have left them behind. It seemed the ones who'd poured back through to our side of the dividing line had vanished, at least for now. Another problem for another day.

Roger's eyes darted back to the place where the line had disappeared, and he grimaced. "What was that anyway? The bright light with all the creepy shadows blasting out of it?"

"How about I tell you about it over a very large, very stiff drink?"

They agreed as the wail of sirens sounded in the background. We exchanged knowing glances. The cops would arrive on the scene before we knew it. How could they not after the giant beam of light in the sky and apparent earthquake? I looked around, checking for evidence of what might have occurred there, but found little.

It seemed that the dividing line had sucked through the bodies of the demon-born, and the demons themselves had either fled, been trapped over the line, or sent back to hell. The only evidence that remained were the strange symbols written in Beaseldorf's black blood, and the large, dried puddles of blood from Tara and the others like her who'd been sacrificed. Thinking about her elicited a pang of guilt and remorse. In the end, I couldn't save her, nor had I been able to save Elias Hunter. I thought of their families, of the futures Beaseldorf had robbed them of, and a ball of angst formed in my belly.

The cops would tie the blood back to the missing people, that much I felt certain of. What would Bethany and her husband say when they found out that Tara hadn't been crazy? That something terrible had happened to her. What about Sarah and Marie, Elias's sister and mother? Their grief would know no bounds. They'd likely feel some level of responsibility, for not believing their family members when they'd had the chance.

But before I could let the familiar feelings of failure and sorrow paralyze me, Gaby grabbed my hand and pulled me away from the growing sound of the police sirens. "We've gotta get out of here. Unless you want to spend the rest of the night in a holding cell, getting questioned by cops."

I gave the port one last scan, checking for any sign of Remus and Khamden. But I saw nothing. With a frown of disappointment, I noticed Roger sprinting over to a nearby shipping crate, picking up their discarded weapons, and hurrying back to us.

Gaby and I turned as Roger reached us and I bent down, sweeping up the katana—no way I was letting this baby go. Once we'd collected everything incriminating, we put on a burst of speed and ran between shipping containers and cranes, over to where I could only hope that Gaby's car was parked. Because otherwise, things were about to get real awkward real quick with the cops.

We hurried into a second parking lot as the squeals of stopping police cars sounded from the dock we'd just abandoned. I spared a glance over my shoulder and saw Luke step out of an undercover cop car, Bud on the opposite side of it. Luke had his gun drawn and his muscular arms flexed with tension. His head turned toward us just before we darted behind the warehouse at the far end of the dock and he disappeared from view. I felt another pang of guilt, knowing that he'd never have any real answers about Tara's disappearance. It wasn't like I could tell him everything that had happened. Not that he'd believe me even if I did.

As we hurried, I saw Gaby's car parked in the lot opposite from where the cops had come from and I thanked the Lord for small blessings. She unlocked it with her remote and we all jumped inside, Roger in back, Gaby in the driver's seat, and me in the passenger seat. She fired up the engine and punched the car into reverse, steering us out of the lot as quickly and quietly as she could manage. We hopped the curb and turned onto the main drag, making it a mere ten feet before the cops turned a corner and blew past us on the other side of the street.

I watched them in the side-view mirror, praying that they wouldn't flip a bitch in the middle of the road and detain us, because getting caught with our nigh arsenal of weapons sounded like a bad end to the week.

But they kept driving, peeling out in the parking lot, as we turned onto Del Rio Street and headed toward the freeway. When we merged onto Eastbound 70, heading toward downtown and no cops followed, I knew we were home free.

"Holy shit," Roger breathed in the back seat. "My heart is pounding like a jackrabbit in heat." He let out dramatic breath and Gaby and I exchanged amused glances. Glad to know the world nearly ending hadn't affected his good humor. He leaned forward so that his striking face popped out between our seats. "Did we just save the world? We totally just saved the world, didn't we?"

I let out a low chuckle, my heart tumbling from adrenaline. "Yep, we sure did." In a sudden rush, I could feel Khamden's presence in my head, a niggle in the back of my mind reminding me that we hadn't done it alone. Something told me that I hadn't seen the last of him. My skin heated and my chest fluttered as I considered the possibility of coming face-to-face with him again, and I didn't know how I felt about that.

Gaby held out her hand for a fist bump, and all thoughts of Khamden, along with his presence, left me. "We are badass motherfuckers, am I right?" She grinned from ear to ear, and my lips curled too. We didn't leave her hanging, and I made sure to explode my fist because, deep down, I liked that shit.

She, of course, didn't know about what happened to Tara. How could she? Tara's body had disappeared when the line had formed. I'd tell her later, and we'd probably cry together. But I wanted us to have this moment of joy and triumph before I went and ruined it.

"You know, it feels wrong that we aren't getting paid for our services, doesn't it? I mean, saving the world should be worth something, right?" Roger asked, leaning back against the cushions as we took the exit for 17th Street.

I looked down at the sword on my lap and smiled just a little wider. "Well, I did get paid a dollar." Then I wrapped my fingers around the hilt of the fine, deadly sharp blade. "And as you may remember, mama did need a new katana."

Epilogue

Khamden

I sat at the bar in the historic Oscuridad Hotel in downtown Santa Sombra and ordered a whiskey on the rocks. After swirling the liquid in the glass, I sipped it thoughtfully, peering out the window as I watched the people pass by, umbrellas open against the rain. I'd managed to stop the merging of the two worlds, but I hadn't been quite as successful as I would have liked.

My power, stronger than I'd felt in decades, radiated around me, and I couldn't help but notice the women at the bar and restaurant casting furtive glances in my direction. It didn't interest me, because lately, my interests remained fixed on one particular woman.

The only one I couldn't have.

Why did I feel so drawn to her? What about her made me lose control? Made me want to kiss and lick and taste every inch of her delicious body, and not just in her dreams? I already knew the answer to that, and it was far more complicated than I cared to admit.

My magic didn't just affect her, it soaked through her, and she reveled in it in a way that made me burn with need whenever I was in her presence. And her lust? It tasted more divine than any I'd ever encountered. Tart, sweet, and fucking intoxicating. That mixed with her sharp tongue and her reckless bravery, and I found myself intrigued.

For the hundredth time since that day she'd fought at my side, I'd asked myself why she'd bothered to intervene on my behalf. Beaseldorf would have taken me over that line if she hadn't forced him over it instead and almost sacrificed herself to save me. I was a demon, the son of Lucifer, and yet she'd put herself at risk to keep me here. So why did she do it?

The idea of surprising her in that bar she worked in to ask her that very question flowed through my mind again. But that would be a terrible idea.

Fucking hell, I needed to get a grip. If that interaction went anything like how I imagined it, and the other Nephilim found out, I'd end up getting her killed.

Getting us both killed.

She didn't understand the full depth of our world, having only operated on the outskirts of it her whole life. Nor did she understand the consequences of fraternizing with the enemy.

But I did.

As though summoned by my darkest thoughts, someone entered the bar and a familiar presence washed over me. A presence I hadn't felt anywhere close to me in an age, at least until that night when the dividing line had almost fallen. I let out a long, resigned sigh.

No, things had definitely not gone according to plan.

Power rippled over me as he sat down beside me, feeding my own magic and filling it to the brim. "Vodka martini, two olives." His low voice rumbled through me and the bartender immediately began making the order. She looked between the two of us, apparently unable to keep her gaze away, and set the finished drink on the bar.

She shook her head, a shy grin pulling at her full lips. "I'm sorry to stare, I just can't believe the similarities. You two look so much alike. Are you twins?"

"No," the being next to me said, draping his arm over my shoulders and squeezing, the threat in the gesture clear. "Actually, this is my son."

The End

Other Books by Loryn

For the Love of Series

- For the Love of Demons and Katanas (Book 1)
- For the Love of Witches and Whiskey (Book 2)
- For the Love of Angels and Mayhem (Book 3, ETA Fall 2026)
- For the Love of Satan and Stilettos (Book 4, Coming soon)

Diary of a Deity – A complete romantasy adventure series

- The Burning (Book 1)
- The Rising (Book 2)
- The Darkening (Book 3)

- The Dawning (Book 4)
- Prefer it all in one? Get the omnibus (ebook) instead: Diary of a Deity: The Complete Saga: Books 1,2,3,4

Want to Keep in Touch?

The story doesn't end here. Join Loryn's newsletter and get a FREE short story in the For the Love of world that explains why Luke finds Jenna so dang suspicious. You'll also receive a look into Loryn's Diary of a Deity universe, with a free short story and an insider's world guide:

https://lorynmoore.com/contact-loryn/

A Quick Note About Reviews

Reviews are never expected, but always appreciated. For indie authors like me, your words help others discover our stories. If you feel moved to leave a review, please know it means the world to me.

Acknowledgements

Jenna's story has been a long time in the making. I've had the near-final draft of For the Love of Demons and Katanas on my computer for years now, and I'm so happy I finally got to share her book with the world! Without further delay, I want to take a moment to show my gratitude for everyone who made this book possible.

First, I want to thank my husband who supported me and put up with me when I just needed those days to write and edit. Thank you, babe!

As always, thank you to my amazing plotting buddy and friend, Leoneh Charmell. Your feedback and keen sense for plot are invaluable and more appreciated than you could possibly know! Also, thank you so much for the gorgeous cover art for this book that is near and dear to both of our hearts!

Thank you to Kimberly Dawn for a thorough and speedy line edit and proofread! I appreciate your attention to detail and enthusiasm for the story.

Thank you to my sons, who inspire me to be more and do more. I hope to make you both proud.

And last but certainly not least, to everyone who continues to support my journey as an author, thank you. You guys make the late nights and writing frenzies worthwhile. Without you, none of this would be possible.

About the Author

Loryn Moore writes stories where power awakens, danger lingers, and love is never the easy choice. Her fantasy romances blend magic, mystery, and forbidden desire that drawing readers into hidden worlds where destiny is tested and passion can change everything.

Secret worlds that could exist just beneath the surface of our own has drawn Loryn to stories of magic woven into everyday life. She writes for readers who love high emotional stakes, morally complex relationships, and romances shaped as much by choice and consequence as by fate.

Loryn lives in North Florida with her husband and their two young sons, the men who serve as her greatest inspiration. When she's not working on her next story, she and her husband can usually be found tackling DIY projects, tending their backyard garden, or escaping to the beach whenever possible. Those quiet, ordinary moments are often where her most beautiful and magical ideas begin.

Subscribe to Loryn's Newsletter or follow her on social media:

https://linktr.ee/Lorynmooreauthor & on TikTok, Instagram, & Facebook: @lorynmooreauthor

www.ingramcontent.com/pod-product-compliance
Lightning Source LLC
LaVergne TN
LVHW100506110826
845146LV00002B/534

* 9 7 9 8 9 9 1 5 0 4 5 4 6 *